STRATEGOS

BORN
IN THE
BORDERLANDS

GORDON
DOHERTY

CANELO

MIX
Paper from
responsible sources
FSC
FSC® C004072

First published in the United Kingdom in 2011 by Gordon Doherty

This edition published in the United Kingdom in 2022 by

Canelo
Unit 9, 5th Floor
Cargo Works, 1-2 Hatfields
London, SE1 9PG
United Kingdom

A CIP catalogue record for this book is available from the British Library.

Print ISBN 978 1 80436 043 9
Ebook ISBN 978 1 80436 042 2

This book is a work of fiction. Names, characters, businesses, organizations, places and events are either the product of the author's imagination or are used fictitiously. Any resemblance to actual persons, living or dead, events or locales is entirely coincidental.

Cover design by Black Sheep

Cover images © ArcAngel; Depositphotos

Look for more great books at www.canelo.co

Printed and bound in Great Britain by Clays Ltd, Elcograf S.p.A.

1

This book is for my loving wife, Sarah. Quite simply, without her constant support and patience throughout the long writing process, this work would not have come to be.

I'd also like to thank my mum, Jean, who has been unwavering in her support of my efforts in writing and in everything else I have done in my life.

Thanks must also go to the fine users of youwriteonline.co.uk, not least Anthony Armitt and Simon Turney, who have proved to be writing gurus as well as good friends.

Finally, for their expert knowledge in all things Byzantine and Seljuk, and their generous help and advice, I would like to offer my thanks to Dr Timothy Dawson, Burak Sansal from allaboutturkey.com, Jill Guest in representation of the Turkish Culture and Tourism Office and the knowledgeable users of historum.co.uk.

Thank you all!

A set of maps and diagrams to accompany this novel can be
viewed at the author's website: www.gordondoherty.co.uk

Prologue

AD 1026: The Pontic Forest, Chaldia

I circle the grey skies, surveying the thick carpet of autumnal forest below. Then it is broken by a clearing and I am numbed by the sight of the still-smoking ruins and charred bodies strewn in the grass. It is only a small village in the borderlands of Byzantium, but it underwrites a truth that has been with me all my years: man will destroy man.

And in this part of the world it is like watching Prometheus live out his agony day after day as civilisations shatter against one another: the Greeks and the Trojans, the Hittites and the Assyrians, the Romans and the Persians. Now Rome's heir, Byzantium, teeters on the brink of war with the burgeoning Seljuk Empire.

My age is almost past and my power cowed, thus I am little more than an observer of cruel fate, and fate has it that Byzantium is mortal. Yes, like all empires, Byzantium will fall, but I believe in the vision I had: the dark leader, not yet born, the one man who can prevent the devastation that fate has in store.

The Haga!

I sweep over the treetops, following the dirt path that snakes through the woodland. Then, some distance down that track, I sense them, Seljuk warriors, poised in the undergrowth like asps, waiting on their prey; proud men, unaware of their part in the everlasting cycle of destruction.

I sense a soul on horseback, approaching the waiting ambush. Then I feel it: he is part of the vision; he is why I was drawn here today. I cannot make this man or any other do my bidding; like a mirror to his soul I can only present to him what he already knows. But I must speak with him so that one day, when the Haga has risen, man can stand against fate.

I

Tepid rain fell in sheets, churning the forest path into mire before the depleted column of iron-clad riders. Only seven remained of the twenty-five *kataphractoi* that had set out that morning. At their head, Cydones blinked the rainwater from his eyes and tugged at the beginnings of his dark beard, twisting it into twin points. With the light fading, the forest was becoming an army of shadows.

He shrugged to adjust his *klibanion*, the weight of the iron lamellar vest biting into his collarbone. *Set an example*, he chided himself and sat tall in his saddle. The men needed their leader to be strong after the events of the day. They had intercepted and slain all but the vanguard and rearguard of the Seljuk raiding party, but had lost many friends and colleagues in the process. Yet there was no time to dwell on this latest incursion; the kataphractoi were few and precious and Chaldia was vast, the borders of the *thema* encompassing an area far greater than the skeleton garrisons and scant collection of full-time riders could hope to protect. As the raindrops rattled on his knuckles, he wondered at his choices in life that had brought him to this daily and brutal conflict.

Cydones' life so far had been based on simple ideals and these were in stark contrast to those valued by the rest of his family. He thought of his older brother, Agapetes, and the wealth and luxury his sibling had amassed back in Constantinople in the family trading business. Cydones had never bonded with his brother, a cold-hearted boy and then a snake of a man who always sought to serve himself first. Agapetes had followed in his father's footsteps and used his business nous to tap into the riches of the capital's trade markets. That the poor bastard had died in an overloaded trade cog caught in a storm just off the Hellespont was a bitter irony, but that his father could only grieve at the loss of Agapetes the business partner and not Agapetes the son was a cold reality that Cydones just did not understand.

While his father and Agapetes had worked hard to take from the empire, Cydones had only ever wanted to fight for her. He traced a finger along the edge of the bronze Christian *Chi-Rho*

2

on the chain around his neck. The symbol of God pierced the skylines of Byzantium's cities and was painted on the shield of every imperial soldier; it was the symbol that his mother had taught him to respect and obey. His mother had been the only soul who seemed to understand him, her heart touched with warmth. When she died, his father had remained stony-faced and dry-eyed throughout the funeral, often neglecting his part in the ceremonies to attend to business. Cydones finally realised that his time with his family was over the following summer, the day he saw his father weep with joy at clinching a deal to bring regular shipments of wine and honey in from the groves and hives of Southern Anatolia.

So Cydones had left the capital and travelled east to the borderlands with only the tunic on his back, the Chi-Rho around his neck and a sling. Coinless, he had caught fish, raided beehives and trapped rabbits on the road to the region known as Chaldia, one of the easternmost themata of the empire. He had then signed up as a regular thema infantryman, a *skutatos*, committed to working an arid patch of land and then defending it with his life when the empire called upon him. When he had lifted the *spathion* and *skutum*, the Byzantine sword and shield, for the first time, it had been like a final closing of the door on his life back in the capital. From that point on, he had patrolled, fought and bled for the betterment of his people, quickly leaving the agricultural half of the soldier-farmer life behind as promotion after promotion came his way. And now he was a cavalry *komes*, in charge of fifty riders. This was his calling, and a brutal one it was. In the borderlands blood was readily spilled; brigands were a constant menace but the relentless westward progression of the Seljuk hordes was like a spear driving into the empire's gut. They were only getting stronger year on year while the empire faltered under the squabbling of the power-hungry in Constantinople. He had seen an estuary flow crimson after one hinterland battle with the Seljuk riders; so many men dead and all just to limit the loss of imperial territory.

The clopping hooves of another mount shook him back to the present.

'Lovely rain, hides from us all year, lets the sun scorch our crops, has us trailing halfway across the thema for a bucket of water... then this!'

Cydones blinked. The young, blue-eyed rider, Ferro, had ridden ahead of his ten to draw level.

Ferro closed his eyes. 'Now I see a fire roaring back at the barracks; a plate of roast lamb and a tray of honey cakes.'

Cydones could not contain a wry chuckle. 'I'll add a keg of ale to the table, Ferro, when we get back... but keep your eyes on the treeline while we ride. Another night in this mire, then tomorrow, once we're out of this damned forest, we can ride at a decent pace...' His words trailed off at the screeching of an eagle. He glanced up at the canopy of forest above; what he could see of the sky was an unbroken grey. When he looked forward again, his eyes were drawn to the undergrowth. A fern shook and then settled. The breath froze in his lungs.

'Sir?' Ferro cocked an eyebrow, hand resting on his pommel.

Cydones made to raise a hand for a full stop. Then a roar pierced the air.

Two packs of men burst from either side of the undergrowth; at least thirty of them, dark-skinned and moustachioed. *Akhi*, Seljuk infantry, hoisting broad-bladed spears and wearing felt caps and jackets. Immediately, two of his men toppled from their horses, impaled on the spears.

'To arms!' Cydones roared, ripping his spathion from his scabbard as his horse reared at the oncoming swell of spearmen. He snarled, hacking through the flurry of spear thrusts aimed at him before chopping down on the nearest attacker, snapping through bone and gristle, lopping the man's arm off in one blow. A hot arterial spray coated his face and the Chi-Rho dangling on his chain.

'Come on then, you *whoresons!*' he bellowed, storming into the fray. He turned to the growing roar of a spearman rushing

4

for his back. He hefted his spathion up to strike and heeled his mount round to face his attacker, but his blood ran cold as his horse struggled to turn in the mire under hoof. He felt time slow as he tried to pull his foot from the stirrup to twist in his saddle. The spearman's eyes bulged, spear point only a pace away from Cydones, when a sword point burst through the spearman's neck. The man toppled like a felled tree to reveal the snarling Ferro, dismounted, clutching the hilt of his spathion, the blade coated in crimson gore.

Ferro leapt back into the melee and Cydones turned to hack off the spear point of the next akhi before swiping his sword back round to behead the man. The grating of iron on bone was disguised only by the whinnying of horses and the screaming of men. The fine armour of the kataphractoi ensured the skirmish was swift, and as the akhi lost their numerical advantage they broke for cover in the forest. At this, the kataphractoi were quick to nock arrows to their bows, felling all but one of the retreating men. Ferro leapt on his mount again and charged after the last of the fleeing akhi. With the flat of his sword, he smashed the man on the back of the head, toppling him like a sack of rubble.

'Easy!' Cydones roared as Ferro leapt from his horse and lifted his sword to strike again.

'Just being careful,' Ferro countered, kicking the dagger from the akhi's hand and digging his boot into the man's throat.

The felled man groaned, rolling round to face the encircling kataphractoi unit.

'Your head will sit on a spike on the walls of Trebizond by nightfall,' Cydones spat.

The Seljuk had looked bleary but then his face curled into a sneer. 'And all of your people will cower under the *Falcon*'s blade before too long.'

Cydones slid his helmet from his head, running a hand over his bald pate and biting back the instinctive reply that came to his lips, the spiteful rhetoric seeming foolish as his heartbeat calmed. Sultan Tugrul, the *Falcon*, had indeed cast a shadow across these lands, a shadow that was growing with every passing year. This lone spearman's life or death would not change that. This must be the rearguard of the raiding party, he realised, lost and terrified in a foreign land. The man he had hoped to catch was gone: Tugrul's young protégé, the shrewd Seljuk rider who had continuously beaten, and beaten well, the armies of the thema in the last year would be long gone with the vanguard. *Enough blood*, he thought.

'Should we just stick the bastard, sir?' said the bull of a rider by his side. 'I don't fancy taking him all the way back to the barracks.'

Cydones glared at the rider, who dropped his gaze and took to studying the nearest tree intensively. 'Bind his hands,' he said, then jabbed a finger at the big rider. 'He rides with you.'

—

As night cloaked the forest, the rains stopped to present a clear sky above the small clearing. Due to the humidity, the remaining five kataphractoi had chosen not to erect their pavilion tent. They lay instead in their quilted blankets on the soft bracken of the forest floor, spears dug into the ground in readiness should there be a night ambush. The Seljuk prisoner was bound to a tree and had fallen into an exhausted sleep. Snoring from the soldiers and the occasional snort from the horses could be heard, breaking the constant rustle of the overhead canopy and the sporadic hooting of owls.

Cydones yawned, then muttered a curse at his selfless offer of taking the middle watch. Yet he knew the men respected a leader who would not balk at hardship. His belly rumbled; they had eaten a simple meal of toasted bread and salt beef washed down with water, but the rations barely compensated for the full day of riding.

Focusing on the toppled beech just a handful of paces ahead, he felt his eyelids droop and his thoughts dance freely, and an instant later, his head lolled forward. Then the piercing screech of an eagle wrenched him to his senses. He leapt up and felt for his spathion but then he realised he had been dreaming and settled back against the trunk with a nervous chuckle.

Then he saw her.

She stood only paces away, wearing a grey robe that clung to her knotted figure. Barefoot, her face was puckered, her eyes were clouded milky white and her hair was perfect silver. He felt an unexpected sense of ease and no compulsion to raise the alarm.

'Be at ease, soldier,' she said, crouching. Her tone was soft, like a mother's words to a child. She looked nothing like his mother but he felt a familiar warmth touch his heart as she spoke. He made to reach for his Chi-Rho neck chain, but his arms felt curiously leaden.

Cydones cast a glance around the forest. There was nobody else.

'You fought well today,' the woman spoke.

'You were there?' Cydones asked as she sat on a tree stump across from him.

'I saw it all.'

'Then you were with the akhi?' Cydones asked, suddenly aware of the prisoner, but a glance reassured him that the Seljuk akhi was still safely bound and asleep.

'No, but I feel for them.'

'You'll have seen us butcher the rest of them?'

'As they would have done to you, had you not been on your guard,' she said. 'Much blood was spilled and that was a great pity, but you also made a fine choice,' she nodded towards the sleeping prisoner. 'That man could have been easily slain and left to rot on the forest floor.'

'Two of my men died today at the hands of his party,' Cydones countered. 'So his head will still end up on a spike.'

'Perhaps, but that will not be of your doing. You made a choice that was unpopular with your men, when it would have been so simple to make things easy for yourself.'

Cydones shrugged. Inside he hoped she was right. Then he noticed her bare feet and gnarled toes; they were clean despite the damp forest floor. 'Why have you come here? There are no settlements for miles around,' he asked, thinking back to the incinerated settlement they had passed that morning. 'You must have walked for...'

'You are a young man, Cydones,' the old woman cut in. She did not flinch when he gawped at her use of his name. 'You are bound for a long career; some would call it glorious, some would call it ghastly.'

'What do you know of my future?'

'Little more than you do. You know in your heart that the empire is in great danger from the peoples of the east. The years ahead will be troubled and dark for Byzantium. How dark only the actions of men will decide, but no matter what happens, you are a good man. You must remember this and stay true to yourself and your ideals. Now, you must listen to what I say next and listen well.'

Cydones nodded, uneasy as the woman's features became taut.

'When the falcon has flown, the mountain lion will charge from the east, and all Byzantium will quake. Only one man can save the empire.' She gripped his wrist. 'Find the *Haga*!'

'The *Haga*?' Cydones frowned, thinking of the old Hittite legend: the mythical two-headed eagle. It made no sense. 'How, where, would I find such a man?'

She leaned in to his ear. 'You will know when you meet him. He is one man torn to become two.'

He shook his head, frowning, searching for questions. Then he saw that she stood away from him, past the fallen beech. He rubbed his eyes and then saw that she stood even further away, arms outstretched to the sky. Then he blinked, realising he was looking at a sapling beech, two branches sprouting either side. He was alone.

An eagle shrieked high above.

His thoughts echoed with her words.

Find the Haga.

Part 1: AD 1046

CHAPTER 1

Trebizond

The squat innkeeper furtively eyed the figure in the shadows. This customer had sat silent and motionless, recessed in the darkest corner of the cellar inn most of the morning.

'Another one?' the innkeeper grunted, poking a finger at the near-empty cup of water on the table. A moment passed and the innkeeper wondered if he had yet another corpse on his hands. Then the shadows rippled as the customer leant forward. He was a man nearing fifty, swarthy, heavy-set and moustachioed, with an expression of stone. He remained silent, only waving a hand by way of reply.

'Hmm,' the innkeeper barely disguised a sneer before waddling off to prise business from the rest of his clientele.

Leaning back into obscurity, Mansur rubbed at his temples. Out of the blistering heat up above, the brackish water had at least washed the dust from his throat after such a long journey; though even after rest and refreshment, his sweat-bathed tunic remained stuck to his generous figure. He pulled off his blue felt cap and wiped the perspiration from his brow and grey stubbled scalp, then fixed it back in place and tidied his moustache with a wipe of the hand. Then he glanced to either side: his garb was the same as any other Byzantine citizen and only his darker skin would give him away, but nobody yet had noticed the Seljuk in this imperial drinking hole. The tension along the borderlands had grown palpable in recent years as Seljuk pressure intensified, and the Byzantine citizens were quick to channel their fear into anger and turn upon strangers. Especially in a hive like Trebizond. Especially in a cut-throat drinking hole like this.

It had been a long day so far; a full morning driving his wagon under the glare of the midsummer sun. He sighed, remembering the worn axle that made the wagon judder violently at every bump in the road. Another neglected task and one of many that would stay neglected. Since he had made the decision to come to Trebizond, everything else was secondary. He thought of his daughter Maria and swallowed his guilt. *Everything*.

Yet he had been sitting for some time now; noon had come and gone and still no sign of the boy. Perhaps the information had been phoney? How long had he worked to earn the six *nomismata* it had cost to hire that mean-eyed investigator? Two moons, two moons of blistered hands, eating beans and roots and precious little else to pull together those six gold coins. Not that it had tempered his bulging waistline, he mused. But it all added up, every piece of extra produce he could keep and sell. Now he had just enough left to complete his objective. *But where was the boy?*

Suddenly, the ambient murmur of drunken chatter was shattered with a crash from the far side of the inn. Mansur tensed and shot a sideways glance: in the murky half-light pooling by the foot of the timber stairs, two men grappled like snarling dogs, one hooded and dressed in filthy rags and the other, long-haired and wearing some kind of cloth militia tunic and both very drunk. Bar stools crumpled under them and cups toppled and crashed to the floor as they wrestled.

'Oi!' the innkeeper roared, slamming a balled fist onto the bar, but the pair carried on pulling and kicking at each other as they spilled around the floor. Drinkers shot up, barking at first in protest and then in amusement as the brawl gathered momentum.

'Not in my place, you filthy whoresons!' The diminutive innkeeper vaulted across the bar, a club in hand. Then, as if materialising from the shadows, two bald-headed brutes of men appeared to flank him like turrets, one bearing a short sword and the other unsheathing an axe. The crowd parted and their heckling died to a murmur at the sight of the doormen. Then, with an animal shriek, the fighting pair broke apart. The hooded one stood, arms wide as if pleading innocence, then turned and bolted upstairs and into the sunlight.

'Leave him!' The innkeeper lifted an arm to either side as his men made to lurch after the hooded brawler. 'That one'll get what's coming to him. Deal with this fellow for now, looks as if he's military.' He nodded to the second brawler, hunched against the wall, panting.

Mansur stood to watch, brow furrowed.

The two doormen flanked the soldier and pulled him round to face the innkeeper. A collective gasp of disgust filled the shadows at the gaping crimson grin stretched across the man's throat. Blood washed down his tunic, consuming the faded Chi-Rho embroidered on the front and even in the half-light Mansur could see the man's narrow features turn white and then grey, before his eyes rolled in his head and his life was gone. In a few beats of the heart, the body crumpled to a heap.

'Bugger,' the innkeeper spat on the floor then snorted a lungful of air, his eyes wide in fury, 'there's going to be all sorts of shit to deal with now.' His two doormen looked at him expectantly. 'Longibardus, take message to the city barracks. Speak to the *strategos* and the strategos only. Make sure Cydones knows we tried to stop this.'

Mansur's ears perked up at the mention of Cydones. He wondered how his old adversary had fared since last they had faced one another.

As the first doorman set off up the stairs, the innkeeper turned to his second man. 'Choniates,' he grunted, 'get out there and catch that whoreson who thinks he can spill blood on my floor,' then his eyes narrowed, mouth curling up into a rapacious sneer, 'and take the sword... bring him or bring his head!'

Mansur sat back down, his nose wrinkled briefly at the metallic stench of black blood drying in the heat. He had been ready to eat, even in this cesspit, but not now. He dug his fingernails into the table; it was getting on in the afternoon, the establishment was a fetid cave for drunks and crooks and little else, surely a boy could not survive in this place. No, he affirmed, he had been conned of his hard-earned coins. Time to leave, to get on the highway and back to the farm before dusk. With a laboured sigh, he stood, pushing his stool back. Then he froze at the dull crack of knuckles on flesh from the room behind the bar.

'Get out there and clean it up!' the innkeeper's voice rumbled. Then there were uneven, sluggish footsteps mixed with the tapping of wood on the floor. Mansur's eyes locked on the figure of a boy that hobbled out from behind the bar: face hidden behind a curtain of amber hair, carrying a mop and resting his weight on a crutch, dragging one leg as if a great weight was attached to it. He wore a filthy hemp garment from shoulder to ankle and on one wrist was a frayed prayer rope.

The boy stopped by the thick gloop of dark blood, half soaked into the dirt on the floor. He pushed his hair back, tucking it behind his ears to reveal a thick red swelling on one temple. His brow was furrowed and jutting, eyes masked in shadow either side of a knotted aquiline nose as he contemplated the blood and the corpse in turn. The boy stared, trembling.

At this, the watching punters finally returned to form, exploding into a chorus of fervent heckling. 'Mop it up, boy. Then drink it!' one roared, slapping his thigh at his own wit.

'Aye,' the innkeeper added, drying cups with industrial vigour, teeth clenched, 'clean it up or your blood'll be on the floor too.'

Mansur stepped forward to join the ring of onlookers. The shadows had hidden him and his features until now. He had hoped to have a quiet word with the innkeeper later, one to one, but that chance was gone. He had to face the crowd, all of them. It was all about the boy.

Stood like a sapling in the breeze, the boy's chest shuddered. His cheeks swelled and then a torrent of grey-orange bile erupted from his mouth and soaked the floor.

'Eurgh… you bloody fool!' the innkeeper bawled, while the onlookers groaned, shuffling back from the mess, covering their wine and ale cups. 'If I can't knock sense into you then you're of no use to me!'

The boy shot a pleading look at the innkeeper.

'Out of my way, idiot,' the innkeeper snatched the mop from the boy's grip, then kicked the crutch from under him. A chorus of jeers filled the inn as the boy stumbled back, crashing through a pile of stools, his cloak falling to the floor. Now dressed only in a sleeveless and short tunic, a furious red, scabbed and serrated welt was revealed, running from his heel all the way up his leg, disappearing under the frayed hem of his tunic. The boy cowered, pulling the threads of his tunic down, covering the scar with his hands.

'Useless, this one!' The innkeeper jabbed a finger at the boy while grinning at his customers. 'The crook that sold me him in the market told me everything about him: son of a pure-blood Byzantine kataphractos; mother from the northlands of the Rus; only ten years old. Oh aye, told me everything, everything except that he's a bloody cripple!'

The crowd roared. 'Seen you comin'!' one drunk cackled.

'He was sitting down when I saw him!' The innkeeper stabbed a finger at his customer and then cast a glance over his shoulder to the boy, 'and you can forget about eating tonight, you little runt… you're fast buying yourself a ticket to the salt mines. If I can be sold a lame-leg like you then I can sell you on just as easily.'

Mansur readied himself as the innkeeper mopped at the gory puddle. He touched a hand to his purse and took a deep breath, stepping from the shadows. 'How much for the boy?'

The innkeeper stopped mopping for a moment, resting on the end of the pole, then turned to face Mansur with a wrinkle of incredulity twisting his features. 'Eh?'

'The boy, I want to buy him. He is a slave isn't he?'

The innkeeper stalked forward, eyes narrowed as he examined Mansur. Then his pupils sparkled in realisation and a predatory grin split his face. 'So what business does a Seljuk have in a place like this? This isn't the fiery hell of a desert your lot call home. You're in the empire!'

All around him, the crowd murmured, noses wrinkling as if a plague was in the air. Mansur kept his face expressionless. 'Yes, I'm in the empire and I have been for years, tilling the lands, paying my taxes like any of you... and I've got money to spend. Now, the boy?'

The innkeeper's lips trembled for the briefest of moments, then his eyes fell on the purple purse on Mansur's belt and his face brightened at once. 'A slave... aye... and a damned good one.'

Mansur swallowed the urge to belly laugh at the transparency of the man. 'Well I'm sure he is. How much?'

The innkeeper poked out his tongue to dampen his lips, shooting glances to Mansur's purse, weighing it in his mind. 'So young boys are your thing, eh?' he sneered, wringing a chorus of cackling from the listening drunks.

Mansur's face remained stony, eyes fixed on the innkeeper.

Finally, the laughter around them died and the innkeeper's face fell firm. 'Nine nomismata!'

The crowd roared at this. 'You're 'avin a laugh!' one shrieked.

Mansur suppressed a sigh and braced himself for haggling. Four gold coins remained in his purse. 'You clearly don't want the boy so let's be realistic. What's a slave from the salt mines worth?'

'Ah, no; I said I was going to send him there but he hasn't been there yet! Still plenty of time for him to develop into a big, strapping lad.'

'You just described him as a cripple, did you not?' Mansur cut in.

'He'll never be a runner but...' the innkeeper started.

'I could buy three child slaves for nine nomismata at the market square.'

'Well, why don't you? Door's open,' the innkeeper countered.

Mansur cocked an eyebrow. 'Well, it seems I'm in for a bargain at the market then, three slaves for the price of one.' He waited until the glint in the innkeeper's eyes dulled, then strode for the staircase. One stair creaked under his weight, then another, then he lifted his foot again…

'Er… wait,' a deflated voice grumbled from behind him.

Mansur paused, then twisted around. 'Your price?'

'Six nomismata,' the innkeeper sighed.

Mansur turned and continued to climb the stairs.

'Alright, four!' the man barked.

Mansur suppressed a grin and turned to descend the stairs. 'Why the long face,' he asked the innkeeper as he counted out the coins, 'you're still getting more than he's worth?'

The innkeeper scowled at Mansur as the circle of punters leered at the exchange of currency. 'Just be on your way.'

With a whimper, the boy shielded his eyes as he limped up one stair at a time with the aid of his crutch, Mansur slowing to match his pace. The light betrayed the savage discolouring on his leg all around the wound and the fetid mess that was his tunic. They pressed to one side of the stairs as Longibardus the doorman came thundering back with an entourage of four skutatoi from the city garrison in tow.

As they stepped out into the full glare of the mid-afternoon sunlight, the bustle of the city enveloped them. The salty tang from the nearby waters of the Pontus Euxinus mixed with the arid, red dust that clouded the air and caught in the throat, thrown up by the throngs of determined citizens and wagons that pressed past the pair and into the market square. All around them was an incessant rabble of shouting traders, barking skutatoi, whin-nying horses and cackling drunks. Clusters of verdant green palms and beeches stood fastidiously in the swell of activity, providing precious shade in the wide street between the sturdy structures of the church and the granary. At the end of the street, away from the market square, the baked battlements of the city walls shimmered, punctuated by iron-garbed skutatoi and cotton-armoured *toxotai* bowmen. The boy looked up, eyes glassy. Mansur followed his gaze; towering above all other buildings and the high masts of the warships at the city dock, the Chi-Rho atop the red-tiled church dome pierced the eggshell-blue sky.

Mansur put an arm around him. 'Come with me, lad,' he whispered, turning to push back through the crowd towards the south gate. 'You can trust me… and I hope in time you will.'

The boy looked up at him, his emerald eyes meeting Mansur's at last.

'I'm Mansur.' He squatted to be level with the boy, who was already tired from the effort of walking this short distance. 'So what's your name, lad?'

The boy licked his lips and pulled in a deep breath before replying.

'I'm Apion.' He jolted free of Mansur's arm, steadying himself on his crutch, eyes searing under his frown. 'I'm Apion… and I am nobody's slave.'

CHAPTER 2

The Anatolian Highway

'You alright back there, lad?' a gravel voice called back from the wagon drivers' berth.

Apion sat in the corner of the cabin, a timber box, closed on all sides with a door on the right. He heard Mansur's words but his mind remained elsewhere. Early evening sunlight flitted across him through the slats in the wagon roof, illuminating the crimson of long dried blood and red dust from the road crusting his tunic. The wagon sunk and then lurched on a pothole and a streak of white-hot pain burst from his scar, engulfing his leg in an invisible fire. He clutched at his thigh and winced, grimacing through the worst of the pain before slumping back. As the pain subsided, he peered through the slats on the side of the wagon, gazing at the speeding countryside outside. At first, the land was a patchwork of farmhouses and crop squares worked by stooped forms of the soldier-farmers of the thema, but these settlements thinned as they headed southwards.

He noticed the landscape growing more uneven on either side of the road. The colour of the land was changing as well, the verdant blanket that hugged the northern coast drying out into baked terracotta and gold hillsides, strewn with rocks and dappled with bursts of green shrub, gatherings of lazy palms and shimmering olive groves. The wagon jolted again as it hit a lone flagstone, harking back to a time when the road from the city had been well-maintained. Now only a dirt track remained, weaving across the hills and never straying too far from the rapids of the

Piksidis, the river that snaked to Trebizond through the southern Parhar Mountains. A sad familiarity gripped his heart; the rush of the water, the rolling hills, and the old rope bridge up ahead – it was just as he remembered.

Then he realised what was coming next. He twisted round and pressed his eyes to the gap in the slats. Then he saw it: some fifty paces from the road and the riverbank was a mound of rubble, coated in lichen and almost swallowed by long grass, the visible patches of bare stone still charred. He craned his neck as the wagon sped past, eyes hanging on the ruin until he could see it no more. He longed to shout for Mansur to stop, but the words would not come. He slunk back down, biting his lower lip until he tasted metallic blood. One word echoed through his mind.

Home.

He traced his forefinger back and forth over the knotted prayer rope on his wrist, remembering the day mother had tied it there, but the words of the Prayer of the Heart would not come to him. His sorrow swirled into anger and at once the image that plagued his nights shot to the fore: an arched door, floating in darkness. A harmless scene, he had reasoned a thousand times, yet he could not work out why it chilled him with foreboding. With a grunt, he forced the image from his mind. The wagon slowed momentarily.

The gravel voice called again from the front. 'You need to stop to do your business or something?'

Apion stared at the timber slats separating him from the driver. He could make out only the outline of Mansur's portly figure. Why he could not respond, Apion was not sure. How many words had he spoken since that awful night, then throughout the following year at the slave market and then the filthy inn? A handful at most. Perhaps it was the fear of breaking some spell, perhaps speaking would mean it was all real?

'Just rap on the front if you want to stop, you hear?' Mansur waited again for a few breaths before the wagon accelerated.

Apion did not reply, instead tracing the knots on his prayer rope once more, eyes on the sliver of skyline visible through the roof.

After some time, the sun had turned a darker orange and the wagon slowed again. This time there were voices. Foreign voices.

'Halt!' one called in a jagged Rus accent.

'*Bracchus...*' Mansur grunted, his words tapering off with a growl. 'Stay quiet back there, lad, you hear? You've got to keep out of sight, yes? I'll deal with this.'

'Ah, it's Mansur,' another voice cut in, baritone and abrupt.

With a frown, Apion leaned forward to the gap in the slats. He saw two figures stood by the driver's bench; Byzantine kataphractoi, armed and armoured well. One was young, with ginger eyebrows and stubble, standing by his mount, tall and broad and wearing a battered iron helmet. The other remained mounted and had a pointed face and was tall and lean, probably in his mid-twenties. This one's garb was noteworthy; the helmet with a tuft of golden plumage and the leather gloves with iron studs on the knuckles.

'Bracchus? We have no business together, so why do you stop me?' Mansur addressed the plumed soldier, his gravel voice dry. 'You want to examine my wagon, check for trading papers like a good officer?'

Bracchus shot a leaden glare at Mansur. Apion felt his mouth dry as the rider then reached to drum his fingers on his spathion hilt, his razor of a nose bending over a sharp grin.

'You know very well why you have been stopped. Hand over your coins, they will be used for a... higher purpose.' Bracchus beckoned with his free hand.

A moment of silence hung in the air before a purple purse slapped into the dust by the big Rus soldier's feet with the thick clunk.

'I'll be going now,' Mansur spat.

'And you'll be thankful your throat is not opened,' Bracchus snarled, weighing the purse in his hand, eyes fixed on Mansur as the wagon moved off. 'Remember your place in this land, *Seljuk scum!*'

Apion shuddered as Bracchus' words cut through the air and he stared at the man's expression. Anger crackled in those eyes.

'Don't be afraid, lad. That one rears his head every so often, but I know how to handle him,' he spoke over the rumble of the road. But despite Mansur's words, the old man's tone suggested he had been rattled by the encounter with the rogue kataphractoi. 'Anyway, we're nearly there,' Mansur added. 'At my house you can eat, you can sleep and you will be safe. I promise you.'

Apion could only stare at the back of Mansur's head. Promises were cheap.

They travelled south for some time until the land was cast in a rich orange glow and striped with shadows as the sun dipped into the western hills. Eventually, they entered a wide valley, the ubiquitous terracotta and green valley sides arcing out to frame a wide and sheltered oval of flatland, the Piksidis flowing broad and calm at its centre. The wagon slowed to cross a stone bridge before wheeling round at a canter through a pair of gateless posts. The nutty scent of barley and the bleating of goats filled the air, then a farm building rolled into sight.

The squat structure was ramshackle at best, baked brickwork subsiding, crumbling and unpainted, the roof missing almost as many tiles as it possessed. Nature had kindly done her best to disguise the state of disrepair with clematis and ivy tendrils hugging the walls and framing the shutters. Crop fields lay behind the house and stretched for a good quarter of a mile up to the slope of the valley. In front of the house there was a yard with an axe and a pile of chopped logs lying in the centre. The yard was framed on one side by a small, rectangular storehouse adjoined to the main house and a simple timber goat pen hemming in some thirty woad-marked animals, and on the other side by a little chicken coop built on the end of a small stable shed packed out with hay. As the portly figure of Mansur leapt to the ground to untether the horses, Apion eyed the place for some clue of what this next chapter of life was to hold, fear and doubt stabbing at his gut. He traced the barley- and hay-strewn path up to a cracked oak door, lying ajar. Then a rattle of footsteps filled the porch inside and a delicate, fawn hand, smaller even than Apion's, wrapped around the edge of the door, low down, to pull it open.

'Father!' the girl squealed. 'You're late! I was worried, even the goats were worried!' The words tumbled from her, trilling as she skipped forward to throw herself into Mansur's arms.

Apion squinted: she was probably his age. All he could make out from the distance was a toothy grin framed with tousled charcoal locks, her knees black with dirt and her hemp robe frayed as though the goats had been chewing at the hem.

'Maria, you worry when you shouldn't. I said I would return before sunset, and here I am, you silly girl!' Mansur squatted to be level with her, taking off his felt cap to wipe the sweat from his brow.

'But it *is* sunset! Well... nearly,' she protested. 'I've had food on the table for ages; I've made salad *and* stew *and* I've gathered fresh eggs *and* I've opened a cheese!'

Mansur nodded, a wide grin lifting his moustache as he stood and ran a hand down the mane of each of his horses, muttering words of comfort to them as they munched from their troughs. He turned back to the ever-less-patient girl, now grimacing, hands pressed into her hips. 'Sounds delicious and my belly's roaring already... but before we sit down to eat, there's someone I'd like you to meet.'

The girl pursed her lips and frowned, then stared at the wagon. She couldn't see Apion but he returned her gaze through the slats.

'A boy.'

'A boy?'

'Same age as you, I reckon. He's not well and,' Mansur paused, 'he needs looking after. He'll stay with us. Our house will be his home.'

Home. Apion thought of the sorry heap of rubble downriver. *Somewhere I can never return to.*

Mansur flicked his head towards the wagon. 'Come, I'll introduce you.'

Apion's heart hammered, his mouth drained of moisture and anxiety needled his skin. Reality beckoned.

He braced himself as the wagon door swung open with a groan and the dying evening sunlight fell upon him. His eyes narrowed and he pulled a hand over them, peering through the cracks.

'He's a Byzantine,' she uttered almost accusingly, taking a step back.

Apion bristled, proud of Mother's Rus ancestry, proud of Father fighting for the empire. A retort formed in his mind but the words lodged in his throat.

'He's a boy who needs a family,' Mansur sighed, placing his hands on her shoulders.

Apion's eyesight tuned into the brightness at last and Maria's face was the first thing he set eyes upon. She was boyish, her eyebrows fuzzy and unkempt, her nose broad and her chin rounded like her father's.

'Well his hair's a funny colour – like the sunset.' She wrinkled her nose and pursed her lips, her head tilting to one side as she beheld him and then the sun as it slipped behind the hillside.

Apion felt a surge of self-consciousness, reaching to brush his locks from his brow, sitting up straight on the wagon bench.

'Aye and he might think you're a bit different too, madam,' Mansur added with a chuckle. 'Maria, I'd like you to meet Apion. Apion, Maria.'

Maria continued to eye him in a petulant standoff.

'Well, you two are welcome to stand out here till it gets dark,' Mansur sighed, 'but I'm going in for supper… as ordered! Join me if you wish.' Mansur fixed his cap back on his head and strolled towards the farmhouse, whistling. He pushed open the door, revealing a simple hearth room with three cobbled chairs around an oak table bedecked with Maria's feast. He glanced back at Maria, who remained fixed to the spot, scrutinising Apion, then he groaned and went inside.

Apion held Maria's glare with a mix of terror and defiance until, with a dismissive sigh, she turned, following her father's steps with exaggerated strides and made for the farmhouse too. He watched her matted hair swing behind her all the way to the door, which she slammed behind her with gusto. He stared at the farmhouse, mind awash. A gust rattled the wagon, bringing with it the first bite of night chill, then he glanced up as a lone bat rapped across the sky, black against the coming twilight. A shiver danced across his skin.

Suddenly, the farmhouse door was pulled open again and an exaggerated sigh pierced the air. Apion blinked: Maria stood in the doorway, arms folded, face creased with impatience.

'Well are you coming in or not?' she scowled. 'It's extremely rude not to eat what someone has cooked for you!'

CHAPTER 3

The Strategos

The Seljuk *ghulam* dipped to the right of his saddle as his mount thundered forward through the melee, then he pulled his scimitar to one side and let loose a guttural roar.

Time slowed for Cydones. Grounded, his mount crippled and whinnying in terror in the slop of blood, flesh and bone underfoot, the ageing strategos felt the moment pass where long ago his nerves would have shuddered. The ghulam had it all: armour, high ground, momentum and morale. For Cydones, klibanion torn and hanging from one shoulder, spathion bent and shield lost in the fray, his years of bitter experience were all he had to counter the attack. He pushed to his feet and braced.

'*Allahu Akbar!*' the ghulam cried.

Cydones stood firm, squinting in the sunshine until he could see the red wetness at the back of the rider's throat, neck muscles clenched, scimitar held aloft and ready to lop off the strategos' head. The split instant flashed before him: the ghulam's blade scything for his neck but both mount and rider's flank lay exposed and undefended. Cydones shot his twisted spathion straight up in a two-handed grip to catch the scimitar blow. His shoulder jarred, a spray of sparks stung his face and his ears numbed at the metallic din as the two swords screamed at one another. The blow parried, he pirouetted and lunged to punch his blade into the gelding's chest. In a high-pitched whinny, the beast threw the ghulam rider forward then splattered down into the gore, thrashing in the foam of its own blood. Cydones stalked over to the rider, lying motionless in the bloody swamp. The Seljuk lay with his face pale and his eyes closed. Cydones made to turn for the next man to fight, when the ghulam's face burst back into life in a fervent rage as he whipped a dagger from his boot, thrusting up at Cydones' thigh.

The pain barely registered. A sharp blade it must have been and on the classic weak spot of the armoured body of a kataphractos. Hot blood flooded over his thigh and his limbs trembled but he held firm to turn his spathion over, blade down, to thrust it through the ghulam's throat with a crunch of vertebrae and sinew. Then he crumpled to his knees, eyes fixed on the ghulam's final gaze. Together, their blood pumped into the scarlet mire that had only this morning been a verdant plain.

The battle was won and Byzantine victory cries rang out over the atrocious scene. Cydones felt his mind wander and his vision dull.

'The strategos!' one voice called out. 'The strategos has fallen!'

'No,' Cydones croaked, raising a hand. He had felt the tearing near-certainty of an arterial death blow before, the angry welt of scar under his thick forked beard a testament. This thigh wound was a sore one but not one that would kill him. Heart thundering, a chill sweat bathing his skin, he shivered and rose to stand. The handful left from the hundred he had led out that morning stood, panting, exhausted, some throwing up into the bilious swamp as the battle frenzy drained from their limbs, the Christian Chi-Rho on their battered crimson kite shields spattered in blood. They had fought for their emperor and for God. Now they looked to their strategos to vindicate them for the lives they had taken today. Cydones acknowledged this all too familiar numbness in his heart but he raised a fist and mustered all his strength to roar the holy victory cry.

'*Nobiscum Deus!*'

A torch burst into life on the short timber platform the men had erected on the hilltop plateau and the two men on the first guard shift watched the pitch-black countryside manfully. A roll call had been taken and it had been worryingly swift: three kataphractoi and twenty-one skutatoi were all that was left of the hundred that had marched from the barracks at Argyroupolis that morning. A score had fled when the Seljuks had attacked but the rest were cold and dead. The truth was, Cydones mused grimly, the remaining and spent handful were also as good as dead if another Seljuk raiding party decided to investigate the firelight. The imperial maps might say otherwise, but this far east it was definitely borderland. Thanks be to God for the loyalty of the Armenian princes, he thought, without their subjects, the borders would be threadbare of manpower.

He ran a filthy hand over his bald scalp and pulled at his forked beard, swigged water from his skin and then let his thoughts drift. He thought back to his old stamping ground, Constantinople: the tales of the rise and fall of emperors, often in inglorious circumstance, reached these outlying themata all too frequently. He still shivered at the report of the last emperor's demise: the feckless Michael the Fifth had been pulled from his horse as he tried to flee the city, his pleas for mercy going unheard as the populace pinned him to the street and prised his eyes from his sockets. Emperor Constantine Monomachus now sat at the pinnacle of Byzantium and so far he had proved only how short-sighted a leader could be, disbanding garrisons all across the land in order to line the bare imperial treasury with a few pounds of gold.

All the turmoil at the heart of empire meant that the border themata were left to fend for themselves, Cydones himself juggling the scant funds raised from the lands of Chaldia to mount an increasingly threadbare defence against the ever more frequent Seljuk incursions.

You're getting too old for this, a voice whispered in his mind. At forty-six years old he couldn't disagree; the crudely bandaged thigh wound snarled rhythmically, every bone was racked with pain and his muscles seared even now, a half-day after the battle.

Despite the fire, heaped high with kindling and brush, he felt the night chill more than ever. He had passed out shortly after the victory cry but fortunately Ferro had been on hand to grasp an arm and disguise the fall. The men had gathered the bodies of their comrades in an exhausted silence and then dug grave after grave. Cydones had narrated the Christian rites as his men buried each body.

'Eat up, sir, there's plenty spare,' Ferro spoke hoarsely as he sidled over, easing his athletic frame down onto the earth to rest his back on a rock, pushing fingers through his dark curls. He threw a chunk of salt beef to his commander.

Cydones examined the stringy strip of meat with disdain. Some wretched animal had died to provide this, but rations were plentiful only because so many men had died in this defensive sortie, men who would not be returning to their farmlands or their wives, mothers and children. 'Aye,' he smoothed his beard, 'I've never felt so hungry and yet not, Ferro.' He handed the beef back; a week with no meat or wine was his usual act of penance after so bloody an encounter.

Ferro nodded gently, gazing around the campfires dotting the plateau, his eyes sparkling in the firelight. 'I'm dog tired, sir, but I'd prise out my own teeth to see the sunrise right now and to be headed for safe ground. Training and gathering supplies for the warehouse would be a pleasant task, for once.'

Cydones grinned wryly. Ferro was his touchstone to reality. If the *tourmarches* was feeling the grind of being on a sortie then they truly were in a bad way. Ferro relished every chance to muster and set out with his infantry, temporarily freeing himself from the mire of *tourma* district administration that came with the role. He and the other tourmarchai were vital in allowing Cydones to run the Chaldian Thema as a whole. His mind chattered with the legal and taxation wranglings he had left neglected back in Trebizond and worse, the tense diplomatic meetings with the neighbouring themata. Not quite the ideals he had once strived for, he mused, touching the dull bronze Chi-Rho on his neckchain.

29

His mind wandered back, as it often did after battle, to the lady of the forest all those years ago. Sometimes he felt sure the whole episode was just a dream, yet a twinge in his heart would see the words repeated over and again in his head. *Be true to yourself*, he wondered how closely he had followed that mantra. How many mass graves of Seljuk warriors could he really absolve himself of in the name of defending the rotting hulk of the empire? Killing one thousand to save one hundred. Worse were the times when those graves contained fellow Byzantines; the ever more frequent and bloody in-fighting between rival themata was especially repugnant to his ideals yet he had still obeyed orders. He dipped his head to rid himself of the bitter imagery. Then the lady's other words trickled into his thoughts: *find the Haga*. Now that was still a mystery to him. A riddle as murky as life itself and one he reckoned he might never solve before the reaper came for him.

Age had come on fast in the last few years for the strategos. Cydones looked over to his tourmarches and wondered if Ferro would be the man to replace him and take on the burden of guilt when he retired gracefully. *Or when I end up gurgling on the end of a Seljuk scimitar!* He chuckled to himself.

'Sir?' Ferro cocked an eyebrow, mumbling through a piece of salt beef.

'Just letting my mind wander.' He stretched his arms, fatigue enshrouding him. 'Tell me, Ferro, how many of our lads do you think are officer material?'

'Them?' He jabbed a finger over his shoulder, sweeping across the tattered men behind. 'What rank? *Dekarchos*? Komes?'

Cydones frowned. 'It doesn't matter whether it's a ten or a full *bandon*, Ferro. Just look at them.' He lifted a hand to the group of three gangly soldiers who huddled around the fire.

'They're not the bulkiest of lads, true, and maybe a bit too young to be officers?'

'None of that really matters, Ferro. What I see when I look at them is fear. They are scared. They need men to lead them, Ferro. *Good* men.'

Ferro coughed. 'Well, sir, I think I'm a bloody good fit to that description. Give me a spathion and a good stallion, any number of men behind me. They'll follow me, I tell you.'

Cydones' shoulders jostled as a gravelly laugh tumbled from his chest. 'I know you would, only too well.' He rubbed the angry scar under his beard. If it wasn't for Ferro's counterattack all those years ago in the eastern desert, the Seljuk horde would have slaughtered Cydones and every single one of his men. The tourmarches had spurred his five hundred riders into such frenzy that they had charged nearly four times that number of Seljuk ghulam and spearmen, shattering their ranks like glass.

'It's the fact that you're a dying breed that worries me, Ferro. You're never going to be beaten, even on the day when somebody does manage to get a sword under your ribs. But the rest of the men in the ranks these days… well, you can see it in their eyes, they don't believe in what they're fighting for anymore.'

'For God?'

'We all have our ideals,' Cydones' brow creased, 'and I would never question the faith of any of them.'

'Then for the Empire?'

'Exactly,' Cydones nodded. 'The men need to feel like the empire is theirs to fight for, but it is not. The themata were founded on the principles of the old Roman levies; soldier farmers willing to fight and to die to protect their lands. Then our emperor decrees this exemption tax and he has hamstrung his borders with it. I know many men who would have made great soldiers but have taken that option, handing over a few coins to tend their lands and grow fat at home. It is a foolhardy and short-sighted mindset that will lead to not only poverty but destruction and the end of our empire.'

Ferro nodded. 'And out here in the borderlands we will always go unheard.'

'Until it is too late,' Cydones said. 'One day our riders will be too few to stave off the Seljuk incursions, there are less than five hundred of us in all Chaldia. A Seljuk invasion is only a matter of time, Ferro. When that day comes, the infantry of the themata will be mustered; they are a far cry from their ancestors, the sons of the legions. Perhaps the emperor will be there to see their impoverished state? I fear that when the sun sets on that day Byzantium will be no more.'

'I wish there was an answer to it, sir.'

'There is, Ferro,' Cydones leaned forward, 'a brave and loyal soldier will stay brave and loyal if he is led by a competent and fair officer, while those with fear in their hearts will be lost to us. But if a leader is tenacious, tactically shrewd and willing to fight on the front line… then the brave and loyal will fight with all their hearts and the fearful will start to forget their fears. That, Ferro, is the key. Good men at the helm.'

His words were cut off with a *plunk* as Ferro pulled the cork from his skin of wine and took a swig, then offered it over the fire. 'Good men!'

Cydones' face wrinkled into a grin as he took the skin and swigged. The sour wash cleared his head of thought momentarily but then his own words echoed inside him.

When the sun sets on that day Byzantium will be no more.

CHAPTER 4

The Farm

Apion sat on a cool rock that soothed the biting pain of his scar. He flexed his bare toes in a dewy patch of grass underfoot, drinking in the vista of the valley yawning below him: the farmhouse, the river and the terracotta and green lands glowing in the breaking summer dawn. He was alone; nobody around him except the goats, crunching into the thick islands of grass of this, the best grazing spot near Mansur's farm. He decided they had the right idea and reached into his canvas satchel for the flatbread, still warm from the oven, that he had picked up on his way out. He bit a piece off, comforted by its chewy texture and charcoal flavour, and let his eyes linger on the landscape.

Over the last month at the farm he had come to cherish this time when the land would turn from darkness to dawn, the light bringing the valley to life as he watched in silence, feeling the first heat of the sun stretch across his skin. The spectacle allowed him to briefly forget the murky voices and images that swam in his head at all other times. Being up here and bereft of fellowship was like a tonic for his mind. Not that Mansur the farmer had been anything other than a benevolent and warm person since his arrival. Indeed, far from his expectation that he was to be a landslave, he had been treated like a son by Mansur, who provided him with a fresh and hearty meal every night and had given over to him a small but comfortable and clean bedroom. Maria still scowled at him in a mix of suspicion and curiosity like something she had dug from her ears – of questionable hygiene in any case – but he had come to understand that this was just her way.

33

Mansur had tried to talk to him on the first few days, usually over meals at the oak table. It was throwaway chatter: about the lands and the prospects for the harvest; about Kutalmish, the farmer over the hill who grew the ripest nectarines and figs in all Anatolia. Apion had shunned the conversation, instead staring through the open shutters, his gaze searching northward; his thoughts on the charred pile of rubble that used to be his home.

Every evening after eating he would go to his room and kneel by the foot of the bed, clutching the prayer rope to his forehead, the words of the Prayer of the Heart tumbling out as he recited the lines again and again, seeking a moment of truth, an answer. Neither was forthcoming.

It was the nights that truly haunted him. He had managed a single night of sleep since arriving. On that first night it had felt as if he had rested his head on the pillow and then plummeted into a deep well, all thoughts evaporating from his mind. It had been a full day later before he wakened. But every night since, that apparition of the dark door floating in the blackness visited him, drawing him towards it. The door was closed, and only more blackness could be seen through the cracks around its edges. Every night he would wake, bathed in sweat, trembling.

'So that's where my other bread went?' a voice said from behind him.

Apion's heart leapt and he bit into his tongue. He swivelled to the direction of the voice. Maria stood behind him, breathless from climbing the valley side, hair clinging to her face, her red robe was, as usual, soiled with grass and earth stains. She was grinning but her eyes showed apprehension and Apion still sensed her unease around him. He was a stranger in her home, after all. Perhaps Mansur had urged her to approach him, he mused.

'Maria,' he mumbled, gulping down his mouthful of bread, cracking what he intended as a warm smile but felt more like a wide-eyed grimace.

'So you do speak?' Maria's face twisted into mock disbelief.

'The bread is delicious! I hope I didn't leave you short in taking it?' he finished.

34

'No, there are another three rounds, but they are in the kitchen and I am here,' she stated austerely, reaching over to tear a piece from the bread in his hand. With that, her wariness evaporated and she sat down on the rock beside him and nudged her hips into his, moving him along.

'Your skin is so pale, it's like goat milk,' she mumbled rather ungraciously through a full mouth and spray of crumbs. 'Father says all Byzantines start pale but get burnt brown like us over their lives.'

Apion gave a half nod, chewing. What did she want him to say to that, he mused?

'Then there's your hair; it's a really strange colour, like sunrise over our barley fields. And your eyes, they're green like precious stones hidden under that brow.'

Apion flushed in self-consciousness.

'You look... really strange,' she finished and then ripped another chunk of bread from him. 'Not in a bad way, of course.'

'Of course.' Apion cocked an eyebrow.

'Why're you up here so early anyway? The goats are happy to wait and graze mid-morning you know.' She cocked her head to one side.

'I like being alo...' he hesitated. 'I like to see the sunrise.'

'Well I like to sleep until it is light,' she smiled, tucking her hair behind her ears, 'though maybe one morning I'll rise early and come with you?'

Apion saw the hopeful look on her face and nodded.

The farm was fully illuminated now, a patchwork of green plenty and brown fallow, hugged by the burnished red of the Anatolian landscape. A lowing of oxen drew their eyes to the tiny shape that was Mansur driving the beasts across the field, ploughing the earth for the next sowing of rye. Then, to formally announce the day, the cicadas broke into song, building towards their trilling crescendo that would last until dark.

'And so begins the new day,' Maria whispered. 'I've been bringing the goats here for years but I've never stopped to take it all in like this. It's like seeing your world like God would, looking down on everything and everyone at once.'

God. He wondered at her use of the word, unconsciously thumbing the knotted prayer rope. The farmhouse was devoid of religious matter. In a land riven by the religious zeal of Islam and Christianity that was almost unheard of. His own home had been typical of the soldier-farmers of the thema, devoutly Christian at every turn. He recalled Mother recounting the holy tale of the blind beggar and the tax collector at bedtime, her lilting tones would eventually turn to the lines of the Prayer of the Heart and the calming aroma of her violet scent would send him into a peaceful sleep. The memory was pleasant at first but then his scar tingled and he remembered that night, the screaming, then the charred rubble. Why would God deal a good Christian family such a hand?

'Father says you come from a family just like ours – farmers?' Maria asked, her voice inflecting uncertainty.

Apion nodded. He couldn't look at her as she spoke; terrified that she would see it all in his eyes. He wanted to say something about his mother and father but again the words choked on his lips, and he hated himself for it. Instead, he pretended to gaze at the wagon haring along the dirt road far below and gripped his prayer rope until his fingers turned white.

'Father says I've not to ask you too many questions,' she started, biting her lip. 'You can talk to me about them if you want though… when you are ready.'

Apion nodded.

'Look!' Maria yelped.

She pointed excitedly to the silvery column entering the northern end of the valley. In silence they watched the clutch of twenty or so kataphractoi that led the procession: iron helmets, iron klibania hugging their torsos over crimson tunics, each rider mounted on a fine warhorse, some of which even wore armour plating over their heads and bodies. Every rider bore an arsenal of iron: the spathion hanging from their belts, crimson skutum like a shell on their backs, hiding a bow and quiver. Each rider also carried a *kontarion*, the lengthy and broad-bladed spear over twice the height of a man, and one also carried the crimson Chi-Rho standard of the thema. Behind the riders, a bandon of just over three hundred skutatoi infantry marched, some garbed in iron helmets and klibania but most wearing padded vests, jackets and felt caps. They too carried kontarion, spathion and skutum. Behind the bandon a mule train followed obediently, laden with supplies. 'My father was a soldier,' he heard himself say as they disappeared from the other side of the valley.

'Your father was one of them?' Her face puckered a little, then she shook her head. 'We see armies set off through this valley all the time. They head east to war with... our people.'

Apion felt a flare of anger in his chest. 'And your people come here to spill blood too!' he barked, the dark door flitting across his thoughts. Then he gawped at Maria, who stood and shuffled back from him, face paling in fear. 'I'm sorry,' he stood to reach out to her but his scarred leg flared with a fiery pain. He fell to the ground with a roar, clutching at his thigh. She dropped to kneel by him, hands hovering to help.

'Leave me, there's nothing that can be done for it,' he panted. The pain subsided and he looked up into her eyes. 'Look, I'm really sorry for what I said.'

She offered a hand and helped him to his feet. 'It doesn't matter. They can fight all they like. We're all just people in the end.'

He offered her a smile. 'Can we walk a little? I find walking helps a bit.'

'Very well, the goats will be fine on their own for a while.'

They headed down into the neighbouring valley, away from Mansur's farm. She took his arm so he only needed the crutch for the trickier parts of the descent. His gaze was lost in the ground in front of him as they walked. They didn't speak but it was an unexpectedly comfortable silence. He found himself gazing into the horizon as they reached the valley floor and walked through the tall grass. Then he heard a crunch.

'Mmm… best nectarines in Anatolia.' Maria grinned, mouth half full, juice dripping down her chin, the orange flesh of a fruit glistening in her hand and an overhanging branch quivering.

Apion blinked, realising they had wandered to the edge of an orchard. 'It's beautiful,' he marvelled at the vibrant red-orange fruit dotting the trees. Then he noticed the fence posts encircling the orchard, tucking around the tree trunks. He leaned on his crutch and scratched his head. 'Isn't that someone else's fruit?'

'Kind of…' Maria mumbled, licking her fingers.

'Isn't that stealing?'

'Doesn't matter, it's old Kutalmish's farm, he's rich and old now; he won't miss a few nectarines.' She pointed to the edge of a well-kept farmhouse peeking out from behind the orchard. It was everything Mansur's was not; neatly tiled roof, freshly white-daubed walls and well-tended gardens. On the porch, a white-haired old man lay snoring in a hammock while Maria munched on his fruit. When she took another bite, Apion noticed that a blob of the fruit had stuck to the end of her nose, then realised that for the first time in so long he was grinning.

Maria frowned. 'What?'

Apion felt the laughter bubble up through his chest and couldn't stop it; it felt good, like honey in his throat. But Maria was furious; he reached up to touch her arm and reassure her, when a snapping of bracken from inside the orchard caught their attention.

'Who goes there?' a gruff voice pierced the air.

Maria grabbed his arm and hauled him away from the opening, pulling him down behind a red rock. His scar protested at this sudden movement, white-hot pain rushed through him and he gulped back a roar. Then Maria added to his misery by digging her elbow into his gut and then wrapping a dirty-nailed hand over his mouth, a faint smell of sweat emanating from her robe.

'Shut up if you don't want a scimitar wound to go with that,' she hissed. 'That was Kutalmish's oldest son, Giyath. I don't think he seen us but he's always keen to fight, he's twice the size of me and you put together… and he's armed.'

Apion stilled as he saw the fear in Maria's eyes. From the other side of the rock, crunching footsteps marched towards them and then stopped dead. Then the rasp of a scimitar blade being ripped from its scabbard sent a fiery dread crawling over his skin. His eyes bulged and his scar burned at the sound of the weapon that had created it. The terror of that night, that dark night, raced back to him.

'I said who goes there?' the gruff voice grunted. 'You're trespassing, so whoever you are, you'll not be walking out of here! It'd better not be you playing games again, little brother?'

Apion edged his head to one side: stood only paces away was a stocky and swarthy young man, shaven-headed, stubble-chinned with a broad and flat-boned face. The man wore a grey tunic and clenched a scimitar as he examined the hillside for movement.

'Whoever it is, show yourself! My blade is dirty and I'm keen to wash it in your blood!'

Apion turned to Maria; she hurled a jagged lump of rubble that flew from her hand and bounced from another chunky boulder around twenty paces away. Giyath's eyes locked onto the disturbance. Then, with a growl, he thundered towards it, his gait clumsy but determined.

'Come on!' Maria hissed and yanked Apion by the wrist.

At once they were hobbling up and around the orchard fence, out of Giyath's line of sight. Then Maria wrenched him towards Kutalmish's farmhouse. His body roared, his crutch meeting the ground only on every second stride, his vision spotting over and his scarred limb searing as though it was being sawn off. They stumbled past the snoring Kutalmish and into a field of tall barley, still dewy and mercifully cool on his searing scar. They were moving only at a fast walk but his body was spent and then, through dimming vision, he realised they were climbing the hill to the valley top and the goat herd once more. He reached out blindly, mouthing silently, knees shaking, when at last she stopped. He crumpled to the ground, panting.

Maria crouched beside him. 'We're safe now. I'm sorry, Apion. It's just that Giyath is... well father says he was a nice boy until...'

Her words trailed off. 'Anyway, he is now a moody and violent man.' Then she looked riddled with guilt as she eyed his trembling leg, biting her bottom lip.

Apion sought strength enough to push himself to his feet. 'It's fine, I'll be fine.' He stopped as he saw her eyes bulge, looking over his shoulder.

'Apion!' she screamed.

When he turned to see what was behind him, a cold hard shock to his cheekbone sent sparks of brilliant light through his eyeballs and bloody phlegm shooting from his nose and mouth. His world rolled in front of his eyes and he groaned, realising he was prone again.

A shadowy figure loomed over him. 'Raiders of Seljuk blood I can take but a Byzantine?' the figure boomed.

Apion shuffled back on the palms of his hands. Vision blurred, he could make out cinnamon skin and a flat-boned face. If it was Giyath then he was surely in big trouble. His eyes focused instead on a pony-tailed boy: younger than Giyath, perhaps his own age, nostrils flaring, eyebrows dipped in the centre like an angry bull. He looked like Giyath but without the broadness or the stubble, his gangly shoulders scaffolding a red, long-sleeved tunic.

'You think you can take from my father? I think you're a fool.' The boy stalked forward and shook his fist, the knuckles bloodied.

'I...' Apion stammered as the boy stalked forward, fists clenched.

'Nasir! No!' Maria screamed.

The boy wheeled around. 'And you, you call yourself a Seljuk? You could have your pick from the orchard, Maria, if only you'd not associate with his type!'

With that, the boy Nasir spun around again and thrust his foot into Apion's stomach. Bile leapt from Apion's mouth and he curled into a ball, croaking for the breath that had been kicked from his lungs. His eyes seemed to pop from their sockets as he retched, his world on its side. Nasir stomped over to Maria, remonstrating with her and Apion saw only the whites of Maria's bulging eyes.

'Nasir, you idiot, you're acting like your ape of a brother!' She shoved him in the chest.

Apion felt his hands scrape on the ground and at once he was up, hobbling towards Nasir's back. A roar pierced the air and he barely recognised it as his own as he clasped his arms around the boy's neck, pulling him down. The pair tumbled to the dust, spilling over in a flurry of elbows and knees. Nasir ended it by pinning Apion to the ground, knees pressed into his shoulders.

'You lay a finger on her and I... I...' Apion spat, struggling under Nasir's weight.

'Hold your tongue, Byzantine.'

'Get off him, Nasir,' Maria squealed, shoving him clear of Apion, 'you're hurting him!'

'What?' Nasir scrambled round to stand over him again, then snorted at the sight of the angry welt of scar on Apion's leg. 'A cripple? Well I won't waste my strength on you. What happened to your leg? Were your parents crippled too?' he mocked.

A fury erupted in Apion's chest and he hobbled forward. 'You filthy Seljuk *whoreson*!'

'Apion!' Maria slapped a hand across his neck. 'Stop it, both of you,' she gasped. 'Animals!'

Apion glanced at her and then shared a breathless and venomous glare with Nasir.

Maria sighed, screwing her eyes shut tight and running her hands through her hair. 'Apion, if you want to continue to share my family home then you'll apologise to Nasir. Nasir, you behave more like yourself and less like your idiot brother and we might speak again.' She wrinkled her nose. 'Make peace,' she demanded.

As the tension ebbed from his veins and the crushing pain from his scar replaced it, Apion looked at the boy Nasir. He was no more than that; just a wiry boy, but whose words had stirred a murky anger deep inside him.

Nasir cast him a mirror image, narrow-eyed stare. 'For now, Byzantine,' he growled.

Apion bristled. 'Likewise.'

'Come on,' Maria hissed, tugging Apion by the elbow as he and Nasir remained locked in a fiery gaze. 'Move or Giyath will come up here and he won't be so easily talked out of skewering you.'

'Talked out of? I had the beating of Nasir!' Apion protested as they descended the hill to Mansur's farm, the goats skipping alongside.

'The beating of him?' Her words cut through his indignation like a razor. 'We were on his property, trying to steal his family's food...' Her words trailed off as she saw the hole she was digging. Her skin darkened a little around the cheeks. 'Well, enough about who's right and who's wrong,' she grumped, pushing back through the barley stalks.

'Agreed.' Apion couldn't contain a weary grin. Before he followed her into the barley field, he cast a glance over his shoulder. Nasir stood like a sentinel on the hilltop, watching them.

CHAPTER 5

Night

Apion stirred from thick sleep. The farmhouse was still and silent. A winter draught tickled his ankles and he pulled them up and into the welcome heat under his hemp blanket. He prised open an eye; it was pitch-black inside and out apart from the pristine crescent of moon hanging in the triangular gap between the shutters, just below the carved Christian Chi-Rho mounted above the window. It was well into the night, he mused, knowing the path the moon took at this time of year. A gruff choking snore from Father startled him; then the subsequent weary groan from Mother sent a smile easing across his face. 'Could wake a bear in hibernation,' she said of Father. He sighed, hugging the edge of the blanket and studying the features of the moon until his eyelids began to droop. Sweet, thick sleep was overcoming him again. Then a shadow darted past the shutters. He sat bolt upright.

It was fleeting, maybe even never there, but he was awake now and his skin rippled with a sense of unease. He blinked hard, rubbing his fists into his eyes. He leaned forward to scan the crack in the shutters, his blanket dropping from his shoulders, the icy air shrouding him. Then, outside, an eagle screeched like a demon, its claws raking at the roof tiles. It sounded pained, as if it had hurt a wing or lost its baby. The bird finally left, its screaming fading. Once more all was still, all was silent. He felt for the creature but welcomed the return of the placid night, then smiled and sank back down onto the bed. He rested his head on the pillow and pulled the blanket back up to his neck. His thoughts began to wander into sleep.

Then a trilling and utterly foreign scream filled the night air. 'Loukas! Your time has come!'

43

His feet slapped on the deathly cold flagstones as he leapt to standing in one movement, eyes bulging, prying at the darkness through the open door of his bedroom, heart crashing against his ribs. He crept forward and poked his head out into the hearth room: the shadowy outline of the table sat inconspicuous as always. Another imagining, Apion hoped? But he knew in his heart something was terribly wrong.

'Apion, get back into your room!' his father croaked, stumbling from his bedroom, pulling on his tunic by the hearth. Then the thick timber door leading out to the yard smashed inwards as though struck by a battering ram, his father stumbled back and at once, his home was invaded by the dancing flames of bobbing torches. Dark towering shapes and jagged voices flooded into the hearth room along with the acrid stench of burning pitch. At once, Apion felt his skin pulled tight, eyes fixed on the intrusion, terror awash in his limbs. He ducked back into his bedroom and watched them from the shadows. There were four of them, each wrapped in thick black robes, heads and faces covered by thin cotton scarves and each wore a sword belt that bore the dreaded Seljuk scimitar. Then a fifth walked in and barked at the other four in the Seljuk tongue, then broke into Greek, the other four obeying his orders. Apion stalked back into the shadows of his bedroom, cowering, Father would protect them, surely.

'Can't find your sword, Loukas?' The leader spoke in a muffled voice through his veil. Then an awful rasping filled the room as three of the four intruders drew their scimitars from their scabbards, the curved blades glinting in the torchlight. 'Lucky we remembered ours!' A nightmarish orange illuminated the blades as three of the figures stepped forward to surround Father. The fourth remained fixed by the door, sword sheathed.

'Loukas? What's happening?' Mother shrieked, her voice trailing off into a series of sobs as she ran to grasp Father's arm. 'Where is Ap...' Father turned and struck her hard across the cheek. Instantly she was silent, one hand on her stinging face and eyes wide in shock, blood dripping from her lip. Father glared at her, terror and urgency contorting his features.

'Rest easy, Loukas, for tonight you will all die for your sins,' the leader purred, flicking a finger either side of the cowering pair. The three armed henchmen stalked around to encircle them. Then the leader stopped, twisting his head back to the fourth intruder. 'What about you?

Why are you suddenly so shy, hero?' The fourth intruder remained stock-still. *'So maybe your reputation is exaggerated? So be it,'* the leader spat, then turned his glare back to Mother and Father. *'Slaughter them and then torch this hovel!'* Then he nudged at the wooden blocks and carved toy soldiers on the floor. *'There is a boy in this house; make sure you find him… and stick him like a pig!'*

Apion could only watch as Mother's scream filled the farmhouse before it was cut short in a single swipe of a scimitar across her neck. Her body collapsed like a sack of rubble, head dangling behind the gaping wound and crimson soaking her night robe in a heartbeat. Father roared, thrashing out at his opponents with balled fists, but the intruders danced back easily from every blow.

'You have brought this upon yourself, Loukas!'

Father could only muster a pained snarl in reply.

'Take him down,' the leader sneered, *'make it slow… then bring me his head.'*

Apion's stomach lurched at the words. He stepped forward from the shadows but his feet froze on the floor as one of the henchmen jabbed his scimitar hilt into Father's face. A dull thud of metal on cracking bone was accompanied by the light patter of blood on the flagstones. Apion's throat clenched, mouthing a silent scream, as Father toppled to the flagstones, sprawled across Mother. The henchmen flicked their scimitars over and over in their hands and circled Father, like butchers eyeing a fresh slaughter. Then Apion felt a change, like a roaring river suddenly drying to a trickle, his fear was gone. What was there to fear when all was lost? His eyes fell on Father's battle gear resting in the shadows by the table. The helmet, the klibanion and the spathion.

Apion strode from the shadows, taking the helmet and placing it on his head, the rim resting on the bridge of his nose and the mail veil icy cold on his face, the leather aventail dangling around his neck and shoulders. The flickering torchlight bathed him but the intruders were captivated with their work as he approached them, prodding Father with the razor tip of their scimitars, puncturing his flesh, showering the hearth with blood. Father roared in pain at each prod but his face was drawn and exhausted as he cradled the bloody form of Mother underneath him, his spirit conquered.

Father's eyes were dimming but as Apion took up the spathion, their eyes met. Father extended a hand out past the legs of his torturers, reached out, then shook his head, his mouth haemorrhaging blood.

'No,' he spluttered as Apion lifted the weighty blade.

Then the leader stepped in between them, still oblivious of Apion, and snarled. 'Now finish him!'

One of the henchmen wrenched Father's head back by the hair and the other swept his scimitar down. Apion's stomach turned over at the ripping of sinew as Father was beheaded, eyes staring, mouth agape in shock. Apion's mouth gaped likewise to scream but his voice was simply not there.

'Now find this dog's child and bring him to me!' The leader turned to the silent intruder. 'And you, you useless whoreson, go outside and make sure nobody gets in or out of this place before we burn it to the ground.'

In a nauseous blur, Apion moved back into the shadows, to his bedroom; this would buy him a precious few seconds of life before he joined Mother and Father. No! Then they would have died in vain, Apion fretted, eyes darting around for any sign of hope as the henchmen emerged from his parents' bedroom. He realised he still held the spathion but what use was a weapon he could barely swing against these two brutes?

'He's not in there,' one henchman grunted and then extended a finger at the very shadows in which Apion hid, 'so he must be in that room.' Together, they stepped forward, scimitars in hand.

Apion realised escape was his only option. If he could flee into the night, wake the soldier-farmers in the next valley, then these raiders could be trapped. He turned to the shutters, ready to unbolt them as quietly as he could. But when he turned he froze, they were already ajar, punched open from outside. Was this some kind of trick? Then he sensed the presence of the two henchmen behind him.

'Too late to run! Ready to join your Father, boy?' one henchman hissed.

Apion spun, poised with the sword in a two-handed grip, trembling.

'Now put that blade down,' the second henchman hissed, his breath reeking. 'Just close your eyes and it'll all be over.'

Apion felt the terror boil in his veins. He roared and swung the sword wildly, the blade glancing from the walls, showering sparks across the room,

46

the henchmen leaping back. Suddenly, the leader stormed into the room and stopped, masked features examining Apion.

'Is this Loukas' runt behind that veil?' Then he pointed a finger at Apion. 'Take his head.'

Apion was frozen momentarily, eyes hanging on the tarnished ring on the leader's finger, a snake winding around the band. Then he roared and wrenched the spathion up, the blade caught the leader's finger, chopping clear a chunk of skin and bone. The leader staggered back with a roar while the blade flew from Apion's hand, plunging into the gut of the second henchman, who touched the hilt in stunned silence, blood gushing from his mouth, before toppling like a log, dead.

'Finish him!' the leader rasped, his voice laced with fury as he clutched the bleeding stump of his finger and ducked back out of the bedroom.

Apion staggered back as the first henchman lurched forward, sweeping his scimitar down. Spinning away, he leapt for the open shutters, then his mind flashed with a white light as the henchman's blade hammered down on the back of his helmet then ground into his flesh. He felt a hot streak of agony like nothing before, the blade tearing at his back, ripping through his thigh and hacking all the way down his calf to his ankle.

Then he could see only the floor and a dark liquid pooling around him. His body grew cold and needled towards numbness. Blackness swam over him. He could hear only a dull ringing and the murmur of the intruders.

'Now drag him outside, I want to see all three heads on spikes.'

Apion felt his ankles being grappled and an unearthly agony stung him to his core.

Then another voice called, the fourth intruder, from outside.

'Imperial riders!'

'Then leave him,' the leader spat from the hearth room. 'They can all burn where they lie.'

Everything around Apion seemed to be growing distant. He could hear splashing, and the smell of pitch grew thicker. Then there was a dull clatter of a torch being hurled to the floor, followed by a roar of fire and anxious yells as they ran from the building.

The heat intensified until it stung through the numbness and was accompanied by the stench of crackling flesh. From somewhere, Apion

47

found the energy to prise apart his eyelids: there, in the corner of his bedroom, lay the staring and unmasked features of the man he had struck down; a Seljuk man, engulfed in the inferno, the skin on his face blistering and exploding like a roasting pig, eyes clouded over. Apion turned away in disgust but all around him was a raging orange; the flames had engulfed his home already. Death was coming for him. He searched for the opening line of the Prayer of the Heart and made to close his eyes, when he caught sight of his own reflection in the blade of the spathion, still lodged in the burning Seljuk's guts. He grimaced at the image, the weakness he portrayed. Behind the blade, he saw two charred masses where Mother and Father had fallen, the flames having consumed their flesh already. Were they to have died for nothing? Did their killers deserve to walk free? A desperate cry rasped from his lungs and he lurched to prop himself onto his elbows and then pulled his torn body forward, the searing hot iron helmet tumbling from his head and rolling into the inferno. The heat pulled the air from his lungs as he tried to breathe and the room above him seemed to be solid with a jet-black smoke. With a grimace, he pulled himself on through the hearth room on a black slick of his own blood, a smoking timber beam crashing down by his side barely registering as he fixed his eyes on the doorway.

The roof groaned as he clasped a hand to either side of the doorframe. The intruders were gone and there were no imperial riders to be seen. The night lay in front of him and out there he would find the creatures responsible for this.

All of this.

Tears stung his cheeks as he hauled himself clear of the doorframe. He roared out into the night. Then, behind him, the roof groaned and shuddered. Then it collapsed. The cloud of flames hurled him through the doorway, then a glowing beam crashed down on top of him, landing with an unearthly pain up the length of his butchered leg, gouging into his back with a rapacious sizzling of flesh. His lungs had nothing left in them to scream with and he felt darkness rush in.

An eagle's cry high above pierced the night air and at once he was gone from the world.

He awoke to the sound of lungful after lungful of screaming. His own. He had the prayer rope clasped with both hands across his heart.

'Apion!' a voice echoed. A broad moustachioed face emerged from the misty confusion. Mansur shook him by the shoulders.

'Father?' Maria scrambled to Apion's bedside.

'Get out, Maria.' He waved a hand at her. 'Please, start the fire and prepare some *salep*.'

'Apion, be calm, please, you are safe, you are safe.'

He felt his chest heave more slowly and the screaming had died to a whimpering. His face was wet with tears. Glancing around the room it was all so peaceful, so quiet: the fire crackled through in the hearth room and the shadows of his bedroom danced lazily in the half-light from the flames.

'Mansur, I'm sorry. I, I saw it all. As if I was there again...'

'Easy, lad, take a deep breath.' Mansur frowned, brushing a thumb across Apion's cheeks, wiping the tears clear.

'It was all like it was happening again for real. I felt every blow, the fire... their bodies...'

Mansur's eyes looked lined and heavy and he shook his head. 'You have a heavy burden on your shoulders, lad. It is time you shared it with me. Come, let us have a drink and talk.'

The hearth room was pleasantly warm, the fire freshly loaded with logs. A rather grumpy Maria had prepared them each a cup of salep, a hot milky drink spiced with cinnamon and orchid root, and then trudged back to her bed to leave them alone. Apion had told Mansur everything, eyes hanging on the gentle flames as he did so. The old man had remained quiet while the story was told, even during the long pauses as Apion composed himself. As the grim tale progressed he found his words flooding out like a river, the images flitting before his mind's eye.

'I was dead. I swear death took me.' He shook his head, gazing into the speckled surface of his salep. He took a sip, the creamy sweetness of the drink coating his throat, comforting him. 'When I woke, my wound was cleaned and dressed and I was resting in a shaded dell, way up on the hills, miles from the farmhouse, a pleasant breeze cooling my skin. Everything was silent apart from a lone eagle calling somewhere high above. I did not feel the pain of my wound at first. My mind was blissfully free of the memories of what had just happened.'

Mansur frowned, confused. 'The slave traders had found you and bandaged you?'

Apion shook his head, his face wrinkling. 'If they had found me then, in the smoking ruins of my house, I would not be alive. No, only a woman was there; silver hair and eyes that were pure white – she must have been blind. She was old, older even than you.' He paused a moment, checking to see if he had caused offence. Mansur issued a weary smile so he continued. 'She dug at roots in the earth and hummed a tune to herself. Her voice was comforting to me in my state, something about it made me think of Mother. Then she came over and removed my dressing. I couldn't look at the wound but she rubbed the root against my flesh and it took the pain away. I asked her who she was and she just laughed. Not at me, just a little laugh as if she had remembered a joke.'

Mansur was captivated. 'Did she tell you how she had got you to this place?'

'No, but she spoke to me while she reapplied my dressing. She said the burning timber that fell on me had saved my life, cauterising the flesh.' He stopped and frowned. 'She gave me my crutch and told me it was time for me to carry on with my life, but she had a single piece of advice for me.'

Mansur leant forward, nodding.

'She said I would choose a path. A path that leads to conflict and pain. She told me to go anywhere I wanted. Anywhere except... home.'

'Where she found you?'

Apion nodded.

'Then you left the dell.' Mansur rubbed his moustache, imagining the scene. 'Where did you go next?'

'Well I found myself hobbling on my crutch a long way from those hills. The pain came back gradually as I made my way back.'

'Back?'

'I went home, Mansur, despite what she told me.' A tear forked from his eye. 'The place was a charred mound of rubble. I kept looking at it, trying to see it, as if the ruin was not real. I spent days there, just sitting, staring into the ash. When the slave wagon came by, I barely noticed them as they shackled me. They packed my wound with salt, knocked me unconscious and took me into the city. I woke in a cellar, insects running through my hair, rats biting at my flesh. I survived in that place for over a month until the trader took his slaves to market. That's when I ended up in the inn; one stinking cellar for another. Every day for the best part of a year they would beat me, spit on me, yet all I could see was the blackness of the ash. All I could think of was righting the wrong.'

Mansur held his gaze, the old man's eyes were red-rimmed. 'It's over now, Apion. You are here and you are safe under my roof. Perhaps the old woman who tended to you was right. As dreadful as what you have just told me is, perhaps you should try not to dwell on what happened at your old home. I realise that what I am suggesting would be far from easy, but to let go of this could be to give yourself a chance to live a happy life? Ask yourself what your parents would have wanted of their son; a blackened individual, joyless and bitter, or the boy they knew, the boy they loved and who loved them back?'

Apion looked at him solemnly and shook his head. 'You speak wise words, Mansur, but I can't even remember who I used to be before that night.' He had tried so hard to remember the past as it once was: Mother preparing a meal of stew and bread for Father's return from campaign. When he arrived, dressed in a leather klibanion, iron helmet and boots, Apion saw him as a model kataphractos. Then the three of them would spend the time outside of campaigning season tilling and sowing the modest farmland. Hard work, but happy times. Yet the memories were becoming flatter and more hazy over time.

Mansur's face saddened at this and he gazed into the fire. 'I know where you are, lad. Loss; it takes a long time to come to terms with it. Indeed it drives you to seek answers from the darkest of places before you finally make peace...' His words trailed off, his voice breaking up.

Apion noticed that Mansur's eyes glistened now. 'Your wife?'

'Ten years ago,' Mansur spoke flatly, his grey crop shimmering with sweat, his face stony as he gazed into the fire.

Apion nodded. So Maria would never have known her mother. Suddenly he felt heart-sad for her. Mansur's grief was there but not there, like its rawness had been chipped away and polished down to a smooth burden that he bore without question. He pulled at his prayer rope and wondered at his next words, whether Mansur would appreciate them.

'Does it help to know she is with God now?'

Mansur did not look round from the fire but his face hardened a little. 'God, if such a thing exists, makes our lives a constant struggle.' He lifted his salep and supped thoughtfully.

Apion frowned. 'You must have loved God once to say such a thing?'

Mansur turned to him and nodded. 'When you lose what is dearest to you, you have a choice: worship or reject. I have made my choice.'

'My mother and father, they were Christian. I am Christian. But, and I don't know if I am betraying them in saying this, I can't see why God could let what happened to them happen.' His eyes darted around the flagstones as he searched for his feelings, then he looked up to Mansur.

'That's what makes me doubt it all, lad,' Mansur replied. 'If God created man, then why are we so foul and blinded? We live our lives for a few handfuls of seasons and we spend most of them making mistakes, terrible mistakes. Only when we're grey and withered do we realise where we should have turned and when.' He shrugged his shoulders and lifted one side of his mouth wryly. 'By then, our children have grown into their own cycle of pig-headedness, doomed to blunder on until we are all merely dust.' A log snapped in the fire.

Apion nodded as he considered Mansur's words. 'Father would have taught me and guided me well. I know it. He always showed me things and said that when I was old enough he would teach me all that he had learned. He promised that after the next campaigning season, he would teach me to tame a horse and make it my own, so I could become a rider like him. Now I will never learn from him.'

The old man held his gaze for a moment longer then shook his head and took a deep breath. 'As I say, learning is usually a matter of making mistakes. Well I am grey and withered and I've made many mistakes in my life. I can help you learn.'

'You'd do that for me? A slave, not of your blood, not even of your kin?'

Mansur finally broke into a weary smile. 'You're no slave, Apion, just as you told me that day in Trebizond. So, the learning begins tomorrow; the grey mare is about the right size for a lad of your age and build. After breakfast we will get you used to life in the saddle, how does that sound?'

Apion grinned.

CHAPTER 6

The Horseman

Dawn had not yet broken and only the moonlight outlined the land. The fresh wind rushed over the pair riding on the grey mare.

'Slow down!' Maria cried out, grappling her hands together around Apion's waist and hugging herself to his back.

'Are you joking? This is like having wings! Anyway, we're nearly finished.'

He leant forward on the saddle and focused on the dark-blue dappled eastern horizon, then heeled the beast's flanks. 'Ya!' he bellowed. The mare accelerated before they hit the uphill slope to the tip of the valley side separating the two farms, heading for the hilltop.

At first, the very act of staying on horseback had proved difficult for him, his scarred leg stinging as he clung to the beast, but the rush when he rode was unmatched and only a few weeks after Mansur had first shown him the basics of handling a horse, riding felt more natural to him than walking.

This morning he and Maria had raced at full pelt down the banks of the Piksidis, before turning in and up to the tip of the valley side. Then they had sped down the opposite side, rounding Kutalmish's farm, Apion shouting a pox on the boy Nasir – much to Maria's chagrin – and then galloping back up the valley side. Now they were coming to the hilltop just north of the farm. Apion had discovered this hilltop on his first solo morning gallop; it was probably the highest point near Mansur's farm, and afforded a fine vista of the breaking dawn.

As they reached the hilltop, they rounded the small beech thicket and then the mare slowed just by a terracotta boulder cairn. Apion's eyes were drawn to the topmost boulder, sporting a faded etching of some creature with two heads, broad wings and dagger-like talons. The etching was very old by the look of it, but the fierceness in the creature's eyes still made his spine tingle every morning when he saw it.

Then Maria cuffed his ear. 'Have you lost your mind? I was terrified we were going to be thrown to the ground and dashed on the rocks!'

Apion laughed; this was the first time she had ridden with him. She had begged him to take her with him because Mansur – who had forbidden her from riding as she was too small – was away to market today. He turned to her, grinning, but his face fell as he noticed that she was shaking. He put a hand on her knee. 'I'm sorry, Maria, I didn't mean to frighten you. It's just that I've never felt more in control than when I'm riding.' He patted the mare's mane and the beast snorted in reply, breath clouding in the dawn air. 'I'd never be able to make it up here on foot with my crutch.'

She glanced at his withered leg and he felt the usual shame. His leg had at least formed a pink welt of scar tissue since leaving the squalid conditions of the cellar inn, but this scarring held the limb bent at the knee, forcing him to walk in a lop-sided fashion. To stretch the scar and stand tall sent a furious agony through his body, so riding suited him perfectly.

'It's alright,' she said softly, 'I know you didn't mean to upset me.' She looked around, the wind dancing through her hair. All was still dark apart from the band of light blue to the east. 'Anyway, why have we stopped here?'

'You said you would watch the sun rise with me one morning, remember?' He pointed to the glimmer of red on the eastern horizon. 'Well, here we are.'

She rested her chin on his shoulder and they remained in silence as the glimmer swelled and spread, growing into orange until the light spilled through the valleys, illuminating the burnished terracotta hillsides, silhouetting the farms and mills that dotted the rich soil flatlands in between and igniting the Piksidis like a silver asp.

They watched until the sun was fully over the horizon, their breath slowing at the majestic transformation.

Maria sighed contentedly, finally breaking the spell. 'It's beautiful.'

'I never tire of watching the land come to life. It washes away all the worry from my mind,' Apion replied.

'It's a wonder you get any sleep at all – you're up before the goats!'

Apion laughed. It had taken him a while to realise but life on the farm had kept him engaged at all times: riding, goat herding and farming absorbing his days and every night was ended with a welcome cup of creamy salep. Even the nightmares had begun to subside in the last few weeks, and the resulting rest had been most welcome. Every morning he had found himself refreshed and calm, rising before dawn to come up here, basking in the beauty of dawn.

His thoughts were interrupted as he noticed Maria shuffling in discomfort. 'It is beautiful, but there will be many more mornings… and I'm hungry. Are you not?' she reasoned, jabbing a finger into his ribs and grinning.

'Aye,' he chuckled, 'let's go home.'

He heeled the mare to turn towards the farm and they set off at a canter. When they got back, they prepared a platter of goats' cheese, bread, yoghurt and figs, and a now unmissable cup of sweet, creamy salep to wash it down. The goats had struck up a chorus of enraged bleating as they ate.

'You'll get your food once we've had ours!' Apion chirped. Through the open door he could see two kids, born in the last month, jostling for position at the front of the pen, ears flopping over their faces, eyes wide in anticipation. 'Anyway, I thought you were goats, not pigs?' he chuckled.

'You're one to talk; you get through the cheese faster than I can prepare it!'

Apion spun round to see Maria stood, the hint of a smirk edging her lips. 'Ah, it's only because I graze them so well that the cheese is so tasty!' He pulled a handful of blueberries from the branch in the middle of the table, popping one in his mouth, the tangy juice inside the fruit bursting across his tongue. The house was quiet and Mansur's dark-blue felt cap was conspicuous by its absence from the peg by the door. It warmed him that the old man trusted him, a Byzantine boy, like a son. It warmed him more to reciprocate that trust. He looked to Maria, wolfing bread in a less than delicate manner, crumbs lining her lip. She was either black or white; she'd snarl at him in a temper then she'd grin at him and he felt good, like everything was well.

'You'll come out with me again one morning?' He munched on the last of the blueberries.

'When I grow taller I'll be riding the fawn mare… on my own,' she replied, looking past him austerely.

'Then we can race!' Apion grinned.

'You're becoming more like Nasir every day. Is that what happens to all boys as they grow up?'

Apion thought of the cinnamon-skinned boy and frowned. Nasir and he had clashed on a regular basis, usually on the valley side when he was grazing the goats. The first time, Nasir came past and mocked him, saying that Apion was a cripple and not even worth fighting. Apion had stayed quiet, refusing to meet the boy's glare and maintaining an air of disinterest. It was only after the boy left him alone that Apion let his fury boil over. Taking his crutch into his hand like a sword and smashing it time and again against a tree. The last time they had met, just last week, Nasir had introduced himself by means of bouncing a stone off the back of Apion's head. His ears ringing, he could only lip-read the obscenities the boy hurled at him until his hearing recovered.

Nasir's face had been a sneer and a grimace at once. Then his expression had dropped as Apion stood and hobbled over to him, eyes burning. Nasir was a good half-foot taller but at that moment he felt level. He had pushed the boy in the chest and saw Nasir's fists ball as if to retaliate, but instead the boy had simply snorted and walked away. 'I've already told you: I won't fight a cripple,' he had thrown over his shoulder derisively. That was when Apion had challenged him to a horse race along the banks of the Piksidis. 'If you won't fight me and you won't race me then I begin to think you are afraid of me,' Apion had growled, hubris coursing in his veins yet well aware that in any such race, Nasir would ride on his father's stallion, a good hand higher than his own grey mare. Regardless of this, the race had been set up for the following week.

'A pox on him!' Apion waved a hand as if swatting an invisible fly.

'Apion! He's a nice boy. He just tries really hard to act like a fool.'

'Like his brother?'

She nodded. 'Exactly like his brother. Father says Giyath himself used to be a nice young man and it was only when his mother was…' She looked away, eyes to the floor.

Apion frowned and sat forward. 'Maria? What happened to their mother?'

'She was killed. Father says I must not speak of it.'

'Why?' Apion said. 'The truth could never be as terrible as what happened to my parents, Maria.'

She looked up to him, eyes glassy. How much of his past Mansur had told her he did not know.

'Nasir and Giyath's mother, Kutalmish's wife, was killed,' she said. 'A Byzantine patrol fell upon the caravan as they came here from the east to settle.'

Apion pulled his chair around and put a hand to her shoulder, nodding.

'They lashed out with their swords without question, assuming the caravan was some Seljuk military supply line. I was there, Apion. I can't remember it as I was but a baby, as was Nasir. Before they realised we were civilian they had killed his mother and… and…'

58

Realisation dawned on him 'Your mother was there too, wasn't she?'

Maria nodded.

Apion pulled his arm around her and let her sob gently into his shoulder. So Kutalmish and Mansur had been widowed on the night they had made the bold step to abandon soldiery and embrace a life of peaceful agriculture in the empire they had once fought. No wonder Giyath was an aggressive beast, and Nasir's rage was understandable. He wondered if the dark door lived in the minds of them all. Did they seek retribution as he did? Did they see every Byzantine being as he saw the masked men from that night?

'I didn't even know her,' Maria spoke softly, wiping her eyes, 'it still hurts to think of her though. Father won't talk to me about her. It's as if I never had a mother.'

'He hurts, deep inside. I know it,' Apion rubbed her shoulder. 'I think he finds it difficult to talk about his past.' Apion realised the irony of the statement; it was Mansur's patient ear that had listened to the tale of Apion's dark past. 'You can talk to me about her, any time you want to.'

'I will.' She offered a hint of a smile but her eyes remained sad. 'But I know that you suffered a terrible loss, as cruel as ours. I want you to talk to me of your family as well.'

Apion nodded, cupping Maria's hand, searching her eyes for a glimmer of happiness.

Instead, Maria straightened in her chair, eyes growing wide, staring over his shoulder and through the doorway. Then she pushed back on her chair, shaking. 'Maria?' Apion's blood iced. He twisted in his chair, following her stare to the vision trotting up the dirt path, rippling in the morning heat haze. Two horsemen approached, armed.

She stood, whispering, eyes searching the floor of the hearth room, fingers grappling at the hem of her dress.

'Who is it?' Apion pushed up from the table, head darting from Maria to the riders until the sunlight splashed from their conical iron helmets and he noticed one wore a golden plume. He recognised the garb: kataphractoi, defenders of the empire, just like father; so why did his gut ripple in unease?

'Stay inside,' she barked, stepping to the doorway, shifting her diminutive figure into the space and bristling, attempting to fill it out in vain. Apion felt only one need at that moment; to protect her.

He shuffled forward on his crutch, then barged past her, out of the doorway and into the growing heat of the morning. Then the gold-plumed soldier slipped down from his horse and strode forward, a smile etched under his blade of a nose that ill-fitted the malevolent grimace worn by his bull of a partner. At that moment Apion recognised him: Bracchus, the soldier who had mugged Mansur that day in the wagon and the big Rus who had accompanied him.

Bracchus sucked in a lungful of air and blew it out again with a groan. 'Oh dear, Mansur really has run out of tricks this time, eh, Vadim?' His voice boomed, belying his tall but lean frame. He turned to his partner, flicking his head towards Apion. 'Seems to have fled the scene and left a boy to deal with his problems. A Byzantine boy living and working for a Seljuk... what's your story?'

'What have you come here for?' Apion said, noticing a glint of coinage from the packed hemp sacks hanging beside Vadim's saddle.

'Whatever I want, boy, whatever I want,' Bracchus chuckled, then pulled off his helmet, the mail aventail rustling. He flexed his fingers, the iron studs on the knuckles of his leather gloves chinking, then ran his hands over his crop of fawn hair. 'I would advise you to be agreeable to my demands.'

'What is an imperial soldier doing on a Seljuk farmstead?' Apion spoke evenly. 'Mansur has paid his taxes well in advance. I ask you again: what do you want?'

Bracchus simply glared at him.

Then Vadim interjected in his jagged Rus accent. 'Stubborn little shit, eh? Ah well, not to worry. Fancy goat for dinner?' With

60

that, he thumped down from his mount, and then strode over to the goat pen.

Apion balled his fists, but Bracchus stood steadily over him, eyes unblinking.

'Aye, a fat old one for more meat or... or what about the kids? Tender and tasty,' Vadim continued.

'No!' Maria squealed, sprinting from the shade of the doorway, spreading her arms across the big soldier's path. Vadim simply leaned over her and scooped a bleating kid out by the neck, its mother crying in panic. In a flash he tore a dagger from his belt and slid it across the animal's throat. The kid kicked and spluttered as a wash of crimson covered its body and pooled on the ground below its dangling hooves. Within moments it hung limp, eyes staring. Maria leapt at the soldier with a sob but with a shovel of a hand, Vadim swept her back, sending her tumbling to the ground.

'Maria!' Apion yelped, lurching for her, but his leg jarred as he turned and he fell to the dust with a groan of agony.

Bracchus snorted in derision and then crouched so his eyes were level with the prone Apion. 'Now you listen here, boy. Mansur knows full well that when I demand, he pays.'

'He has already paid you more than once this year, yet still you won't leave us alone,' Maria seethed.

'You forget your place in this land, Seljuk whore.' Bracchus stalked over to her, grinning. Then he coolly scraped his spathion a few inches from his scabbard.

Apion's skin writhed, that murky image of the dark doorway flitted across his thoughts. 'You spill a drop of her blood and I'll kill you!' he screamed, forcing the words from his lips and heaving himself to standing, lumbering towards Bracchus. Then Vadim pulled his sword round to block Apion's path, and he stopped just in time, the blade pricking his throat and a warm trickle of blood shooting down his neck and onto his tunic.

'Brave move.' Bracchus snorted. 'Worth a shot but all it gets you is an open throat. Finish the little Seljuk-loving whoreson, Vadim, his corpse will be a fine statement of debt for Mansur.'

Apion saw the gleeful malice in Vadim's eyes and knew it was the end for him. He closed his eyes and waited. Then a clang of stone on iron rang out beside them.

'What the…' Vadim staggered back, doubled over, hands clutching at his forehead. Then his helmet slipped from his red-stubbled head and landed in the dirt, a sharp dent in the brow glimmering in the sunshine. At the same time, a smooth pebble bounced away across the dirt path. Vadim's left eye was swollen and purple and one nostril spouted blood. The big Rus roared, chest heaving, blade held out as he circled on the spot. 'Mansur? Come face me! I will tear you apart like a goat!'

Bracchus scanned the surroundings like a cat, poised, spathion drawn and ready to strike.

Apion hobbled over to Maria, wrapping his arms around her. Together, the pair frowned in confusion.

Bracchus' icy eyes darted around the farm, looking for the one who had cast the stone. 'Whoever that was, they've made the biggest mistake of their life, and their last!' he snarled, eyes tracing the path the stone had taken from Vadim's helmet and then up, up to the red tiled roof of the farmhouse. There, almost imperceptibly, was a tiny blur of movement behind the apex of the roof. 'Vadim, go around the other side of the house!'

The groaning Vadim hobbled round to the back of the farm-house.

'Is that you, Mansur? Well, you've done it this time. There's no way out for you,' Bracchus purred. 'Two sharp swords are waiting for you down here. We might be kind and let you die on them, after you have watched your daughter die. Or you can be executed in the city for striking an imperial soldier; your filthy Seljuk head would decorate the city walls nicely.'

Then a whirring penetrated the thickness of the air. It grew and grew into a hum and then a buzz like an angry hornet swarm. Suddenly, a figure shot up to standing on the roof, his form blurred by the heat haze, one arm a smear of spinning colour – a loaded sling.

'You think? I'd like to see what your swords can do from down there. This, on the other hand,' the figure gestured to the sling, 'will dash out your brains before you take even a single step.'

Apion's eyes narrowed: the burnished skin, the pony tail. Nasir!

Bracchus pulled a shark-like grin, his eyes red with rage. 'There are two of us though and by the time you loose a shot and load another, one of us will be upon you. So you will still die and I promise you, it will be slowly.' Vadim remained poised, ready to strike. Bracchus' eyes never left Nasir. Then the ground rumbled, the distant thrashing of hooves growing. Each of the group shot glances at the three horsemen who approached along the highway at a gallop. Then one of the approaching riders bellowed.

'Soldiers!'

Apion eyed the man who had spoken: a mounted, green-cloaked soldier, wearing a klibanion, leggings, leather riding boots and thick, iron-plated gloves, plumed like Bracchus but with green feathers on his shoulders as well as his helmet. A narrow hooked nose curled out over a forked beard, black flecked with grey, and his mouth was firm and straight. His eyes gave nothing away. Two soldiers flanked him, also on horseback, but the man in the centre seemed to dominate the trio.

'Bracchus, what's your business here?' the man boomed.

Bracchus slotted his sword back into his scabbard. 'Attacked by these locals here, sir; militant Seljuks. The situation is under control.' His tone was lacking the urgency the question had demanded and instead inflected disdain for the mounted officer.

The mounted officer studied Bracchus, then eyed Maria and Apion. 'Well they match you for numbers at least,' he snorted.

'But sir, on the roof,' Vadim interrupted.

The roof was bare. The buzzing of the sling had stopped.

'Needs a bit of repair, yes. What of it? Has there been some kind of misunderstanding?'

Bracchus barely suppressed a grimace. 'There is no misunderstanding here, sir,' he muttered.

63

'Then be on your way. A patrol is a patrol; it means you're expected to be on the move. Unless there is an incident, a real incident... somewhere.'

'Sir!' Bracchus replied, without salute. Vadim pulled his dented helmet back over his swollen eye. The pair mounted their horses, Bracchus' glare staying on the mounted officer. Then they heeled their mounts into a gallop.

The mounted officer watched their dust trail, shaking his head slowly, lips muttering silently.

'Strategos!' one of his guardsmen barked. 'We must make haste to the rendezvous!'

Strategos. Apion's ears pricked up at the word. He remembered Father telling him of the select few men who led the armies of Byzantium, the regional themata and the prestigious mobile armies of the central *tagmata*. Mounted and plumed, they were the thinkers of the army.

The officer turned to his guardsman, nodding. 'Aye, haste as always, but these citizens deserve a moment of my time first.' He turned to face Apion. 'What is your name, lad?'

'Apion.'

Cydones nodded. 'And did you strike that big Rus?'

Apion eyed the officer in suspicion, his throat tightened and he made to point to the roof, then thought better of it. The tension of the encounter ebbed from his veins and his thoughts steadied. 'I did not, though I wish I had.'

The strategos removed his plumed helmet and wiped his shining bald pate with a rag tucked into his collar. 'No matter, Vadim's a good fighter but one who cannot be trusted; he has it coming to him if he's going to throw his weight around. But Bracchus? All I will say is be on your guard, lad. I won't always be around to keep him in check.' As his two guardsmen moved away at a canter, the officer rummaged in his purse and threw down a gold nomisma.

Apion stared at the thin gold coin that had wedged into the dust, stained with drying goat blood.

64

'This is for your goat. I hope it covers you for the loss of milk and cheese.' He looked at the lifeless corpse of the tiny animal. 'And I'm sorry this happened.' He held Apion's gaze for a few moments, brow wrinkling.

Then he was off, accelerating to a canter and then a gallop, green cloak billowing. Apion watched his dust trail then turned to Maria.

'Cydones,' Maria whispered. 'Leader of every fighting man in Chaldia.'

'Yet he accepts such corruption?' Apion spat.

'Father says he is a good man, but only one man. He can only do so much.'

'So providing a few honest men policing the roads is beyond him?'

'Father says honest men are only a few coins away from dishonesty.'

'You believe that?'

'There are many who extort from the Seljuk farmers around here, Apion. Like father says: let them have their coins, so long as we are safe and well every night.'

He turned to her. A tear hung in her eye as she beheld the slaughtered kid and the tortured bleating of its sister and mother tore at his heart. Then a voice split the air.

'You should have ridden off with him, Byzantine filth!'

Apion's eyes shot up at the rooftop again. Nasir stood tall once more, his sling hung from his belt.

Apion searched for a reply, then words tumbled from his lips.

'Why would I?' he roared, stabbing a finger at the ground, realisation washing through him, laced with guilt. He saw Mother and Father's faces in his mind, and prayed they would understand. 'This is my home!'

Mansur steadied himself and then lunged forward, stabbing out. Apion leant back on his crutch and parried, the clack-clack of their wooden poles echoing out across the valley in the still summer air.

As he tired and his scar burned ever more furiously, Apion fuelled his efforts with that shadowy image of the dark door, until a guttural roar poured from his lungs as he lunged forward, putting all the strength of his shoulders into a strike.

Mansur parried then panted, resting on his pole for a moment, holding up one hand. 'Easy, easy! This was supposed to be about learning self-defence, remember?'

Apion nodded sheepishly. Mansur had been reluctant in agreeing to this, but equally, the old man felt terrible guilt over having left Apion and Maria alone on that day of the visit of Bracchus and Vadim. Apion had sworn that he wanted only skills enough to be able to defend Maria and the animals at the farm, arguing that if Nasir had not been there that day, it could have been far worse than a slaughtered goat kid.

'Anyway, I think that crutch gives you an unfair advantage over an old man,' Mansur puffed, sweat glistening on his brow.

Apion allowed himself to relax, stabbing his pole into the ground for extra support as he caught his breath. At first the bouts had been short, with Apion flailing, ending up in the dust in seconds, Mansur calmly holding the wooden pole to his throat. But his good leg had grown gradually more taut and lean with every day of practice and riding and this allowed him to improve little by little. Firstly he learned how to parry. This gave him time to watch the old man's movements and spot patterns. It had taken him weeks, but now whenever Mansur attacked he could react, ducking, dodging or executing a good, solid parry, sometimes with the pole and sometimes with the crutch itself, taking his weight briefly on the scarred leg.

He held the crutch up. 'Maybe you need one of these for yourself?'

Mansur looked briefly outraged, then grinned wickedly. 'There speaks a boy who is confident in himself.'

Then a whinnying pierced the air from the top of the valley.

'Hiding?' a voice called out.

Apion twisted to see Nasir, bathed in sunshine, mounted on his stallion. 'Ah,' he murmured to Mansur, 'it is time for another challenge – the horse race!'

'Boys: never happy when not locking horns!' Mansur sighed. 'Go easy on the old mare will you?'

'Of course I will. She will be fed and watered well tonight.' He hobbled over to the stable, remembering how Nasir had snorted in derision when Apion had tried to thank him for warding off Bracchus and Vadim. *It was for Maria, not you*, he had spat. This was the chance to shut the boy up once and for all.

He pushed up with his crutch, sliding his good leg onto the saddle and then slipping into place. He ran his fingers through the mare's mane. 'You and I will teach this arrogant whoreson a lesson today.' Then he heeled her into a trot.

'Ride well, but ride safely!' Mansur called to him as he passed.

Apion turned to him and grinned mischievously. 'Have you taught me any other way?'

The summer sun was at its zenith as the two boys sped on horseback along the lush green banks of the Piksidis.

The grey mare's chest pumped frantically. 'Keep it going, girl!' Apion yelled, hair whipping back in the rush, throat dry from Nasir's dust trail. The pony-tailed boy's mount was growing steadily more distant up ahead and then, as had happened several times already, the boy slowed to stay in sighting distance of Apion and his mare, then hurled abuse and roared with laughter. They were only half a mile from the bridge, the finishing post, when Nasir sped away once more.

He had thought it through last night: in a flat-out race Nasir's stallion would romp to victory, but Nasir didn't want to just win and win well, he wanted to win in a way that punctured Apion's pride as much as possible. That, Apion decided, was the one weakness he could exploit.

With his constant dangling of victory before Apion, then snatching it away again, Nasir was playing into his hands. Yet his own mount had given everything and had galloped faster than ever, but would she have the energy to execute his plan? The mare glistened with sweat and foam gathered at the corners of her mouth. He felt the beast's exhaustion as though it was his own, his scarred leg burning from gripping the mare's flank. He wondered if he should abandon his scheme; what did it matter if Nasir won, he thought? Perhaps the boy would leave him alone if he was allowed his victory. Then he saw Nasir whoop up ahead, punching the air. His brow dipped and he shook his head; no, victory today was a must.

He leaned flat on his saddle, legs cupping the mare's flanks, arms around her neck, his chin resting on her mane. 'This is it. Come on, girl!' The difference was instantaneous. With Apion and his mount at full pelt and Nasir slowing in his certain victory, the gap closed to half in a few heartbeats. 'Come on!' he roared, heeling just another drop of power from the mare's flanks. Nasir turned in his saddle as he slowed to a trot before the bridge, his face stretched into a wild grin that quickly soured as Apion bolted past him.

'Hey! Ya!' Nasir yelled, heeling his mount back out of its gentle trot.

Apion burst across the bridge and punched the air, the mare whinnying and rearing to add to the occasion. He panted, breathless from the agony in his leg, but he still managed to offer a smug grin to Nasir as the Seljuk boy trotted over beside him.

'Byzantine dog! There's no way you're having that victory, I could have run that race twice over in the time it took you to gallop flat out in my dust trail!'

'Yet I finished before you,' Apion spoke evenly. 'You held back your mount for your own reasons,' he stroked the mare's neck, 'and so did I.'

'You'd still never have beaten me if I hadn't held back.'

68

'That's why you lost though. I stayed as close to you as I needed to. I could have pushed my mount on earlier and led for a short while, but then I would not have won.'

'You did not win, you tricked me.'

'Right, you show me these rules that I've broken then.'

Nasir's face curled into an angry scowl and with a roar he leapt from his saddle and punched into Apion's midriff, butting the pair onto the grass.

Apion screamed as he thudded down on top of his scar, a blinding light filling his head.

'Get up! Get up and let's finish this!'

He heard Nasir's words as though through a wall of water. Yet he forced himself to stand, pushing up with his hand in the absence of his crutch, head spinning. He saw Nasir's face drop, ready to dismiss Apion as a cripple again. The fury of it all boiled inside his chest at this and he pushed forward from his good leg, shoulder crunching into Nasir's stomach and throwing the pair to the ground.

They rolled over and over, fingers gouging, fists and legs flailing. Then they were still, with Nasir sitting on his chest, knees pinning his shoulders to the ground. The boy uttered a roar of pure rage then rained blows on Apion's face. The dull thudding was quickly accompanied by a metallic wash of blood down Apion's throat, and with only his good leg for leverage he could offer no defence.

He wriggled until one arm worked loose from under Nasir's knee. Reaching out, Apion grasped around for something, anything. He ripped a fistful of some weed from the earth, ignoring the searing agony that engulfed his palm to whip the weed up and across Nasir's face. A pained warbling sounded, as if some creature had been harpooned, and suddenly his chest was free of weight. He rolled around and propped himself up onto all fours. Nasir lay on the riverbank, cursing, one hand cupped over his eyes, the other splashing water on his face.

Apion looked to his hands and the clutch of nettles in his grasp, dropping them immediately. 'I'm sorry, I didn't realise they were...'

'A dirty, whoreson, Byzantine move all the way,' Nasir spoke over him.

Apion noticed Nasir clutching at his belt and an empty dagger sheath. He stepped back in apprehension, then trod on something – the dagger, lying in the grass by his good leg. He picked it up, thoughts spinning out of control.

'Think you're brave enough to finish the job do you?' Nasir growled as he stood, but his stance was uncertain, his eyes on the dagger.

Apion stared at the angry red puffs that were Nasir's eyelids. Despite his own battered face and stinging hand, he felt no urge to attack the boy.

'Have your dagger, you fool.' Apion was startled by the assertiveness of his own words. 'I've got no wish to hurt or... *kill* you,' he spat. 'Don't you think I've had enough blood in my life?' The dark door flitted across his thoughts. He tossed the dagger to the ground by Nasir's feet, then clutched at his prayer rope until the images abated.

'You have the upper hand and you don't use it. You're a fool!' Nasir spat back, his chest heaving as he regained his breath and snatched up the blade, tucking it into its sheath.

'No, I'm no fool, I pick my battles carefully,' Apion snarled. 'You can hurt me as much as you need to if it will make you feel like the bigger man. I won't stoop to that level though,' he paused, realising he was shaking, partly from exhaustion, partly from rage. He jabbed a finger back upriver towards Mansur's farm, 'but I *would* kill you, in an instant, if you were to cause any harm to my family!' His last word rang in the air and his mouth froze. Guilt snaked around his body and his lips stung. *Mother, Father, what have I said?*

Nasir blinked open his red-raw eyelids. He squinted at Apion. The tumult of the river was the only noise around; Nasir stood still

70

for a moment and then mounted his stallion and stared upriver, frowning, eyes searching the horizon.

'We are done for today,' he spoke softly, and then heeled his mount into a gallop.

That evening, Apion's body was aching and his nose was still stinging and swollen. Indeed, Maria had kindly told him that he looked like a monster when he staggered in after his race with Nasir. 'Since when does a horse race involve fists?' Mansur had sighed; Apion could tell the old man was disappointed in him. 'Nasir brought the fighting to the race, not me!' Apion had been indignant; how could Mansur scorn him when he had done nothing wrong?

Despite this, he dutifully helped the pair prepare and then devour a hearty meal of root stew, bread and cheese accompanied by a steaming cup of creamy salep. Then, bellies full, they sat around the fire in a tired silence. When the fire began to dim, Maria volunteered to fetch some kindling for the fire. Apion made to smile at her, to thank her for her cooking but, as so often was the case, she simply issued an exaggerated sigh and looked away from him. He was fond of her, whatever she thought of him. Then he noticed Mansur's eyes were narrowed in mischief, the old man pulling over and unlocking the tarnished pine box that was always sat in the middle of the table.

'Now, as you seem to be bent on filling your days with fighting, I'd like to introduce you to a more rewarding pastime. Have you played *shatranj*?' he asked, unfolding the box lid to reveal a smooth polished surface of black and white squares that glimmered in the firelight.

Apion gazed over the collection of carved wooden pieces piled at the centre as Mansur laid them out carefully one by one. 'What is it?'

'A game,' Mansur replied.

'Games are for children,' Apion shrugged.

Mansur shook his head slowly. 'This is a game like no other; this is the game of the strategos.'

Apion's ears perked up. He thought of Cydones. 'The strategos can wipe the enemy army from the field, can't he? He's the man who can win the battle?'

Mansur nodded. 'He can. He is also the man who can lose the battle and ensure his army is annihilated.'

Apion shrugged. 'A good strategos would not lose to his enemy though.'

'A good strategos would not engage with his enemy unless he was certain of a victory.'

Apion turned the words over as Mansur put in place formations of opposing black and white pieces, two rows of each on either end of the board. 'If both sides have equal numbers, how can a strategos know if victory is certain or not?'

'Good question!' Mansur smiled. 'The answer is simple: he must study his enemy, see the weaknesses that may not be immediately apparent. For those unfamiliar with shatranj, the instinctive urge is always to attack, attack, attack, race to victory by brute force. This game lets a budding strategos see, all too quickly, that such an approach often leads to a heavy and embarrassing defeat, and all without a drop of blood being spilled… and that's one of the reasons that this game came about, to tame the hot-headed and power-hungry young men who would otherwise take to the field raw and unprepared. To win at shatranj, you must learn to use your mind. The sword comes later.'

The door creaked open and Maria came in with an armful of kindling.

'You're not playing that game at this time, Father?' Maria moaned, resting her free hand on her hip. 'It'll be light by the time you're finished!'

Apion smiled at the familiar tone; so disapproving, so serious but so contrasting to that day, two months ago, when they had raided Kutalmish's farm. Her poise and tone reminded Apion of Mother when she would chastise Father. He smiled and then blinked away the pain that came with the memory and the increasing guilt he felt as he realised that his thoughts of them were becoming less frequent. He supped at his salep, the sweet and creamy liquid rolling across his tongue like velvet and warming his heart, soothing his guilt. He had grown to cherish the times when the three of them were together like this, the fire crackling in the background.

'It will be a short game tonight.' Mansur turned to her with a grin.

'Well if I have to wake you in the morning...' she said, wagging a finger.

Mansur pulled Maria onto his lap and kissed her cheek. 'Where would I be without you? You are certainly your mother's daughter.'

The smile faded from Apion's face. He saw that lost look touch Maria's features again, just as it had when she had spoken to him of her mother.

'Now rest your eyes and your head, dear,' Mansur continued. 'You've had a busy day.'

Apion watched Maria drop the kindling by the fire and then slink off into her bedroom, her shoulders rounded, hair tousled and her dress smudged with those ever present dirt and grass stains. He wondered quite how she managed to look so scruffy given that it was he who now tended the goats out in the countryside.

'So the game,' Mansur stated calmly, tapping the board, 'is a means of warring without bloodshed. It is not a direct represent-ation of a battlefield, but it allows honing of tactical thought.' He placed a finger on the tall, central white piece on the back row nearest him. 'Primarily we are concerned with the kings: they see far across the field, though do not move vast distances; instead, they relay these movements to their troops. Though, vitally, if they are captured then the game is lost.'

Apion sipped at his salep and admired the intricately carved crown adorning the two opposing king pieces placed on the board, watching as Mansur showed the king's range of movement, one square in any direction.

'His counsellor stands by his side, barely mobile like his king, he is there to advise and protect. Flanking them is the strength of the war elephants!' Mansur's voice inflected his love of the game as he placed the elephant pieces either side of the king and the vizier. 'They shield their king and his vizier and can move to stave off attacks or charge the enemy with thunderous momentum, although with limited agility.' Mansur proceeded to place two horse-headed pieces either side and two turreted pieces either side again. 'The knights are the king's finest cavalry, able to race in and flank opponents at speed, just like the kataphractoi of Byzantium and the Seljuk ghulam riders. Finally, we have the rooks; they hark back to a bygone age when bronzed chariots ruled the battlefield, able to race from end to end in a single manoeuvre!'

Apion looked to the uniform pieces on the front row of each side. 'The front line, they are the infantry, yes?'

Mansur looked up and nodded. 'The meat of any army. The skutatoi infantry of the themata are the front line for the Byzantines, they take the brunt, they take the damage, unquestioning, unheard.' He swept a finger to the white pieces on the opposite side of the board. 'In the Seljuk ranks... exactly the same. The Seljuk akhi clash with the skutatoi of the empire, they can only rush headlong towards one another, like warring brothers to the last.'

'Then their only purpose is to die, isn't it?' He shook his head at the thought.

Mansur nodded stonily. 'That is why this game is so vital. Better to take a pawn on the shatranj board than to spill a brave and noble man's blood.'

Apion looked up, nodding. The old man's expression was deadly serious.

The fire crackled in the background. Finally, Mansur tapped on the shatranj board; a weary grin worked its way across his lips. 'Come on now, let's get this game underway. We don't want Maria in a rage come the morning, do we?'

CHAPTER 7

Wolf River

The tail end of summer had baked Chaldia's terracotta landscape and the midday cicada song filled the air. On the dirt road heading south-west to the neighbouring Thema of Colonea, Mansur and Apion sat at the front of the wagon as it rumbled along on well-worn axles. The wagon cabin was packed with barley, cheeses and wool; a decent day of bartering at the market town of Cheriana would see them come home with a supply of oil, tools and a purse of coins – enough to keep the farm in working order for another few weeks.

Apion scoured the landscape for every detail; Mansur had promised him he would see a bit more of the empire on this trip, and he was eager to take it all in. When they travelled the high roads, he would look across the snow-capped mountains, the yawning plains and the clouds of tiny white specks that were goat herds, but most of all he would examine the valleys below, envisioning the land like a giant chequered board, plotting his strategy for the next shatranj game: the stretches of tall grass were the pawns, the olive groves the cavalry and the rockfall the war elephants. The games against Mansur were still very one-sided, but Apion had learned something from each defeat when Mansur had explained his mistakes.

He was shaken from his thoughts as his belly rumbled. He touched a hand to his satchel, feeling the eggs, bread and honey Maria had packed for the pair of them. Guilt touched him at the thought of her being on her own. Mansur had assured him

75

though that Giyath and Nasir would take turns at checking on the farm. Apion wondered about Nasir; perhaps the boy had a decent heart under all that bluster. He wondered if they would ever be on agreeable terms. Then he shook his head with a wry grin.

He mused over this as the road dipped to round the base of a small cliff-face, then noticed a faded carving in the rock. As the wagon rolled round the cliff, his skin tingled as the carving came into view: a two-headed eagle, eyes on each head dipped in anger, wings spread wide and with dagger-like talons. He uttered a gasp; it was a giant rendition of the etching on the boulder cairn by the farm.

'Ah, the *Haga*!' Mansur chirped, noticing Apion's amazement. 'I felt the same the first time I saw it.'

'What is it?' Apion asked, head twisting round to watch as it rolled out of view behind them.

'Long ago, before Byzantium, this land belonged to the empire of the Hittites. They had their own gods and legends. The *Haga* was one of them; a ferocious, two-headed eagle that would swoop down from the cliffs and mountains and could kill a bull in each claw.'

'These people, they are gone, long gone,' Apion said, 'yet their legends remain, etched into the landscape?'

Mansur nodded. 'The emblem adorns many a cliff-face and mountainside across this land. Whatever else they believed in, the Hittites certainly reckoned with the power of the *Haga*.'

Apion tried to imagine such a beast come to life from the rock. He shivered at the thought. The ferocity in those eyes…

As the afternoon wore on, they came to a region of rolling hillocks. Then he saw something up ahead: atop a baked red hill, the stone edifice of a fort stood proud, seemingly baked into the earth as if it had been there for all time. His father had been stationed at such a fort for a whole year. Apion remembered playing by the hearth, building wooden blocks into an enclosure and then lining up carved soldiers, pretending he was one of them, protecting the walls. Then he realised the walls of this fort were unmanned. He looked to the wide gate but could see only the blue of the sky through it. Then they rounded the hill a little further to see the crumbled ruin that was the other side of the fort. Unmanned, meaning this vast tract of imperial land was left undefended.

'The man in the purple seems to think that the east needs no funding for such garrisons,' Mansur said as if reading his thoughts. 'Perhaps if he lived here and experienced the uncertainty it creates, he might think otherwise.'

Apion nodded, eyes hanging on the stark image of the skeletal fort. 'Is it the same in Seljuk lands?'

Mansur shook his head. 'No. My people ride the wave of expansion. Riches are abundant and the lands are well policed. Such prosperity is like a drug, and I fear it is often confused with glory.'

Apion thought over the old man's words as they rode on, the breeze dancing through his amber locks as he tried to imagine what the land must have been like in more prosperous times of the past.

They rode on for some time, then Mansur whipped the horses into a heady pace as they passed through forest. Apion noticed the old man's eyes were narrowed and scouring the undergrowth in suspicion, but he could not see why. It was a pleasant setting; leafy shade, brooks and squat waterfalls snaking through the undergrowth. The whole setting made him feel cooler and more relaxed. Then he remembered he had finished his water some way back.

'Can we stop so I can fill my skin?' He looked up at Mansur; the old man was still examining the road and the treeline. Apion wondered if he had gone unheard. He pulled on Mansur's sleeve, pointing to the stream coming up on their left. 'Can we sto—'

'No!' Mansur barked.

Apion pulled back.

'No,' Mansur repeated, this time in a calmer voice, looking at Apion, his face firm but his eyes friendly. 'When we get to the river we can slake our thirst.'

Apion nodded. 'Very well. What if I need to empty my bladder?'

Mansur's vexation washed away in a tense chuckle. 'Then you do it from the side of the wagon. I hope you have good balance and good aim!'

Apion's shoulders slumped as he thought out the logistics of balancing on his crutch. Soon they rode clear of the trees and Mansur seemed to relax after that as the countryside opened up again.

A long and gentle downhill slope led to a smaller patch of beech forest, behind which the land gave way to accommodate a mighty river, its shimmering waters flowing calmly west. The sheer girth of the river made the Piksidis seem like a stream in comparison. 'What do they call this water?'

'When its current is gentle, the Lykos; when it grows turbulent, the Wolf River. Many men have lost their lives trying to cross this river. That's why we come to this particular crossing point.'

'Is there a bridge?' Apion frowned, scanning the waters for sight of such a structure.

'No, but there is a fine ferryman,' Mansur grinned, 'a dizzy old goat by the name of Petzeas.'

The rush of the rapids drowned out the cicada song as they approached and sure enough, they reached a rudimentary ferry dock. The wagon slowed to a halt by a post with a horn tied to it.

Forgetting his thirst, Apion placed his crutch on the ground and slid down from the drivers' berth, biting back the spasm of pain that shot through his scar. Meanwhile, Mansur groaned and shifted his bulky frame to standing, then dropped down from the wagon and hobbled over to the post, lifted the horn, filled his lungs and blew. The wail of the horn echoed across the land.

Mansur's gaze then fell on the small wooden hut on the other side of the river. All was still for a moment and then the tiny shape of the elderly ferryman emerged from the cabin and waved, quickly flanked by his two sons.

'Well, you've got ample time to slake your thirst now, lad,' Mansur mused, waving back as Petzeas set about rigging up his vessel. They settled in the shade by the wagon and shared a meal of boiled eggs, followed by bread and honey, washed down with freshly drawn water.

'I'm sorry I was terse with you on the forested road. It's a notorious stretch,' Mansur spoke, wiping his hands on his robe.

Apion raised an eyebrow. 'Brigands?'

'Aye,' he snorted, 'bane of any empire.'

Apion thought back to the journey from Trebizond. 'What makes a brigand? Bracchus and Vadim, they robbed you did they not, on that day you bought me? Then they come to your home and rob you again, threatening your family... and they are soldiers?'

'You saw the pitiful state of the forts on the way here, lad. The highways are long and empty these days. The few men assigned to protect the travellers are easily turned by the thought of taking an extra income. It's the nature of soldiers to misbehave when they are not engaged on the front line, especially when their wages don't show up on time.'

'But those two, they seem to have some personal vendetta against you?'

Mansur looked to Apion, but before he could reply, a snapping of branches caught their attention.

'Shhtand back!' a voice called.

Apion twisted round to see the figure of a skutatos stumble from the beech thicket, clumsily pulling up his woollen leggings and fumbling his padded cotton vest back over his waist. The man's dark eyes were at odds and his stride was erratic. He was probably in his early twenties, tall, of medium build, with rounded features and chestnut locks tumbling from his felt cap. Apion felt the urge to laugh at the comic appearance of the soldier, then his face dropped as the man pulled his spathion from his scabbard and brought the point to hover near Mansur's chest.

'Get away from the boy, you… you dirty Seljuk!' The man's breath reeked of wine.

Mansur stood, not letting his eyes leave the man. 'Waiting for the ferry?' he asked in his usual gravel but affable tone, jabbing a thumb over his shoulder to the very slowly approaching Petzeas.

The man's face tightened into an exaggerated frown and he swayed like a sapling in a stiff breeze. 'A Seljuk talking G… Greek?' The man erupted in laughter, looking to Apion as if to share his joke. Apion balked at the man's drunken manner; a memory of Father came back to him: in that last year when his wages could not keep the farm in operation and the lands had run dry of crops, he would turn to drinking soured wine unwatered until he became a different person, joyous for a brief spell and then surly, hot tempered and rash.

'I've always used the mother tongue of this land since I came here,' Mansur replied. 'I've been tilling the lands of the empire for many a year now.'

'Really? Well you look a lot like the Seljuk whoreson riders who wiped out my bandon two days ago. Nearly two hundred infantry, good men, gone! Skin that colour, moustache as well. The buggers ambushed us then slit the throats of the wounded.' The soldier tightened his grip on his sword, his teeth gritted, saliva bubbling through them.

'*Ghazi* riders, this far west?' Mansur shook his head. The Seljuk light cavalry hunted in packs, swift and designed to harass, but they rarely penetrated past the area around the Piksidis. 'I'm truly sorry it came to bloodshed, soldier. Let's have no more of that today, eh?'

'If you were one of them…' the soldier snarled.

Mansur shrugged and gestured to his bulging waistline. 'Me, a rider? Is there a horse in all the Byzantine or Seljuk Empires that could take my weight?'

80

A scowl hovered on the drunken soldier's face, then his expression wavered and melted and finally he laughed despite himself.

Mansur smiled. 'You're heading back to your barracks, one of the forts across the Lykos, right?'

'Might be. Might be waiting on the rest of my lads to catch up first.'

'I don't think so.' Mansur shook his head with a friendly smile. 'Your boots are dried out, ragged and caked in dust; you've been walking for some time. Your water skin is empty; with no colleagues to borrow some from you turned to your wine ration unwatered. Now why don't you come across the river with us? I'll take you in the wagon as far as your fort; you can sleep off the effects of the wine and be fresh to face your commanding officer.'

Apion felt a tense moment pass, the soldier eyeing Mansur as he swayed. Mansur's words were full of reason, but the wine had boiled the soldier's brains. He patted a hand to his own full water skin and then stepped forward, holding it out to the soldier.

'Here, have some of my water,' he said.

The soldier shot a glare down to Apion, saw the prayer rope and then lowered his sword point into the dust to rest his weight on it, rubbing at his eyes. 'Aye… aye, fair enough. I'll go across the water with you.'

–

Petzeas' story of his eldest son's first attempts to harvest the honey from his hives was entertaining in its delivery if a little stale by the third time of its telling, but Apion enjoyed the ferry crossing regardless. He munched on the bread loaf Petzeas had on board for his passengers to enjoy, watching the waters of the Lykos shimmering all around them while the ferryman operated the tiller and his sons, Isaac and Maro, rowed on either side of the ferry. The flat-bottomed vessel held the wagon, wheels fixed with wooden blocks, the horses, with sacks over their heads to keep them calm, and the six passengers and crew with ample room to spare. A squat timber ridge around the sides added stability to the craft and prevented items rolling off.

The soldier, whose mood had lightened, slurred an introduction as Tarsites, then happily accepted a chunk of bread from Apion. Then, after roaring at Petzeas' first rendition of the hive story, Tarsites toppled into a dead man's sleep, his snoring almost drowning out the rush of the rapids. After that, the ferryman's tone had grown bitter as he told of the brigands who had been operating in the forest but had recently turned to flexing their muscle near the riverbank.

'Damned parasites! That's what they are, wriggling like maggots on the body of their own empire! I tell you, if I was twenty years younger and I still had my skutatoi armour...'

'Maybe you should leave that to your boys, Petzeas?' Mansur mused while the two sons carried on rowing regardless. 'They are of age to serve in the thema within the next few years, are they not?'

'They are. I worry for them as they are of the age where young men die on the sword easily. Yet I worry that if they stay here the parasites will see them as some kind of threat.'

'Whatever happens, you should feel safe here. You're providing a service to the empire, so,' he glanced over to the slumbering form of Tarsites and cocked an eyebrow, 'the empire should protect you.'

Petzeas issued a deep throaty sigh. 'Aye but we both know what direction this empire is heading in. Like an ancient candle guttering its last.'

His tone sent a shiver over Apion's skin.

They docked on the opposite bank and Petzeas waived payment, insisting that Mansur could settle with him on the return journey. With that, they set off again, down the track that clung to the southern banks of the Lykos. Some distance later, Apion wondered at Mansur's ease in what was effectively a foreign land. He lived as a citizen of Byzantium, had friends in this empire of his one-time enemies, spoke fluent Greek – more fluent than some of the natives, he mused, eyeing Tarsites, who now sat wedged between Mansur and he, twitching and grunting happily in some inebriate fantasy dream. Indeed, if Mansur had not been able to speak Greek to the man, blood would surely have been spilled.

Later that day, they dropped Tarsites by the roadside. The man was weary but an altogether more pleasant character without wine in his blood.

'I can only apologise for my behaviour... before.' He patted his wineskin and raised his eyebrows. 'I normally don't touch the stuff; I just carry it so I can use it for barter.' He turned to Mansur. 'How can I repay you, farmer?' He rummaged in the purse hanging from his belt.

Mansur raised a hand in refusal. 'Those roads are part of your empire. They need to be policed. If you could lobby your commander on that front, it'd be appreciated. It'd see old Petzeas and I at ease.'

The soldier cast them a weary but genuine grin in return. 'Couldn't agree more, I'll see what I can do.' With that, he set off to his hilltop fort, one of the few with iron speartips and Byzantine crimson Chi-Rho banners adorning the battlements.

'Don't you fear they might take you up on that suggestion?' Apion asked as they set off again. 'The last thing we need is another Bracchus and Vadim.'

'As I said, that is the nature of a soldier far from the front line, and better a corrupt Byzantine than a cut-throat brigand.'

They rode on until the sun turned a tired orange, dipping below the horizon. It was a clear and fine night when they pulled over at a small brook running by the roadside and into the river, leaving Cheriana within an easy ride in the morning. They set up a fire by the wagon as the land dimmed and the navy blue of the twilight sky yawned over them, sparkling with stars. Apion's energy levels were low after such a long day and the gathering of the kindling was enough to make him think of sleep. But first, Mansur insisted, they would eat and then sleep better on a full belly. So they prepared a meal of cheese on toasted bread, followed by figs with honey for dipping.

Apion sipped his skin of stream water, watching Mansur in the firelight as the old man examined the stars to the east, his eyes distant. 'Why did you come to live in Byzantine lands?'

Mansur blinked, hesitated, then gave a wry chuckle. 'For a fresh start, lad. At least that was the plan.'

Apion thought of all Maria had told him of the attack on Mansur and Kutalmish's caravan. A fresh start that had ended in the most harrowing manner. He hoped one day the old man would want to talk about it with him. 'I think you were incredibly brave to come here. Every time you face a man like Bracchus, or Tarsites – before we calmed him – do you not crave to be where you are not a stranger in a foreign land?'

'To feel like a stranger in a foreign land, a man must first have a place he can call home, in order to miss it.'

'You don't miss the east?'

'In ways, yes, perhaps I miss the east as it was when I was a boy, but not the east as it is now. I became tired of the constant warfare and bloodshed.' His eyes hung on the fire. 'The Seljuk people have become something alien to me; in many ways they are as belligerent and power-hungry as the Byzantines whose land they crave. No offence intended.' He winked.

Apion smiled. 'What was it like when you were a boy?'

'We were a simple people. Born on the steppe, living our lives on horseback, hunting in the tall grass of the infinite plains, riding in the surf of the Aral Sea. Simple pleasures still held for us then: returning to the yurts of the tribe at night with the spoils of the hunt. I remember that vividly; in the saddle with my father, the women and younger children rushing to greet us, their faces bright with joy at our return.'

'Why did it all change?'

'Even then it was changing, lad. The tribes were living in the old way but they were being united, for the first time, to act as one people, one military.'

'By Tugrul?' Apion leaned in over the fire. The name of the Seljuk Sultan had been spat like a poisoned grape by the drunks at the inn where he served as a slave, but behind their merry hubris, fear had laced their words. Tugrul, the *Falcon*, the warlord who had harnessed ancient Persia and all the peripheral kingdoms, was coming to topple Byzantium.

Mansur shook his head. 'No, it was Tugrul's father and the elders of the tribes who started the push for unity. Tugrul was a boy, just a little older than me, at this time. He has grown to lead them now on their incessant hunt for glory.'

'Did you ever fight under Tugrul's banner?'

Mansur looked off to the east again instead of returning Apion's engrossed stare. 'I was a Seljuk boy who grew up with a mantra to seek glory in the name of Allah. I served my time in the ranks while Tugrul rose to power. I saw what it did to him; he became a great and lethal leader, but a bitter and troubled man. I could feel the same thing happening to me. Coming west was my attempt to leave all that behind.'

Apion nodded and wondered at the corpulent old man sat across from him now, anything but soldierly. 'You did a fine job of talking Tarsites round. I was terrified that he was going to strike you. We had no weapons to attack him with.'

'Even if we did, Apion, Tarsites was not looking for blood; he was looking for help. A desperate soldier on the road, on his own without food or water. I could see the good-hearted and articulate man inside the drunk that swayed before us. The answer does not always lie with the sword and today was a prime example of that.'

Apion nodded, then eyed his scarred leg. Perhaps if he ever found himself confronted by a trouble-minded Seljuk, diplomacy could be his only real option. 'You said you would teach me, Mansur?'

'Yes, I did.' Mansur cocked an eyebrow wearily.

'Then teach me to speak the Seljuk tongue,' Apion asked.

Mansur grinned at this, then pulled his cap over his eyes, lay back and sighed. 'Tomorrow, lad. We'll start tomorrow.'

Apion rolled over onto his side. He untied and kissed the prayer rope and mouthed the Prayer of the Heart, searching for an image of Mother and Father.

After a long day of trading and a welcome night's sleep at the inn, they were ready to leave Cheriana. The wagon was so full that the wheels groaned as they turned around in the market square under the shadow of the town church's red-tiled dome.

'She's good to go!' Mansur nodded, watching as Apion drove the horses forward just a little. Then he pulled himself onto the drivers' berth with a groan.

Apion lightly whipped the horses and the wagon moved off. The townsfolk meandered casually, only steps away from the wagon. Then, with a chorus of squealing, two pigs scuttled loose from their owner and barged across the road. Apion's heart leapt as both wagon horses tensed and then reared up, whinnying in terror.

'Whoa!' Mansur grabbed the reins from him. 'Easy there!' he cried and then reached forward to pat each of their flanks. 'One of the reasons we don't have pigs on the farm, the horses are terrified of them – terrified!' He looked to Apion. 'Almost comical when you think about it, eh?'

They set off again and the wagon settled into a rhythm and he took one last look around the town as they left. The place was walled with a rudimentary wooden palisade, the original stone walls of the town having fallen into terminal disrepair. The place was about a quarter the size of Trebizond, he reckoned. Apart from the wide main thoroughfare from the entrance gate to the market square, the dusty streets were narrow and the buildings closely packed, none more than two storeys high and most looking very makeshift in their construction. The people were a mixed bag: mainly Byzantines but also tall Slavs, charcoal-skinned Africans and pale westerners punctuating the crowd. All these cultures seemed to blend into the market environment as one people, but Apion had noticed a distinctly frosty attitude towards Mansur as he had bartered. Mansur always spoke to the traders in a warm but assertive tone, much as he had done with Tarsites, and the underlying hostility of the traders never surfaced because of this. He grinned, reciting the words of a simple greeting in Seljuk that Mansur had taught him that morning as they rode into town. Then a voice barked in front of them.

'Halt!'

Apion yanked on the reins, startled. Two skutatoi stood either side of the gate, their spears raised, faces twisted.

'Your business?' the first sneered.

Apion looked to Mansur, eyes wide. On entering the town it had been just after dawn and the night guards were weary. Now they were clearly spoiling for trouble.

Mansur replied to the guards. 'Trade; tools and oil.' He jabbed a thumb over his shoulder to the wagon cabin.

The guard scrutinised him. 'Your kind ain't welcome here, you've been told before. Now go.'

Face straight, Mansur nodded to Apion to whip the horses onwards.

As they rode clear of the town, the throngs of traders on foot and on horseback thinned, but Apion was still troubled by the confrontation with the guards. 'Don't they realise you are a citizen? Farming, paying taxes to the empire?' he asked Mansur.

'If they sat down and thought about it they might realise that, lad. But no, they see a Seljuk and they hate me.'

–

It was nearing the end of the day when they reached Petzeas' ferry crossing again. Mansur reckoned they could get across and bite another few miles from their journey home before it would become too dark. Apion had agreed, despite his rumbling gut demanding that they stop to camp and eat sooner.

'Ah, Petzeas is ready!' Mansur pointed to the figure of the old man, sat on a bench by his docked ferry.

87

Apion's heart lifted at the prospect of the old man's banter and the possibility that he would have some bread on board again. As they approached, Petzeas looked up to them but instead of rising from his seat and hailing them warmly, the old man remained seated, his face drawn and his eyes weary.

'What's wrong, ferryman, you're almost acting your age?' Mansur chirped.

Petzeas cracked a smile but seemed to be wearing it like a mask.

'All is well?' Mansur asked, this time with concern.

Petzeas nodded with a long sigh. 'My youngest, Isaac... he is unwell with a fever. It will probably pass but...'

Mansur glanced to the timber hut. 'We have honey if he is weak?'

Petzeas shook his head quickly. 'He cannot hold anything down, time and rest should bring him round.'

Apion noticed the ferryman's unease and fleeting eye contact. Something felt wrong. 'Is there nothing we can do for him? Perhaps even just a visit might lift his spirits,' he asked, shuffling his withered leg and crutch towards the wagon edge.

'No.' Petzeas seemed ruffled. 'I fear it is contagious and it is a wonder I myself haven't been stricken yet. Perhaps he will be well... the next time you come by this way.' The ferryman glanced across the water briefly as he said this.

'Very well. Our thoughts are with you,' Mansur spoke gently.

Apion noticed Petzeas held a necklace bearing a Chi-Rho in his palm. He held up his wrist with the prayer rope. 'May God bless him with good health soon,' he offered solemnly. Petzeas looked up only for the briefest of moments to acknowledge the sentiment and Apion saw something raw in his eyes. Defeat.

Then the ferryman stood. 'Come now, draw up your wagon to the pier and I will summon Maro. I will need one of you to operate Isaac's oar.' He hesitated, muttering to himself, eyeing Apion's scarred leg. 'Mansur, if you will?' he asked and then turned away to go in to his hut.

Apion let the burning sensation of shame and inadequacy pass; the old ferryman had enough on his mind and meant no offence.

Something was most definitely wrong here. He drove the horses forward onto the pier then slid down off the wagon using his crutch, biting back the searing pain that shot through his body, then hobbled to walk alongside Mansur. He looked up to voice his concern but Mansur spoke first.

'I saw it too.' Mansur's eyes were scanning the surroundings of the hut and then the opposite riverbank. He wore a sharp expression like a preying cat. 'Do not press the ferryman on it. I will have my back to the far bank as I sit at the oar so you must keep your eyes on the treeline as the ferry comes to dock. I will keep watch on this side as I row.'

Apion's blood ran cold. Suddenly, he felt like a lost cub in the wilderness as the sky dulled and the rapids of the Wolf River seemed to roar.

Before long the ferry had set off across the river, Maro and Mansur striking up a rhythm fairly quickly. Petzeas' eldest son seemed naturally shy and taciturn so it was difficult to tell today whether he shared his father's unease. Apion sat near the leading edge of the ferry and pulled at a piece of bread, looking up to the approaching riverbank as frequently and as casually as he could manage. He saw the beech thicket where they had eaten two days previously, empty, as was the rest of the riverbank.

They docked on the muddy bank. Silently, Petzeas hobbled from the tiller to step onto the ground and began tying the vessel to the post with the horn attached. The ferryman looked anywhere but at his two passengers. Apion looked to Mansur, giving a faint shake of the head. Mansur whispered to him as he readied to climb into the drivers' berth. 'Climb into the cabin, lad, make room for yourself in there and shut the door.'

Apion gulped. 'What's happening?'

'Just do as I say, please.' Then Mansur turned to Petzeas. 'See you soon, ferryman.'

Apion's dread grew as Petzeas croaked a farewell and then stood back, head bowed. He climbed into the wagon cabin and clipped the door shut from inside and then Mansur whipped the horses into a canter, off the ferry and on towards the beech forest. His eyes jumped to every fluttering leaf, every branch that shuddered as crows left their nests, but all was as normal. Apion frowned, looking through the slats, back to the shrinking figures of Petzeas and Maro.

Then a roar pierced the air.

Footsteps thundered across the ground and more gruff shouting broke out. Apion pressed his eyes to the slats then leapt back at the sight of the hooded man dressed in filthy rags who raced for the flank of the wagon. The figure held a dagger in his hand, and sprung like a cat to clamber onto the wagon roof.

Three more men rushed for the wagon, each bearing longs-words and running straight for Mansur on the drivers' berth. The horses reared in panic and the reins tangled. The wagon crunched round against a thick oak trunk and Apion was hurled forward, an amphora shattering against his shoulder and throwing him head over heels. It was all he could do to stifle a scream. Then all was still. He glanced up, dazed. Then the scream of iron on iron shattered the silence. Through the slats he saw flitting glances of the brigands stabbing and hacking at something. Then one of the brigands issued a gurgling cry, blood spraying from his mouth, hands clutching at a curved blade that had pierced his belly and burst through his back. The curved blade was ripped back. Apion scrambled forward, pressing against the slats to see it all.

Mansur stood holding a bloodied scimitar; the dirty cloth that had concealed it behind the drivers' berth lay on the ground. He was hacking at the next man's sword thrusts, cutting the blade around to his sides whenever the dagger-wielding thug tried to attack his back. With a roar, the dagger man rushed him. Mansur stepped back half a pace and brought his sword hilt crunching into the man's jaw, then scythed the blade around to cut through another swordsman's throat. The swordsman's face wrinkled and he touched a hand to his neck in the instant before dark blood jetted from the wound, pulling the colour from his skin and weakening his legs until he toppled, dead.

Mansur turned to the last swordsman, his brow knitted, eyes burning. The swordsman lurched forward and Mansur parried. This thug was slighter than the first but more skilled with the weapon and the pair circled each other, clashing again and again. Mansur's chest began to heave as he tired. Then Apion noticed shapes emerge from the trees behind Mansur. More brigands.

Five of them, screaming, three bearing swords, the fourth and biggest one flat-faced and hefting an axe and the last of them approaching on a fawn stallion, wearing a cloak, mail vest, helmet and mail veil. Mansur glanced back at them, and then shoulder charged the swordsman onto the ground, whacking the flat of his scimitar to the man's temple to knock him out before turning to face the five.

As the five surrounded Mansur, the felled dagger-man struggled to his feet, eyes locked on Mansur's unprotected back, blade in hand. Frozen in a mix of fear and anger, Apion's thoughts flitted with the image of the dark door. Then he saw something else: a blurred image of a hand, reaching forward for the door. He blinked and realised he had pushed forward to punch the wagon door open. His eyes seared under a frown, and he hefted an amphora in his arms and dropped out onto the ground and hobbled forward. Without his crutch, the pain was untold. Then, with a cry, he hurled the amphora at the back of the dagger-man's head, the vessel exploding on contact and the man dropping like a sack of rocks, blood trickling from his nose.

'Apion, stay back!' Mansur gasped through shortening breaths, trying to shield him from the approaching five.

Then a desperate cry filled the air from behind them. Apion spun round: Maro stood, a snapped oar held in his arms like a club, Petzeas beside him bearing the other, lighter half of the oar. 'We have your flanks, Mansur,' Old Petzeas cried, the ferryman and his son hurrying forward to stand alongside Mansur and Apion. Then he roared at the approaching brigands. 'Come on then, you dogs!'

'Petzeas?' Mansur uttered.

'Forgive me, friend,' Petzeas apologised, breathless. 'They have taken Isaac hostage. I prayed you would not come back today...'

Mansur nodded. 'Save your apologies, just stay close to me!'

Then the brigands rushed in, swords raised while the veiled horseman followed behind them, eyeing the skirmish. The ferryman and his son were able only to parry the sword cuts of the brigands and Apion watched, helpless, as the relentless axe blows of the big brigand sent Mansur staggering backwards and then down onto his knees, chest heaving, face bathed in sweat. Then the big brigand's leg stamped into the ground before him and Apion pushed with all his strength to jar his shoulder against the man's calf. The brigand buckled and fell, the axe blow aimed for Mansur's head falling wide, but in an instant he was up again, enraged, spinning to face Apion, axe lifted, ready to strike. Apion fell back, awaiting a death blow, but the big brigand's roar was cut short when an arrow thudded into his eye. He was still like a statue for a moment, a grotesque wash of eye-matter and blood coating his face. Then he toppled, dead. Another brigand was felled, back peppered with arrows. The mounted brigand, who had stood back until now, shot looks into the trees, eyes wide with panic as a thudding of hooves grew louder from the thicket. He barked a gruff order to the remaining two thugs. Then the foliage parted and a horseman wearing a leather klibanion burst into view. Flanking him on foot were two toxotai, distinctive by their bows and felt caps.

'Tarsites!' Apion roared, seeing the rounded features of the skutatos, ducked in his saddle, spathion held out to one side. At this, the two brigands on foot broke off and ran for the trees. The mounted brigand then wheeled to take flight as well. Tarsites rounded on one runner and stabbed him through the chest when he tried to fight back. The other stopped running and dropped his sword, realising the two toxotai had their bows trained on him. The mounted brigand raced for Tarsites and drew a spathion, hefting it round to sweep it down at the skutatos. Tarsites only just brought his own blade round in time to parry and instinctively, as the brigand galloped past to break for the forest, Tarsites brought his sword up and round, the blade scything through the veiled rider's arm with a sharp snap of bone, lopping the limb clean off. The rider screamed, then toppled from his mount, body crunching as he landed on his head without the arm to break his fall. He lay still and silent. The fight was over.

Panting, Apion stood. With Petzeas' help they lifted the shaking Mansur to his feet.

'Why didn't you tell us, Petzeas?' Mansur panted. 'We would have helped you!'

'I am so sorry, Mansur. I was blinded by fear for Isaac.'

'Your boy is safe,' Tarsites said, riding up to the group as the toxotai bound the surviving brigand. 'We found him gagged and bound in the brigand camp about two hundred feet into the trees. Though I've got a terrible feeling they were not brigands…'

Petzeas looked at Tarsites, open-mouthed for a moment and then took the skutatos' hand and began to weep. 'You saved my son. God bless you, soldier. God bless you!'

Apion looked up to the horseman. 'Tarsites, you did what Mansur asked, didn't you? You asked for these roads to be policed?'

Tarsites grinned. 'You showed me kindness, and I don't forget things like that easily. I've been assigned to a new bandon and when I raised the suggestion to my new komes, he was all for it, especially as I was volunteering to scout these roads personally. I don't think I ingratiated myself with the rest of the lads,' he shrugged, 'then again, I didn't bargain on getting a scout horse out of it, but there you go.'

'You're a good man, Tarsites,' Mansur spoke, his breath returning.

'As are you, farmer,' Tarsites replied, clasping his leather-gloved hand to Mansur's outstretched palm. 'Again I can only apologise for my drunken behaviour the day before last.'

Mansur nodded, then looked around to each of them; battered, shaken but alive.

Then a rasping voice startled them all.

'Do you realise what a black mistake you have made?'

Their eyes fell to the felled rider, still veiled, only his bloodshot eyes visible. He hissed as his lungs filled with blood. They moved to stand around him.

'Cleared the roads of your likes,' one of the toxotai spat, but Tarsites raised a hand to hush the bowman.

'You're as good as dead, rider,' the man gurgled, 'when they find out what you've done. I'm untouchable.' With that the rider convulsed and was still at last, eyes staring as death took him.

'Was he delirious?' Apion asked, flicking glances to Mansur and Tarsites; both men looked troubled.

'If only that were so. No, his threat was very real.' Tarsites spoke through narrowed lips, eyes falling on the rider's severed arm, and then he pointed at the hand. 'He is no brigand. The emperor is his only master. Look, he is an *Agente*; a dark soul indeed, given licence to disrupt to his liking and cause whatever pain he so chooses.'

Apion looked to the index finger of the hand on the severed limb. Something inside him refused to accept what he saw: a tarnished ring, a snake winding around the band, just like the lead raider on that awful night. 'No, it can't be…' Apion rocked where he stood.

How could the ring be the symbol of some shadowy group of imperial agents? The men from that night were Seljuk, he was sure. The one he had struck down certainly was, so surely the rest were too? *They were dressed as Seljuks*, a dark voice rasped in his mind, *but they were masked*. He shook where he stood. Did the man who had slaughtered his parents, shattered his life, lie before him? Had justice been served?

His heart slowed and dizziness washed through his mind. Then he found the answer. There was no missing finger. This could not be the man.

Yet the ring held the truth. One of these Agentes led the raiders on that night and ordered the death of his parents. A Byzantine. To find the man with the ring and the missing finger meant justice, no, revenge, would be his to take.

His heart beat faster and faster as the rage welled up inside him. At this, something sparked in his soul. That murky image of the dark door floated into his thoughts. The arm outstretched for the door was less blurred now; it was knotted, scarred and sun-darkened, with a band of whiter skin around the wrist, and some dark-red emblem on the forearm. Then something behind the door ignited, the crackling of fire sounded from behind its timbers, orange light flitting around the edges.

—

Tarsites and the two toxotai had helped mend the wagon, and then they had readied the ferry to cross the river with Petzeas and his sons. At that point Mansur and Apion had said their farewells and set off for home. As they rode Apion noticed Mansur yawning more frequently, his eyes red and weary, so he offered to take the reins and the old man was only too happy to accept. As Mansur slept, snoring violently, Apion tried to empty his mind by focusing on the road, but his eyes were drawn to the scimitar. It was wrapped in the cloth again, but a sliver of the blade poked from the end. It sent shivers of awe and disgust through him at once. It was a scimitar that had been used by raiders on the awful night to strike down his parents and to score his body indelibly. Yet those raiders were seemingly led by a Byzantine. An Agente. Added to this, it was a scimitar that had been borne by a Seljuk today to save him. To save him from the dark rider, another Agente. His mind continued to chatter in turmoil at this cruel riddle.

The shadowy image of the dark door continued to surface and he wanted to stop the wagon, to take the scimitar and to hack and hack at the bark of a tree until he could feel anger no longer. He thumbed the knots on his prayer rope and then looked back at the blade. God would not be pleased with his thoughts, but his soul was restless. He gritted his teeth and focused on the road ahead.

—

The following day, as they were nearing the valley, Mansur awoke in the late afternoon. 'I feel as if I've slept for a thousand years,' he groaned, and then winced, rubbing his shoulder, 'and I feel as if I've lived for a thousand more.'

'I could have helped you, you know,' Apion offered, keeping his eyes on the road ahead, 'when you told me to hide in the back of the wagon. I might be lame but I could have helped.'

'You did,' Mansur replied in an even tone.

'But I could have fought alongside you from the start. Just because I am not mobile doesn't mean I can't lift a sword. I have lifted a sword before and used it, just as I told you, remember?' The memory of the dead Seljuk raider, face melting in the fire, on the floor of his parents' farmhouse came flooding back and he shivered.

'I have not forgotten,' Mansur replied, stonily.

'You were like a master with the sword yesterday, and you are a fine teacher of many things. So will you teach me to use the sword?'

Mansur sighed. 'For what reason? This thing, the Agentes. I trust you will not dwell on it? That is a dark road to go down, lad.'

'Fine, then teach me so I can defend myself at least. We've been play-fighting with wooden poles for long enough now. Look what happened today – I could have been far more useful if I had a sword in my hand. Surely you can't deny that?' Apion insisted.

Mansur sighed wearily. 'So be it. Next time we fight, we fight with the scimitar. Though I pray that you never have call to use it.'

Apion waved a hand over his scarred leg. 'It is for the best. Am I not at disadvantage enough?'

Mansur sighed and shook his head. 'Your leg, the scar, it is a serious wound. Although it hurts badly, the skin is pink now. Remember how it was raw and bloody when you first came home with me?'

Apion was chastised by Mansur's even tone. The scar had indeed sealed somewhat. 'What of it?'

'Something of unspeakable agony, something seemingly lost has become... better, it has grown stronger.'

'Marginally. I am still weaker than a lamb, Mansur. I'll never be strong, never.'

'That's all up here lad.' He tapped a finger to his temple. 'With your mind focused, you could overcome your ailment.'

Apion chuckled dryly. 'I wish that were true, Mansur. However, if you were in this body you would understand the frailty I feel. You said you felt two thousand years old? Well I feel ten thousand years old when I try to walk on this thing!'

Mansur laughed. 'Perhaps in the years to come you may see things differently, lad. I truly hope you do.'

Apion looked to the old man. 'I would welcome it, Mansur.'

'Then that is the first step,' Mansur grinned. 'Now, let's try speaking the Seljuk tongue, you can surprise Maria when we get in!'

Apion nodded. The thought of seeing her made him feel warm inside, momentarily silencing the dark chatter in his mind. Then the light caught the scimitar blade again and he remembered the Agente ring. The need for vengeance.

His future was simple: with Mansur's help, he would learn the basics of the sword, and then he would seek out the ring-bearer with the missing finger.

The truth would out, he vowed to himself.

CHAPTER 8

Glory

War horns keened across the Seljuk horde. The Daylamid city of Isfahan was to be theirs today, bringing to an end the year-long siege. The ranks roared their holy battle cry as the elite, iron-clad ghulam cavalry rumbled into place on the flanks, making the ground quiver. In the sweltering heat haze, the bowmen lining the baked city walls appeared to shrink at the noise and at the thousands of Seljuk banners that hovered outside the city, the horizontal bow emblem still and stern in the dead air.

At the centre of the Seljuk horde, Sultan Tugrul was saddled on a white stallion. He sat poised with rigid majesty, grey-flecked hair curling from under his ornate helmet, the crafted nose-guard adding to his austerity. Now in his fifty-seventh year, he had united the tribes and led the Seljuk people from the steppe and on to glory, toppling the Ghaznavid Empire. Now he was in the cusp of controlling all Persia. Beside him, saddled on a fawn-dappled gelding was his young nephew, Muhammud.

'They fight for you, *Falcon*!' Muhammud enthused.

Tugrul looked round, letting a wistful smile touch his stern expression for just a moment. 'I command them, but they fight for Allah!' He noticed his nephew's gaze was fixed on one point on the city walls and followed it; a Daylamid bowman waited there in silence, impotent to quell the storm that was coming for him. Beneath the iron helmet of the bowman, he could see only the glimmer of a nose-guard and shadow for his face, a bronze tipped crossbow resting on the wall. He sensed the question forming on Muhammud's lips.

'If you take the city, Uncle, what will you do with the people?'

Tugrul laughed at this and his officers around him joined in. 'When we take the city, Muhammud, when,' Tugrul replied. At that moment the ground began to shake and the groaning and snapping of breaking rocks filled the air behind them.

Muhammud twisted in his saddle: the trebuchets at the back of the ranks were dwarfed as twelve war towers on gargantuan wheels rumbled towards them, swaying, the ranks parting to let them through. The timber walls were featureless but at the top, a squat enclosure was perched, covered to the front and sides. Hundreds of heavily armoured akhi spearmen would be packed in there, waiting to burst onto the battlements when the towers reached the walls. Armoured engineers hung from the back, toppling buckets of water down the sides of the towers, soaking the wood to protect it from fire arrows.

Tugrul smiled at the eagerness of his protégé. 'The city-takers will give us the walls, after the trebuchets have cleared the battlements.' He looked back to the bowman atop the wall, just as the first trebuchet bucked and loosed a mass of rock, which flew over the heads of the Seljuk army. The rock exploded through the battlements. The army roared at this as the dust cleared and the gouged battlement was revealed, spattered with red stains where the defenders had stood. He saw his nephew shudder.

'If there had been a field battle, Muhammud,' Tugrul leant forward to speak in his nephew's ear, 'many men would have died, probably in a single day. They would have earned glory and the death would have ceased after that, but these people choose to shun the glory of meeting my army in the field and instead hide behind their walls. A year of famine and pestilence and then inglorious defeat is their reward. Every man inside those walls will die today. It has to be that way; otherwise all our enemies will barricade themselves away like this. A field battle is glorious and swift. Remember this.'

'Then why do you choose to end this with a siege on this day?'

'Because, Muhammud, victory today will end the Daylamid threat. What is left of their armies will march under our banner.

Then we march against our next foe and our next again… until the Seljuk people and her lands form an empire that none can threaten, dominating this ancient land.'

'What happens when we achieve this, Uncle?'

Tugrul grew a sly grin at this. His nephew was thinking ahead already. 'Then we cast our net ever wider; there are two fruits ripe for the picking. The Fatimids to the south and ancient Byzantium to the west. They are still strong right now, but one of these proud civilisations will flinch at our presence. Flinch, and then fall.'

Another volley of trebuchet fire exploded against the walls, huge sections crumbling to dust leaving yawning chasms in the bulwark. The defenders were impotent to retaliate with only short-range bows and bolt throwers that barely reached the Seljuk front ranks, instead concentrating their fire on the city-takers that now rumbled close to the walls. One of the towers stumbled into a spike pit that had been dug to trap infantry, its structure shattering and scattering hundreds of men from the ladders and enclosure on the top, dashing them on the ground, cutting their screams short. Another tower was riven by a bolt that caught the structure in the corner, splitting the timber walls, which fell away to reveal the akhi packed inside – easy prey for the Daylamid bowmen who fired volley after volley into their mass. With a chorus of screaming, the tower slowed to a halt and then toppled forward with the weight of the dead inside. The remaining ten towers carried on relentlessly until a great wail rose up from inside the city as they clunked into place by the battlements, peppered with arrow shafts but undamaged.

Muhammud watched the carnage with a puzzled look. 'Byzantium; that is the empire of the western god?'

Tugrul shook his head. 'Of the one and only God. Byzantium holds on to a tradition of invincibility and I would relish the chance to teach them of their own mortality. But it will be a long journey, one of many years, like our longest shatranj duel… we are positioning our pieces now to fortify our homeland before we can strike out at these distant empires. By that time you will be a grown man, Muhammud, and you will not shudder at scenes like those you will see before you today. Men will revere you and you will bring glory to Allah. Our destiny is foretold: glory waits on us!'

With that Tugrul raised his banner and bellowed, spotting the Seljuk banners flooding the city battlements. 'The walls are ours. Forward!'

The war horns sounded and as one, the Seljuk army surged forward like a tide.

—

'Watch, Muhammud.' Tugrul twisted his nephew's head to face the execution.

Muhammud shivered at the screams of the Daylamid prince, whose face had turned pale at the sight of the wide, squat and roughly hewn stake set up in the square at the centre of Isfahan. The dipping sun cast a long shadow from the execution device as two akhi spearmen grappled the prince's shoulders and marched him forward. The crowd of Daylamid citizens – the women and children who had survived three days of butchery since the city had fallen – and Seljuk conquerors watched in a near silence.

'He has to die. If he lives, he presents a threat of rebellion. Thus he *must* die, and in a public forum so that his people will know what awaits them should they take up his mantle.'

Muhammud kept his expression stern. He knew his uncle was right, despite the horror of the spectacle. He shook free of Tugrul's grip. 'I understand. Do not treat me like a boy, Uncle.'

Tugrul nodded with a faint hint of a smile. 'You are growing into the young man I knew you would. One day they will give you a name to match your greatness. To become what I know you can, you must shun all doubt. Know you are invincible and do not squirm at the brutality of war.' He looked wistfully towards the west. 'I once had a protégé who could have been great, yet he let feebleness guide him, preferring to shun the reality of war.'

'What happened to him, Uncle?'

'He went west, to settle in Byzantine lands,' Tugrul snorted, 'as some kind of statement of his pacifism. He could have been great, but he was meek, Muhammud, meek like your father.'

Muhammud's skin crawled in shame. His father, Chagri, was content to rule as a weak sibling, defending and consolidating in the wake of Tugrul's conquests. He loved his father but felt shame at the contrast between him and Tugrul. He knew from the first time he rode with the armies that it was his uncle's path in life he wanted to follow.

Yet his own actions in proving himself to Tugrul caused him far more shame. He remembered the old slave, a quiet and unassuming man, happy to receive reward from Muhammud and repentant after punishment. One day, Tugrul had called Muhammud to the palace rooftop, and there he found the slave kneeling, weeping in the centre of a circle of his uncle's trusted men. Tugrul had announced to his men that Muhammud would one day lead them to ultimate glory, then he had handed his nephew a knife. Tugrul had roared that Muhammud would now show his ruthlessness by executing the slave. A year had passed since that day and he could still feel the rasp of the blade sawing into the flesh, the warmth of the blood spilling over his hands, the confusion in the slave's eyes, staring up at his young master.

He looked up at Tugrul, realising he hated and loved his uncle with every breath. 'I will never shirk glory,' he spoke sternly.

Tugrul's expression remained stony.

Then a groan of terror sounded from the centre of the square.

The two akhi spearmen strained to push the prince forward towards the waist-high wooden stake; the man, who that morning had been a royal member of the Daylamid Dynasty, began to claw at his fine-skinned face, throwing laments to the sky and begging his previous subjects for help.

Finally, the two spearmen got each of the prince's legs either side of the stake. They looked up to Tugrul, who nodded. The prince's eyes bulged and he mouthed silent pleas now as he was pushed down by the shoulders. A ripping of clothing and then a cracking of bone and sinew was all there was to be heard as they pushed him down further and further, the stake impaling his rectum and crunching through his gut, then parting his organs. Finally, his legs were splayed out on the ground, the tip of the stake resting somewhere in his chest cavity.

Muhammud refused to look away as the prince's breathing grew shallow, blood running from his mouth, eyes, nose and ears. But the man was very much alive, and he would be for the rest of the day and most of the night until his heart grew too weak to pump blood around his horribly compacted and distorted body.

'Now gouge out his eyes!' Tugrul barked.

Muhammud did not flinch.

This was the other side of glory.

CHAPTER 9

The Trail

The market square in Cheriana was abuzz in the spring haze. Under the towering, red-tiled church dome, the place was alive with activity; heckling, barging, swearing, all to the rhythm of a kettledrum beat and the ubiquitous aroma of cooking meat and horse dung.

Apion looked to the trader behind the stall once more and gestured towards the clutch of hoes. 'Come on, your prices are surely a joke?'

'You offer one nomismata when I ask for two? I won't be beaten down because I am far from home!' The swarthy trader shook his head with a fastidious grin and Apion noticed that the man looked like a younger Mansur with a tidier moustache.

Apion thumbed the single nomismata in his purse. He saw the trader was not for budging and racked his mind for another approach. Then he realised he was thinking in Seljuk; nearly a year of learning the language meant he could now use it interchangeably with Greek. He looked up with a glint in his eye and switched to the Seljuk tongue. 'I'll give you one nomismata and a bag of orchid root.' He pressed the coin into the man's hand, unclipped the hemp sack of root from his belt and nodded. 'Makes salep sweeter than honey.'

The trader frowned, then broke into a grin and then a chesty laugh. 'As sweet as the mother tongue? Then we have a deal.' Then he rummaged under his stall and produced a similar purse-sized frayed sack. 'Here, fresh almond flakes; you are obviously a man of good taste.'

Apion grinned and took the pouch, clipping it onto his belt. 'I'll be back here regularly and I'll make sure to stop by your stall and give you my trade.' He scooped up the hoes under one arm and hobbled back to the wagon on his crutch, the trader whistling to two of his hands to pick up the plough-blade and fodder Apion had also purchased.

When the goods were loaded into the cabin and the trader gone, the grin fell from Apion's face, the facade of light-heartedness was as close to happiness as he had come since last summer. The image of the ring on the dead Agente's finger had stayed with him, vivid behind closed eyelids, absent only when his anger piqued and he saw the dark door. Mansur had grown weary of his obsession over the Agentes and Maria rarely looked happy these days, troubled by his dark and brooding moods and shunning of her fellowship. She deserved better than this, as did Mansur, he mused. He looked to the drivers' berth and the side where Mansur usually sat. But not this time: this was the third solo trip Apion had undertaken. The journey here had been uneventful, yet his guts had been in knots the whole time and he could not even bring himself to relax at Petzeas the ferryman's tall tales.

For today he was to cross paths with an Agente.

He had met an investigator on his first solo visit last autumn, and paid him to find out all he could about the Agentes, and it was on his second visit in the winter that the man had informed him of the Agentes meeting that was to take place here, today, and Apion planned to spy on the proceedings. He looked up to the sun. Midday. It was time.

He set off for the meeting point, his eyes narrowing as he hobbled towards a tight alleyway: beyond the blacksmith and tannery there was a dilapidated inn, crowned by two floors of crumbling tenements. Then, down at the end of the alleyway was a building in an even worse state – the old imperial warehouse – the door hanging from its hinges and two burly skutatoi flanking the entrance.

The alley narrowed as he hobbled down it, the walls towering above him, dulling the noise from the market square. A one-legged man sat by the inn clutching a carved wooden Chi-Rho, eyes staring through the begging bowl in front of him. Apion recognised the filthy tunic that barely remained in one piece – military issue. He thumbed the remaining coin in his purse and eyed the empty bowl, when a whinnying and grinding of cartwheels filled the alley. He stumbled back as a black-painted wagon rushed through the cramped space, halting at the ramshackle warehouse after the inn. The skutatoi at the warehouse doorway stood to attention at this. Apion ducked back into the doorway of the inn.

The wagon door opened and a broad, scar-faced figure dressed in a scale vest stepped down, followed by a slim man in a black cloak, black felt cap and dark-green silk shirt and leggings. The slim man seemed to hold himself with an air of arrogant majesty and the skutatoi at the doorway were instantly obedient, pulling the warehouse door open. The party disappeared inside and the skutatoi visibly slumped in relief.

Apion frowned, eyes burning into the spot where the cloaked man had stood. The prey was in his sights.

He turned and hobbled inside the inn, ignoring the stench of vomit and the red-eyed clientele who hugged their cups and huddled around the bartender. For it was at the back, near the kitchen area, that there was a hatch leading into the derelict warehouse next door. At least that was what the investigator had told him. Apion's blood fired as he considered how he would tackle the cloaked man. A quick death or a slow one – it all depended on whether the man had a full complement of fingers or not. Then something thudded into his shoulder and he looked up to see a toothless drunk staggering back, wine swilling over the edge of his cup, face contorted in a scowl.

'Watch it... hold on, what's a young lad doing in here on his own?' Then his eyes fell on Apion's leg and crutch. 'Where's your minder, boy?'

Apion's skin burned as a few of the drinkers looked up, squinting at this twelve-year-old boy lurching through their drinking hole. His plan had been to slip through the inn to the hatch unnoticed. Now even the bartender was flicking glances towards him, eyes narrowing, mouth opening as he turned to his hired muscle sat by the bar.

Panic setting in, Apion stopped where he stood. Then his hand brushed against the small pack of almond flakes the trader had given him. An idea sparked in his mind. He pulled the pack from his belt and held it up. 'Kitchen?'

The drunk shrugged, grunted and turned away. The barman's features relaxed and he jabbed a thumb to the door at the rear of the inn. 'Through there.'

Apion hobbled on, eyes fixed on a latched, cobwebbed timber half-door rising only to waist height, just before the kitchen door. Then as soon as he was beyond sight, he ducked down, unlatched the door and pushed through, closing it behind him.

The darkness of the space between the walls was complemented by the musty tang of damp timber and brickwork and the air was stale and thin. He saw a dot of light further on through the wall space, and moved gingerly towards it, careful to feel his way in the blackness with his crutch. His eyes were gradually adjusting to the blackness, so he could make out the dim outlines of the cavity, when an icy drop of water splashed on his neck and trickled down his back. Then there was a flurry of movement around his boots and a high-pitched shrieking. His heart thundered when he saw a myriad of glimmering eyes. Rats. He glanced back to the faint sliver of light from the hatch door, then screwed up his eyes and shook his head. To get this close and then succumb to fear, like the fear he had felt that awful night, would be unforgiveable. He sought out the dark door in his thoughts, sure that his fury would overcome any fear he felt. As the image came to him, he saw the arm again; the white band of skin around the wrist and that curious red emblem on the forearm. With that, he realised he was comfortable in the darkness. His breathing slowed to normal again.

Then, from the opposite wall, he heard a groan. His skin crawled. Then there was a hoarse yelp, followed by a nauseating snapping then shredding sound. He looked to the tiny spot of light up ahead and hobbled forward, straining to stand on the toes of his good leg, pressing his eye to the coin-sized hole looking into the warehouse. It was lit by a pair of oil lamps and in the centre stood a group of four men; the cloaked figure from outside, his scarred bodyguard and two more skutatoi. They were encircling something hanging from the rafters. Apion squinted to see what it was, then one of them moved to reveal it. The breath froze in his lungs: a figure, barely recognisable as a man, hung, bound by his wrists to a rafter, toes scraping at the ground but unable to take his weight. The man was naked yet wore a coating of dried blood; long hair matted brown and stuck to his face. His chest would expand, snatching in breath, then his whole body would shudder as he exhaled, whimpering. A stack of bloodied tools lay on a table nearby: a dagger, a hammer, a sickle and a spathion. Lying on the floor beside the man was a pair of fleshy masses, sinew and blood disguising their identity.

Then the cloaked man shook his head. 'A pitiful end for you, isn't it, soldier? You might be wondering how you can bargain with me to make this quick, to put an end to your miserable life without further suffering? Well, there is nothing you have left to bargain with. You borrow money from me, you belong to me. If you cannot pay me back, you die... slowly.'

With that the cloaked man nodded to his bodyguard who squeezed his knuckles and hammered a right jab into the man's ribcage, the cracking of a rib echoing throughout the warehouse. The tortured man spun on the rope and Apion saw the raw crimson triangle where his nose had been and the bloody dark patch that used to be his genitals.

He ducked back from the eyehole and clamped a hand over his mouth, bile coating his tongue. Then he bit back his disgust and forced himself to look again, for if the cloaked man had a missing finger and the ring...

The cloaked man nodded to one of the military-dressed figures. 'Keep him here. Make sure he lives for another day.' Then he rummaged in his purse and pulled out a pair of coins. Apion's eyes widened as the man's hands were illuminated in the lamplight, the tarnished ring catching the glow, but it was all too clear; the man was missing no fingers.

Apion closed his eyes. The torturing of this soldier was despicable, yet he felt only guilt that it was somehow lessened in importance now that this Agente was not the man responsible for the slaughter of his parents. He bit into his lip, tasting blood. *No*, he resolved, *I can do good here. When they leave I will free the tortured man.*

Then he heard the cloaked man continue. 'We travel for Trebizond tomorrow, to meet with my master. We will be back to finish this wretch's life before we depart.'

Apion's eyes darted around the darkness; so the Agentes had a master, back in the city where he had served as a slave. Trebizond held the key.

He shot up to press his eye to the coin-sized hole again; the four men had turned their backs on the tortured soldier and were discussing something in hushed tones. But the tortured man was not still, no, his wrists were wriggling. Apion willed the man to find strength and had to stifle a gasp of delight when the soldier did this, slipping free of his bonds and crumpling to the floor. But the four spun around at the noise. The tortured soldier pushed to standing, his limbs wobbling like a drunk man such was his pain. But he managed to stagger over to scoop up the spathion from the table. Then with a hoarse and pitiful cry, he lunged to punch the blade down through the shoulder of the first military man, the sword disappearing up to the hilt and the military man's eyes rolling in their sockets. The tortured man struggled to pull the blade free with his shaking arms, and in a flash of iron it was all over, the second military man swiping his sword across the tortured man's neck. The tortured man was silent; his head tilting back from the gaping wound, his remaining blood soaking him in an instant. Then he crumpled to the floor and was still.

Apion stifled a gasp of disgust.

The Agente was still and silent for a moment and the silence seemed to cause the military man to shrink. 'Keep him alive. That was my order. A simple order.'

The military man shook his head. 'No, sir, I was just protecting you, he would have come at you next...' The man's words ended with a grunt as the Agente's bodyguard thrust a dagger up through his jaw, piercing his brain. With a sucking noise, he ripped the dagger free, clutched the man's lifeless body just long enough to wipe his dagger blade on the man's sleeve, then dropped the body like a sack of rubble.

'Most... disappointing,' the Agente said. 'Come; let us leave this mess for the two outside to deal with. We should now depart for Trebizond today instead of tomorrow.'

With that, they were gone. Apion was all alone in the stinking wall space. The air seemed to grow short again and his mind spun with a thousand voices. He staggered back to the hatch and burst into the inn, ignoring the shouting as he barged past one table, spilled ale foaming from knocked-over cups and mixing with blood-red wine.

He staggered out into the alley just as the black wagon hared past and despite his panting, he still could not find breath. To tackle these shadowy figures would be far harder than he had ever imagined. Cunning, lethal and underhand they were, without morals or conscience. They were not just lone-operatives hiring brigands, like the Agente killed by Tarsites; the Agente today clearly held sway in the ranks of the thema as well. To face them he would have to embrace the darkness within himself. He questioned his motivations, rubbing his prayer rope as he hobbled.

He threw the remaining nomismata into the bowl of a one-legged beggar in passing.

'God bless you, boy,' the beggar called.

Apion hobbled on and did not look back. When he pushed into the centre of the market square, something caught his eye from atop the town gates. He stopped and looked up. His blood ran cold and the bustle around him fell away.

Three new heads adorned the spikes above the gate. His heart wept as he recognised the features of Tarsites and the two archers who had accompanied him that day by the river.

It was mid-morning and the valley air was pleasant under a thin veil of cloud. Mansur strolled over to the wagon and rummaged in the box behind the drivers' berth, the chickens and goats clucking and bleating in misguided expectation of being fed. 'Your mood troubles me today, lad. I'm not so sure sword practice is the best idea?'

'I am sure,' Apion replied. He had returned from Cheriana yesterday and found his thoughts incessant and chattering, but one thing was sure: if he was to find and face the master Agente, then he would need to be ready to fight and fight well. He and Mansur had been practising for the best part of a year now, and Apion's good leg and both arms were leaner and stronger for it, but he knew he had not yet stretched himself to his full potential.

Mansur threw one of the two scimitars to him and Apion caught it by the ribbed and well-worn ivory handle. He hefted the light blade in his grip and eyed the edge: this was Mansur's scimitar, while the old man used Kutalmish's, from years past when they had both been Seljuk soldiers. He remembered Mansur's words when they had first practised with the weapons. *Now I beg you, be careful; they call this weapon the lion's claw for a good reason. The curve means that all the force of a strike is channelled into the section that makes contact with your foe – it can cleave a man's head in one blow.*

'So do you want to practise or admire your reflection in the blade?' Mansur smirked.

Apion issued a half-grin in return as Mansur began to circle him slowly. Then Mansur executed a flurry of swipes, lightning fast, before Apion's face. Apion tried his best to disguise a flinch and kept his eyes on Mansur: the old man's movement and poise exactly as it was back when they had fought with poles, but there was something different when practising with the blade, an icy reality that one slip, one slow parry and he would be spliced open. His scar flared, the damage of a scimitar was already written all over his body. Added to that, where Apion had once found his crutch a steadying centre point, it now felt like a hindrance and he wanted to throw it to one side, to bring his other hand round to hold the blade steady, yet he knew if he was to do so he would crumple to the dust after a few moments of agony. He shook his head clear of the thoughts and glanced to Mansur's footsteps, knowing that the old man's right knee always bent a little before he lunged.

When Apion noticed Mansur's knuckles whiten on his sword hand, he shot a glance to the old man's knees and saw the left knee bend. Confused, his body tensed and he pulled the scimitar up to parry but with a flash of sunlight on iron, he found himself empty-handed, his scimitar spinning through the air to land by the point in the dust, quivering.

Mansur's scimitar tip hovered by Apion's heart. 'Never, *never*, assume anything of your opponent, lad.'

Apion gawped at the glinting blade, frowned and then squinted up to Mansur. 'I will master this. It might take time, but I will.'

Mansur stabbed his own blade into the ground then wrapped an arm around him. 'I know you will. You possess a sharp mind, lad, and I wish you would not put it to use only with the sword. But if mastering the sword makes you the happy boy you were before this obsession you have with the Agentes, then I will teach you all I know.'

Summer turned to autumn, dappling the green lands of Chaldia with gold. Every day Apion focused his efforts on sword practice and every night he pored over what little he knew of the Agentes. This night, however, Mansur and Apion sat opposite each other at the table, the shatranj board separating them, each with just a few pieces left in the game that had run into its sixth night. Apion examined every possible move again but there was no option that would not result in exposing his king, neatly tucked into one corner behind his pawns and flanked by a rook.

The game was a welcome distraction to him. It had been three months since that day in Cheriana, but the image of poor Tarsites' severed head still sent a shiver through him every time he closed his eyes. Every fortnight since, he had taken Mansur's wagon into the market at Trebizond. On those visits, he had spoken with more rogues, racketeers, assassins and swindlers than he could remember, all to no avail, the unsavoury characters dismissing him as just a boy, or falling silent and tight-lipped at the first mention of the Agentes. The backstreets of the bustling city held the answer to it all, an answer that was as yet utterly elusive. His knuckles whitened as he ground them into the table, seeing the dark door in his mind, the knotted arm reaching for it.

'It's tortuous, isn't it?' Mansur grinned.

'Sorry?' Apion looked up, startled.

'The game.' Mansur nodded to the board.

Apion shook his head. The old man was worried for him, he could sense it. 'Every move I plot in my head looks good,' Apion spoke, his words echoing both the puzzle of shatranj and the riddle of the Agentes, 'until I see the move after that and then the next. All moves lead me to a place I don't want to go.'

Mansur nodded. 'So do you sacrifice a piece to take one of mine, perhaps? Is it worth it?'

Apion frowned, looking the old man in the eye. 'No, that opens too many doors.' They held each other's gaze for some time.

Finally, a piece of firewood snapped and Mansur nodded, then tapped the board with a sigh. 'In shatranj, sometimes sacrifice is the only option. Imagine how the strategos feels, he must make such choices when it is not wooden pieces that are at stake but living, breathing men: whether to send a unit of infantry to their deaths to allow the rest a fighting retreat; to have his cavalry pierce an enemy flank knowing that it will slow their advance but then the horsemen will be hopelessly lost in a nest of speartips as a result; whether to leave his bowmen out front for one last hail of arrows knowing it will critically thin the enemy charge but that the archers will die for it. These are the choices of the strategos.'

Apion frowned and shook his head. 'I don't envy the man who has to make that call and then to try to rest at night with the knowledge of what he has done. But I would rather take up the mantle and face the guilt that comes with it and stand against fate, than wander blindly to my death at the whim of another.'

Mansur grinned wryly at this. 'Then take up that mantle – make your move!'

Apion studied the board again: he had his king, a knight, a rook and three pawns left; Mansur with his king, vizier, a chariot and a pawn. Mansur was positioned around Apion's bunkered pieces and the onus was on Apion to break forward and make the most of his numerical advantage. He had soon learned the lesson to avoid rushing to victory on impulse, but also that hesitation could sap confidence. 'Protect the flanks,' he muttered, 'but to win I must expose them?'

Mansur smoothed his moustache and considered the comment. 'Such is the nature of the game. Expose the flanks if you must, but develop the centre in doing so, forcing your enemy to defend.'

Apion studied the board, mapping out the moves his pawns and his knight could make. Then he thought of the oft-passing columns of Byzantine thema soldiers, always the same make-up of a head of kataphractoi cavalry, a body of skutatoi infantry and a tail or flanks of toxotai archers with a mule and wagon train to the rear. No elephants, chariots or other such exotic units in sight.

'Cavalry and infantry; that's what a real strategos has to work with, isn't it? That's what Cydones has in his ranks?'

Mansur looked up as though he had heard a long forgotten voice. 'Cydones?' The old man nodded. 'He is a fine strategos. He manages Chaldia well and leads the fighting men like a lion. His tools are indeed the infantry and the cavalry; the anvil and the hammer. Yet those tools are not enough. No money comes from Constantinople to fund the defence of the empire anymore. Still, that man has been the thorn in the Seljuk advance for over two decades!'

'The Seljuks won't stop, will they? Cydones can never win.'

'As things stand, Cydones can only delay the coming of my people. This will remain the case while the Byzantine Emperor chooses not to support his outlying themata adequately and the Seljuk Sultan believes war and conquest is tantamount to glory. The *Falcon* is a driven individual; Tugrul sees every moment of hesitation as a drop of lost glory.'

Apion wondered what would become of the borderlands if the expected invasion occurred. If the Seljuks were to sweep over the land then his life and his quest would be swept away with their charge. Then, as his eyes hung on his pawns, he saw the killer move. He picked up a pawn and moved it away from the other two, pinning Mansur's chariot against his king. He looked up, grinning.

Mansur pushed his vizier one square forward then cocked an eyebrow. 'Checkmate!'

Apion's heart sank; he had exposed his own king and trapped him in the corner. His brow knitted. His first victory over the old man remained elusive. 'It's impossible!' he fumed.

'Then how is it possible for me to win time after time?' Mansur asked calmly.

'I don't know, our pieces are of equal power, I've tried matching your sequences of movements, and I've tried striking out with my own patterns...'

'Our pieces are of equal power, but we are not.' His words were blunt.

Apion stared at Mansur. Was the old man mocking him?

'The most powerful weapon in shatranj is the mind of the man who controls the pieces.' Mansur tapped a finger to his temple and then moved his vizier back to the square it had been on. 'You are getting better and better. I haven't been that close to defeat in a long, long time. Had you moved your knight around my flank, you would have limited my next move,' he pushed his vizier forward, 'and I would have been forced to expose my king just as you did.'

Apion saw the pattern like a ray of sunlight.

'You would have won. A boy of twelve years beating a man on his last clutch of summers. You should be proud.'

'I could have won... *should* have won.' Apion's spine tingled.

Mansur swept a hand across the board. 'You are starting to see the board from above, like an eagle, soaring on a zephyr, looking down on the formations. The higher you soar, the greater your eye will be for weaknesses in the enemy line.'

Apion held Mansur's gaze as the old man's eyes sparkled in the firelight. 'Like a strategos?'

'See like the eagle and you *are* the strategos!' Mansur grinned.

'Better to be the *Haga*, with two heads to see the battlefield?' Apion grinned in return.

Mansur laughed at this. 'Well put.' Then the old man held his gaze. 'To see you smile is like a tonic for me, lad. Does it not make you feel good when you smile, when you let go of your troubles?'

'It does,' Apion nodded. 'But I do not seek out the thoughts that trouble me. Since that day by the Lykos, they come to me incessantly, they will not leave me alone.'

'You can change that, lad. Let go of this obsession over the Agentes and live the life you have now. Do you think you can do that?'

Apion saw the hope in Mansur's eyes and held his gaze for a moment, then glanced away to the hearth, and nodded. 'I will try.'

Later that night Apion could not sleep and went to the stable, brushing the mane of the grey mare and speaking to her softly. Then he heard the clopping of hooves. The mare's ears perked up. Apion looked out into the darkness.

A black-robed and veiled rider trotted up to the gateposts, stopped and waited.

Apion eyed the figure, uncertain, then hobbled forward. 'What do you want, rider?'

The rider was stock-still. 'You wanted answers?'

Apion's eyes narrowed and his skin prickled. 'Who sent you?'

'My boss will tell you what you want to know. Tomorrow, noon, downriver by the old mill. Bring five nomismata and come alone.'

With that, the rider heeled his mount into a gallop back downriver and was gone.

Apion watched the dust trail in the moonlight. Of all those who had scoffed at his enquiries, or fallen silent at the first mention of the Agentes, there was one who had offered him just a sliver of hope. At the dockside inn, Apion had placed a purse of coins on the table and old Kyros had eyed it in silence. After what felt like an eternity, Apion thought this was another dead end. Resigned, he stood, scooped up the purse and began to hobble away. But Kyros called him back. The old rogue nodded to Apion and said he couldn't promise anything, but would see what he could do, insisting that more money would be needed. Apion had expected that he would never hear from Kyros again, but it now seemed that the old rogue had been serious. If money was what it took then so be it, Apion thought. He had acquired a purse of nomismata through bartering for just this purpose. But one question hung on his mind.

What price for revenge?

CHAPTER 10

Oath

The warm valley winds let me soar high over the farmlands. Here and now, all is peaceable, but I know this cannot last, for I have been drawn here for a reason. Then I see him, the solitary figure on horseback, and at that moment I know what he is to become.

I cannot bend his will, but my heart weeps when I see what fate has in store for him, from this moment and on through the years. So wretched that this being has it in him to be the saviour of an empire but must also dwell in an ill-deserved perdition. If his life is to be as fate will have it then I can only try to prepare him, to show him what lies in his path.

Downriver from the farm, the air was still and tinged with the scent of honeysuckle as the land bathed in the early autumn heat. Only the rush of the Piksidis pierced the serenity. As Apion rode at a canter on the grey mare through the placid scene, he wished for a future where his mind could be free to enjoy such calm.

He slowed his mount and once again glanced over his shoulder, eyes narrowed. Ever since he had set out he hadn't been able to shake a distinctly uneasy feeling that he was being followed. He shook his head of the thought and checked his equipment again: he wore just a green knee-length tunic, satchel, leather boots, a belt equipped with Mansur's scimitar and his crutch strapped across his back. If he found this elusive master Agente, he wondered, would he be ready to tackle him? He had a good technique with the sword, his sword arm muscular and precise, and his crutch arm sturdy and robust just like his good leg. His mind was sharp too; he had beaten almost everyone he had faced at shatranj: Kutalmish, Petzeas and his sons and many an over-confident trader at the market towns. But not Mansur, he mused with a shake of the head.

Scanning the land ahead, he lifted a linen parcel from his satchel and unwrapped a goats' cheese round, biting from it as he turned over the possibilities of the meeting at the mill. When an eagle screeched somewhere above, he looked up, but could see nothing other than unbroken blue.

'You are a long way from home?' a voice spoke.

Apion turned to the voice. A woman was crouched by the riverbank, back turned. Her silver hair hung to her shoulders and her body was frail under an off-white robe. He moved a little closer and saw she was bathing her gnarled feet. He could not see her face but a warm familiarity touched his heart.

'I am, though maybe not for too much longer.' He frowned, looking downriver.

'Where are you headed?'

'North, trading,' he lied.

'Ah, very well. You have no goods to trade though?'

Apion saw her reflection in the water but the ripples hid her features. 'I'm hoping to buy something valuable.' He patted his purse.

'Be careful what you value,' she cut in sharply. 'Remember what happened the last time you ignored my advice?'

'It is you, isn't it, the old lady from the dell?' Apion's spine tingled as he remembered her distant humming of a tune when she had nursed his wound. If, he mused, he had taken her advice and resisted the instinctive urge to return to the burnt-out farm-house, he would not have fallen into the hands of the slave traders. 'You saved me. I'm sorry I didn't listen to you before. I was lost in those days. I never thanked you for what you did for me.'

'Don't thank me, just heed my words.' She turned to him; her puckered face was longer, sadder than he had remembered, but those milky white eyes remained all seeing and utterly blind at once. She stepped forward and grasped his arms. Then her shoulders sagged and she looked resigned. 'You must know where your choices will take you.'

'I don't understand?'

She turned back to the river and crouched to bathe her feet again. 'You may not see it now, but you will choose a path. A path that leads to conflict and pain. Much pain. Fate teases you with that illusion of choice.'

He frowned. Once he had found the master Agente and dealt justice, Apion intended only to live a quiet life on the farm, to bring happiness to Maria and Mansur for all they had done for him and to make up for this last year of his foul moods. How could that bring such pain? 'Then what you foresee is false. Conflict and pain? I have no wish for such a future.'

'Really? Then where are you headed right now? And spare me the rot about trading!'

Apion shook his head. 'If you know where I am going then you'll know why I am headed there. I will never be able to rest and accept the happy life I want until I have resolution on what happened that night, before you found me. I'm closer to achieving it now than I've ever been. All I have to do is go north and meet...'

She raised a hand and cut him off. 'And fate is victorious again. When the falcon has flown, the mountain lion will charge from the east and all Byzantium will quake. Only one man can save the empire... the *Haga*!' Her tone grew dry. 'Are you ready for what lies ahead, Apion?'

He scoured the riverbank, seeking words in reply. Then the lone eagle screeched again and Apion shot a glance up to the sky. Again, nothing. When he looked back to the riverbank it was empty, just the base of a felled beech lying where the woman had been, its spindly roots dipped in the water. He stood, gazing at the spot, turning the woman's words over in his head, a chill dancing across his skin. She was deluded, he thought, surely a man's actions defined his destiny, and he was free to choose those actions? Then he looked north. Conflict did indeed lie ahead for him but only for a short while. He heeled his mount on and tried to clear his thoughts. Then he stopped and listened; was there another set of hooves somewhere behind him? He shot a glance round, expecting to see another traveller, but there was nobody. He was alone on the road.

Morning became noon and finally he trotted into the valley where the ruined mill lay in the midst of the carpet of long grass, swaying in the breeze. High mountains enclosed the valley, streamlets of mountain water trickling down their steep sides to fertilise the grasslands and then to add their strength to the Piksidis' current. Despite the recent drought, the broad river was ferocious here, knots punctuating every part of the surface and the tumbled stone bridgeheads downriver stood quietly in disrepair, alluding to the full strength the waters could muster.

He stroked the mare's mane and slid down onto his crutch, then moved to the riverbank. There, he stooped and cupped water into his mouth, washing the dust of the ride from his throat, then pulled another handful over his amber locks, soaking them and cooling his scalp. He examined his reflection, rubbing his jaw, wondering if it had become broader like his shoulders in recent months. Then he blinked at the other dark reflection in the water's surface.

'So, you are alone?'

Apion spun up and round, wincing and righting himself on his crutch. It was old Kyros. The old man was just as he remembered: short and slight, wearing a felt cap and padded jacket that reached his shins. His face spoke of a hard life: a crooked nose and a heavily wrinkled, withered chin and teeth that were a motley collection of charred bumps peeking from his gums.

'I am,' Apion replied. 'So, you have information for me about this man, the master Agente?'

Kyros smiled and nodded. 'Yes of course, boy. If you have the nomismata, as discussed, we can talk… and I have much to tell you.'

Apion instinctively moved his hand to pat his purse, hanging by his buttock, but stopped. Something wasn't right; Kyros stood here in the valley with no horse or wagon nearby. 'How did you get here?'

'I got here,' Kyros grinned, 'and that is all that matters. Now, the money...'

Apion's gut fluttered in unease at the glint in the little man's eyes. 'The money is nearby and you will have it when you tell me what you know.'

At this Kyros erupted in laughter and then shouted towards the bridge. 'Cockier than a veteran rider, this one, and he's only a boy... a crippled boy!' At this a whinny of horses and chorus of gruff laughter split the air. Three hulking men in grubby felt vests and woollen leggings moved from under the bridgehead to flank Kyros and encircle Apion, pinning him to the riverbank. They all bore longswords.

'Ah, don't mind my men, they travel with me always. Just in case things get a little rough.'

Then, as suddenly as they had started laughing, all four fell silent and Kyros' face fell stony. 'You come into the city asking about the master Agente. You are a fool, boy. Nobody knows his identity and only fools seek it. I simply pay my dues to him through his underlings and hope never to stray across his path. I could have raised word of your enquiry and believe me you would be cold and dead long before now if I had. However, I did not. I thought I could take care of this business myself,' he pulled a dagger from his belt, 'and take your purse into the bargain.'

Apion's skin crawled as the other three drew their swords, grinning.

'Like slaughtering a lamb...' Kyros purred, then stepped forward and slashed his dagger at Apion's face. The blade stung like fire, ripping across his cheek. 'Now, hand over your purse, boy.'

Shaking, Apion reached round to his belt. Then he hesitated, noticing the glint in Kyros' eyes, realising that as soon as he handed the purse over, they were certain to kill him, throw his body in the river and carry on with their business. At that moment he felt like such a fool and it was all of his own doing. He had been safe at the farm, with the people who cared for him. Yet he had sought out this meeting, kicked the hornets' nest. *A path that leads to conflict and pain.*

'I understand,' he whispered to himself. 'But I do have a choice. If I survive this, I will seek another path.'

'What's that, boy? Come on, hand over your purse and we'll give you a quick death, tear your throat out maybe.'

Apion affixed the old man with a glare from under his furrowed brow. His top lip curled into a snarl and he clutched a hand to his belt, but not for his purse. Instead, he grappled the scimitar hilt and ripped it free of the scabbard with an iron rasp. The blade glinted in the sunlight and the four stood back in mock fright.

'Well, now the odds have changed,' Kyros cooed. 'Now we have to kill not just a cripple, but a cripple with a sword!'

The words did not register for Apion; instead he saw only the dark door, the fire behind it growing intense, orange tendrils licking under the timbers.

Kyros nodded to one of his men. 'Take that dirty Seljuk blade from him.'

The big man walked forward and reached out for the scimitar. Apion swiped the blade up, scoring the man's arm, causing him to fall back with a howl.

'Bad idea, boy.' Kyros clicked his fingers and the other two men came for him.

The first of the men hacked down with a powerful blow and Apion could only pivot on his crutch to dodge the blade. Then the second man swiped his blade from the side and Apion ducked just under its arc. He shuffled back as the first man with the bleeding arm rushed in to join them. 'He's mine,' the man spat, then rushed for Apion with a roar, sword arcing to strike. Then Apion saw the moment: the man's arm was raised, armpit exposed. Crumpling to his knees, he punched the scimitar up with all the strength of his well-trained arms. There was a dull grumble of sinew, cartilage and bone being torn apart and blood showered over him, accompanied by the foul stench of innards. At that moment he saw only the dark door in his mind, smashed back on its hinges, a wall of hellfire on the other side, the knotted arm reaching out like talons into the flames. He heard screaming; only realising it was his own when his lungs were spent. A stunned croaking came from the man, his dead weight resting on Apion's sword. His scar flared in agony as he pulled the scimitar free and pushed back to standing, the thug's lifeless body crumpling.

The other two men were frozen for just an instant and even Kyros' expression had changed. Then the old man coiled into a crouch and stalked forward with his dagger raised to eye level. 'So the cripple can use a sword? You will pay dearly for that, boy; it'll cost me another two coins to hire another to replace him. A slow death waits for you now. I'll put your eyes out first, then cut out your tongue.'

At that the two men flanking Kyros lunged for Apion and Apion could only parry each blow, the tremendous power shuddering through his body. His scarred leg weakened with every strike and he was being pushed back, one foot in the shallows of the river. He glanced back and was ready to leap into the water, to let the current carry him away; the weakness of his scarred leg would surely see him drown but at least he would deny these cretins their kill. Then Kyros scuttled round to splash into the shallows. 'No escape that way, boy. Your eyeballs will burst on the tip of my dagger.'

Apion parried again but now his vision was spotting over, his strength sapped by his weak leg, and he could see Kyros readying to strike at his unprotected back.

Then a whinny pierced the air.

In the gaps between the two big men smashing at him, Apion saw a stallion racing for the melee, a veiled and capped rider flat in the saddle.

'One of you, turn!' Kyros rasped, eyes widening at the newcomer, but before either of the big men could spin around, the stallion wheeled past them, the rider swiping a sword across the back of one. The stricken man fell, screaming, a section of white bone and pink lung visible in his cleaved back; he shuddered, blood haemorrhaging from his nose and mouth and then he was still. At this the melee broke apart and Apion hobbled from the riverbank, gasping for breath, readying himself for the next attack, eyes darting from the last big man to Kyros.

As the rider circled to come back, Apion could see the doubt ripple across Kyros' face. 'Now it is you who should pray for a quick death, old man.'

Kyros set his face into a grimace again, then lunged forward. Apion readied his scimitar to parry once more but the old man slid onto one knee and stuck his other foot forward to kick into Apion's crutch, the wood snapping instantly. Apion felt his own weight pull on him like an anvil and his scarred leg trembled and then buckled. Prone, he saw the big man and Kyros rush for him. He lashed out with his scimitar but the big man smashed his sword down, swatting the curved blade from Apion's hand.

'Gut him!' Kyros snarled, darting a glance back to the approaching rider. 'The horseman's not going to save you this time, cripple!'

The big man raised his sword over his head and roared as he hammered it down. Apion felt only sadness at that moment, wishing he could say goodbye to those he loved and had let down. He closed his eyes and heard the whirring of a sling, a thwack and then a gurgling and a thud of something large hitting the ground. He opened his eyes: the last of Kyros' thugs lay shuddering in the grass, a rock embedded in his temple, grey matter and blood sputtering from the wound.

Kyros froze momentarily, then turned and leapt on top of Apion, pushing the dagger down for his heart. The old man was more powerful than he looked, and all the strength in Apion's arms was not enough to resist as the blade pierced his tunic and dug into his flesh. He roared as it ground against his ribcage, splintering the bone. He summoned his failing strength to smash his head forward, his jutting brow crashing into Kyros' nose. With a crack of cartilage and a yowl, Kyros relaxed his grip on the dagger momentarily. Apion grappled for the blade and turned it on Kyros, pushing the old crook onto his back, but Kyros resisted for what seemed like an eternity until, suddenly, there was a crunch of iron piercing bone and a warm wash engulfed Apion as the blade sunk into the little man's chest.

'You've just signed your own death warrant, boy,' Kyros hissed, grinning maniacally, teeth flooding with blood. With that, the life left the man, his eyes growing distant as his body stilled. Apion scrambled back, panting, staring at the dagger, embedded up to the hilt in the old man's chest.

Apion checked himself. He was drenched in blood with cuts to his ribs, cheek and arms, but there were no mortal wounds. The rider slowed to a trot and stopped beside him. Apion, shivering, looked up as the rider dismounted. He recognised the stallion and the sling, then looked up to the veiled rider's eyes.

'You saved me again, Nasir,' Apion said.

Nasir removed the veil from his face, his expression cold as usual. 'Maria asked me to follow you. She knew you were up to something and was worried for you.'

'Still, you risked your life for me.'

Nasir's face finally fell with a sigh of relief. 'What were you doing, Apion? Chasing these Byzantine Agentes?' He slid from his mount and crouched next to Apion then handed him a water skin. 'Why do you pursue this? You said it to me yourself, you have a loving family. Do you know how hurt they would be if you were killed today? And do you know how much you have upset them with this insane quest?'

Apion nodded, holding the boy's gaze. 'I thought I was only a step away from having vengeance for what happened to my parents, Nasir. You must understand how that would feel.'

Nasir looked guarded momentarily.

'Maria has told me, not in any detail, but I know you lost your mother to the sword.'

Nasir nodded, glancing away as his eyes glassed over.

'But then I met someone today. She talked to me about choosing a path.'

Nasir frowned but nodded.

'Now I realise that I will never find the truth I seek. There will be no happy resolution. So I have chosen my path.' He glanced around the corpses that surrounded them. 'I am leaving all this behind. My family is what matters.'

Nasir smiled at him. It was the first time the boy had done so in all the time he had been at Mansur's farm. 'I never thought I would say this, Byzantine, but for once, we agree!'

Apion smiled back then spat on his hand and held it out. 'I owe you my life. Not just for today. I will be there for you when you need my help. That's something my mother taught me and that's the best way I can honour my parents.'

'I'll watch out for you too. Until we're both dust?' Nasir cocked an eyebrow.

'Until we're both dust,' Apion nodded.

The pair clasped hands, grinning.

—

A spark of hope touches my soul as I see the two boys, vowing to pursue a life of virtue, but that spark is quickly snuffed out as I see what is to come: Apion will learn to live in the coming years, but the dark future will find him, then fate will be served.

Part 2: AD 1053

CHAPTER 11

The Creaking of the Door

Six more winters passed over Anatolia, each one as bitter as the summers were unforgivingly hot. Five years ago, Tugrul had marched his hordes west and hammered against a staunch resistance from a combined force of the Scholae Tagma, Cydones' Chaldian Thema and the Armenian themata, led by their loyal princes. Tugrul was stopped but certainly not defeated, yet a deal was struck to put in place a truce. All had been quiet for the next four years with fewer and fewer ghazi raids. Then rumours started of a rejuvenated Seljuk war machine. Far to the east, Tugrul had swamped the lands of old Persia, revitalising the ancient cities and studding the landscape with garrisoned forts. All the armies of the Abbasid Caliphate, once bitterly opposed to Sultan Tugrul's expediency, were now under his control. The *Falcon* was now at the helm of an army more numerous than the world had seen in centuries, and people said that now he looked east to Byzantium and south to the Fatimid Caliphate of Egypt, weighing the ripeness of each like fruit.

Then, as the harsh winter set in again, official word spread across Byzantium like a blizzard: Emperor Constantine Monomachus had seen prudence in effectively disbanding the Armenian themata, the loyal buffer states that had patrolled the eastern lip of the Byzantine Empire throughout the truce. Fifty thousand loyal men at once became estranged to Byzantium. Tugrul's decision was made for him: the *Falcon* was set to march on Byzantium and take his glory.

High up on the narrow cliff path, sat on the wagon, a winter wind whipped around Apion's legs, even through the woollen leggings he had bought at market. He lifted the extra cloak and placed it around Maria's shoulders.

'I'm fine!' she grumbled. The wagon horses spluttered in a supporting chorus of agitation.

He replaced the garment with a cocked eyebrow and then drew his own cloak tighter. Then he turned back to the problem: an obstinate rock filled the road, smugly insisting that they turn back. The earthquake had felt little more than a tremor a day's ride downriver in Cheriana, but up here, he could see the countryside littered with new features: chasms, landslides and rockfalls like this. Nevertheless, in Maria's eyes their predicament was his fault for trying this new shortcut. He hopped down onto the road, wincing as the iron brace around his knee bit at his scar.

The crutch had been like a living limb to him for that first year at Mansur's farm but as his body developed, growing muscular and lean from his riding and swordplay, his scarred leg remained withered and underdeveloped, as if trapped in time. Eventually, the crutch had become a burden and another solution was required. So, five years ago, Mansur had paid a blacksmith in Cheriana to smelt a mail vest and use it to mould a brace to the shape of Apion's knee. The result had been revitalising. Although he was still stooped to one side, slow and easily tired, he could walk without the aid of the crutch and for that he was eternally grateful to the old man.

And much else had changed for Apion in those years since he had discarded the crutch. Now in his eighteenth year, he had grown broad in the jaw and shoulders, his plaited amber locks draped down his back and the wispy beginnings of a beard had sprouted on his chin. His brow had grown prominent like his father's, casting his emerald eyes in a permanent shade and his aquiline nose was now even more battered and knotted from his adolescent misadventure. For all the physical changes in his life, Apion was grateful only for the peaceful years he had enjoyed: teasing Maria; indulging in horseplay with Nasir; pushing for that still-elusive shatranj victory over Mansur and relishing his trips around the thema market towns. For this simple and pleasant life he had thanked God every morning and night.

He hobbled over to the rock: the impact of the thing had created a hairline fracture in the surface of the road, marking out a crescent from the base of the rock to the cliff edge and bedding the monolith into the road surface ever so slightly. He sighed: he was an experienced hand at dealing with problems on the roads and working a deal at the markets; his Seljuk tongue was now fluent and if the trader was from the east then a few words of the native tongue usually clinched a healthy discount. But no amount of experience could have prepared him for the comedy of disasters this trip had been: a splintered wheel, a horse with rampant diarrhoea and then a thief in the market inn who stealthily relieved him of his purse while he played shatranj with the innkeeper. Now this; a rocky path with a towering cliff-face on one side and a gut-churning plummet on the other. Both he and Maria's hands were scraped and bruised at their attempts to move the monolith, so far without success. The strength of another big lad was just what he needed right now. He thought of his good friend.

Where are you when I need you, Nasir?

It had been a long year since the boy with whom he had shared so many days of play and mischief had upped from Kutalmish's farmhouse and rode east to enlist with the Seljuk riders. The boy had accepted Apion and shared his will to leave the dark past and the death of his mother behind, but his heart burned with a desire for a slice of the glory that the mighty Tugrul was taking in his relentless push westwards. Invasion was the word on everyone's lips and the pull of war won, dragging Nasir into its midst.

'Look, we should loop back and go the other route.' Maria leant forward, hissing as if to disguise her words from the horses, startling Apion from his thoughts. 'You've gotten nowhere so far,' she jabbed a finger up at the early afternoon sun, 'and I don't fancy being stuck out here when it gets cold and dark.'

A tad melodramatic, Apion thought, gulping back the snarling response he wanted to give. He watched as she cooed soothingly into the horses' ears, brushing her cheek against their faces. His frustration quelled.

He would never have recognised this girl seven years ago. She was still short, her eyes only level with his shoulders. However, her matted tufts of hair had blossomed into sleek charcoal locks, her chocolate eyes had stretched into a fine almond shape – probably helped by the kohl from market she had begun to line them with – and she now kept her eyebrows plucked to a fine arc. She was not what others might call beautiful but in another sense that he couldn't quite grasp, she was just that in every way. Over the last few years he had begun to notice how her body moved as she walked, the generous curve of her hips rolling smoothly with each step. So smooth, so soft. An idea sparked in his mind.

'The oil!' he yelped.

Maria shot him a disparaging glance. 'Eh?'

'The oil will shift it!' He hobbled around to the rear of the wagon, pulled the door and jabbed a finger at the neat row of amphorae containing freshly pressed olive oil.

'Or the original route home?' Maria added stoically, hands on hips.

'It'd take us the rest of the day; this way will take us half that time.' He grabbed an amphora and two stakes of wood.

'Oh, going to do some cooking?' Maria cooed as he hobbled over to the rock. 'Why if I'd known I'd have brought a wineskin.'

'Look, if this doesn't work we go your way. It won't take long. Here we go.' Apion popped the cork and let the amphora tumble over behind the rock, the slick green-tinged liquid coating the ground instantly, breaking around the base of the obstacle. 'Come on, give me a hand.' Apion handed her one of the stakes. He wedged the first in under a tiny crevice near the base of the fallen rock. 'Now you do the same.' He pointed to a similar crevice a few hand widths along the base. He looked at her as she sighed, lifting the winch as though it was cursed, her nose wrinkling in distaste. Then the savoury tang of olive oil evaporating hit them both at that moment and a rumble pierced the air.

Maria's face darkened in embarrassment and she clutched her belly. 'Look, I'm hungry, and this is all your fault, so get on with it.'

Apion grinned. 'Then let's get this moved and we'll be back home and eating in no time.'

She shrugged, muttering, then stabbed the winch into the rock.

'On three: one, two… *three!*'

With a grunt, they pressed down onto the winches to lift the rock by the tiniest distance and at once the oil flooded into the gap.

'That's it,' Apion yelped with the last scraps of air in his lungs, 'it's moving!'

The rock reluctantly swivelled on the slick of oil, its weight no longer invincible. Apion ground the stake in and forward, driving at the mass and Maria followed suit. It gathered speed and slipped like soap, silently and without fuss, plummeting over the cliff edge. Apion panted, then stood tall and made to punch the air in victory.

Then, with an almighty crack, the earth shifted under him. He glanced down as the hairline fracture at the edge of the road disintegrated under his feet, rubble tumbling over the cliff edge, pulling him and Maria with it.

'Apion!' Maria screamed, flailing.

'No!' He lunged to grab her, his hand clasping hers just as her legs slipped from the edge. She shrieked, nails splitting the skin of his forearm. He fell to his knees, clawing at the disintegrating road, but each piece of rock he caught hold of came away in his hand. In desperation, he ripped his dagger free of its sheath and stabbed it into the edge of the track. Maria's piercing scream abated. They were halted at last.

'I've got you,' he panted. 'I've got you, now pull up, come on, pull up on my arm.'

Whimpering, Maria clambered up and over Apion, then he hoisted himself up and onto the solid, remaining section of the road.

They sat in silence for a few moments, gasping for air. Time skipped past as they avoided each other's eyes, limbs throbbing, giddiness ruling their minds, until at last Apion stood up, sheathing his dagger. 'We did it, we can go home now!' he panted, grasping Maria's hand to lift her.

As she rose, she slipped and he steadied her by cupping the small of her back. He felt her warmth, her softness against his chest.

Her face wrinkled. 'You idiot!' she spat, her fist crunching into his jaw. 'You could have killed us both!'

Apion reeled back, metallic blood coating his tongue.

'Next time, we do it my way.'

'I'm sorry,' he groaned. 'I didn't think it would...'

'You didn't think? Then we agree on something. Now let's get the road cleared so we can get the wagon over this mess safely.' She turned from him with a groan and strode over to the horses.

Apion held a hand to his stinging jaw and watched her hips sway.

––

The wagon rumbled into the yard at the front of the farmhouse and Apion's heart warmed at the sight of the place, the excited clucking of chickens and bleating of goats filling the air as they slowed. A thick scent of root stew – Mansur's speciality – curled from the kitchen. The old man had become quite the cook since Apion had taken over the majority of market trips. A bowl of this and a hunk of fresh bread would ease his aches and pains and maybe wash the guilt from his thoughts over the oil idea. He fired a quick sideways glance at Maria, who was still sitting, arms folded, lips pursed and staring straight ahead, just as she had the whole way home from the cliff path. He opened his mouth to speak to her when a troubled whinny sounded from the stable.

Apion and Maria shared a confused glance; both of Mansur's horses were with them, tethered to the wagon.

'Visitors?' Apion quizzed, his stomach tightening. He thought of Bracchus and his bull of a sidekick Vadim. Every visit of the pair had seen Mansur hand over a purse of coins. At first Apion had wished for the strategos, Cydones, to call and catch his men in the act. Then, as the extortion had continued unchecked, he felt a sense of shame at standing by as his family was mugged time after time, every exhausting trip to the market towns, every day working the fields counting for little after the vile kataphractos and his mutt had their way. Every area of every thema had just this problem, Mansur insisted, never losing his cool. The irony was that two years ago, the pair had suddenly stopped coming round, just when Apion felt his physique was such that he could stand up to them, despite his braced leg. Rumour had it that the two had been promoted to run some border outpost, something that smacked of bribery or some such underhand measure given their corrupt ways and blatant disrespect for the strategos. Whatever the reason, they were gone, or so he had thought.

Then something moved by his side. 'Maria!' he hissed, seeing her hop down from the wagon, ignoring him as he knew she would. Apion grimaced, lifting the cloth-wrapped scimitar from behind the bench and sliding down gently onto his brace to go after her.

Maria skipped from the wagon to glance round to the stables. She held up one finger.

One horse: that ruled out Bracchus, who would never turn up unaccompanied by his Rus partner. He inched forward and then stopped dead: the front door was ajar. He caught Maria's eye and pushed a finger over pursed lips. Then he motioned for her to stay round to the side of the house. She hesitated, then her face tightened into a defiant sneer and she stepped primly back past the front door. Then something moved in the shadows inside, just behind the oblivious Maria. Apion's flesh crawled.

A flash of iron blinded him as a towering, armoured figure bolted from the door, roaring like a lion to grasp her, lifting her from her feet. 'Maria!' Apion gasped, stumbling forward, clutching the scimitar.

A gaggle of laughter interrupted his run. The armoured figure grinned, spinning Maria in circles. She was laughing. Apion stopped in his tracks, realising he held his scimitar ready to strike in his trembling hand.

'You idiot!' Maria yelped, slapping at the armoured figure – Seljuk armour, Apion realised. Then Mansur strode to the doorway, grinning, watching the pair.

Apion frowned; someone had forgotten to share the joke with him. He moved forward, cocking his head to one side as he recognised the face inside the pointed Seljuk helmet. The dark skin, broad nose, ash-grey eyes and pony tail were unmistakable. His sword arm fell limp. 'Nasir?'

Nasir spun to face Apion, flashing a full grin. 'Apion!'

Before he could gasp or utter a mouthful of relieved abuse, Nasir had him in a bear grip, squeezing the air from his lungs. The scent of sweat, dust and oiled leather entered his nostrils.

Nasir jabbed a fist into Apion's chest. 'Well?' Then he turned to Maria, cocking an eyebrow. 'What a welcome, eh?'

Apion grinned but felt uneasy, noting how much his friend had bulked up. His shoulders, albeit draped in a mail hood, were broad and solid like oak branches and his chest seemed eager to burst from the scale vest hugging his torso. Even his face seemed so different, his jaw had broadened and his chin was shaded with stubble, Apion mused, subconsciously scruffing his fingers through his own sparse amber growth. 'You're a brave man for riding through from the east in your armour. If a Byzantine patrol had sighted you...'

'I'd have outridden them!' he beamed.

'Sounds more like his brother Giyath than the boy who left us last winter, eh?' Mansur chuckled as he strolled from the farmhouse and sidled alongside them. 'Well, any boy's a fool to

138

take to the sword but let's be thankful that he's back and in one piece. You should think yourselves lucky; he hasn't been round to see his father yet, have you? Came to see us first!'

Nasir shrugged his shoulders. 'Well this place was first on my way home. And don't tell Father I said this but Maria is a far better cook than he. So what's on the menu?'

Maria swiped a hand at him, a ferocious grin etched on her face. 'Goat poo if you're not careful!'

'That'll do me nicely. Life with the riders means eating what you can get and when you can get it, drinking anything that doesn't make you gag and sleeping in some of the most... interesting of places.' He shot a wide-eyed glance to Apion, cocking an eyebrow.

Apion half grinned in return as if all-knowing but really his chest felt itchy with envy at Nasir's easy manner.

'Come inside,' Mansur beckoned, 'I knew Maria's goat-poo pie wouldn't go down too well so there's a vat of root stew and an urn of salep waiting on us.'

Apion followed the three inside, feeling hidden behind Nasir's broad frame. They settled at the table and Mansur began ladling his stew into bowls as Maria broke a freshly baked flatbread into quarters, curls of steam rising from its centre, while Nasir lifted off his mail hood and rested it on the chest by his side.

'So you're back for how long, until next moon?' Mansur munched on his bread.

'Just until the *bey*, our leader, comes for us again. The whole unit is on leave.'

Apion wondered what Cydones the strategos thought of the Seljuk army levying troops from within imperial borders, walking freely from the east to come off-duty on Byzantine land.

'So with the riders, have you bloodied your sword yet?'

'Apion!' Maria mumbled in disapproval, through a torn piece of flatbread held in her lips. Mansur's brow creased almost imperceptibly.

He shrugged, wide-eyed.

'Come on,' Nasir snorted, 'you were all going to ask that one eventually.' He glanced at Apion then dropped his eyes to his stew, stirring it with his wedge of bread. 'We rode for three months around the east of Armenia. Building wells, protecting the villages from bandits. Good people, those Armenians. They still can't believe the Byzantine Emperor has abandoned them.' Nasir shook his head, taking a mouthful of stew. 'So that part of army life was good. After that, we headed south for a few weeks. Then we moved east until the world dried up under us.' Now his expression fell. 'Out east it is a different world. Definitely not like here.' He shrugged his shoulders. 'With sand in every direction, burning your skin and blinding you, every man out there seems to distrust every other man.' He stirred his food. 'Byzantine and Seljuk patrols pass each other at times, under orders not to engage, what with the truce. Yet all it takes is one sly look from either side, one petty insult hurled over the shoulder...' he moved to tap his sword hilt, '...so, yes, I've bloodied my sword.'

Maria put a hand on Nasir's arm, then looked up at Apion with a frown. Apion's skin burned.

Mansur cleared his throat and cut in. 'Well, you two boys have a lot of catching up to do, I imagine?'

Both looked up at Mansur, then at each other, finally sharing a smile.

'So what better way to do that than with a trip to Trebizond? Late winter market starts tomorrow and is on all week. It'll take you a day's ride on the wagon to get there,' Mansur munched. 'Spend a day there and then head back – Kutalmish and I need some good iron tools to plough the frozen fields.'

Nasir nudged his elbow. 'Apion?'

Apion grinned back at his friend. With Mansur and then on his own, he had travelled far and wide but not for six years had he been to the thema capital. The buried shadow of his old quest for revenge touched his thoughts momentarily, but he shook his mind clear of the image.

Then he glanced at Maria, who was still studying Nasir's broad jaw. His chest itched.

He affixed Nasir with a sincere look. 'Whenever you're ready, I am.'

It was colder than Apion could ever remember and he and Nasir were perched on the drivers' berth of the wagon, tucked into thick woollen leggings, leather boots, tunics and woollen cloaks. The incessant snowfall continued, adding to the thick blanket of white on the ground and ensuring their progress was slow, night already having descended upon them. Despite this, there wasn't far to go and they had both agreed to carry on.

'Is there no end to it?' Nasir shivered as clusters of snow whipped across the wagon, carried by a deathly wind. He shot a furtive glance at Apion, before shuffling to pull his cloak tighter around him.

'I've never seen weather like this.' Apion shuddered. 'Mansur says his father's father used to tell stories of the steppe, where the snow lay higher than a man on horseback at times.' He screwed up his eyes to peer at the ground ahead; the snow was still only knee deep, he guessed, but the camber of the road was lost under it and it was only the frozen waters of the Piksidis that had kept them on course in the whiteout. 'I think we're still on the road,' he muttered, 'but there might be an easier route.'

'Another shortcut?'

Apion wrinkled his brow and cast a disdainful glance at his co-driver.

Nasir was smirking. 'She told me all about it, the fallen rock. She said you saved her life,' he began with a keen tone.

'Yes. Sharpness of thought, that's what I used. That and a bit of muscle...'

Nasir cut him off, '...saved her life after nearly killing her with some idiot plan involving lacing a mountain road with oil?'

Apion's skin burned under the carapace of cold as Nasir roared with laughter before breaking down in a coughing fit, almost

141

choking on an inhaled snowflake. Enjoying his friend's discomfort, the glow on the horizon went almost unnoticed.

Then they both blinked at the sight, then turned to grin at one another.

'Trebizond!' Apion chattered.

They approached in silence, only the crunching of wheels in fresh snow could be heard. The crenelated city walls grew more massive as they neared and then Apion realised that what he thought were skutatoi lining them were in fact six spikes with a shapeless mass stuck on the end of each. The torchlight up above guttered and the features of the severed heads were momentarily apparent; empty, staring eyes, mouths agape, flesh grey, hair matted with blood and sinuous matter trailing from the neck. A distant memory of poor Tarsites touched his thoughts.

They passed inside the arch of the city's main gate, Nasir staying quiet as agreed while Apion explained the purpose of their visit to the gate guards. Inside the city was muted, the raucous babble he remembered was but a distant echo from neighbouring streets, the weather seemingly having herded the populace indoors. He shivered and looked up to the skyline, the structures of the packed city outlined faintly by the torchlight from the streets. The great church still dominated the centre of the place as he remembered, the snow-covered Chi-Rho on its dome stark against the night sky. A city of god? He felt the urge to scoff at the idea, remembering his time in the cellar drinking hole.

They parked the wagon on the market square, across from a small inn that Mansur had recommended as being Seljuk-friendly. Nasir headed inside while Apion locked up the wagon and tethered the horses in the empty stable nearby. 'Feed them well,' he said, tossing two bronze *folles* to the shivering attendant. He stroked the grey mare's nose and petted the other's mane, eyeing the snow heaped on the market stalls. 'You two huddle

142

together; I'll see you get plenty more fodder tomorrow morning.' He turned to stride across the street for the inn when a clopping of hooves stopped him in his tracks.

'Single file,' a voice barked.

He twisted round: a column of kataphractoi bedecked with crimson Chi-Rho banners trotted across the market square. One rider trotted more slowly, falling back to the rear as the column passed Apion. The trailing rider wore a green cloak, green plumage on his helmet and shoulders and had a forked beard. Apion's eyes widened as he recognised the garb – the strategos! He straightened up to disguise his lameness, taking the pain in his withered leg.

Cydones nodded, eyeing him. 'Mansur's farm boy, Apion, isn't it?'

Apion nodded.

'Well, you've come a long way since I last saw you. You were walking with a crutch, were you not? And the scimitar? That's a fine and somewhat controversial weapon for a Byzantine boy to be carrying in the capital of the thema.'

'It is Mansur's weapon,' Apion replied.

Cydones smiled. 'I know it is, by God I would recognise that blade at a hundred miles. Has he been teaching you the art of swordfighting?'

'He is a fine teacher.' Apion nodded, wondering how Cydones knew the old man. 'You must have fought against him, when he was in the Seljuk ranks?'

'In the ranks, is that what he told you?' Cydones chuckled.

'He was!' Apion was indignant.

Cydones lifted a hand. 'Easy, lad. I know he was a fine warrior in the past, but he was more than a man of the ranks. He was an *emir*, a Seljuk strategos. Led Tugrul's armies like a lion. Probably the finest tactical mind that has ever crossed the imperial borders. His ghulam wing shattered an entire tagma, left them ragged and bleeding with one feigned charge that disrupted their lines and then a real one that finished them.'

'Mansur? A strategos?' Apion's mind reeled. Mansur the peaceful farmer, the waddling old man, the caring father. Then he remembered that day at the Lykos, the ambush, Mansur's swordfighting was awesome, not like that of a common soldier of the ranks.

'Yes, a leader of men, and a damned fine one too. With his right-hand man, Kutalmish, they were nigh invincible at times. He taught me a lot too, you know, had me in a few close scrapes!'

'You speak of him warmly,' Apion commented.

'I hold my former adversary in such high regard because he was a good man. Simple as that.' Cydones nodded. 'I remember the time when he had a battle won and he spared Byzantine lives, let men walk home to their families.'

Apion nodded, his mind reeling. The old man had ghosts, but this was a revelation. 'If he was so glorious a leader of men, why did he leave that life?'

Cydones smirked wryly. 'Every man has his reasons. You would have to ask old Mansur himself.'

Apion frowned. 'Then how do you feel about having a Seljuk strategos living in imperial lands?'

Cydones looked at him, confused. 'I welcome him. He gave up military life to come here, to settle on these lands and farm the soil in peace.' The strategos shook his head. 'I don't live for conflict, Apion, I live to prevent it. It's God's cruel game that in this world we only seem to be able to win peace by warring until we are exhausted or until too few live to fight anymore.' His words trailed off and he thumbed his bronze Chi-Rho neckpiece as he spoke.

'Mansur's crossing over the borderlands to settle amongst those he once considered as his enemy was an example I hoped more would follow. There are other Seljuk settlers in the empire – and I welcome them too – but not nearly as many as I had hoped.' He pointed to the semi-constructed dome near the old library. 'One day soon my engineers will complete this mosque and erect the crescent on its peak. Way west in Constantinople they have many mosques and a myriad of cultures and peoples. It is these borderlands that are so poisonous, but we're making small steps. One day our people might become one, with no need for war or conquest. Until that day, if it ever comes, we must live by the sword. We need good men in our ranks, Apion. Good swordsmen are in short supply. I am well aware that Mansur pays his exemption taxes in full and on time but if you are deft with that weapon then you would be most welcome under my banner.'

Apion felt a surge of pride at this, then remembered the old lady by the river. *You may not see it now, but you will choose a path. A path that leads to conflict and pain. Much pain.* He looked the strategos in the eye and steadied himself; it still took great effort to face the choice he had made since that day he had clashed with old Kyros. 'When I was a boy I dreamt of riding with the kataphractoi, just like my father. Then my parents were slaughtered before my eyes.'

At this, Cydones face fell stony, his eyes weary.

Apion continued. 'I spent a long time after that, too long, chasing revenge and seeking out violent justice. I can only thank God that one day I realised that in doing so I was pursuing ghosts and destroying the second chance at happiness that I had been given in Mansur's home. That day I resolved to stay clear of conflict. It was the hardest thing I've ever done, sir, but the best. I'll help Mansur pay the exemption tax, and I'll even seek to purchase fine weapons and armour to equip another in my place, but I won't be joining the ranks. Even if it were not for my resolution, it would not seem right, for I am a Byzantine and at the same time a Seljuk. I could not fight with such a mindset.'

Cydones' eyes narrowed at this. 'That saddens me, Apion, but at least your reasoning is well thought through, so I can only respect your conviction.' He sighed and then continued. 'Still, though, the thema army is to be mustered in the coming months. Five years of demobilisation makes it an onerous task indeed, but the emperor is expecting us to tackle the advance of Tugrul and his Seljuk armies and he expects us to do it alone as well. In disbanding the Armenian themata, the man in the purple *buskins* believes the Armenian princes and the fifty thousand men who marched with them under the imperial banner are no longer required. The borders are now here,' he pointed to the ground, 'right where we stand. Tugrul's eyes are upon us. Just existing here in Chaldia means that you will be part of the war, whether you are in the ranks or not.'

Apion thought of the shatranj board, the front ranks, and the expendable blades. 'The *Falcon*'s forces, are they not as large an army as has ever approached the empire?'

A smile touched the edge of Cydones' lips at Apion's interest. 'Rumours are dangerous, Apion. Rumours can defeat a man before he even takes to the battlefield. I have heard such talk, but I hold little stock in it.'

'But surely their number would dictate whether the thema faces them in the field or invites them to break on her city walls?'

'A wise question and one my officers and I must mull over in the coming weeks. So Mansur has taught you to think with a tactical mind?'

'Shatranj is my battlefield; we pit our wits against one another almost every night,' Apion nodded, feeling the chill bite through his clothes. 'I have still to beat him though.'

Cydones smiled wistfully. 'That sounds very familiar, he always was one step ahead at that game. Perhaps if you are not to fight in my ranks then we could at least pit our wits over the shatranj board one day?'

Apion nodded, teeth chattering as a fresh batch of snow began to fall silently around them.

'In the meantime, I invite you to spend the evening with my men at the inn up by the docks; they have a crackling fire, hot food and limitless wine and ale to warm the heart!'

Apion glanced back at the inn they were supposed to be staying at. The place was comfortable when he had looked inside but the ovens were off and the fire low. The inn by the docks sounded far more inviting. Then he thought of Nasir. He looked back to Cydones. 'My friend, he is… Seljuk.'

Cydones nodded. 'You tell them the strategos sent you; they'll treat you and your friend well.'

Apion shivered. 'Then I'll take you up on that offer!'

Cydones trotted on after his men. Something the boy had said lingered in his thoughts. *I am a Byzantine and a Seljuk.* Though it had been many years since the crone had come to him, he often thought of her words. He looked back, his gaze hanging on Apion, hobbling around the wagon.

When the falcon has flown, the mountain lion will charge from the east, and all Byzantium will quake. Only one man can save the empire... find the Haga!

He is one man torn to become two.

His eyes narrowed and for a moment he wondered... then he shook his head with a weary chuckle and heeled his mount onwards.

Twin flutes piped out a lilting ditty and kettledrums thumped like horse hooves. Smoke from the roaring fire coiled under the cracked timber ceiling and laughter and babble packed the little space left in the dockside inn. A grinning, rotund lady, eyes smudged black with kohl, stumbled across the legs of three rugged and rosy-cheeked skutatoi. She emitted a staged shriek as she landed in the welcoming arms of the tallest of the three. The soldier wiped ale froth from his lips and cracked a stumpy-toothed grin as one of the woman's breasts spilled loose from her frock and her pristine blonde sculpted hair tumbled loose of its pins. The countless skutatoi and kataphractoi crammed into the alehouse cheered at her exposure. She slapped the bewildered soldier and then planted a wet kiss on his lips, before struggling up and away, leaving him gazing like a lost but happy lamb while his comrades slapped his back and shoulders.

Apion squinted at the frothing golden liquid that swam near the base of his jug. 'Tastes… funny,' he slurred.

Nasir shook his head. 'That's one of the reasons my people don't drink the stuff.'

'Maybe you need it to appreciate the, er, atmosphere in here?' Apion mused.

Ferro the tourmarches had been quick to welcome Apion and Nasir into the inn with the soldiers and almost before they were seated, a pair of foaming ales were slammed down in front of them. Nasir had politely refused his. Apion drunk both greedily though. And he had practically inhaled the platter of duck meat and carrot stew the soldiers had bought for him, the tenderness of the meat and the rich, salty gravy flooding through his enervated limbs. Now, belly full and on his third jug of ale, he felt distinctly woozy.

'Ale is sweet most evenings, but tonight,' Ferro nudged him with an elbow, 'it tastes like honey from God!'

'Aye, and it'll burn like the piss of the devil in the morning!' a fellow skutatos roared in reply, conducting another cacophony of shrieking laughter.

'It feels as if I'm swimming, but inside my own head?' Apion wondered, feeling his thoughts run wild.

Amidst another crash of laughter, Apion squinted up at Nasir, supping honeyed water steadily. His friend was nervous in the presence of the men of the thema.

'Another ale for the boy!' Ferro yelled at an emaciated maid as she threaded her way through the throng. She winked in acknowledgement, growing an instant, well-rehearsed and over-the-top expression of gratitude before turning to move off.

'Not sure if I can take another.' Apion stood to stop the maid but his hand seemed to thrash out wildly as if belonging to someone else, knocking the cups from her tray. They crashed in a foamy wash on the grime underfoot. 'Sorry.' The blood drained from his face and he slammed back onto the bench, elbows thudding onto the table, head flopping into his hands.

'With that charm and wit, you'll pull the women all night long,' one soldier yelped.

'Aye, he's got a way with them, eh?' Nasir replied nervously.

Apion squinted up, his vision blurring. 'Hold on, what about Maria; she likes me, laughs at my jokes. Likes the ones about the goats best.'

'Maria? I think you're kidding yourself,' Nasir mused, looking off into the distance with a smirk.

Apion fired a glare at his friend, and then tucked the last swill of ale down his throat. Bitter at first, it now slipped down, tasteless. 'You've got something to say about her?'

Nasir flicked his eyebrows up in mock alarm. 'Think about it. She was pleased to see me the other day.' At this the surrounding skutatoi leant in, cooing in a sudden interest. '*Very* pleased.'

'And? She and I have grown close over the last year.' Apion spluttered. '*Very* close,' he mocked.

At this, Ferro clapped his shoulder with a chuckle and stood. 'Sounds juicy, but I'm off for a piss. Try to stay in one piece till I get back.'

Nasir threw his head back in laughter as the tourmarches upped and left for the latrines. 'She likes you, aye, but like a brother!'

The skutatoi let out a series of mocking gasps. 'A fight over a bit of pussy? What a surprise!' one of them cackled, slurring. 'What's she like, eh? Slutty?'

Apion's blood fizzed and he pushed up to standing, barging the table back, refusing to wince as his brace cut into his scar. Drinks toppled and foamed around him. 'You shut your mouth!' he roared at the soldier, who stared back wide-eyed, his face slack as he leant back in his stool. It was only then that Apion felt the weight of his sword hilt in his hand, the blade part-removed from its sheath. A wash of fiery confusion consumed him as he saw the faces of the men around him: gone was the ruddy bonhomie and in its place were frowns of disgust. He tucked the blade away and rubbed his temples.

'What're you doing with a blade like that?' one red-faced soldier growled, then jabbed a finger at Nasir. 'And you, your face doesn't fit in around here.'

'Leave it,' one kataphractos from the column shouted him down. 'The strategos sent them here tonight.'

'Aye?' The ruddy-faced soldier's expression changed, and then he nodded, kicking a pair of stools out from his table. 'Then I let my words get the better of me. Sit, have a drink with us.'

Apion and Nasir sat, gingerly at first. Under the influence of the ale, the soldier's moods seemed to spiral like leaves on a breeze as they bantered. Apion refused any more of the ale and supped water instead, listening as the conversation turned distinctly bawdy.

As story after story was told, he found his thoughts wandering. He looked over to the corner of the inn, happy to find his vision had sharpened again despite the onset of a burning headache. Then he frowned, noticing a sharp-faced figure sat in the shadows in the corner, flanked by four massive soldiers either side. A short, bald tradesman sat in their midst talking with the sharp-faced man. No, not talking, pleading. The sharp-faced man leant forward to rest his chin on steepled fingers wrapped in iron-studded gloves. Apion's heart skipped a beat. It was Bracchus.

'Keep your head down around that one, lad,' the skutatos by his side nudged him. 'Bad news follows him like a plague. I've only been in this city for a year but I know to keep from his path.'

But Apion's eyes were fixed on Bracchus as he reached forward to grip the tradesman's jaw. Then, from the side of the gathering, a big, shaven-headed man stepped forward, a citizen. He barged in and reached out to pull Bracchus' hands from the tradesman. At once the giants surrounding Bracchus stood, hands on their sword hilts, teeth bared. The tradesman's bodyguard, dwarfed by these men, stepped back. Bracchus pulled his arm back and then swept his knuckles across the tradesman's face with a crack that was disguised by the babble of drunks.

The skutatos by Apion's side continued. 'He's pulled whatever strings he needed to and is now a tourmarches. He runs the garrison and the town of Argyroupolis like a mini-kingdom, or so I've heard.'

Then, as the tradesman and his bodyguard beat a hasty retreat from the inn, Apion saw Bracchus wince, rub his knuckles, then pull off his glove to rub his hand. All the noise and activity of the inn fell away for Apion.

'I said don't look at him!' the soldier hissed by his side.

'Apion, what's wrong?' Nasir's voice echoed nearby.

But Apion's eyes were locked on only one thing.

Bracchus' index finger was but a stump. On the stump was a tarnished silver ring with a snake winding around the band.

In his mind, the dark door roared, rushing towards him, the arm reaching out for it, muscles taut, seeking the inferno.

CHAPTER 12

Leaving

The thick blanket of snow clung to the land for the next two weeks, but Apion shunned the warmth of the farmhouse, spending his days trudging through the drifts, wrapped in his cloak, shivering. He sought solitude, poring over the newfound truth, and the blanket of white all around him seemed to help him focus on his thoughts. He searched for the resolve he had known previously, to bury his need for vengeance deep within. He sifted through every possible alternative, but none rested easy with his heart. No, now he could see only one future for himself.

After weeks of such sombre thinking, a sudden thaw ushered in spring. The land was quickly turned green and mild and Apion knew what he had to do; he stopped a wagon one day on the road and brokered a berth on the vehicle, heading east in three days' time.

When he returned to the farm that night, he left his meal untouched and sat in silence, despite Maria's attempts to drag conversation from him. Finally, she went to bed and he was left with Mansur in the hearth room.

The old man cut a lonely figure behind the shatranj board, untouched since before the Trebizond visit. 'Your mood is troubling me, lad. You won't eat, you won't talk with me, and you haven't slept for weeks. Tell me, what do you want?'

The fire crackled in the hearth and a sweet woodsmoke puffed across the old oak table. Apion glared into the flames. His mind had been in turmoil since they had returned from the city. The rest of that evening at the inn had been numb for him. Every inch of his being wanted to rip his scimitar from its sheath and run for Bracchus, to plunge the blade deep in his heart and look into his eyes as the life slipped from them. Nasir had been worried for his friend, but at first when Apion tried to tell him what he had seen, he found his voice simply was not there. As Bracchus left the inn, flanked by his brutish bodyguards, Apion had watched him, a thousand voices screaming at him to act. But he didn't and that made him feel all the more reprehensible.

'Talk to me, lad. Remember how that has helped in the past. Play shatranj with me?'

'I'm leaving the farm, Mansur. I'm joining the thema.' He waited for a reaction but none was forthcoming. 'You want to know why?'

Mansur was silent, staring. Then at last he spoke. 'Nasir told me. He said you think you have found the man responsible for what happened to you, to your parents.' His voice dried a little and then he croaked. 'He said you seek to kill Bracchus?'

'He is dead already, Mansur. He is a walking corpse. I found out what I need to know from the men of the thema, he sits like a peacock in his lofty post as tourmarches in the frontier town of Argyroupolis, buttressed by giants who kill for him on a whim. They say he is an Agente, the master of all other Agentes seeded in the eastern borders. Untouchable, a killer endorsed by the emperor himself. I will prove them wrong. For all he has done to me and all the crimes he has committed.'

Mansur dropped his gaze to the floor at this, rubbing his temples, eyes shut tight. 'Be careful what you seek, Apion. It may not bring you happiness.'

'I don't seek happiness. I seek revenge.'

'In the ranks of the thema? Have you thought it through, lad? I am not sure you are ready and I don't mean because of the weakness in your leg. No, you are a fine swordsman in a duel with me, but you cannot imagine the reality of the battlefield, your body coated in blood, skin and bone all around your feet.

Around you a thousand men scream and a thousand more are dying. Blades and spears hack through the air all around you. Yet you can only pray to your God that they do not fall upon you as you remain utterly engaged in combat with the man before you. Combat, to the death!'

'You forget that I have killed before.' He thought of the Seljuk on that awful night. He thought of Kyros and his men, though Mansur knew nothing of that incident. 'I have spilled blood and it did not trouble me,' he lied.

Mansur shook his head. 'You will be fighting my kin. You could find yourself fighting Giyath or Nasir.'

Apion looked up. 'Some of the men who killed my parents were Seljuk,' he spat.

Mansur's face fell stony at the venomous riposte. 'Your words are fired with anger,' he replied evenly. 'Your quest for revenge is understandable, but make no mistake: Tugrul's hordes are vast and committed to conquest, lad. The years of skirmishing and raiding are over, for they have served their purpose of testing Byzantium's defences. The *Falcon* is going to war. I fear you would lose your mind, if not your life, in the bloodshed that is to come.'

'Is that why you left your post as an emir?'

Mansur's eyes darted up. 'I see. Nasir also told me you had spoken with Cydones.'

'He told me there was more to you than you let on.' Apion felt his anger dissipate just a fraction. 'Why didn't you tell me?'

'What difference does it make? I fight in the ranks, I see blood. I fight as an emir, a strategos, I see blood.'

'You fought under Tugrul's banner?'

'I did.'

'Is he the war-hungry creature they talk of, the *Falcon*?'

'He was and still is a sharp mind, Apion. He taught me to play shatranj. He lived with dreams that were spawned years before either he or I was born. To unite his people, to seek out glory for Allah.'

'Then he is not all bad?'

'Are any of us, lad, are any of us?' His gaze drifted to the fire. 'The early years of glory were seen as justified as we consolidated our grazing lands and removed the threats hanging over our people. I accepted the reasoning at that time. Yet as the years went by I had to ask myself why I was leading ever-growing armies against cities further and further south than our people had ever been before.'

'Cydones says you were one of the finest tacticians he has ever faced.'

'And he was one of the bravest young lions I remember. When we clashed, he was like a demi-god; he fought not for spoils or for glory but purely for his empire; a rare trait.'

'He said that one day you let him and his men go home unharmed when you had beaten them. This is true as well?' Apion leaned forward.

'That day, I let my enemies go home unharmed,' Mansur shook his head, 'but there were many other days.'

Silence filled the room, only the crackling of the fire breaking the stillness. Apion felt a growing shame at his behaviour. Mansur was the last person who deserved his wrath over Bracchus. He pushed back from the stool and hobbled over to the hearth, pouring two cups' worth of goat milk into a pan. He dropped a few pinches of dried orchid root into the milk, stirred it and then sprinkled cinnamon over the surface and placed the pan over the fire. Salep would soothe their wounded hearts.

'So is it Argyroupolis you will be headed to?' Mansur spoke at last.

Apion nodded, eyes fixed on the bubbling drink. 'Yes, I will be leaving in three days' time; I have paid for a berth on a wagon.'

'A wagon? No, you shall ride into the fort at Argyroupolis on horseback. The grey mare, she is yours, always has been since the first day you rode her.'

Apion felt his heart clench at this. The old mare was tired, fit for wagon work but not any more for hard galloping. A loyal friend, he could never take her into danger. 'You need her,

Mansur, you know you do. For the farm to operate, you need two horses. My pay will be coming home to you, of course, to help with the upkeep of the farm and feed the two of them. But no, I will be walking into the barracks at Argyroupolis. This brace will not stop me.'

'So it is to be,' Mansur sighed.

Apion looked to Mansur, realising that talking with the old man had indeed calmed him. He wanted to thank him. His eyes fell on the shatranj board. 'Shall we?'

They played long into the night, trancelike, until a grating snore filled the air. Both of them jumped.

'Snores like a boar, that girl.' Mansur grinned, nodding to Maria's bedroom.

Apion realised his eyes hung on the door a little too long and he glanced down at the table again. What would it be like to be away from her? She was a friend like no other and barely a night passed without him dreaming of her. Was Nasir right, he wondered, was he just a brother to her? His gaze fell on the shatranj board as he contemplated this. Then he noticed the gap in Mansur's lines. He lifted his war elephant and placed it two squares away along a diagonal from Mansur's king.

They were both silent, then finally Mansur raised his eyebrows and let out a puff of breath and chuckled.

'Checkmate!' Apion grinned.

His first ever victory over Mansur.

After a long pause, Mansur looked up with a wry smile. 'Well played, lad. You've got a knack of counter-flanking there. Risky,' he jabbed a finger at the two chariots, isolated and exposed wide of the main force, 'but bloody effective.'

Apion nodded. 'One of many strategies I have learned.'

Mansur chuckled, his chins folding and his eyes creasing. 'Well put, lad, and well won. Today. But try that again tomorrow and you'll see how easily that move can be countered itself.' He stood and groaned, stretching his arms. 'Now, it is time to sleep!'

'Until tomorrow, when we play again?' Apion said.

'Until tomorrow, lad,' Mansur chuckled.

Apion watched the old man waddle into his bedroom. Sadness touched his heart when he realised that he only had a few more days before he would be gone from this place. He traced a finger over his prayer rope, seeking the first words of the Prayer of the Heart. He sought out the happiness he had known before he had uncovered Bracchus' true identity. Instead, he only found the fury inside him. The name rasped in his mind again. He dug his nails into the table until one snapped.

Bracchus!

His lungs rasped and his eyes stung from the wash of fresh sweat. But he had made it to the top of the hill, this time without the grey mare. He hobbled onto the beech-wooded plateau and pushed through the foliage until he came to the clearing, with the tumbled red boulder cairn at its centre. Here, he tore off his tunic and collapsed, the cool dewy grass soothing his naked body. One hill and so much fatigue and fiery pain in his leg. The ranks of the thema would hold far tougher challenges, he realised. His eyes fell on the stern etching of the *Haga* on top of the cairn. Its glare seemed to burn into him.

Back at the farm he had laid out his kit on the bed: a spare tunic, brown woollen leggings, boots and a brown hemp cloak. In his satchel he had packed food: bread, salted meat, a pot of olives, a round of goats' cheese and a skin of stream water. Mansur had also insisted he take with him a miniature shatranj set. *Keep your mind honed, lad; make your mistakes on the board and not on the battlefield.*

Leaning against the bedstead was Mansur's scimitar, tucked into a sword belt. The thema would issue him standard arms and armour on joining them but additional weaponry that the state

157

didn't have to pay for would always be welcome. If they scorned his use of the Seljuk blade, he would just have to learn to handle a spathion. And all this was only a day away, he mused, eyes fixed on the *Haga*.

Once his breathing had slowed, he stood to get dressed. He was suddenly all too aware of his nudity. Fortunately, the beech thicket obscured him from the highway down below.

'Well, you do need better feeding, I must say; there's no danger that the wolves will be preying upon you!'

Apion's skin froze and he pulled his tunic across his crotch. The voice was light, lilting. Maria. 'You followed me?' He spun around, unable to locate her.

'No, I came up here before you.'

'How did you know I would be...?'

'Yes, amazing, isn't it. You've only been coming up this hill for years. You didn't need the mare to get up here today though, did you?'

Apion's cheeks burned.

'You're pretty flustered though, I thought you were in prime condition for the thema?' she mused, visible at last as she strolled from the trees towards him. She looked different, wearing a rich red robe – clean for once. Her hips swung hypnotically.

He touched a hand to his burning face; at least the effort of the ascent had disguised his embarrassment. He tried to straighten up, to look nonchalant about it all, but his plaited pony tail tracing against his bare back wouldn't let him forget he was naked and she wasn't. 'I was hot, so I took off my tunic.'

He felt the old shame at his scar being fully exposed, the serrated flesh snaking from ankle to midriff, and was expecting the usual frown of disgust when she saw it. Instead, her hazel eyes stuck on his, the glance became a gaze as he saw her, so close now: her eyes were richly kohl-lined, her lips stained with ochre and curled into a decadent smile.

'I think you're a fool for what you're doing, Apion, but you've been in such a foul mood for so long now that I wonder if serving

158

in the army will do you good. But I came here because I want you to know something.' Her words were softly spoken. 'I will miss you. You are like a brother to me, but more than that...'

A thousand reasons why she should not come any closer flooded to his mind, but she took just one more step and stopped. Then they embraced and she pressed her mouth to his, their lips rapacious as they tasted one another.

Maria ploughed her fingers through Apion's hair as he hugged her to him. Inside he felt a myriad of fires raging. Fear and a deep, unknown excitement blossomed in every inch of his body. Without a word, they were prone. He pulled her to sit on top of him, lifting her robe, his hands cupping the warm smooth flesh of her hips, sliding up over her stomach and settling on the underside of her heavy breasts. She lifted the robe off at last, and then uttered a shuddering gasp as he entered her.

He had dreamt of this, countless times. Now it was so real, so natural. Her face was creased, eyes screwed shut, biting her lower lip and she moaned with every thrust. All the way from his lips down through his heart, stomach, all along his legs, he tingled, the sensation building ever more intense until, like an explosion, the climax flowed through both of them, Apion shot to sitting as he moaned, pulling Maria to him so each panted into the nape of the other's neck.

Time seemed irrelevant as the sensation ebbed into a placid calm. Then at last Maria rolled to one side to lie flat. Apion lay so his eyes were level with hers. What to say? He simply took her hand in his and smiled. The light of the rising sun came through the beech thicket, a touch of warmth blanketing them. Every birdsong was a precious melody and every breath tasted rich and full. Now this was the thing he had been missing, Apion mused, losing himself in Maria's eyes.

Suddenly, Maria shot upright and grappled for her robe. 'Well, that wasn't at all bad,' she muttered casually, looking off into the sunrise.

Apion felt his euphoric world crumble. *Wasn't bad?* It sounded as if she was talking about an under-flavoured cup of salep. Was this something she did every day? The fuzzy warmth in his chest turned abrasive and he frowned. 'Sorry?'

'What's wrong, can't take a compliment?' She shuffled to standing. 'Come on, we'd better head back, I need to finish making breakfast.'

Just like that? Inside he was furious, furious that indignation had swept away the utopia of moments ago. He wanted to shout and swear, yet he found himself grinning at her inanely.

Maria looked at him as though he was a troublesome stain. 'Tchoh! Will you put your clothes on and come on!'

—

'Raise your drinks!' Kutalmish roared, his voice echoing around his hearth room as he lifted a cup of salep. The likeable, white-haired old man was barely visible over the feast-laden table piled with cheeses, grapes, apples, figs, vegetable stew, salad, fresh breads, yoghurt and jugs of chilled fruit juices. Nasir sat by Apion on one side, Maria by Giyath on the other. Mansur and Kutalmish made up both ends. This was it: the big send-off for Apion, Nasir and Giyath, as they prepared to set out the following morning, Apion with the thema and Kutalmish's sons with the Seljuk riders.

Apion's stomach squirmed at the luxurious spread. He hadn't eaten all day, not even at breakfast. His head was awash with conflicting emotions: revenge lay on his horizons and he would have to immerse himself in the conflict to take that revenge. Then there was Maria; their encounter at dawn had left him in a spin, his emotions rolling up and down like the hills. He had stumbled back down to the farm, weak and unable to keep stride with her in her purposeful march. When they had got back it had been just like any other day by the way she had acted, munching through her breakfast in a perfunctory manner, refusing to meet the giddy gaze he had fixed on her. The rest of the day had been a spiral of thoughts until now, with the sun setting, he would spend his last night at the farm with those who made up his world.

'Not hungry?' Giyath grumbled through a mouthful of yoghurt, shooting a glance from under his thick brows.

'Oh I'm hungry, just not sure where to start!' Apion replied, shrugging at Nasir's older brother. In the years since Apion had first laid eyes on him, Giyath had grown to become a rock of a man, his head shaved, further emphasising the anvil of a chin and broadening his bull-like shoulders. He was every inch the fighter, the kind of man you would want as the beating heart of your front line. Apion had never quite clicked with him in the same way he eventually had with Nasir, perhaps because of the age difference or more likely because of the personality clash. This man was a shrill echo of the stubborn, belligerent persona that Nasir had been when Apion first came to Mansur's farm.

'Well get your fill because you'll be on swill and rat meat with the thema!' Giyath chuckled at his own joke, before breaking down in a coughing fit.

'You think he's joking?' Nasir shot Apion a grin.

'Enough that all three of you should do your duty with honour and, most importantly, return safely,' Kutalmish cut in. 'I trust my sons will do me proud and, Apion, I hope you will...' the old man frowned, lost for words momentarily as he glanced to Mansur, '...find what you are looking for. War will be upon us soon enough, so let tonight be a night we can remember. All of us sat around the table as one big family. All of us,' Kutalmish repeated, a warm smile growing across his features, directed at Apion.

Apion felt all eyes fall on him, a shyness crackled on his skin. He wondered what they all felt of the unspoken truth: that Kutalmish's sons were to pursue the life of warfare that their father had shunned; that Mansur's protégé was to walk from the valley with a thirst for revenge and blood. Then he glanced up at Maria; he and Mansur had resolved not to tell her of the matter of Bracchus. Her face was radiant, light of troubles. She winked at him. He smiled in return. Maria prodded her tongue out then grinned; a ridiculous, toothy grin and one that Apion found hugely infectious. He could not suppress a snigger.

'Something funny, is there?' Giyath grunted, his brow set like stone.

Maria widened her eyes in mock terror.

'Of course not, I...' Apion started.

'My father welcomes you as a member of our family and you laugh at him? You'll do well to stay clear of the ghulam riders,' Giyath's tone was grating. The man angered easily and sought conflict and Apion had just handed him another point of contention on a plate.

'Enough, Giyath.' Kutalmish waved his hands over the table. 'Let us eat tonight in peace.'

'Agreed.' Mansur raised his cup. 'Let us rise above all that is to come and remember what bonds us together. Strong bonds, stronger than blood.'

Apion felt a warmth cloak him and he too raised his cup. 'And those bonds should never be broken,' he said. Every face lit up, apart from the wrinkled frown of Giyath. Then, with a screeching of his stool on the flagstones, Giyath rose, tossing his knife down, then turned and stomped from the hearth room to go outside.

'I'm sorry, was it what I said?' Apion stammered.

'No, Apion. Let him be controlled by his moods, the foolish boy,' Kutalmish muttered, shook his head, then slowly began eating again.

The tense silence that ensued hung heavy in the air and Apion found it difficult to eat when every bite echoed through the hearth room. He wished he was back at the farm, alone. Or maybe with Maria in his arms? He suddenly realised that Mansur did not know of their encounter. Would he object? He glanced up at the old man, realising a gentle chatter had begun between him and Kutalmish. Mansur loved Maria but he loved Apion too. Perhaps it would be best to keep their relationship to himself for now, he mused. Yet he couldn't shake the image from his mind: Maria, naked in his arms. He shot a wicked glance up at her. She winked, but not at him.

Apion followed her impish grin. On the other end, Nasir's gaze was fixed on her, expressionless apart from his eyes, which sparkled with mischief. Apion's skin burned and his chest clenched. *What was she doing?*

Mansur supped the last of his salep and chuckled. 'Well, Kutalmish, I can only thank you for your hospitality again. The dates...' He shook his head as he pulled his cloak on from the back of his chair. 'My word, the soil in your orchard is blessed! Now we should be on our way, to let the boys sleep well before tomorrow.'

'Pleasure to have you,' Mansur. Pleasure to have all of you, but please, leave your robes. It's cold and dark outside and very late. There are enough rooms for each of you to sleep here tonight.'

Mansur patted his stomach. 'Aye but a walk would probably be best for me.' He glanced out of the open shutter at the darkness and raised an eyebrow. 'Then again...'

'I'll get the fresh bedding?' Nasir pre-empted his father, barely disguising a sigh.

Kutalmish nodded.

The bed was soft and warm, but Apion found sleep hard to come by, his stomach gurgling over what little he had managed to eat, his mind turning over the flashpoints of the evening. He tried to relax, breathing deeply. Eventually, sleep teased his thoughts into a collage of memories and images. Then one forced its way to the front; the dark door rushed for him, the knotted arm swiping out to push it open. *Revenge!* The rasping voice in his head grew louder and louder, jolting him awake.

With a groan, he slid from the warm comfort of the sheets, the brace clicking into place under his weight as his soles rested on the cool flagstoned floor. He slipped on his tunic and hobbled out of the room: the floor of the farmhouse was a forest of shadows in the moonlight but his eyes locked onto the door of the room Maria was sleeping in, two along from his own. Every one of his steps seemed to land on a loose flagstone, causing a clunking and grating. Fortunately, Mansur's snoring more than drowned it out

163

as he crept past the old man's door – he had some cheek to talk of her snoring! Then he stopped. Maria's door was ajar. Was she expecting him?

His blood raced as he reached out to push the door, the smell of her hair, the touch of her skin dancing in his memory. Her room was dark but he could sense her, waiting under the blankets, as he patted them from the foot of the bed. Until he reached the pillow. The bed was empty.

Then a distant shriek from outside echoed through the house. It was faint but it jolted him all the same. The sliver of moon outside, the darkness, the screaming. A nauseous swell touched his guts as his mind was cast back to that awful night. He thought of waking Mansur, Kutalmish. No, that would take precious time and he would not stand back and do nothing *this* time. He made for the door and hobbled out into the night.

–

The shriek had come from the highest hilltop. Apion, breathless, struggled through the last of the scree and up onto the hilltop, his strength deserting him already: whoever had Maria had taken her away from the farmhouse and up to this spot – his spot – in the midst of the beech thicket. He crouched to rest by the first of the beech trunks that encircled the small clearing in the centre. Apart from the hum of crickets, all was silent. Then a groan echoed through the trees. Apion narrowed his eyes and stalked forward.

Then he heard her. She moaned rhythmically, but there was someone else, grunting in tandem. Realisation dawned before he saw them, but denial kept him stalking forward until he saw the two shapes, writhing.

Maria grasped Nasir's back, her legs wrapped around his thighs, while his buttocks thrust forward again and again. Apion felt a cold sliver of pain in his heart.

He fell back onto the bracken.

'What was that?' Maria hissed, suddenly breaking from their embrace.

From the shadows, Apion's eyes hung on hers. He longed for her and loathed her in one sorry pang of self-pity.

'A fox, probably,' Nasir grunted in annoyance, before nuzzling into her neck and pushing her down again.

Apion stumbled back from the thicket, his brace clanking.

'No, I know that noise,' he heard Maria say.

The stinging precursor to hot tears itched behind his nose. He hobbled down the hill, roaring out into the darkness.

His scar flared in a white-hot agony as he threw himself forward, exhaustion gripping his muscles and spots swimming in his vision, but he continued, stomping towards the banks of the Piksidis, begging for the wagon that was to take him east in the morning to be there, right now.

As he approached the riverbank the blood froze in his veins; someone was sitting there, upon a rock, silhouetted in the faint moonlight. Apion crouched, ready to turn and hobble away.

'Relax,' a gruff voice grunted. 'We're not enemies, yet.'

Giyath. Apion's skin prickled.

'I can never sleep the night before joining up either.' He eyed Apion furtively. 'And all that talk at the table, it boils my blood.'

Apion moved to sit beside Giyath. The man's face was a crease of untended fury for an instant and then his head dropped. He ran thick fingers over his shorn scalp.

'It's all very well to talk as if we are of the same blood.' He looked at Apion, his eyes glistening in the moonlight. His words were weighted but his face was solemn now, unthreatening.

Apion wondered how many times he had actually spoken with Giyath over the years. Him aside though, there was Maria and Mansur, Nasir and old Kutalmish. They were his blood in every sense other than the physical. He relaxed with a sigh. 'We practically are.'

Giyath cut him off, ripping a dagger from his belt with a rasp of iron. 'I respect you as Mansur's boy, but you've got to understand, for your own sake, if we ever met in the field, then I wouldn't blink before sliding this into your guts—' he grabbed Apion by the collar, pulled him close so the pair were nose to nose and Giyath's breath stung in his nostrils, '—to split your veins, to tear your organs, spill your blood into the earth.'

Apion's heart hammered and his eyes darted from Giyath's dagger, pressed against his ribs, to his burning features. He saw the inky depth of sadness in there, if only for a flitting moment. Then Giyath roared in an impotent fury and shoved Apion back from the rock.

'Well then I pray we never meet in the field,' Apion spluttered, prone, touching a hand to the pool of red trickling from the narrow gash on his ribs. Then boldness laced his blood as he stood. 'For your sake as much as mine.' He jutted his chin out in defiance.

Giyath stabbed his dagger into the ground and laughed a hollow laugh. 'It's not about me being better or stronger than you, Apion. That's not the issue here.' He looked up, now his eyes were glassy. 'It's the cold, hard truth of the battlefield. You're with the thema. So even if you were a brother...' tears rolled around his anvil chin and dripped to the ground, '...it would be just the same: your blood or mine.' He wiped angrily at his tears and turned away. 'Now leave me, I want to be alone!'

Apion felt cold at the thought of returning to Kutalmish's farmhouse. In the oddest way, he felt his only bond with another was this wretched one he had with Giyath, right now. 'Why don't you leave, Giyath, leave the Seljuk ranks? Here in the borderlands you could be neutral. You could tend the farm instead, make Kutalmish proud. War is coming but you don't have to be part of it. You could be neutral, just like your father, just like Mansur.'

Giyath looked up at him once more. This time though, his eyes were dry. 'Leave the ranks?' he whispered and then slowly shook his head, eyes fixed on Apion. 'Oh, no. You can never leave. You ask my father or Mansur and they will tell you so.' He turned back to the river. 'Now leave me.'

As Apion walked away, Giyath's words circled in his thoughts.

Then a lone eagle cried, piercing the still of the night. He felt a presence nearby, but the land was empty as he peered into the darkness. Then he heard it from all around him and inside him at once, a whisper.

You may not see it now, but you will choose a path. A path that leads to conflict and pain. Much pain.

A dust storm raged in the dark outside and buffeted the timbers of the imperial waystation, making the space inside feel almost welcoming. The cloaked and hooded Bracchus cupped his gloved fingers around his watered wine and studied the clientele: punch-drunk, hunched and haggard seemed to be the common theme. These hovels were supposed to be a sanctuary to weary travellers, a place where imperial scouts and messengers could exchange their mount for a fresh one after a restful night's slumber. Why anyone would feel safe enough to blink let alone sleep in this place was beyond him. Yet in the candlelight, three bodies lay slumped and snoring in the bunks to the rear, veiled from the bar area by only a filthy curtain.

Here he was; the master Agente, executor of the emperor's bidding and now a tourmarches, one step away from a strategos. He stifled a snort at the absurdity of it: unlimited power was within his grasp yet he was sitting amongst filthy rogues. He twisted at the snake-band ring through his glove and for a moment, he remembered the time before, when he had no power, when people could take from him what they wished. Some took things that could never be replaced.

He heard her voice. *Don't look, son, go with them, please, don't look back.*

But he had looked back. He could see that stinking alleyway in the backstreets of Trebizond; the three thugs had paid their bronze folles to have their way with Mother and Bracchus had left them to it, heavy-hearted as always. She had explained to him every day since he was old enough to understand that this was the difference between them living and dying of starvation. But still it felt to him as if she died a little every time she sold herself this way.

He waited the usual short while it took and then made his way back round to where he had left her. But when Bracchus turned in to the alleyway he froze to the spot: his mother stood naked and bleeding, one thug stood behind her, gripping her shoulders, the other hurled blows into her face, already swollen and discoloured. They laughed, laughed like they were playing a game. He made to sprint for her when a third thug hooked an arm around Bracchus' neck and dragged him away. It was then she had pleaded with him. *Don't look back!* But the gruff tones of the thug drowned her out. *Forget about 'er, boy, you've got a whole new life ahead of you. You're goin' to fetch a pretty sum at market,* he slurred and then ripped from Bracchus' neck the bronze Chi-Rho, his only possession of value and the one his mother insisted he could not sell for food. It was the last time he had ever contemplated God. Bracchus sunk his teeth into the man's forearm until he tasted blood and heard the man roar. Then he wrenched free, twisting to go back for his mother, but froze as he saw the knife tear out her throat. Then the blood. Dark blood. The shrieking laughter. The finality of her body crumpling onto the scum of the alley floor.

A pang of sorrow stabbed his chest and then he thudded the table with a fist, clearing himself of sentiment. The drinkers nearest him in the waystation shot furtive glances his way, and then returned to their drinks. They were ignorant. Ignorant of the debt the empire owed him.

It was a debt that could never be settled; the urban guard were absent when they should have been there to protect his mother. The empire could at least be grateful for the fact that he had focused his initial vengeance on the vile underworld, like the racketeer under whose protection those three thugs had operated; safe until they had underestimated the filthy, homeless son of a prostitute.

He had found the thug who had tried to drag him away, talking of slavery; the fool was staggering down the very same alley, blind drunk, only two nights after the incident. Bracchus had knocked him from his feet with a wooden club, then hacked off the man's arm, tore out his tongue and left him to bleed to death. The next thug, the one who had held Bracchus' mother by the shoulders, was found nailed through the shoulders to the doorway of the racketeer's headquarters, his ribcage ripped open, organs pulled free and left on the street for the rats to feast on. The last one, the thug who had slit his mother's throat, disappeared one night, then his severed head was sent crashing through the window of the racketeer's headquarters, empty eye sockets cauterised with a red-hot blade. The racketeer himself had paid his dues with interest; the rumour had spread that they found only his skin and a sea of blood on the floor of his office.

Bracchus felt the dagger clipped under his tunic onto his thigh. It had served him well over the years and his heart had blackened with its every use until now, when he knew only darkness. In that time he had channelled his spite, using shrewdness to rise into the emperor's favour. Now he had licence for his deeds, as black as he wished to make them. The Agentes were sent far and wide in the empire with licence to ignore the law, to spill blood, plot subterfuge and instigate unrest to suit the emperor's whims, and the man in the purple now desired that the eastern borders stay volatile, limiting the power and reputations of the outlying strategoi. So it was a dark role for the darkest of people. But did the empire know what a demon they had hired in him? Now he was in a prime position to become a strategos. With that role combined with his role as master Agente of the east, who could curb his power? No, nobody would take from him ever again.

The slats lifted and a gust whipped around his ankles as the door opened. Another hooded, hemp-robed figure strode in, face in shadows. The figure cast a glance around the tables until his eyes fell on Bracchus. Bracchus supped his watered wine and nodded to the seat opposite.

Both of them sat, faces in shadows.

'What do you wish of me, master?' the Agente hissed like a snake.

Bracchus felt a surge of exhilaration; some Agentes resented being led by any man other than the emperor, but this one was totally obedient. He fixed his gaze on the man's eyes, shaded under his hood. 'The strategos, Cydones, is mobile, mustering and taking stock of the thema,' Bracchus paused, toying with the idea that he could just as easily order the strategos dead with his next sentence. Perhaps the time for such an order would come soon, he mused, but for now, all that mattered was that he and he alone would be left to rule Argyroupolis, free from the meddling of so-called superiors. 'He must be kept from Argyroupolis for some time, until next spring at least. Keep him busy; pay our Seljuk friends well to keep him from the town.'

A wide grin spread across the Agente's features. 'Consider it done, master.'

CHAPTER 13

Argyroupolis

The wagon had found every pothole in the road that wound through the Parhar mountain pass and a dust storm had blown all day, puffing the contents of the land through the slatted wagon cabin with gusto. Apion's plan of sleeping through the journey to Argyroupolis after his wretched night's rest had been blown away with the storm. He groaned, wiping his eyes as if he could clear the fog from his mind, then peeked from the slats of the cabin: the sky was now showing patches of blue as the wind seemed to ebb at last. Then he caught the familiar scent of market: salted and fresh meats, cooking stews and roasting vegetables, all mixed in with the less savoury cocktail of dung and sweat. Then the squabble of the traders, the tinkling of goat bells and the gentle chords of a well-tuned lyre.

This was Argyroupolis. The gateway to the northern coastline and one of the key fortified settlements on Byzantium's eastern flank. He surveyed the town: about a third the size of Trebizond and ringed by a squat limestone wall. Its position, snug in the mountain pass leading to the northern coast and western themata, meant it was always going to be a critical stronghold, the slopes of the Parhar Mountains towering above the walls like flanking titans, defying those who tried to enter the imperial heartlands beyond. Outside the town there was a run-down archery range and a series of dilapidated timber huts, but the town was very much the oasis of life in this mountain wilderness.

'Alright, lad, get your kit together,' the hoarse driver called from the front. 'You'll be handing over another two folles, by the way.' He stopped to hack up another lump of phlegm. 'My horses are knackered. I'd never have driven them through that normally!'

'Right,' Apion croaked, realising his own throat was coated with the dust. The storm had sprung up in the morning as he left Mansur's and the wagon driver had rolled his eyes and tried all he could to dissuade Apion from hitching a ride. *You'd have to be a bloody maniac to travel in this weather!* But Apion had made his down-payment for the journey the previous week and a further clutch of six folles had swayed the man pretty quickly. All the while, Mansur and Maria had stood by the farm doorway, watching him in silence. Mansur couldn't understand his mood that morning. Maria, however, could. She had almost winced when she set eyes on his torn expression and then had avoided his glare after that. He loathed himself for it but he still wanted to hold her, to smell the scent on the nape of her neck.

Then the wagon driver barked to pull him back to the present. 'Move it! I've got to be in and out of here and back in Trebizond by tomorrow or I'll get my balls cut off!'

Apion slung his satchel over his shoulder and braced himself. He winced into the brightness, then slid gingerly out of the wagon.

He stood under the shadow of the main gateway, which was three times the height of a man, the iron-studded timber gates lying pushed back and pinned there by a dune of dust. The wind still had a bite to it, lifting dust that stung the flesh. He pulled on his cloak, aware of the glare of the two skutatoi stood at either side of the entrance and another two stationed above them on the crenelated gate towers. They looked as tired as he felt, dust lining their tunics and packing the cracks in their leather klibania.

'Here.' He tossed the coins to the driver, then his shoulders slumped as he realised he only had one more follis left.

'Hmm.' The driver weighed the coins in his hand and eyed him furtively, a sour whiff of wine on his breath. 'I might need another two. That back wheel took a pounding on some of them roads, and the horses need fodder and a good watering.'

Apion frowned. 'Well sorry about that, next time I'll fill in the potholes before we set off!' He tucked his purse into his belt in refusal. 'Make sure it's the horses that get a drink and not you.'

'Cheeky runt!' the driver snarled, and then whipped his horses on into the town.

'Quite right, lad. He'd rob his grandmother blind, that whoreson,' one skutatos offered with a snort of derision. 'You're here to sign your life away, eh?' he added, eyeing the sword belt.

Apion winced and tried to straighten up, hoping to disguise his lop-sided stance. 'I am. The strategos, he is here?'

'The strategos? He is with the *protomandator*, chief of heralds, mustering the thema. He will be gone for some time. At least until next spring. Until then…' the skutatos rolled his eyes and shot a glance at his colleague, '…well let's just say that since that new tourmarches took charge here,' he shook his head and sucked air through his teeth, 'things have been harsh. Damned harsh, eh, Peleus?'

'Aye,' the other skutatos added wryly, casting an eye into the town. 'Stypiotes is right. Cydones used to run this town, and if you thought he was a hard bastard…'

Apion nodded. 'But until the thema is mustered there must be a place for new recruits to the permanent garrison?' He waited until both the soldiers shrugged. 'Then I'll take my chances.'

'The new tourmarches has made this place his kingdom. He won't give you any chances.' The guard called Stypiotes shook his head with wide eyes.

'Thanks for the warning.' He gave the pair an uncertain nod and passed in under the shade of the walls. Mercifully, the tiresome gale outside dropped away once inside. The interior of the city fell somewhere between the might and grandeur of Trebizond and the ramshackle chaos of Cheriana: in the centre of the town, a granary and a red-domed church bookended a row of three-storey tenements and a line of workhouses, smiths and inns completed the border of the market square. The market square itself was a tight squeeze with colour and noise crammed in to make best use of the limited space of the flat ground between the mountains; traders, shoppers, animals, slaves, spices, textiles, exotic fruits, farming tools and crop stores all mixed in a swirl of commerce. A pair of chickens scuttled around his feet, their owner cursing in Armenian as he chased them, stooping to catch them only for each one to flutter clear of his grasp.

Apion hopped clear of them, his shoulder barging into something.

'Watch it!' a burly, red-faced man snarled, grappling the wicker basket of vegetables he carried.

'Sorry, I…' Apion started.

'Oi!' a saucer-eyed woman screeched as he stumbled back onto her bare toes.

'Sorry!' he yelped as she hissed and hared past him.

'Get out of the way, bloody idiot!'

Suddenly the market town seemed to be writhing around him as traders poured to and from the bottleneck leading to the main gate. The place was alive with purpose and it was as if he was the only soul who had no business being there. Every face was creased with importance and every body moved in haste, while he bounced between them, clutching his satchel, his heart pounding at every bump or curse. His braced knee trembled from weakness already and he felt cold inside and out. *This isn't home*, he almost retched. Then a thundering of hooves rumbled through the dusty ground and a whinny pierced the air together with the familiar cursing of the wagon driver. He spun just as the crowd parted.

'Whoa!' the wagon driver howled, his face stretched in alarm as he reined his horses back but it was too late, Apion could only shudder at the two mounts' bulging and bloodshot eyes as he crumpled under their flailing hooves, throwing an arm across his face. Then he felt the shuddering blow of a pair of hands hammering onto his side, knocking the wind from his lungs, throwing him from the horses' path.

Prone in the dust, Apion winced, clasping a hand to the grating agony that rose through his scar. He sat up: the street was cloaked in a cloud of dust and a general babble of excitement filled the air as the crowd slowed momentarily, no doubt eager to witness some mangled body under the hooves. Instead, they groaned as they laid eyes on Apion.

'Pah! Not even any blood,' one well-wisher commented. With that, the crowd began to melt into a stream of people in a hurry once more.

'Fool!' the wagon driver spat, then peered down at him. '…It's you! Would've served you bloody well right to get trampled.'

'On your way, traveller!' a baritone voice bawled across the sea of heads from the other side of the street. The wagon driver's head snapped round to glare at the source but then his face fell and he grumbled, nodded and then urged his horses on.

Apion stood, teeth gritted at the fiery pain running the length of his scar. He peered across the crowded street to see who had spoken. There, on the opposite side, stood a man with a typical Byzantine felt cap, but under the cap were broad, charcoal-dark features, eyes fixed on him, white as snow with piercing silver irises. From the distant lands of Africa, Apion guessed, he had seen men with the same skin in Trebizond, selling exotic creatures from their homeland to the rich of Byzantium. He had the fresh features of a man in his early twenties and wore a rough off-white and sleeveless tunic with a red sash around his torso and he rested his athletic frame on a spear. The crowd thinned a little and Apion hobbled across to the man.

'You saved me?'

The African nodded, then pointed to Apion's sword belt. 'Conscript?'

Apion's skin prickled. Was it that obvious? Then the man's expression creased in dismay as it fell on his quivering leg. His leggings may well have disguised the scar and the brace but his weakness was not so easy to hide. Apion pulled his cloak over his legs. Maybe this was all a mistake. A distant part of him longed to say no to the African, longed to chase after the wretched wagon driver and beg to be taken back home to the farm. Mansur would welcome him back, surely. Then he screwed his eyes shut tight until he saw the image of the dark door, of Bracchus. He tensed and fixed his eyes on the man. 'Yes, I'm here to join the thema.'

The African nodded. 'Sha, dekarchos, leader of ten,' he pulled at the red sash. 'Or I would be if we had a full complement. I'm part of the permanent garrison here.' The African offered his hand.

Physically, he could see why this man was a leader: young, with broad shoulders and a torso that was honed and lean. Apion gripped him by the forearm. 'I'm Apion.'

'Well, we need every man we can get, but...' the African's voice trailed off, his eyes falling again on Apion's withered leg. He shook his head and looked Apion in the eye. 'There are barely four hundred in the garrison, covering the whole of the east of Chaldia.'

Barely four hundred? Apion wondered at this and the size of the thema border, stretching for miles north and south.

'Second thoughts?' Sha's eyes narrowed. 'We need men, but we have no time for passengers.'

Apion shook his head. 'I'm ready.'

'Come with me, I'll get you signed up.' Sha smiled but his tone was one of resignation rather than enthusiasm. As they walked, Sha pointed to the scimitar. 'That's a fine sword going by the hilt. A conscript bringing in equipment is always welcome.'

Perhaps now was not the best time to mention that it was a Seljuk weapon in the sheath, Apion mused. He looked for a change of tack. 'You are from Africa, are you not? Egypt?'

'Close. Mali, in the heart of the sands.' He patted a hand to his chest. 'Been a long time since I was there though. I was taken into slavery as a boy and served many a Persian master. Then one day I was bought by a Seljuk master who thought I was a broken soul. So he neglected to guard the gates of the slave quarters one evening – so I took my freedom. The only way I could run was west and so here I am. What about you, you're from the north or the west?' Sha nodded, eyeing Apion's plaited amber locks.

Apion wondered at this. His heart lay with Mother and Father, yet with Mansur and Maria at the same time. 'Let's just say my roots are here.' He pointed to the ground.

Sha smiled at this. Then they stopped by the barrack compound and the man's smile faded.

The compound was small, squat and unremarkable, tucked into the corner of the town. A smaller northern and western wall met with the sturdy town walls, segregating from the throng an area maybe ninety feet long and wide. The inner walls were thin and had no walkway, only a timber tower by the left of the wide iron spiked gates provided an elevation overlooking the city. Through the spikes, Apion saw shapes flitting across the muster yard in the centre. Skin and metal glistened, orchestrated by the barking of an officer, yelps of pain and then the smash of iron upon iron. A single skutatos stood atop the timber tower, leaning on the edge of the inward facing lip, eyeing the goings-on below with a troubled look.

'Attention!' Sha called up to the skutatos on the tower. The soldier jolted upright, spun and grabbed his spear, then, upon seeing Sha, he relaxed.

'Dekarchos coming through,' he bawled down to the gates. Two more skutatoi eventually shuffled over to unbolt the iron gates and wrench them open.

The inside of the place was as run down and uninspiring as outside: a single storey brick building ran the length of the eastern side of the enclosure resting against the town wall, probably the sleeping quarters and mess hall judging by the size and rudimentary architecture. It had a tiled roof that looked to be teetering on the brink of collapse, the brickwork was crumbling and bleached by the sun, and flaking, cracked shutters hung limp from hinges. By the south-western corner near the gate was a ramshackle lean-to of timber that looked – and smelt – like the latrines. Lining the northern wall was a large and sturdy box building, uncomplicated but for the crenelated roof space, probably the officers' quarters going by the small stable resting against it. The northern wall of the barracks was in fact the side of another building, a hulking brick structure with its entrance next to the officers' quarters. A wagon was parked by its doorway, clothing and shields being ferried inside – no doubt this was an imperial warehouse, where the soldiers would receive their clothing, armour and arms.

But it was the centre of the compound that grabbed his attention: roughly three hundred men – almost the entire garrison going by what Sha had said – stood in a closed circle in only their tunics and boots. In their midst were two soldiers unarmoured apart from helmets, each clutching a well-polished spathion. They alternated between circling each other and lunging against each other in a flurry of sword blows. All this was happening under the keen eye of a barking officer who held a pole and wore a double-headed axe on his belt.

'Are they training?' Apion asked as they walked past the circle.

Sha kept his gaze straight ahead and spoke in a hushed tone. 'They are being punished. The *kampidoktores* will see to that. His role as drill-master barely covers the brutality he employs.'

Apion frowned at this, and then stopped in his tracks as the officer barking at the fighting men removed his helmet and wiped a rag over his sweating ginger stubble. Vadim! At that moment, one of the fighting men stumbled and fell to the dust. His opponent lanced his sword down then stopped, the point hovering at the fallen man's neck. Apion stopped and stared.

The man with his sword ready for the kill looked up to Vadim. 'I can't, sir,' he croaked, 'he is my friend.'

Vadim sighed and shook his head. 'You are both dead. You just need to accept that. Now finish him!'

Apion shivered, noticing the dark and damp crimson patches in the dust all around the pair. The man relaxed his sword-grip and stood back, chin out in defiance. Vadim took his sword from him, hefted it over, eyeing the blade with narrowed eyes. Then in one stroke the big Rus punched the spathion through the reticent man's chest, letting him gurgle and then slide free of the blade, crumpling to the dust like a sack of rubble. As an afterthought

Vadim stabbed the sword underhand through the other man's throat, cutting his pleas for mercy short and pinning him to the ground. The watching crowd were silent, simply dropping their heads in dismay. Then, at Vadim's command, they dispersed, brushing past Apion and Sha. Apion hobbled forward to the scene of the two dead men, being solemnly lifted by a team of spectators.

'Do not draw attention to yourself,' Sha hissed, pulling him back.

'Death bouts?' Apion hissed, shaking free of his grip. 'This is allowed?'

'They were caught sleeping on watch,' Sha said. 'Punishable by death.'

'But that was no punishment; that was vile, animal entertainment.'

Sha gripped him by the arm, the African's face creased in concern. 'It is what you will have to live with if you want to serve in the garrison. The tourmarches decrees the punishment for breaches of discipline.'

Then another voice pierced the air. 'Bringing runts in at this time, Dekarchos?'

Apion turned to face the approaching figure. Something shivered deep within him. This officer wore no sash but instead a plume, a golden plume, an iron klibanion and leather gloves with iron studs on the knuckles. Two giant soldiers flanked him. Apion's heart hammered.

'Muster and recruitment will happen on my word. *My word!*' Bracchus growled.

'Leave this to me...' Sha whispered to Apion.

'I gave an order. When I give an order you obey it as though it had been issued by the strategos himself.'

'Tourmarches!' Sha turned to salute, stamping one foot into the dust at the same time, his eyes shot for the horizon and remained fixed there. 'He brings his own weapons. Given the low numbers of the garrison, sir, I...'

'You did as you pleased? Yes?' Bracchus cut him off.

Apion felt that terrible chill creep across his skin as Bracchus leaned forward, the sun falling on his face, the piercing blue eyes and razor nose fixed on Sha. Then he turned to Apion.

'Well,' he purred, 'I thought I recognised that lame gait.'

Apion's skin shrivelled. His hand tensed, fingers itching to rip his scimitar free and plunge it into the cretin's throat, right here, right now. Then he glanced at Bracchus' guards, the bloodied sand and then Sha; he relaxed his hand. Then Bracchus' lips wrinkled and Apion realised what was coming next. *Go on; destroy me in front of them all. Shout to them and show them my withered leg. Then tell them all how I live with the enemy. Call me it again: a Seljuk-loving whoreson!*

Bracchus' eyes seemed to drill into Apion's thoughts, his grin widening until suddenly, he stood tall and nodded. 'Well, perhaps we will make an exception for this one.'

Apion's eyes darted around the enclosure: most were the swarthy and dark-haired so-called natives of the empire. Dotted amongst them there were a few northerners and westerners, distinctive like him by their red or pure blonde locks. Then there were a peppering of Africans, Syrians and even a yellow-skinned man with almond eyes. The people and soldiers of the empire were tolerant and open to other cultures. All except the Seljuks. Now all Bracchus had to do was announce that Apion came from a Seljuk household and he would be hated by a lethal majority of the garrison. What was the tourmarches up to?

Bracchus fixed him with an ice-cold glare. 'Vadim, provide our new garrison soldier with armour and weapons.' He turned to the big Rus and nodded. Vadim beckoned Apion and marched for the officers' quarters.

Apion hesitated and shot a glance back to Sha. The African shook his head briskly. Apion felt an awful dread grip his stomach as he followed Vadim into the dim quarters. Inside, a candle flickered, illuminating the crumbling brick interior and a large square table covered in a mess of paper. A bald and corpulent man was buried behind the pile of documents, trying to copy information from the papers into a tattered leather-bound book and at the same time shield a block of six coin towers from the mess. He would then turn to count coins into purses and then stamp the papers with a lead seal. Apion guessed this was the *protocancellarius*, the man Father had spoken of as being respons- ible for carving up the soldiers' pay. On the wall opposite the doorway, a set of map scrolls hung unfurled, outlining the border themata, the forts, towns and cities represented by solid dots, a red line scored across the disbanded Armenian themata. Vadim flitted through the pile of documents on the table, oblivious of the fat man's scowl.

'When you sign this form,' Vadim muttered, pulling one sheaf from the pile, 'you are owned by the tourmarches. You obey him without question.'

Apion nodded silently. *Only until I cut out his heart*, the rasping voice replied inside his head.

Vadim stopped and looked up. 'You affirm every word from a superior's mouth with a yes, sir! The tourmarches is not to be questioned.'

'Yes, sir!' Apion barked, sincere and aping Sha's fixed gaze from moments ago.

Vadim glared at Apion blankly for a moment, arms folded. Then his jutting brow and ginger-stubbled scalp wrinkled. He touched a hand to the scar running over his left eye and a dreadful grin crept over his features. 'Your friend, the Seljuk with sling; I have yet to spill his blood. Remind him of this when next you meet. Now come with me and we will sort out your kit.' He ducked under a low doorway into the adjoining warehouse.

Apion followed him in. The warehouse was musty and dim, lit only by a pair of open shutters, its walls clad in shelving. Vadim dug around near a pile of klibania, and then turned back to him with a garment. Apion braced for the weight of the garment to pull on him. This would be the sleeveless lamellar vest of rectangular leather or iron plates strung together to form a tough armour. Instead, he grasped the bundle with ease as Vadim dropped it – a padded cotton vest.

'I'm here to serve in the infantry as a skutatos, what's this? This is an archer's vest, is it not?'

'Expecting scale or lamellar? Well you have to earn it in this shithole. Only the front ranks get good armour, and believe me, they need it!' He held up one of the klibania, pointing to a spear-tip-sized hole in the chest, surrounded by an encrusted dark-brown substance. Then Vadim rustled around on a shelf and turned to hand him a rusted conical helmet with a frayed and cracked leather aventail. 'Think yourself lucky you're getting that. The last unfortunate bugger to own it was knifed last week in a fight over a woman. Most of the runts get a felt hat at most, but this is much less comfortable; chews into the scalp,' he grinned.

Apion tried the helmet on. It rested like a cauldron on his head and only sat on his crown momentarily before sliding down over his eyes. When he pulled it up, Vadim stood before him with a pair of square-toed boots, sodden and mouldy. They were split above the knee at the sides so they could be folded down to the shin when marching and folded up to the thigh in battle. Then came the skutum, the teardrop shaped shield; battered and faintly etched with the Christian Chi-Rho on a faded crimson backdrop. He glanced to his prayer rope – his business here was anything but godly.

'What else is standard?' Vadim scratched his scalp. 'Ah, yes. You're going to need a kontarion.' Vadim lifted a broad-bladed spear, nearly twice Apion's height, from the rack. 'You really are.' The giant may as well have issued him with a written threat. 'You do not need a sword,' Vadim glared at Apion's sheath, 'but you can have an axe and you can have a pair of *rhiptaria* too.' Vadim gave him a small hand axe, which he clipped to his sword belt, and two shorter, lighter spears, for hurling at an advancing enemy.

'All for the bargain price of half your first year's pay!' Vadim grinned. 'Now, outside, the tourmarches will be ready for you.'

Apion turned to leave and he could feel Vadim's breath burn on his neck as he moved back through to the room with the desk.

There stood Bracchus, flanked by his giants, stood over a leaf of paper.

'Make your mark here.' Bracchus jabbed a finger into the fresh document on the table.

Apion picked up the quill and dunked it in the pot of ink. He could not write as such and could only faintly recall mother teaching him to print his name. As the quill scratched on the paper, he wondered at the significance. A contract for revenge? Then a stench of garlic hit him as Bracchus hissed over his shoulder.

'In any fort or barracks in the empire the soldier usually signs his name, serves his time...' the tourmarches' nose and cool glare hovered just in Apion's peripheral vision, '...but it will be very different for you. Here I am king and the garrison are obedient to my rule and you will be especially so. You were fortunate my promotion took me from your filthy Seljuk master's path, but now your luck is out, cripple. Now I own you. You obey my every word or you bleed your last into the dust.' He jabbed a finger at the grey body of one of the dead combatants being carried past the door outside. 'You *Seljuk-loving whoreson!*'

The gloomy bunk area was functional at best and the other three of Sha's depleted *kontoubernion* sat around on their bunks wearing expressions that matched the odour of the place, examining Apion as he stood in their midst.

The garrison at Argyroupolis comprised of a single bandon, the primary infantry unit, numbering nearly three hundred men when fully populated, plus a smattering of archers. Apion would be sharing a bunk block, rations, reward and punishment primarily with Sha and these three.

'You've got to be kidding?' the biggest of them scoffed, glancing from Apion to Sha. Blastares was built and scarred like an oak and seemed to have the mood of a bear. He sported a broken nose that shuddered from between close-set eyes and his features were baked into a scowl. He shook his head and went back to sharpening his sword on a whetstone.

'He's lame, he can't even stand straight. What's the point of bringing in a cripple?' Procopius, a prune-faced older skutatos with grey-flecked, cropped hair, added with a shrug of his narrow shoulders, jabbing a finger at Apion's trembling limb. 'He'll slow us down, get us killed. We were better off as a four.' With that, he went back to polishing what looked like an artillery torsion spring.

Apion felt his skin burn and he longed to be out of their gaze.

'Do you want to take it up with the tourmarches?' Sha shot back.

'I think I'd rather shit a mace,' Procopius chuckled under his breath.

Blastares also turned to Sha. 'I've told you before, drop the officer babble. Being in charge of a kontoubernion means nothing; until you're leading a bandon you're just a grunt, like us. In any case, we're all grunts to Bracchus.' Then he cast a derisive glance back at Apion. 'But he's a cripple. No use to us.'

The third man leaned forward from the shadow of his bunk. Nepos was a slender, blue-eyed and angle-faced Slav and his expression was cold. He didn't look at Apion as he spoke, instead continuing to carve splinters from a lump of wood. 'You two just don't see past the obvious. You'd try to make stew by forcing a live cow into boiling water.'

'What're you on about, you pointy-faced bugger?' Blastares growled.

Nepos pulled a mocking, tight-lipped smile, then continued: 'Well I wouldn't complain if we had Achilles as the vanguard and Heracles watching our backs, but let's face it; the army is patchwork, cobbled together from what is available. We're lucky the Pecheneg Turks offer to serve alongside us, so we take what we can get and make the best of it. What I'm trying to say is that sometimes you've got to look past people's limitations and seek out their strengths.'

Blank looks ensued from Blastares and Procopius. Nepos seemed to suppress a sigh and then continued. 'Well look at him; he's got a sword. I can tell from the shape of the sheath that it's not a spathion, so he brought it in with him. His arms are muscular but lean – swordfighter's arms. He's got skill with the blade.'

Apion shuffled in embarrassment at the scrutiny.

'Pah! No use if your enemy is more agile than you, can flit around you, stick his sword in your back.' Blastares scratched at his crotch and cackled.

'He's got a sharp mind too,' Nepos added quickly, his eyes hovering on the wooden shatranj box poking from Apion's satchel.

'Leave it out,' Procopius snorted, 'he's lame! That's the be-all and end-all!'

Sha stepped forward and ushered Apion to the spare bunk. 'Well he's in our unit. We live or die as a unit, remember?'

'Aye, well he can watch your back,' Blastares said to Sha, then flicked a thumb over his shoulder to Procopius as the pair stood to leave. 'I'd rather have this old bastard watching mine, even if he's daydreaming about catapults or whatever it is he spends half his life talking about.'

'Watch it!' Procopius shoved him in the side and the pair left, muttering.

Sha cut a frustrated figure, sighing, then turned to Apion. 'Welcome to the thema!' he said, sardonically, then walked out as well.

Apion turned to Nepos. The Slav eyed him stonily, still carving the piece of wood that was slowly taking shape as a shatranj pawn piece. 'You play?' Apion tapped his satchel.

Nepos nodded. 'I need the distraction; I came to this place to get away from a troubled home life, yet I found that I carried all those troubles here with me in my mind.'

Apion frowned. 'So you didn't come here because you wanted to?'

'Few do, lad. It's a long story, and maybe someday I will tell you of it. But right now you only need to know one thing: you've walked into a hornets' nest here. War is coming this way and soon. You're going to have to prove yourself. You know that, right?' With that, the Slav slunk back into the shadow of his bunk.

All around them, the barracks seemed to shake with the thunderous banter of the other soldiers. Apion rubbed the knots on his prayer rope. He had never felt so lost.

CHAPTER 14

The Gathering of the Storm

The sun-baked city of Isfahan, the jewel in the centre of the Seljuk Empire, shimmered in the midday sun. In the centre of the city stood an ornately blue-and-white-tiled palace that enclosed a courtyard. Inside the courtyard, cicadas trilled, birds chattered and a marble fountain babbled, all framed by the orange trees and grapevines hugging the tiles as if seeking to scale the walls.

Muhammud sat on the bench in the middle of the courtyard, dressed in just a silk robe, his battered armour resting for the day. He took a deep breath and looked up to the eggshell blue sky above. The years of peace and prosperity had faded his memories of the day the city had been taken. The flagstones and cobbles had long ago been washed clean of the gore and the families of the survivors conveniently enslaved and sent to the salt mines or scattered across the now vast Seljuk dominion. The screams of the prince who had died on the stake were but a memory. But while this city had known peace in the intervening years, a tide of bloody battle had washed along with the ever-expanding Seljuk borders, and he could no longer even guess the number of men who had died on his sword or on his orders. Yet it was the gaze of the slave he had murdered as a boy that haunted his dreams.

He shook his head of the morose thoughts and sipped his cup of iced water. The summer had been intense. Even now, in the shade, his skin still prickled and his muscles ached from the ride from the city of Tus that morning. He smoothed his moustache and wondered with a grin if, at the age of twenty-six, this was the onset of old age. He picked up a pebble and tossed it into the fountain, scattering a pair of parakeets. The ripples reflected the sunlight over his face and he wondered what his future held. He was truly his uncle's boy. His father had meekly accepted this just as he had meekly accepted his own peripheral role in Tugrul's empire.

But as Muhammud had grown, he had found the maintenance of the empire dull and unrewarding; it was poring over the maps and debating the expansion of the Sultanate that gripped him. Tugrul's trusted men always bowed before the Sultan's opinion, but now they even deferred to Muhammud, unable to counter his sharp-eyed assessments of tactics and strategy. Those activities were bettered only by the thrill of riding at the head of the hordes, chasing glory for Allah, and his appetite for the chase was now insatiable, like a parasite in the mind. Now they would look to the west; ancient Byzantium would be next to fall. Since Tugrul had been held to a stalemate five years ago, forced into a humiliating truce, his uncle had talked of nothing but putting Byzantium to flames. At this, something twinged in his heart; he had long ago buried the doubts over this glory under the carapace of the warrior and leader he had become, but he still felt the echo of those doubts, somewhere deep down in his being.

'Enjoying the shade, Master Muhammud?'

Startled, Muhammud twisted round on his chair, then he relaxed with a smile as he saw the vizier, Nizam, shuffling into the courtyard. 'Nizam, care to join me?' He lifted the jug of iced water and nodded to the empty cup and space on the bench.

'I fear I will not be able to stand again if I do.' Nizam mopped the sweat from his brow then glanced to the palace rooftop.

Muhammud chuckled. 'My uncle is itching to get back on his horse, I presume?'

'He is already planning the route for tomorrow.' Nizam nodded to the open veranda above with a glint in his eye.

Muhammud felt a surge of invigoration, keen to go and invest-igate his uncle's plans. It was at these times that he had felt

188

a longing to be in control of the strategies and formations of the Seljuk ranks. On the field he had shown an innate mastery in the command of the ghulam divisions; like a master emir, Tugrul had enthused. The ranks of the vast Seljuk army loved him for his leadership, bestowing him with an honorary name: Alp Arslan, the *Mountain Lion*. He smiled, remembering how they had chanted it just a fortnight ago, beating their shields as he rode in front of them before the battle on the plains to the south. The show had weakened the resolve of the massive Fatimid rebellion that had dared to challenge Seljuk supremacy, and victory had been decisive and crushing. Yet despite Tugrul's advancing years, his uncle would still not let Muhammud lead the armies absolutely. Tugrul's reasoning was absurdly simple: Muhammud had yet to beat him at shatranj.

He sighed and looked to the vizier. While Tugrul had swept the lands into Seljuk rule and brought the shining glory of Allah upon their people, Nizam had quietly followed the trail of conquest, setting in place a system of government in the oft-chaotic aftermath of a change of rule. He had overseen the establishment of schools, libraries. And thanks to his ground-work, the Seljuk people were evolving into master thinkers and artisans in architecture, literature, politics and governance. A legacy that would last, and all he asked for in reward was to be allowed to continue in his role. Added to this, the dusty cities they had taken over had been embellished under Nizam's guidance to their current ornate beauty, with cavernous baths, immense mosques, grandiose fountains, flamboyant gardens and fine sculpture commonplace. 'To have you, Nizam, is a blessing from Allah indeed.' Muhammud stood to stretch. 'With your wits and organisational skills, Uncle and I can be what we are supreme at.'

'Your father is equally adept at consolidating,' Nizam replied, 'and I think he would be a fine ruler – in times of peace, perhaps.'

'Perhaps,' Muhammud mused, 'but peace is a long way off, Nizam. Times of peace must be won with years of war.'

'I know better than to debate that with you, Muhammud,' Nizam smiled. 'So Byzantium is ripe for Tugrul's sword?'

'We move west after tomorrow, and we will be gone for some time,' Muhammud nodded. 'We will probe their borders and strike at the weakest point.'

When they had arrived this morning, Muhammud had never seen an army like the one amassed on the plains outside the city. It took them near a half-morning to negotiate a path through the camps to reach the city gates. Hundreds of ghazi raiding parties had been sent off to the west to weaken and reconnoitre the borders of Anatolia before the invasion. Yet thousands of Seljuks already lived in the Anatolian farmland, and he wondered what their perception of the invasion might be.

'They say that Byzantium holds the favour of the Christian God,' he muttered, turning back to Nizam.

Nizam cocked his head to one side as if to half-agree. 'They do, but then that God is Allah, is he not?'

Muhammud smiled. The vizier was a man of logic and he was playing with him. He nodded, his face falling stern.

'Only time will tell.'

'You will be weaker for it, Uncle.' Muhammud grimaced at the irritation in his own tone but he could not preserve a veneer of cool over this humiliation.

'No, we will be stronger.' Tugrul fixed him with a tunnelling glare. His uncle was sixty-two now, the locks of pure white hair hanging loose from his turban a testament to this. But age only served to etch his features with an even more pronounced scowl of determination and his posture was upright and broad, like a proud, young man. The *Falcon* was still strong. Perhaps not as agile as he once was, but still the first to plough into an enemy line, hacking and stabbing from his stallion.

'I am like an extra limb for you in battle, you said that yourself!'

'You are a fine leader of men, Muhammud, but do not become a blinkered one.' Tugrul swept the jumble of shatranj pieces along the strategy map, their shadows long in the orange of the dipping sun on the veranda. 'I alone must go west. My reputation and my pride were dented when the Byzantines contained the last advance. Allah challenges me to take the glory for him.'

Muhammud glared at the map. Each of the twelve pieces represented two thousand men: ghulam heavy cavalry, ghazi light cavalry, camel archers and the masses of akhi spearmen and swordsmen. This was but a fraction of the number the Sultanate could muster, but Tugrul had insisted this force was perfectly sized and composed for the job of breaking Byzantium's borders. All would be seeking the glory of Allah. All except Muhammud.

Tugrul's voice was laced with irritation now. 'This is our heartland,' he stabbed a finger into the table, 'and it is yet young, formative. I will be gone for some time. I hope to return victorious but in that time I cannot risk losing what has been accomplished so far.' His uncle paced to the edge of the colonnaded veranda. 'Usurpers watch my every move, Muhammud, and I need my extra limb here, to crush them should they try to undermine my position.'

'I am not my father! You will not keep me chained back here like a mule as you did with him! He and Nizam can maintain the state, I have told you that!'

'Nizam is what he is but he is never a ruler, Muhammud… and you know the same is true of your father,' Tugrul spat.

Muhammud sought a change of tack. 'You taught me to strive for honour and the glory of Allah, Uncle.' He felt a stinging self-pity as he spoke the words. 'How can I find that, sat here while my brothers spill their blood for the cause a thousand miles to the west?'

'I taught you well, Muhammud,' Tugrul said. 'When Byzantium's borders are shattered and we are established to the west, then I will call for you. The army you see outside these walls is but a fraction of what we can raise against our enemy. I will spearhead this invasion, but it is merely a vanguard, Muhammud. You will lead the main force when I have broken the borders. I have always seen greatness in you.' He clutched his nephew's wrist. 'It must be you who leads the final conquest, for you are to be the successor to the Seljuk Empire, Muhammud.'

Muhammud's heart thundered with pride as his uncle embraced him. Over Tugrul's shoulder he noticed the shatranj board; set up with the game they had been playing for some weeks now. His eyes honed onto the piece that was his uncle's king; beside it sat his chariot and below was his war elephant, both seemingly blocked by Tugrul's pawns. Then it flashed before his eyes: he could sacrifice a pawn, and then within three moves Tugrul's king would be exposed and trapped. He saw victory. He pulled back from his uncle, knowing in his heart he was ready and all because of Tugrul's tutelage. 'Seek out that glory and honour, Uncle. Break the doubters to the west on your blade and shield boss and then call for me. My heart and my prayers travel with you.'

'I will, my heir. When my armies are far from here and doubt strikes their hearts, your legend will inspire my men: Alp Arslan, the *Mountain Lion* is readying to come west and hammer home our advantage!'

'For inspiration, they need only remember that they march with the *Falcon*, Uncle. Crush Byzantium, take your glory!'

CHAPTER 15

The Skutatos

'Keep up, runt!' Blastares roared over his shoulder, his breath clouding in the cool winter air.

Apion nodded, breathless, eyes on his boots, treading the frost-speckled ground. Six months into army life and daily patrol was as gruelling for Apion as it had been on day one. Scouting the area around Argyroupolis was hectic. Since the disbanding of the Armenian themata, the stretch of land east of the mountains was highly volatile with the Seljuk armies moving in to fortify and garrison the previously Byzantine-occupied lands, pressing against Chaldia and Colonea to the south. Raiding parties had become more and more frequent, striking at least once every week; until last month, when everything went quiet. Sha seemed to have some distinct unease at the sudden lack of conflict, but they had stuck to their duty vigilantly: two hours were spent every afternoon marching on patrol around the mountain paths to the east, looking for any sign of Seljuk activity.

Apion had not yet bloodied his sword in his time with the garrison. But he had watched grey bodies of unfortunate soldiers being brought back after their patrols had been caught out by a Seljuk raid, the Christian priest delivering their rites as they were taken to the burial ground outside the town. It was a grim reality, but one he would endure until he had worked the opportunity to sink his blade into Bracchus' heart. Time had shown that the tourmarches was meticulous and would never walk without his grunts flanking him or following close enough to intercept any attacker. The man knew he had his enemies. Did he know how close they were?

Yet every day that passed ended with a bitter nightmare. The dark door burning in his mind, Mother and Father's faint voices calling to him while he could only cry out to them in apology for his inaction. Every morning, before the garrison would pray together at muster, he would pray alone, clutching his prayer rope. But God would soon see a different side to him; when the time was right, he would strike.

Until that moment came, these afternoon patrols did little to bolster his confidence that he could get at Bracchus. They were more like a ritual humiliation, being forced to try to keep up with his unit as they quick-marched through treacherous terrain. Every day that meant two hours of the lip of his boots and his brace biting into his welted flesh, his scar screaming for him to stop, the leather handles of his shield pulling at his arms, and his lungs burning as he tried to keep up with the others. Every day he would be lagging behind after only a short while, sweat blinding him as he tried to train his sight on the rhythmic and perfectly balanced march of the four in front of him. This routine had gone on for the entire summer, all of autumn, and continued now, as winter approached.

Maybe the weather cooling had helped a bit, but he clung on to the belief that he was just a little less far behind each day. Yet at this rate he would be an old man before he could manage to keep up.

'Onto the road!' Sha barked, his voice unnaturally tight, in an attempt to out-shout Blastares. The five filed onto the dirt road that wound through the main mountain pass and led back up to the gates of Argyroupolis. Up ahead, the imperial grain supply caravan of wagons, mules and camels rumbled towards the city at their own pace, flanked by an escort of four cavalry archers.

'Come on, lad,' Blastares growled. 'Don't go showing us up again. Stay in line!'

When Apion grimaced and stretched his bad leg as he would his good one, the pain was enormous, like a fire running from his neck to his toes, needling at his muscle and tearing at his tendons, flashes of white-hot agony bursting across his field of vision. He glared at Blastares.

'That's better. Now see if you can keep it up,' he mocked.

'I reckon he could show you up, Blastares,' Nepos panted, dropping back a little.

'I reckon someone's filled your skin with wine.' Blastares roared with laughter, and then broke down in a coughing fit.

'Well you should never underestimate any opponent,' the Slav countered.

'I'll stick money on the big man, fat bastard though he is.' Procopius slapped a hand on Blastares' shoulder.

'Put a nomisma on Apion for me.' Nepos looked straight ahead as he spoke.

Apion shot a gawping look to Nepos. The man had usually shown good judgement. Until now.

Nepos turned and winked at him. 'A race up to the peak, to the gates of the mountaintop village of Bizye. Wait till the spring though, gives you both a chance to prepare and a chance to get a good book going on it; there's a killing to be made here. In fact, make it two nomismata from me.'

'You really are off your head,' Procopius spluttered. 'Two nomismata on the runt not even making it to the top of the mountain. I bet he falls into a creek or the like and breaks his neck.'

'Listen,' Sha cut in, 'I'll put my whole year's pay on us being put to a death bout if we roll through the gates like this.' He stabbed a finger up ahead to the bulk of the town. 'Bracchus is looking for any excuse – particularly with the lad.'

Apion's stomach tightened at the truth of this: as brutal as patrol was, training was a whole lot worse. The training was supervised by Bracchus and drill-mastered by Vadim, and neither had shown anything but utter contempt for him, singling him out to make an example of him. Running was the staple exercise, then alternating running ten paces with leaping, to keep the joints supple. Apion could only hobble, having to have one foot on the ground at all times, so Vadim called him out to hobble and try to leap alone in front of the garrison. This left him in a breathless heap, his scar split and bloodied, his withered limb trembling violently. Then he had taken to using Apion as the example of what happens when a soldier neglects his strength, making Apion stand to the front again, holding a pair of iron klibania at the tips of his outstretched arms while the sun seared at his skin. There had been sword fighting too. One on one. At this, Apion had accounted for himself well, winning more bouts than he lost. The lingering image of the death bout on that first day had made him hold back though in case he drew Bracchus' attention to his skill with the scimitar.

'Come on,' Blastares repeated Sha's order as his own, 'let's get in formation!'

Sha glowered at the big soldier. Nepos shook his head and rolled his eyes.

Apion struggled to stay with them, every bit of his body screaming in agony. He thought of Nepos' stern advice from that first day.

You're going to have to prove yourself.

He bit down on his lip until he tasted blood and hobbled on. Roughly half a mile more to cover, then he could peel off his boots, unclip the brace and let the air around his bloodied, withered leg, but his vision was closing in as it was. *Can't stop*, he willed himself on, *they'll never trust me if I hold them up.* He threw his head back to take in a gulp of air, hoping it would stave off the black spots bursting at the edge of his vision. Then he noticed something else, out there, coming from the narrow mountain pass off to one side. A forked dust trail, riders at the fore, at least thirty, shimmering with iron. He made out the pointed helmets, the scale armour. The breath froze in his lungs.

'Seljuk riders!' he bellowed.

Sha spun, the others stumbling from their stride as the mini-column disintegrated.

Then Procopius yelled, pointing to another ten haring from the opposite pass. 'They're coming on both sides!'

They were converging on the trade caravan but a handful broke to snare the five skutatoi.

'Catch up with the caravan; otherwise we'll be cut to pieces!' Sha bellowed. Four of the five broke into a sprint.

Apion saw the four of them shrink and could only gasp in his ethereal haze, lifting one hand out to reach for them. Nepos looked to be turning back to help but Blastares pulled him back in the direction of the caravan, and the four mounted the rear wagon and pulled their swords and spears out, poised, ready to fend off the attack. Then the wagon began to pick up speed, shrinking even faster.

Apion stopped. He was utterly alone in the middle of the valley. He hefted a rhiptarion in his hand, trembling with fatigue, resting his weight on his good leg. He readied to face the riders; there were four of them, two on each side. One had broken ahead and lay low in his saddle, scimitar raised and ready to cut.

'*Allahu Akbar!*' the ghazi rider roared, face twisted in bloodlust.

Apion gritted his teeth at this. *You will not deny me vengeance*, the rasping voice spoke in his mind. He saw the ghazi's sneer of arrogant expectation and felt the dark door rush for him, its fires flaring inside and the knotted arm swiping forward to punch it open. Where his body faltered, his mind was fortified. He lifted the rhiptarion to his cheek, frowned along its shaft and hefted it back until he saw the veins in the first rider's neck, then let loose. The spear punched into the rider's jugular, sending his head whipping round to face backwards with a crack. The body went limp and slid from the mount.

In an instant, the second rider was upon him. No time to hoist his next rhiptarion, he hefted his sword by the hilt, took aim and hurled it forward. The blade carried little momentum but the rider's charge was furious and the blade met with his chest in a sickening crunch of bone, exploding through his ribs, sending organs and blood spraying over the grass and knocking the rider to the ground.

Now swordless, Apion took up his kontarion and spun to the three who were almost upon him, jabbing the blade of the spear at each of them in turn. Then the first rider hacked the end of the spear off. Apion threw the shaft away and pulled his shield around to parry the subsequent sword strike, staggering back from the brute force of the blow.

His shoulder jarred at the second strike and then a third hammered into his helmet, sending white light through his head. He crumpled to his knees. He looked up and saw a rider heel his mount around and stab forward with his scimitar. He closed his eyes and held his shield up, waiting on the impact.

There was a crunching of bone and a gasp, then the thud of a body hitting the earth. Then a hand grappled Apion's neck just as a smash of iron rang out beside him.

'Come on, you bloody runt!'

He blinked: the rider lay impaled on Blastares' spear and the big skutatos had dragged Apion clear of the last rider's scimitar strike just in time.

Blastares dragged him back and discarded him like a used rag. He scrambled to try to stand but his weak leg buckled under him. He could only watch as the rider hammered blow after blow at Blastares, the big soldier tiring and roaring as the scimitar got in behind his shield to rip the flesh of his bicep.

Apion fumbled with his dagger. He glanced down the road to the caravan to cry for help, but his heart stilled as he saw the wall of Seljuk ghazis thundering for him. The caravan must already be destroyed, he realised.

The riders seemed to bring the earth to life with their charge and Apion pushed up to stand against them, pulling his dagger from his belt. But the riders broke around him and Blastares like a river, haring on through the main mountain pass, headed east. Apion looked to Blastares, equally stunned. Then the big soldier's face cracked into an evil grin.

'Reinforcements!'

Apion turned to see the thick wall of some one hundred skutatoi who had raced from the town barracks, filling the width of the pass like a set of iron fangs. A handful of scout riders raced on the flanks. The caravan had been saved. They had been saved.

Then he felt Blastares' grip on his collar again. The big man's face was purple, his features torn, body still shaking from the tension of the fight. 'All we ask of you is to bloody well keep up with us! I don't know what we've done wrong to get burdened with the likes of you, but you ever fall behind like that again and I'll put a blade through you myself. Do you hear me? And what's the idea of walking around with that bloody Seljuk sword?' He prised Apion's scimitar from the dead Seljuk's chest, then stabbed it into the dust. 'It's not the weapon of the empire, and you're never a soldier of the empire!'

Apion's head was already swimming and he could only nod as the blackness set in.

He heard footsteps rumbling up to him. 'Leave him,' Sha shouted.

'Come on, Blastares,' Nepos added. 'It's over!'

'I meant what I said. Yes, he can handle a sword, but he's not fit to fight for the empire.'

The words rang in Apion's ears.

—

Apion heard the crunch of boots on frosted ground outside; the first watch. The wail from the *buccina* would be next, then another day in the barracks would be upon him. Patrol was brutal, but training was even harsher, Vadim ever keen to hurt and humiliate him before the garrison.

Hearing the mutterings of the watch outside, he clutched his prayer rope and tried to spirit himself away. He drew on the warmth of the blankets and screwed his eyes shut tight and searched for a happy place. He saw farmland, lush green hillocks with golden crop squares and rich brown fallow fields. He tried hard to remember Mother's scent, the sound of Father's laughter but it was growing ever hazier through time. He could, however, see Mansur's tired smile and hear Maria's laughter echo in his thoughts. Sadness enveloped him that he had parted from them in such a foul mood.

Then the buccina wailed and he blinked his eyes open. The barrack block rustled very gradually into life with the usual chorus of gruff swearing. Apion heard Blastares shuffle from his bunk, break wind violently and then scratch himself. Apion steeled himself and swung his legs from his own bunk. Blastares had affixed him with a stony glare.

'You'd better not let us down again. If you mess up, we all take the punishment.'

He held the big man's gaze. Every day since the ambush, Blastares had issued this warning. The patrols had been mercifully uneventful and Apion had managed to avoid further mishap. He had tried to offer his sincere apology and gratitude to Blastares for saving him from the caravan ambush, but the big man was simply unapproachable that day. Yet Blastares' veneer of gruffness belied his underlying piety; after the narrow escape from the ambush, he had forgone wine and meat the following day in penance for the lives he had taken in saving Apion. Apion decided to follow suit to show his gratitude and the big man had almost shot him a less than furious look when he saw this. But training and patrol meant that it was only a matter of time before his weakness would come to the fore and rile the big man again. 'I can only promise you that I'll try.'

'I'll believe it when I see it,' Blastares grunted and stood to get dressed.

'Take heart; it's formation work today,' Nepos said quietly, 'we're readying for when the rest of the thema are mustered.'

Apion nodded but couldn't disguise a wrinkle of confusion on his brow as he slipped on his padded vest then sat down to pull on his boots, gingerly sliding on the one that seemed to grate at his withered leg, folding the lip down to below his brace. 'Formation work? Is that a good thing?'

'Well, it means no running; it's all about timing.' A semi-grin touched one side of Nepos' narrow lips.

Apion nodded, realising how rarely he had seen the Slav smile. His sharp blue eyes always seemed alert and suspicious. Again, he wondered what the Slav's story was; the man had run from his home thema to come out here, the dusty borderland. He had run from something, but what?

'It's still bloody torture, mind,' Procopius grunted, 'especially when the kampidoktores wants it to be. And we haven't done it since spring, so I expect he's got a whole lot of pain in store for us.'

A crisp day was upon them by the time the winter sun was fully up. The garrison of nearly four hundred – a bandon of infantry and a further clutch of some hundred toxotai archers – was mustered on the flatland of the mountain pass east of the city, near the dilapidated archery range. Apion joined in the chorus of the Morning Prayer, the mountain pass reverberating to the baritone chant. He noticed Bracchus did not participate, instead striding slowly in front of the garrison, eyeing each of them with a disconcerting keenness. Then when it stopped, he whispered something in Vadim's ear, then retired to the shade, watching with his retinue of giant soldiers.

Whatever the tourmarches had suggested, Vadim grinned with glee at the sentiment. 'First, I will tire you out with formation marching: split up into *kentarchia*, then each hundred men at a time, march round the square. Then the real work begins.'

'That's not so bad?' Apion muttered, eyes darting around the four crimson-flagged posts dug into the ground marking out a square three hundred feet on each edge.

Nepos shook his head. 'It's good practice. When you're in a battle, the slightest gap can mean the whole unit can be ripped apart, especially by cavalry. When the thema is mustered we'll be expected to pass this training on. But it's not the exercise that worries me, it's the punishment that bastard likes to give out for the slightest flaw – you know, you've borne the brunt of it all too often, and today I get the feeling it's going to be worse than usual. Now stay tight to those around you and keep pace to the inch.'

'We haven't done this in a while, so fifty circuits today,' Vadim roared. The garrison stifled a groan. The infantry bandon split into three groups of just fewer than one hundred men, each headed up by a *kentarches*.

Apion watched as the first group marched. They bunched together in a square and the first rank, those wearing proper *klibania* lowered their spears to form a wall of spearpoints. Those in the second row did likewise while those behind held their spears vertical. At their komes' order, they set off around the square, every step in perfect time, like a single organism. When they reached the corner of the square they held their shape perfectly, turning in formation without any gaps appearing.

'One!' Vadim roared as they completed the first circuit of the fifty.

Apion steeled himself; it was his kentarchia's turn next and already he could feel his withered leg tiring from standing.

The unit was approaching the last corner on their fiftieth lap of the square when a collective gasp filled the air as one of the marching men fell from his place, having had his heel trodden on by the man behind.

Vadim clapped his hands together. 'Forty lashes for both men. Rations halved for the unit for the next week,' he said as if discussing the weather. The rest of the marching unit began to look ragged at this but a quick, barked order from their kentarches saw them march on to complete their exercise.

Then the kentarches leading Apion's hundred cried as Vadim nodded them forward. 'Ready, march!'

Apion felt a welling terror that every step would see him stumble and every man around him would trip him or barge him to the ground. His chest tightened and his breath grew short at the proximity of his fellow soldiers. He bit on his lower lip to distract from the pain in his leg and focused on his step, drawing breath with each pace, exhaling steadily in between. They completed the first circuit and he knew his body would fail him, his leg trembling already. He caught sight of Vadim as they passed him and moved onto the fourth circuit; the big Rus's eyes were on him like a predator.

'Don't think about the fifty circuits,' Nepos whispered as they came round again.

'What?' Apion blinked; terrified that he would lose his step.

'Take each circuit in turn, one at a time. Trust me; it's a mental victory if you can do that.'

'You don't understand. I'll never make it.'

'Five!' Vadim roared out as they passed him again.

Apion tried all he could to distract himself from the nausea that overcame him, but his vision began to darken at the edges and he saw the man in front's shoulder blades grow closer and closer as he stooped forward, then he felt Nepos and Sha grasp him by the arm either side, righting him just in time. He had been treating each circuit as the last, just as Nepos had advised, ignoring Vadim's counting. But how much time had passed? He glanced to the sun, it hadn't moved an inch.

'Thirty-eight!' Vadim roared, a hint of frustration in his voice. At this he forced himself upright, shoulders back, fixing a steely expression on his face every time he passed Vadim.

'That's it, you show the bastard,' Blastares grumbled from behind him. Apion felt an initial surge of confidence at the big man's encouragement, 'because if you don't and we all suffer for it, you'll have me to deal with.'

'Forty-nine!' Vadim shuffled from one foot to the other.

Apion felt the raw, open flesh of his knee rubbing at the lip of his boot. His skin was bathed in a cold sweat and he knew he had only the next few paces in him.

'Fifty!' Vadim spat the word. As soon as he had, Blastares bundled forward with a curse, the man behind him having stumbled into him. In an instant, the tight square that had been as one for the last fifty laps was a scrambling mess, men rolling in the dust.

'Ah, we have another call for the lash!' Vadim perked up instantly.

The kentarches stood to attention first. 'Sir, we were finished when we fell out of formation!'

Vadim stepped forward to stand tall over the kentarches and lashed the pole he held across the man's jaw. 'You and your unit are a disgrace. If that happened on the battlefield, the whole army could disintegrate. You did complete the fifty circuits though, so perhaps the lash is not appropriate.' Vadim scratched his chin and the kentarches looked momentarily optimistic, despite his bloodied lip. Then Vadim nodded with narrowed eyes. 'No, instead of the lash, your lot will make a fine subject of *foulkon* practice.'

The men around Apion broke into a worried babble. Apion looked around: the other detachments from the bandon and the toxotai looked to their feet at this order. Practising the ancient tortoise formation sounded reasonable, but then so had the marching practice. The kentarches nodded solemnly. 'Yes, sir!' he said to Vadim, then turned to his hundred to bark them into silence.

The hundred formed into a square again in the middle of the training field, while the rest gathered in a circle around them.

The kentarches took his place in the front rank. 'Shields!'

Apion followed suit as, with a ripple of wood, the men of the kentarchia pulled their shields overhead to form a tiled roof, those at the sides and front locking their shields like a wall.

His arms were now trembling and the shield felt as heavy as an anvil. They waited under the canopy, sweating, panting despite the freshness of the winter air, while the other two kentarchia and the archers encircled them.

'Just hold tight and don't let go,' Procopius hissed at him, eyes wide, 'and don't leave any gaps!'

Apion frowned, then heard Vadim roar. 'Loose!'

Something heavy thudded on Apion's shield and he staggered, his shield slipping from the roof. From the momentary gap he saw a hail of rocks hurtling towards them. Arms shuddering, he forced the shield back up just before the enclosed space inside the foulkon was filled by the crashing rain of stone rapping on their shields, splintering the wood. Then there was a scream where someone had left a gap at just the wrong moment. Then another. Apion screwed his eyes shut tight and grimaced until the hail slowed and then stopped.

'Now perhaps next time you will march in good order?' Vadim cooed. 'Now rest and eat your rations. For this afternoon is going to be proper work!'

Apion lowered his shield. The sun was nearly at its zenith and his whole body was racked with agony. All around him, his kent-archia looked pale and shaken and two men lay prone, moaning, one with a bleeding eye socket, the remains of his eye lying in the sand, and another clutching his shattered forearm. The garrison medic hurried over to the men, his shoulders hunched as if fearing reprimand from Vadim.

'Come on,' Nepos pushed Apion away, 'you need to eat and rest.'

Apion shrugged away from him. 'I'm fine,' he lied.

He walked to the nearby cluster of rocks where the garrison sat to eat, ignoring the blinding pain of every step. He sat on the edge of a rock on his own and made to slide his boot off but stopped when he saw the crimson and glistening flesh around his knee. Then he heard booming laughter; he looked up to see Bracchus, in deep conversation with Vadim, two of his brutes flanking him, their eyes sharp and their fingers drumming on their sword pommels. He realised it at that moment: while he was shackled with this brace and the withered leg he would never be able to get at them.

'So you know the brief?' The new protomandator pulled his cloak tighter around him and cocked an eyebrow, breath clouding in the dawn winter air.

'Through the mountains, to the waystation, then hand the papers over to the imperial messenger; same as it's been for the last two weeks?' Apion replied.

'You're fine with that?' The protomandator's eyes hung on Apion's withered leg as if it was plague-ridden.

'I'll be fine, and so will the package.' He swiped the hemp sack from the protomandator's grasp, dropped it in his satchel and left the officers' quarters. They didn't care about the messenger who carried the lesser documents to the northern waystation. If they did, they would have afforded him a mount or a berth on a wagon to go round the mountains as they did with the imperial couriers. No, it was cheaper to send a man on foot. So here he was, on this crisp winter morning, dressed in a faded crimson military tunic, green woollen leggings, bare feet – despite the cold – and carrying only his dagger and his satchel.

He did his best to walk tall as he crossed the muster yard, passing Bracchus and the garrison, formed up for roll call by the sleeping quarters. The tourmarches sneered the first time he saw Apion head out on foot: the last messenger had been killed by brigands as he ran through the mountain passes. But Apion planned on more than survival – he was focused on using these morning sorties to bring vengeance a little closer with every passing day; added to that, he had resolved to prove himself to his kontoubernion.

The barrack gates groaned open and he felt a freedom as he walked through the empty streets to the town gates, no bustle and no attention on him as he limped. The guards on the battlements had grown bored with hurling abuse at him, cheering whenever he stumbled and whooping when he tripped; now they simply opened the gates for him without comment. Once outside he felt truly alone, feeling only the sun on his face, frost underfoot and a fresh morning breeze.

He headed north, through the narrow mountain pass that snaked off from the main east–west pass. As usual, he held himself to hobbling until Argyroupolis slipped behind the mountainside. When this happened he stooped to unclip his brace, tucking the device into his satchel. Then he set off again, grimacing, making each stride a little longer than the last. The skin on his withered leg stretched as he forced himself to use the limb's full length, issuing a fiery pain up his back. But he bit his lip and continued, the absence of the military boots a great relief. He entered the shade of a pass and remembered Blastares' mocking and worse, the bitter reprimand after the Seljuk ambush. His skin burned with humiliation, but the big soldier's doubts over him only spurred him on so far.

Then he imagined Bracchus and Vadim delighting in his pain and took an even bigger stride. Since he had enlisted in the garrison, Apion had witnessed the tourmarches send six men to their ends in those awful death bouts, yet the rank and file of the garrison remained obedient and fearful. His skin stretched taut over his scar and he roared in agony, his cry filling the valley, sending a flock of doves scattering. He doubled over, tears stinging his cheeks. Then he heard Bracchus' words. *Seljuk-loving whoreson!* At this, his eyes burned like coals as he glared to the end of the valley, imagining the man without his bodyguards, armed but alone. Ready for the edge of Apion's scimitar. With a roar, he strode forward again, forcing his weak leg to take his weight. His next stride sent a white-hot wave of pain through him; his next seemed to tear him from within. But on the next stride, both feet lifted from the ground. He was running.

Each morning he had managed this sortie. Every time it had been agony, but each day a little less so and each day he had returned to the barracks just a little sooner. At first, the rider at the waystation had been worried by Apion's lateness, then on seeing him, thought he had been ambushed such was the sight of his bleeding scar, swollen feet and pale, sweat-bathed features. Apion had refused the man's offer of help, instead planting the package in the saddlebag, nodding and turning back to begin the return journey to Argyroupolis. On that first day he had barely managed to return to the town before afternoon patrol. Today he swore to himself he would make it to the waystation before the rider, and back to the barracks before midday.

He had managed to break into a run after five days of walking the messenger sortie at a quick march. On the first day he had tried it, it was not fast at first, barely more than a jog, every landing on his weak leg bringing a yelp from his lungs. But to his delight, his body numbed after a few hundred strides, despite the blood thudding through his head in protest. It felt like the injury was gone from his body and his stride grew longer, his lungs heaving, a sweat bursting from his brow. The ground underneath him even seemed to level out, his limp ineffective. He had woken the next day with callused and bleeding feet and his scar wept and stung with a pain he had never known before. Yet that second day, he did it all again.

Each day he pushed himself just that bit more. The pain later on was doubled and his feet were raw because of that little extra effort. But he continued and now, on the fifth day of running, he sought out that pain. He welcomed the agony, seeing it as the death throes of the feebleness that had shackled him in life until now.

The floor of the mountain pass closed up before him into a series of jagged limestone steps like a winding staircase. With a roar, he lunged onto the first, then up onto the second, then the third. Then he stopped counting until he reached the peak, where he hurtled along the ridge of a small mountain and heard only the wind whistle past his ears, barely noticing the angry grey clouds gathering above.

Along with the numbness in his limbs, he felt a great wash of cool clarity in his mind. All the musty, lingering self-doubt, anger and frustration seemed to be washed away with it, leaving only a shimmering goal in his mind's eye. *I will run, I will prove myself,* he swore, *I will make Mother and Father proud, I will take vengeance in their name.* His heart hammered and tears stained his cheeks, feeling a surge of fresh energy at this point before he descended back into the next mountain pass.

The scree slope forced him to slow to almost walking and he felt his mind cloud over again. The pain would come racing back if he slowed down too much. He tried to keep his eye on his footing, when the piercing scream of an eagle startled him. He shot a glance up, seeing only the bulging clouds, then felt his foot lodge in the rubble and at once he was tumbling. The scree slid under him and he grasped out for purchase, rolling out of control. Finally, he stopped, dust catching in his throat, palms cut and stinging. Prone, he looked back up the slope. Something was wrong. Something quivered in the dust where he had fallen. An arrow shaft.

Fear shook him and cramp gripped his muscles almost immediately. He pressed flat down and scrutinised the mountainside on either side of him. Nothing. Then he heard a whinnying, racked with pain. He leapt to his haunches and drew his dagger, wincing as the scar seared violently, the numbness deserting him. The whinnying sounded again. It was coming from the shallow dip in the track to his left.

Limping over the scree, he gingerly peered into the dip, when a blurred figure uttered a roar and then a flash of iron sent him sprawling backwards. He scrambled to his feet, dagger extended, expecting the figure to come rushing from the dip and at him. Instead, a pained scream rang out, followed by a whimpering.

He stalked forward again, braced this time, ready to come down on top of the figure. But he dropped his stance when he saw a mare, eyes rolling in terror, on its side. Its two front legs were snapped, shards of bone stabbing out from under the flesh. Pinned under the horse was a dark-skinned and moustachioed rider. His eyes were cobalt blue but bloodshot, his hands trembling, clutching a short stabbing sword. A discarded bow lay a few paces from the man.

'You fired on me?'

'Stay back, Byzantine, don't come any closer. You'll regret it!' he growled, his breath coming in short gasps as the mare's weight pressed upon his chest.

Apion slipped into the Seljuk tongue with ease. 'Why would I? You've fired your last arrow,' he panted, nodding to the empty quiver on the ground, 'and you missed.'

'You speak Seljuk?' The man seemed perplexed, eyeing Apion's military tunic. 'Yet you are surely an imperial soldier?'

Apion blinked the sweat from his eyes and tried his best to disguise the rafts of stabbing pain that seemed to be marching over his body. 'Well most of us struggle to speak one language, I'll give you that...'

The Seljuk cut him short. 'My unit will be back this way anytime. You're a dead man if you try anything.'

Apion knelt on his good knee to relieve his pain. He had not eaten his ration as he normally would have by this time in the morning and his body seemed to shake with weakness. He took a look at the mare – a middling pony – and the man's garb. He had a bow and arrow and a simple sword, he was unarmoured. A scout, surely. A lone scout.

'Well I'll take my chances. Now look, your mount has had it, but I can get you out from under her. We'll go our separate ways after that?' As he finished speaking he felt a lightness in his head swell into a distinct haziness.

'You'll save me?' The Seljuk seemed puzzled.

Apion thought of Nasir, the times the boy had saved him. He nodded with a half-smile at the memory, only partially aware of the black spots closing in around his vision. A sudden thirst overcame him.

'Well I can only trust in you, but you don't look like you're capable of lifting a drink, Byzantine, never mind shifting a horse.' The man's brow furrowed, eyes fixed on Apion.

Apion patted his shoulder for his satchel, looking for his water skin, but as he did so, nausea swept across his flesh and through his stomach, then a black wave closed over him.

—

He blinked. The world was on its side. His body still ached but his nausea was subsiding, his mind sharper. Then a dark-skinned hand thrust the lip of a water skin to his mouth. He scrambled up to sitting. The Seljuk recoiled, still pinned under his mare; he had stretched just enough to reach Apion.

'What are you doing?' Apion noticed that his neck and chest were soaked.

'Making you well,' the Seljuk replied, holding up the water skin.

'Why?' Apion checked for his dagger; it was still there.

'So you can save me? You feel stronger now, yes?'

Apion could not deny the tingling sense of focus that seemed to be pushing away the sickness that had engulfed him just a moment ago.

He took more of the water, then pushed himself to standing and gulped down a few cool breaths. Then he worked his way round to the other side of the mare, avoiding her flailing and mangled limbs. He saw a piece of rope hanging from the saddle and snatched it clear, then hurled it over the mare's body. As he did so, the first dark splodges of rain began to mark the ground around them.

'Pass it through to me,' he gestured to the Seljuk.

The man winced and moaned as he batted the end of the rope under his mare's body as she flailed. Apion grabbed the end and made a loop. Then he braced his bad leg against a boulder. 'Ready yourself.' The Seljuk nodded. Apion heaved. The mare's whinnying was tortuous and he felt pity stab at his heart as he dragged her front half towards him. The strain was agonising for Apion, and the beast barely moved under his pull, but was agitated enough to kick out with her back legs, and this was enough to push her whole body off the Seljuk.

'I'm whole!' the Seljuk yelped.

Apion dropped the rope, panting as the man stood gingerly, stiff at first, then stretching tall. Then he dropped to his knees, facing south-east to spread out his arms before him, head bowed, in prayer, oblivious of the now battering rain.

Then the man stood, his face solemn, and walked towards Apion, drawing his sword up above his head. Apion braced in shock, then the sword came down and plunged through the mare's chest, bursting her heart. In an instant, she was lifeless.

Apion felt relief for the poor beast.

'A good companion, she was.' The Seljuk's eyes were misty as he smoothed her mane. Then he looked up to Apion, holding up his hemp sack. 'My name is Kartal. I have food.' He blinked the rainwater from his eyes and nodded to a small cave nearby. 'Before we go our separate ways, will you shelter and eat with me?'

–

Apion had added his bread and dried fruit to Kartal's rations of plump olives, dates and cheese. Despite that odd burst of energy Apion had felt, his stomach roared for attention. They watched the rain's fury without speaking as they gorged on the food and then drunk their skins dry.

Bellies full, he snatched glances at the Seljuk. The man was probably a good ten years older than he, and seemed far more comfortable with the silence. He picked up a shard of rock; it seemed to shimmer like the cave itself.

'Silver,' Kartal said, 'a rich seam as well.'

Apion turned the rock in his hand. He knew there were some mines down nearer the town, having passed their entrances, but up here was relatively untouched. He wondered at the possibilities.

'Iron too,' Kartal added, 'another reason for the Sultan to fix his gaze on this rugged land.'

Apion put the rock in his satchel and looked up at Kartal. The Seljuk was eyeing him.

'You could have killed me, taken my things.' Kartal spoke softly.

'Then your scouting party would have come back and killed me for it.' Apion grinned.

'There is nobody else here, as you well know.' Kartal smiled back. 'I am a lone scout rider and no more. I am still struggling to believe I have been saved by my enemy.'

Apion smiled and shook his head, tugging on his amber locks. 'I may be a Byzantine-Rus halfbreed, as far from Seljuk blood as you can imagine, but I've got, shall we say, a chequered past. My family, they are Seljuk. I have no vendetta against the Seljuk people.'

Kartal shook his head and sighed. 'Then you have not been in this conflict long enough.'

'What do you mean?' Apion frowned.

'My mother was half-Greek,' Kartal grinned, pointing to his striking blue eyes, 'my eyes tell her story! When she married my father, she let her customs and culture sift into the past, embracing the Seljuk way of life. But she taught me much of the western peoples,' he paused, then continued to speak in Greek, 'their tongue, their past, their flaws and their wonders. I once thought I loved all peoples equally. Then, eight years ago, I joined the *Falcon's* ranks. I have seen much since then that makes me doubt everything I once believed in. Sometimes I forget why I joined.' Kartal eyed him. 'And you, with your background, why did you bring yourself under the imperial banner?'

He thought of Father lying on the floor, protecting Mother's corpse while the Seljuk raiders hacked at him like butchers, the veiled Bracchus watching it all. His mood blackened and the dark door cast its shadow on his thoughts. 'It's a calling,' he replied. 'I don't know where it'll take me yet.'

'Does any man know where he is headed?' Kartal chuckled and looked through the cave entrance and up at the sky. 'It seems when we are lost we inevitably end up in conflict.'

'What does your god say about it?' Apion asked tentatively.

'Remember, he is your god as well. I love him and devote myself to him. He tells us to love and respect one another and I search for this in God when I pray. He tells us to fight also; I'm not so sure I want to hear this from him.'

Apion eyed his prayer rope. 'I pray to God, but I cannot help but question him too. I may be new to the war between our peoples, but many dreadful things have happened in my short lifetime.'

Kartal nodded respectfully. 'I understand. Every man has his own journey, his own take on faith.'

They talked of their lives away from the military until, eventually, the din of the rain quietened, easing to a light shower. He thought of his duties; the imperial rider would be approaching the waystation soon. The pair stood and went outside.

'I fear I have a long trek to get back to my camp.' Kartal looked wearily over his shoulder to the pass heading east and then down at his bare feet. 'Still, some of this will keep me strong.' He lifted a verdant and almond-shaped leaf from the chest pocket of his robe, popped it in his mouth and began to chew. 'You seemed to like it too?'

'You put some in the water?' Apion clicked, scrutinising the leaf. 'It seemed to give me focus when I had none. What is it?'

'Betel, it strengthens the spirit and focuses the mind, but only temporarily. Take a leaf and flake it in water or place it under your tongue and let the juices soak out slowly or chew when you need a boost. As I say, it only works for a short while but it will help you,' he gestured to Apion's withered leg, 'when your body weakens. Also it will soothe your joints so you won't feel like you've been trampled by a pony in the morning!' Kartal lifted a stack of five leaves from his pocket and offered them to him.

Apion took the betel leaves, placed them in his satchel and then held out his hand. 'We part as friends, Kartal.'

'We do.' Kartal grinned. 'I hope – and I mean this as a friend – that we never meet again. For the battlefield is calling my people and yours. War is long overdue, like a thunderstorm.'

Apion nodded solemnly. The two continued about their journeys.

CHAPTER 16

The Haga

'Keep your head down!' Sha spat at him.

Apion was flat already; face pressed into the hot, dust-coated rocky outcrop jutting from the sheer mountainside. The summer sun cooked the five where they lay in hiding, perched like nesting vultures halfway up the walls of this narrow pass. The air was treacherously still and he could hear the Seljuk hooves echo through the pass below, the rocks under him vibrating from the movement.

'At least forty of them, Dekarchos!' Blastares whispered from above. Apion twisted his neck around to see the flushed features of the big man jutting out from the overhanging outcrop. He flicked his head towards Procopius. 'Me and the old bastard could take out ten with our bows, maybe more?'

'Then what – we become target practice for them? No, we keep our heads down!' Sha hissed, his voice almost crackling into an audible level.

The dekarchos' face was drawn and his eyes bloodshot. He had sensed the recent raids were building into something more. Yesterday afternoon, not long after they had slaked their thirst by a mountain stream, they noticed a dust cloud behind the mountain ridge to the west, cutting off their patrol route back to Argyroupolis. All hopes of it being a caravan or travellers were dashed with the glint of iron. Raiders this far into the borderlands were always there for one reason only: to wreak havoc, to slaughter patrols, to disrupt the empire's borders and weaken Byzantine hearts. But these riders were different, they carried with them maps and he had seen them survey the landscape keenly. Sha was right, these were no mere raiders, they were on reconnaissance. A prelude to invasion if ever there was one.

For a full day the five had skirted around the raider party, keeping out of sight, hoping to stay with the party until another Byzantine patrol was nearby. Though after a further morning, their ration packs were empty like their stomachs. They had to break off unseen and return to base. Just when it looked as if they might be able to do that, by inching up onto the walls of this pass to let the Seljuk party ride through the floor of the pass, they had watched in dismay as the riders cantered into the pass and stopped to make camp by the stream that snaked along the ground.

One of the Seljuk riders dismounted, pulling a loaf of bread from his saddlebag and tearing at it with his teeth. Apion hadn't eaten since dawn yesterday. His belly turned over with a hollow groan. He clasped a hand to his side and winced as Sha shot him a foul glare.

Apion pulled a betel leaf from his pocket and placed it under his tongue, perhaps it would help him focus through the distraction of hunger. He watched the Seljuks: a few started pulling at dried roots and brush for a fire – no doubt to cook up some salep. These men were ghazi riders, light cavalry; their strength was in their speed, perfect for hit-and-run tactics, to leave a bloody trail in their wake and sap morale from their enemy without ever engaging in pitched combat. In saying that they were probably as well armoured and armed as any of the five skutatoi: each of the riders wore a padded quilt vest, a fine composite bow and quiver slung over their backs along with a short lance. Scimitars and lassos hung from their belts, and some also had a hand axe or a war hammer hanging there too. Finally, a glint of iron dagger hilt peeked from the lips of their leather boots. These men were certainly not poorly equipped skirmishers.

Then something caught Apion's eye: it was the Seljuk commander. He was bearded with sun-darkened cheeks, wearing only a felt vest over leggings and boots, his hair knotted to the back under a felt cap. Unlike his men, he seemed distracted, wary. He crouched by the water, dipping his hands in. He splashed the liquid over his face and then seemed to stare at the reflection on the surface. Then at once he shot up, eyes scouring the lip of the pass. Apion ducked just before the commander's eyes ran past the position of the hidden five.

Finally, the commander's cry filled the pass. 'I want a foot reconnaissance on the perimeter. Sweep the edges of this pass and maintain a watch up there – eight men each side.' Then there was the scuffle of feet and a few barked orders as the riders were divided up into guard parties.

Apion shot darting glances to both Sha and Blastares above him; they still bore anxious stares and remained plastered to the rock. Yet lying here was a death sentence, the Seljuk scouts would be on top of them in moments. Then a shiver of realisation raced up his spine: *of course – they don't speak Seljuk!*

'Sir! We've got to move!' Apion hissed, raising slightly on his hands and jabbing a finger to the jutting lip of the outcrop above Blastares.

Sha simply glowered at him in disbelief. 'Get down!'

'Sir, they're coming up here. If we stay still, we're dead!'

Sha's features curled in the horror of realisation.

'What did he just say?' Blastares grunted.

Just then a scuffle of boots on scree sounded just below them. Sha's face dropped. 'Move!'

At once the five were up and scrambling for the outcrop above, their din disguised only by that of the approaching Seljuks. The climb was haphazard and punishing. Apion's fingers slipped and his knees smashed off the rocks as he tried to reach the edge of the outcrop. His bad leg burned as though being pressed with red-hot irons, but he was well used to this now, after six months of running, and the pain was so much less than it had been in those early days. He chewed down on the betel leaf, sucking the juices from it, and just the act of doing this snapped him back to focus on the climb. With a muted grunt he heaved his weight up and onto the outcrop and collapsed, panting. The ledge provided by the outcrop was small and backed onto the sheer mountain face and only a pile of boulders interrupted the smooth floor they stood on. He turned to see Procopius still labouring to come over the lip.

'Come on, come on!' Sha growled.

Apion grappled the old soldier by the wrists, hauling him over with the help of Blastares, but not before cries of alarm rang out from below.

'They saw us!' Sha gasped.

Apion scrambled back from the edge to join the four of them. Nepos and Procopius braced to the rear, pulling their bows to the ready. Sha and Blastares crouched at the front, swiping spathions from scabbards, grimacing, ready to strike, ready for blood. Apion pulled his scimitar from its sheath. He closed his eyes to compose himself, his thoughts flitting with the image of the dark door, the knotted arm with the white band of skin and the red emblem reaching out for it. His heart hammered, blood pounding in his ears.

A scrabbling and grunting came from the lip of the outcrop.

Sha was crouched with one hand on the ground, the other holding his sword point forward. 'Ready...'

Something moved at the lip, and Nepos' bowstring creaked as he readied to loose.

'Wait!' Sha hissed, raising a hand.

Then a fawn limb and a hoof clawed at the lip, followed by antlers. Then inky black eyes and a panicked face appeared as a stag scrabbled half onto the lip of the outcrop, back legs trailing, just as Apion had been moments earlier. The five had to stifle a gasp. Then there was the twang of a bowstring, the whoosh and then the thud of an arrow punching through flesh. The beast let out a terrible groan, its tongue stretching from its mouth, its eyes searching the Byzantine soldiers for mercy they could not provide, and then it was gone, tumbling back into the pass with a heavy thud. Seljuk echoes of delight filled the air as they celebrated their kill.

'Get back, we're not in the clear yet!' Sha motioned to the outcrop on the opposite wall of the pass, where the other party of eight Seljuks were only just scrabbling up onto the flat. The dekarchos scuttled behind the pile of boulders. Apion followed the other three to join him. The five were barely hidden behind the boulder pile as they huddled around the dekarchos, who panted as he spoke: 'They've got us pinned down here,' he jabbed a thumb at the opposite outcrop, then pointed down, 'and the other group that downed that stag will be bedding in just below us for some time to string up their kill.' He caught Blastares' eye and shook his head, pre-empting a repeat of the big man's suggestion. 'I know we could take a smaller group out but the rest would be on us in moments.'

Blastares grunted and turned away.

'We can't go up.' Nepos craned his neck up but the mountainside above was practically sheer. 'We can't go along.' The Slav shook his head, the mountain face on either side of them was pockmarked with hand and footholds but they would be exposed and easily picked off. 'And we can't go down. They're on horseback; they'd crush us even if we could get down and onto the floor of the pass. So we're pinned down until it's dark at least. Maybe that's it; we should sit tight and slip away in the night.'

Sha glanced around to gauge his men's reaction to this: they were all thirsty, hungry and exhausted. It was only just entering mid-morning now so there was still a long time before the eager sun peaked, let alone dipped. They remained in silence, each man scouring the surroundings in search of another option. Apion, however, gazed not at the surroundings, but back through his memories. He heard Mansur's words: *the answer need not lie with the sword.* Panic welled in his chest at the idea of speaking up, but he gulped and took a deep breath.

'Sir,' he offered, 'we can get out of here before nightfall.'

All four turned to him, glowering.

Apion's initial hubris weakened and then crumbled as he felt all eyes on him, examining his every word. These men trusted each other like brothers, he knew. They did not trust him at all, this was also true, despite his now adequate pace on patrol. His throat felt like knotted rope and his tongue shrivelled, but he knew he had no choice. 'How quickly could you climb along to the end of the pass?' He pointed to the nearest end, where the ground rose to meet the level of the outcrop they were on.

'We can't! Didn't you hear the pointy-faced bastard?' Blastares spat, jabbing a thumb at Nepos. 'We can't go along.'

'Hold on, let's hear him out,' Nepos cut in.

Apion took a deep breath. 'Well, we need a short spell where they're distracted.'

'Right. Not long, I reckon,' Nepos added in his characteristic even tone, blue eyes like slits as he peered at the sun. 'We could scale along there in a count of what, sixty?'

'And how do we get along there without being spotted?' Procopius asked in a doubtful tone.

Apion nodded. 'They've not sighted us yet. They know Byzantine skutatoi are likely to be in the area.' He caught the eye of each of them in turn, one by one, they all nodded. 'But if a lone man, a civilian, was to cross their path, what would they do?'

'Gut him,' Blastares shot back with a rapacious and gap-toothed grin.

Apion couldn't suppress a smile. 'Aye, most probably. But what if he spoke Seljuk?'

'Who knows?' Sha mused.

'A decoy? Fair enough, but where do we find a neutral Seljuk whoreson who feels like doing us a favour at this exact point in time?' Blastares said. 'That sword of yours can't talk can it?'

Nepos smiled, a look of realisation creeping across his face. Then he answered for Apion. 'The decoy doesn't have to be a Seljuk!'

Blastares and Procopius looked back blankly and Sha frowned.

The Slav's arrow-like nose bent under the grin that cut across his face. 'Young Apion here, he speaks the tongue.'

'Eh?' Blastares grunted. 'How's that?' The giant skutatos eyed him in distaste.

Procopius scratched his chin, eyes narrowing. 'Here, you're not some kind of spy, are you?'

Apion hesitated, knowing this wouldn't go down well. 'I... I come from a Seljuk family. My mother is Rus, my father a Byzantine through and through and from Trebizond. But my family, those who have looked after me since I was a boy, they are Seljuk.'

Blastares' eyes widened and Procopius shot a stunned look to Sha. Silence hung over the group.

Sha's features were creased in confusion. Apion held the dekarchos' gaze, until finally, the African's face relaxed into a grin. 'Then may God bless them for teaching you their tongue!'

'Hear, hear,' Nepos added. 'Now can we save the congratulations until we've actually tried the plan?'

'Let's do it,' Sha affirmed.

'Aye, I don't fancy the alternative.' Blastares squinted up at the blistering sun.

Procopius was the last to consent. 'You get us out of this, lad, and I don't care whether you're Byzantine, Seljuk or even a bloody Slav.' He grinned at Nepos.

Apion slipped off his cotton vest, sword belt, leggings and boots so he wore only his tunic. The four each glanced at the angry pink scar winding the length of his leg and the metal brace that clamped his knee. He noticed with a spark of pride that the muscles on his leg were beginning to bulge around the scar and the brace, swallowing both. Regardless of this, he had had enough of shame. 'Not pretty, is it?' He cocked an eyebrow. The four grinned at this.

'Your sword?' the dekarchos suggested.

'No, I'll keep this on me.'

'What about you, Apion?' Sha grasped his wrist, face etched with concern.

'Me? I'll see you back at the barracks,' he concluded.

'It is as I say, Bey Soundaq: he just stumbled down the mountain-side as if he was out for a stroll!' The ghazi thumped a fist into Apion's spine, sending him sprawling forward. His knees skidded and scraped on the stones by the stream, and a slimy gloop of saliva and blood lopped from his lips and onto the mud in front of him. The ghazi had said nothing when they came face to face, simply hammering the hilt of his sword into Apion's jaw then ushering him down to the commander at swordpoint.

Then there was a silence, broken only by the gentle babbling current by his side. Apion hadn't slaked his thirst since the previous evening and his eyes hung on the shimmering water. But he shook his head of the distraction, because, so far, the plan had worked as he had hoped it would.

He had exaggerated his fall to come to the other side of the leader, the one they called Soundaq. As he had hoped, Soundaq turned away from the outcrop to examine him, the rest of the ghazis forming an arc either side of their leader. The ghazis on each side of the pass had been distracted by his appearance; they had jostled to escort him down to their leader by the stream in hope of commendation. The window of opportunity had been opened for Sha and the men but their chances of escape were still slim. All it would take would be one glance to the mountainside from a ghazi, and his kontoubernion would be target practice for the Seljuk bows. His own chances, he realised with a convulsion of his bowels, were even slimmer. He could not bring himself to look up at the ghazis, fearful that the truth would shine through in his eyes. Then a polished curved sword blade flashed towards him, the sun's rays blinding him momentarily as the blade was thrust under his chin to tilt his head up.

'You seem nervous, boy?' Soundaq glared at him along the length of the blade.

Apion squinted up at the commander. His eyes were narrowed, spelling out distrust as he peered down his nose, his skin sun-darkened and lined with age. Apion composed himself to reply:

he was a traveller, out hunting, poaching maybe; these soldiers would surely approve of poaching on so-called Byzantine lands.

'Just out for the hunt.' He nodded to the ghazi who held his scimitar.

'A fine piece of weaponry that,' Soundaq mused. 'One I'd expect to see my commander wear to battle, not one I'd expect to see on an amber-haired boy wandering the mountains. So tell me, what exactly do you hunt with a sword?'

Apion held the commander's gaze. In the background he noted movement across the mountainside; four figures, scaling silently like spiders. One flinch, one dart of the eyes, one hint of a stammer and he was dead, his unit was dead.

'Anything that fills my belly.' Apion tried to sound casual but his throat felt tight. 'Anyway, I'd never be without it. My father gave me it,' he shrugged, thinking of Mansur.

'Then where did *he* get it?' another ghazi spat. The commander silenced him with a raised hand, while holding Apion's gaze.

'He fought with Tugrul, as an emir.' Apion spoke the words with pride and fear.

'He's scavenged it from one of our people's corpses!' one ghazi barked over him. 'Or worse, he's cut one of our brothers' throats himself, and taken the sword from the corpse!'

'Another word and you'll be spitting teeth,' Soundaq snapped, this time shooting a burning glare at the perpetrator, who dropped his eyes to the stream. The commander turned back to Apion, then stopped, his brow furrowed, then he turned, flicking his gaze along the outcrops of the pass.

Apion's heart thundered, then slowed as he saw the mountainside was now bare.

Then the commander shot his glare back to Apion. A silence ensued. Then Soundaq barked at his men. 'I ordered an eight up onto each of those outcrops, yet I find you all gathered around me like dogs looking for scraps? Back to your posts!'

With a grumble, the ghazis dispersed. 'The rest of you, water the horses and get that stag skinned and on a spit.'

Apion wondered if he should wait on permission to stand, then thought that an honest man, an innocent man, should have no reason to kneel. He pushed up from kneeling with the heels of his hands. As he did so, a boulder crumbled from the outcrop, tumbling down the mountainside. Apion's gasp at this sparked realisation in the commander's eyes.

Soundaq leaned in and grabbed his wrist. 'What is this, you dog?' he hissed, darting his eyes to the end of the pass, holding the scimitar up to Apion's jugular. 'You are no lone hunter!'

The rest of the ghazis turned, suddenly alert to their leader's tone. Apion's breath stilled in his lungs, his eyes searching those of the commander. 'A handful of scouts, they will be on their speedy mounts and long gone by now,' he lied. 'To pursue them would be futile.' He fixed Soundaq with a defiant stare and his leg-brace chinked as he steadied himself. At this, Soundaq looked down, frowning at the brace, then his expression split into a wry half-grin.

'Well, well…' Soundaq's grip on him relaxed and he laughed dryly. He turned to his men and waved them towards their posts again. 'Sentries on each outcrop, as I ordered!' he barked. Then he turned back to Apion with a weary expression. 'It's your good fortune that I think I know who you are, boy – the messenger with the leg-brace. You saved a rider of mine, Kartal. I don't know what your story is, but you live to tell it another day. Besides, I've seen enough blood over these last months.' With that, he nodded to the opening of the pass, handing the scimitar back to Apion.

Apion stepped back warily. Was this a game? Would an arrow or a dagger pierce his back as soon as he turned around? Then Soundaq nodded to the end of the pass again.

Soundaq spoke as he stepped back, the words echoing in the pass. 'But heed this message well: a storm approaches from the east, and the *Falcon* soars on its wrath. Byzantium's time is over.'

Apion held the man's glare, feeling the burning looks from the rest of the ghazis, then turned and walked from the pass.

Argyroupolis glowed like a giant firefly in the mountains, the orange of its lights tingeing the otherwise pitch-black night sky. Peleus and Stypiotes the skutatoi stood on the towers flanking the main gate. Their eyes were heavy from the long shift on watch and so they welcomed the night chill that kept them alert.

Peleus mused over the events of the day. Reports of a ghazi warband had come in that afternoon as Dekarchos Sha and his weary and depleted kontoubernion staggered through the gates, parched and coated in dust. One skutatos from his number had been lost; a light price to pay apparently going by the smirk that had touched Tourmarches Bracchus' face when the loss was reported. But word had spread that this one man had sacrificed himself, saving Sha and the rest. The men in the mess hall had been toasting his memory like a hero just before he and Stypiotes had to leave and come on duty.

'Peleus!' Stypiotes hissed across the gate top.

Peleus jolted to life, he gripped his kontarion and spun to his colleague.

'Something's out there.'

'Aye?' Peleus shrugged, screwing his eyes tight to peer into the blackness: the dirt road lay empty, dropping into the inky abyss only a few hundred feet ahead. 'Have you been drinking again, Stypiotes? There's nothing out there.'

'No,' his colleague snarled, 'listen.'

Peleus turned his ear to the road and cupped his hand around it, plugging a finger in the other ear to block out the dull babble from the town tavern. Nothing, nothing bar the singing of cicadas. Then he heard it: the crunch of feet on the dirt road. His stomach churned. A Seljuk army of thousands marched in the shadows of his mind. The guards on the wall were usually the first to be torn to pieces by the missile hail of a besieging army. *Be brave*, he repeated as he gripped his skutum and peered over its rim. Then the slight and diminutive figure of a young man, hobbling and a little lop-sided, trudged from the darkness.

Stypiotes gasped in relief from the other tower, dropping his shield, turning to roll his eyes at Peleus. Then he turned back to face the young man. 'Identify yourself!'

The young man stopped, swaying on trembling legs. Squinting up to the watchtower, he offered no reply.

'Ah well,' Stypiotes shrugged, pulling his bow from his shoulder, 'I'm always game for a bit of target practice. Bit of a challenge at this distance, but hey ho.' He stretched an arrow onto the bowstring and winked behind it, tongue poking out as he took aim.

Peleus winced; the lad was no threat at all, but better to be safe than sorry, there had been decoy attacks like this in the past. But there was something familiar about the grubby figure's faint limp. It reminded him of the boy Sha had dragged in last summer, the one with the far more severe lop-sided gait. Then he noticed the same heavy brow shading the eyes, the bashed nose and the amber hair. Peleus cocked an eyebrow as the pieces all came together: Sha's lot, the missing skutatos.

'Hold it!' he barked at Stypiotes.

'Eh?' Stypiotes moaned, relaxing his aim. 'You havin' a laugh?'

Peleus ignored his colleague and barked down to the gatehouse: 'Man on the outside, just the one. Let him through.'

A skutatos walked with an arm wrapped tightly around Apion's back to support him. The barrack enclosure swam in a dim orange, torches licking the night air every twenty paces or so. Cackling and hoarse laughter spilled across the muster yard, coming from the mess hall and that was where the guard seemed to be taking him. Apion could only think of the damp pile of rags that was his bunk but could not muster the energy to tell the skutatos this.

After fleeing the pass, he had unclipped his brace and run for what felt like a day, carried by the nervous energy of his narrow escape, until his scar burned like hellfire. With no betel

226

leaf remaining, his mind tired quickly, urging him to stop, to lie down. But something deep inside pushed him on at that moment. His destiny demanded that he make it back to the barracks, and he had made it. Now he was past thirst and on to sickness and all he wanted was to lie down, just to close his eyes and let the blackness overcome him.

Then two skutatoi spilled from the mess hall, eyes red with inebriation, faces stretched in an artificial joy as they staggered and bumped against one another. In his condition though, Apion simply stared through them.

Procopius was the first to recognise Apion under his cloak of thick dust, the prune-featured veteran's jaw dropped. 'I'll be damned!'

Blastares' face twisted into an exaggerated frown. 'Bringing beggars in for entertainment? Where're the whores?' Then his face, too, widened into a grin. 'It's the lad! God bless him! He's alive!'

At this, a few more skutatoi had appeared at the door of the mess hall in curiosity. Word rippled round inside and then there was a chorus of stool legs screeching on flagstones. With a rumble of boots, the bulk of the garrison toppled out into the muster yard, wine cups and ale mugs in hand. Word rippled round as Apion felt his legs wobble. The lad with the scimitar. The lad with the Seljuk tongue. The one who saved Sha's lot. The hero.

Then a hand clasped on his shoulder. Through bleary eyes he recognised Nepos. 'You did it, Apion.' He swept a hand back over Procopius, Blastares and Sha. 'You saved us. You proved yourself.'

Another voice called out. 'What is it you said? He scaled down the pass unseen, then drifted past the guards, silent like a gliding eagle, to infiltrate the Seljuk camp?'

'That's what I heard,' another called out, 'as if he was invisible until he reached their leader. Then he spoke in their tongue as if he was one of them and told them he would destroy them all if they did not leave?'

Then Sha stepped forward with a hint of a smile at the soldier's exaggeration and held his arms out wide theatrically. 'Indeed.

He swoops down from the mountainside like the mighty *Haga*, one head looks east, the other looks west, then he overcomes the enemy warriors not with force, but with his Seljuk tongue.'

Apion's spine tingled at the comparison with the ferocious two-headed eagle. He opened his mouth to correct them on the reality of the encounter, but another soldier roared before he could say a word.

'All hail the *Haga*!' the soldier cried. At this a violent and drunken cheer rang out. As Apion was lifted onto a pair of shoulders, the gathered soldiers cheered again.

Then, just as his eyelids drooped again, he caught sight of Bracchus, stood back by the officers' quarters.

The man's eyes crackled with rage.

CHAPTER 17

The Predator and the Prey

Cydones sucked in a breath of summer air as the column moved at a canter from under the canopy of the Pontic Forest and out into the yawning green landscape of south-west Chaldia. The thema had almost been fully inventoried and placed on standby for mustering but it had been a tough task after five years of demobilisation. It had been planned as a six-month task, but distracted at every turn by seemingly relentless bands of mysterious Seljuk irregulars who rode without a banner, Cydones and his retinue were nearly seven months behind schedule. All the while, the threat of Seljuk invasion was hanging over the people of the eastern themata like a dark cloud. The reports from the eastern border towns were coming in thick and fast; organised ghazi raids were ever more frequent and the garrison soldiers were stretched to breaking point.

Despite this, spirits had remained high amongst his three hundred kataphractoi as they toured the lands. They were growing stronger and more numerous every day, and they were soaring now with the promise of returning to Trebizond for a short spell before setting out to engage with Tugrul.

Cydones was about to order them into a trot when he heard the riders behind him chattering, talking of a tale of bravery that had spread around the thema. Something piqued his curiosity and he called the two riders forward and asked them to repeat the story, and they were only too happy to comply.

'So this soldier, he and his men are trapped in a mountain pass by a whole Seljuk army, thousands of them. He swoops down

229

from the mountainside, disguises himself as a Seljuk, goes to them and talks his way to their leader, then he pulls out a scimitar, kills a hundred of them before the rest turn and run. Put his life on the line and saved his men. The whole garrison over at Argyroupolis treat him like a hero!'

The second rider cut in quickly. 'Aye, they say when he first hobbled into the barracks he was lame, like an old man, but now he walks tall and is built like an oak. He's a demon with the sword, too – since that day when he talked the Seljuks down, he has fought off raiders like none other in the garrison.'

'Now what is it they call him again,' the first rider rubbed his jaw in thought and the second one scratched his head.

'Interesting. I'm sure the stories have been embellished some-what, but they need heroes out there,' Cydones replied. 'That town is no longer near the borderland. It *is* the border. When Tugrul comes west, we must be ready to intercept him, otherwise the men on the walls will be the first Byzantines to face them, and as things stand – hero or not – that town will fall.' He thought of the dark presence of the tourmarches Bracchus who ran the town. He had been forced to promote the man, the order coming straight from the emperor. Sultan Tugrul would be but one of this hero's worries, he mused wryly. 'But we need more like him… what did you say his name was?'

'The *Haga*!' the rider yelped, clicking his fingers.

'The Hittite legend?' the other rider quizzed.

Cydones slowed his mount, a hint of a smile touching his lips. 'Indeed, the ancient legend of the ferocious eagle with two heads.'

The column drew to a halt behind the strategos. Cydones studied the horizon; the scimitar, the limping Seljuk speaker, the two-headed eagle. One name echoed in his thoughts.

Apion.

He held up his hand and slowed the column. The riders would not be best pleased at the order he was about to give, but if there was as much riding on his next action as he thought, then he had no choice.

'Trebizond must wait,' he boomed. 'We ride for Argyroupolis!'

Summer's heat had conquered the land and he was bathed in sweat as he ran, but Apion refused to drop his pace. It was barely mid-morning and he had Argyroupolis in his sights, the papers already delivered to the imperial rider in record time. Indeed, he had reached the rendezvous point early enough to kindle a fire and toast some bread before the rider arrived, and he could only wonder at how much he might have broken his record by without the wait.

The sweat droplets gathered on his now thick amber beard and he felt his vision closing in; he reached into his satchel without breaking stride, lifting a betel leaf from the batch he had bought in the market from a coal-skinned Indian trader known to Sha. He slipped the leaf between his lips and chewed until the tangy juices came through. His mind seemed sharpened almost instantly and his stamina steadied a little and then lifted, just a fraction, but enough to keep him going. Kartal the Seljuk had been right about the leaf, it had been invaluable in keeping him going and in making the pain later more bearable. After six months of running every day, his withered leg had swollen with muscle, almost entirely swallowing the scar. Added to this, he found the urge to chew on the leaf come less often. Now in his twentieth year, he could stretch the limb fully to stand tall, at last without need of the brace. More, he could run like a leopard.

He was ready. Bracchus' time was almost over.

As he came within view of the walls of Argyroupolis he slowed, looked up and grinned; the sun was not even close to its zenith. A record by some way; quite an achievement, he mused, feeling the iron weights he had sewn into the hem of his tunic to accelerate his muscle development.

Then the wall guard saw him and broke into a babble of cheering. He heard their chants as he neared. *Ha-ga! Ha-ga!* Changed times, he mused with a grin. Then he looked to his forearm and the red-inked stigma of the mythical creature that the men had insisted on etching there just a few nights previously. He had agreed to this after drinking his first cup of ale in years. But later that night, through bleary eyes, he had examined the design in suspicion. It looked chillingly familiar, he had realised, thinking of that knotted arm reaching for the dark door, with the red emblem on the forearm and the white band of skin around the wrist.

He shook the thoughts from his head and called out to the wall guard. That day at the pass had been a pivotal moment in winning the hearts of the garrison, and on three occasions since he had clashed again with ghazi raiders. Each skirmish had been swift and brutal, with no prospect of diplomacy or retreat. He had fought only as he knew how to, and found himself being heralded as one of the finest swordfighters in the ranks. But what mattered most to him was the trust and respect he had gained from his kontoubernion. Procopius would always be a dry-witted whoreson, but the old soldier's opinion of him had definitely mellowed. Even the bullish Blastares seemed to treat him more like an equal now. *You saved us back at the pass so you'll do for me*, the oak-limbed giant had muttered grudgingly. He still trod carefully around the pair, eager not to push their firebrand and ale-fuelled dispositions too far. Sha and Nepos, on the contrary, were just that little bit more open-minded. They would tease him about his newfound reputation and they could take a joke in return. It was this spirit that made life bearable in the lead up to the moment he would face and strike down Bracchus.

That moment was tonight.

He stopped under the walls to stretch his calves and his quadriceps. He had it all planned: he had watched the tourmarches' movements closely in the last year. Every night, Bracchus would make his way from the mess hall to the officers' quarters escorted only by Vadim and for once without the brutes who trailed around with him at every other part of the day. So it was to be that the big Rus would have to die if Apion was to take his vengeance.

Until tonight, he needed to keep himself busy, to stop fear and doubt from needling into his thoughts. Today would be a fine distraction. The race had been dismissed as a farce at first; the powerhouse Blastares against the cripple Apion, but that had been back in the autumn, before Apion had grown into a broad and muscular young man. Now the odds had tumbled to even and the contest had been talked about all over the barracks as the date neared.

Apion glanced up to the west; the distant mountain peak and the village of Bizye. It was an hour's march away from Argyroupolis. If he could win, it would destroy the power of the serrated scar forever and shatter the shackles of that dark night. *The physical shackles, at least*, he thought, his expression darkening.

The sun was beginning to drop after a hot midday and the air was dry. Sha, Nepós and Procopius stood by the wooden palisade gates of Bizye atop the mountain. The tiny settlement was one of the few patches of land that could support crop and grazing in the mountains surrounding Argyroupolis, and as such the families of over a quarter of the skeleton garrison of the town lived there. The settlement, a good hour's march west of the town, was afforded only a wooden palisade wall, more to break the winds at that altitude than for defence and with Argyroupolis to the east plugging the main mountain pass the threat of attack was fairly light.

Around Sha and his men, at least a hundred villagers, some twenty off-duty skutatoi and a handful of toxotai gathered beside their families, their coins riding on the result of the race. Now all eyes were on the two dots down on the valley floor. Sha lifted a purple rag and waved it over his head three times. A babble of cheering and catcalls broke out from the cluster of soldiers.

The race was on.

Apion and Blastares squinted up at the mountaintop.

'Right, I think he's waving,' Apion said. A grunt and a scattering of scree told him Blastares was already off and running. Apion set off behind the big man. There were several winding paths, man-made and natural, that would take him to the summit but each held their own dangers and detours. They came to the first fork in the path. He would go right, he affirmed, feeling his lungs begin to stretch. Right was a shorter but less stable route, with a narrow and crumbly path further up. Then Blastares cut right. Apion went left.

'I'll have an ale ready for you when you reach the top!' Blastares roared, barely disguising his early fatigue. Then the big man disappeared round the side of the mountain.

Apion laughed and upped his pace, the air thinning as he ascended. Then the bleating of a mountain goat startled him and he jumped past the equally bemused animal. His muscles ached but not at all like they used to. He was nearly halfway up, he realised, glancing up at the mountaintop plateau. He noticed a plume of dust from the eastern edge of the mountain, further up than he was. Blastares was ahead! He felt the urge to reach for a betel leaf but then hesitated; this race had to be won without advantage. Then he noticed another plume, a little further down from him, again on the eastern edge. Odd, he thought, as the villagers only made the trip down to Argyroupolis once a day at dawn and then back up again in the evening, after they had traded their wares. Perhaps it was a goatherd moving his flock along. He shook the thought from his head and honed his mind, trying to garner the same focus that the betel leaves would give him. Running without their aid was another challenge he was determined to win. Only two more zig-zags and he was at the top, where all the paths converged to a single dirt track leading into the village.

He heard Procopius first, the old soldier uttering a guttural roar of joy. 'Come on, Apion!' he whooped. The old soldier had changed his bet on seeing Apion's limbs swell and tone through the training regime.

The mountaintop rolled into view and the crowd pumped their fists and roared, braced, heads darting from one path to the next. Then Blastares appeared at the other edge, his face a shade of plum. The big soldier had less ground to cover but his legs were leaden. Apion sensed his reserves of energy would carry him home in first place. He half-heard a gasping insult from Blastares as he raced ahead, then sprinted for the spear planted in the ground – the finishing post – but then a pained yowl pierced the air just behind him. The faces of the gathered crowd dropped into winces. Apion slowed to look back over his shoulder. Blastares lay in a crumpled heap, grappling his ankle.

'Come on, lad, get over the line! I've got a month's pay on this one!' one soldier bawled.

Apion was now still.

'What you playin' at?' another one roared.

Apion jogged back and crouched by Blastares.

'Get on with it, you nippy bugger!' the big soldier growled at him, the veins in his forehead bulging like worms.

'Nobody's losing today.' Apion wrapped an arm around Blastares' shoulders and hoisted the big man's weight.

'Eh? No way, put me down, I'm no bloody crip…' His words tailed off. 'Sorry.'

Together, they walked to the finishing post. Half the crowd looked relieved, the other half frustrated. 'We'll race again one day soon.' Apion said to them. 'I don't want to win because the big man here took an injury.' He saw they needed more than that. 'Take your bets back. You'll need them. We'll double the stakes next time! Who's up for it?'

Procopius shrugged and then pumped a fist in the air. 'Right, I'm doing the book, who's in?' At once the crowd erupted into a babble, surrounding the old soldier, coins in hand.

Blastares' resolve crumbled and he issued a hoarse cackle in between gasps for breath. 'Next time, you don't get half a year to prepare!'

'Next time, you don't get a head start!' Apion grinned. The big man had the temper of a bear and the heart of a lion. Maybe not a tactician but a man he would always be heartened to have by his side in battle.

Sha and Nepos joined them as they made their way into the village. Procopius hurried after them, tipping his takings for the next race into his helmet, while the crowd of soldiers began to pick up their weapons, ready for the walk back to the barracks, and the villagers headed back to their homes, goats and laughing children trailing in their wake.

Nepos clasped a hand to his shoulder and gave him a firm nod. 'You did it,' he said with a grin. Apion gave the Slav a knowing look. Nepos was a thinker, shrewd and quick-witted, and had supported Apion since his first days in the garrison, the pair often playing shatranj in the evening.

Sha laughed like a drain. 'I never thought it possible, Apion, now you are the strong one!' Apion nodded his thanks. The African had also been there to guide Apion in his early days in the garrison and his shortcomings as a domineering officer were more than made up for by his knack for diplomacy and tact; he had seen the man diffuse many a potentially abrasive situation. Perhaps that was why he had initially been put in charge of Blastares, Apion mused.

Procopius slapped both Blastares and Apion on the back. The old soldier's fleet-footed fighting days were probably in the past but the man was obsessed with siege equipment and artillery. Apion knew that a man doing a job he loved for free was worth ten men loathing a job they were paid for. He wondered why the old soldier hadn't been put in charge of the *ballista* squads.

He beheld the four and wondered how he had ever found them so cold, so distant, like that first day in the barracks. He took his scimitar and satchel from Sha, then rummaged in the satchel to pull two skins clear. 'Before we head back, let us rest for a while... with a drink.'

'You brought wine?' Blastares' eyes grew wide.

'I like this lad more every day,' Procopius chuckled, 'give me a swig!' He reached out to grasp a skin but he froze, his eyes bulging.

'Procopius?' Sha's brow wrinkled. Then the village bell pealed rapidly.

Apion spun around, following Procopius' stare to the plateau edge – the second dust plume. A rumbling of hooves caused the plateau to quiver.

'Get into the village!' he roared, waving at the pack of off-duty skutatoi and toxotai who wandered lazily to the other descending path. They realised what was happening, but they were too late; a pack of some fifty ghazi riders burst onto the plateau and thundered straight for them. The Byzantine soldiers who had brought their weapons and armour had no time to lace up their klibania or padded vests, throwing them to one side, fumbling on their helmets and pulling bows, shields and swords to the ready with shaking hands. Then, with no officer in their number to organise them properly, they formed a poorly constructed line. Heavily outnumbered by cavalry, they stood little chance.

Apion glanced to the terrified villagers who stood by the gates, readying to slam them closed. 'Keep the gates open!' He jabbed an accusing finger at the man with his hands on the locking bar, who gulped and nodded hurriedly. Then he turned to the four; Sha was searching for the right words, the other three were itching to act.

'At them, sir, we must! Or they're all dead!' Apion insisted. 'They need a leader!'

Sha frowned and then shook his head. 'We can't beat fifty cavalry on open ground, Apion; we must get inside the village, the others will have to fight for themselves!'

'Then what? Defend the place, just the five of us, against those same fifty?'

'Either way, we're done for.' Sha's eyes darted, panic setting in.

'No, we make a fighting retreat into the town, save as many of those men as we can!' Apion protested.

Sha looked up, face wrinkled in indecision.

'Then we may have the number to hold out inside the town palisade,' Apion gasped, his eyes on the closing gap between the

237

ghazi riders and the Byzantine soldiers. The toxotai managed to loose a handful of arrows, but their haste meant only one found its target, taking a rider in the chest and punching him from his horse.

Then the ghazi detachment smashed into the trickle of Byzantine soldiers. 'Come on!' Blastares roared to Sha.

Apion grasped his arm and leant into the African's ear. 'Sir, make this your call, give the order. I will fight like a lion beside you, we all will.'

Sha's eyes widened at the burning expression on Apion's face. He nodded, then filled his lungs. 'Forward!' the African roared.

At once the five rushed into the skirmish, running for the flank of the riders. Apion felt fury wash through his veins as he ran, and the dark door was punched open by the scarred and knotted arm, its flames rushing out like a serpent's tongue. He hefted his scimitar and leapt, swiping it past a Seljuk rider's neck, taking arterial wall with it and soaking him and the soldiers nearby in a shower of blood. With that, Apion was pitched into the midst of the fray. He spun on one heel and then another, flashing the curved blade round and up to parry a spear jab and then stab home into a rider's chest. With his legs now equal in strength, he was catlike in his movements. Another rider fell, cleaved from shoulder to heart, then another, belly sliced open, guts slapping onto the ground before the body. He heard a grunt and spun to right himself for a parry from the ghazi whose sword was arcing down on him. Their blades clashed and Apion shouldered into the man's thigh then wrapped an arm around his waist, pulling him from his horse. They fell in a tangle past other bloodied corpses and screaming wounded. Then Apion grappled the man by the throat, fumbled for his dagger and punched the blade into the ghazi's abdomen. Yet the man fought on, pulling a small axe from his belt and swiping, despite the black blood pumping from his wound. Apion leapt back and finally the man's eyes rolled in his head and he was still.

Turning, he saw that the ghazi charge had been absorbed; many riders had been pulled from their mounts. This battle was starting to look winnable, but then he saw another dust cloud coming uphill. Seljuk reinforcements; they had an instant to cheat death.

'Pull back!' he roared. 'Get inside the gates!'

The Byzantines staggered back and the ghazis regrouped and remounted.

'Move!' Apion bellowed. Like a herd of wounded cattle, the Byzantines ran, hobbled and crawled for the sliver of a gap in the palisade gates, the ghazis racing after them.

Then the source of the second dust cloud was revealed as a party of some fifty Seljuk spearmen.

'By God,' Sha stammered as they tumbled inside the gate, pulling in the handful of stragglers who had survived the chase, 'infantry, this far west? Tugrul must be nearby!'

'We can worry about that tomorrow, should we see tomorrow, yes?' Apion bawled over the thunder of hooves. With the shoulders of all those who had made it inside, the gate was slammed shut and the locking bar was clunked into place. Apion took stock of their number: there was Sha, Nepos, Blastares and Procopius, plus eight skutatoi and three toxotai. He glanced over the rudimentary gatehouse, his eyes hung for an instant on its flat roof and he yelled at the archers. 'Toxotai, get up onto that roof!' Then he stopped one of them. 'You, go up there.' He jabbed a finger at a thatch roof on the opposite side of the gate.

'Apion?' Sha looked desperate, glancing from Apion to Blastares, who was already barking orders to the skutatoi, ushering them into a line.

'They're only staying outside of the gate for so long. If we're to make any kind of stand then you need crossfire to cover our flanks.' As he spoke, the whole palisade shuddered as the Seljuk infantry crashed against it, pushing at its fragile frame. Then ropes were lassoed around the carved points of the palisade gates. The ropes tightened and the gates groaned, bending outwards.

'But we're hugely outnumbered,' Sha countered. 'Surely we need every man we have to face them if... *when* they break through?'

239

Nepos cut in. 'Apion's right, sir. All sixteen of us versus that lot outside in a straight pitched fight – we're dead any which way you choose to cut it.'

Apion waited until Sha gave him the nod, then he grasped Procopius' shoulder. 'Procopius, we don't have artillery, but is there anything we could use to slow them when they break through?'

The Seljuk war cry was now dreadfully close, iron hacking into timber like a premonition of what was to come. Then a spear punched through the barrier. Then another and another.

'Eh? Well a ballista would be lovely but…' He shrugged his shoulders.

'There must be something.' Apion glanced around the village for inspiration, but only terrified villagers, pigs, bales of hay and mud presented themselves.

'Hold on,' Procopius purred. 'We can't fire bolts at them but if they're so desperate to get in here then they can kindly run onto our spears.' He dug his heel into the mud and then pushed the butt of his spear in until it stuck, the broad blade pointing accusingly at the now collapsing gate. He looked to Apion. Apion nodded feverishly and Procopius turned to the rest. 'Right, lads, get your spears in the dirt, just like this.' Then the old soldier turned back to Apion. 'Now, those hay bales could also be our friend… if we had some pitch and some rope.'

'You sort it out, Procopius – you're the expert in this kind of thing!' Apion clasped a hand on Procopius' shoulder.

Then he turned back to Sha. 'This spear wall will buy us precious time,' he yelled over the din of the Seljuk roars. 'Pin them down, might even thin them a little but we need to scatter them or we're done for.' A pig squealed as a Seljuk forced his bow through a hole in the collapsing gate and let an arrow loose that skimmed the beast's back. Apion's eyes narrowed: the squeal conjured up the image of that day at Cheriana, when the pigs ran loose, terrifying the wagon horses.

'That's it! The pigs!' Apion cried. A pair of villagers struggled to hold their pen gate in place such was the terror of the animals, running, leaping over one another. 'Release them from the pen when I say, then drive them to the gate,' he roared at them and the villagers nodded, faces white with terror. 'You do understand? They *must* run for the gate.' With that, Apion turned and added himself to the line of skutatoi. Then, with a crash, the gate was ripped down by the lassos and some eighty Seljuks, riders and spearmen poured through the narrow opening. They flooded towards the spears, hacking at them, expecting to be able to brush a path between them, but they remained stuck fast in the mud. A cry of panic rose up from the Seljuks to the front as they realised, just too late, what was happening. The ghazi riders to the back pushed on, forcing their own men, screaming, onto the broad blades. Bones popped, blood bursting down the shafts and the screaming was swiftly ended.

'They're pinned, fire at will,' Apion roared, but the toxotai on the gatehouse roof and the opposite thatched roof were already loosing shaft after shaft into the crush. At the same time, the thin line of skutatoi stabbed through the spear wall, felling the Seljuks who were compressed against the blades.

In the moment when the Seljuks lost momentum, Procopius batted a hand against the shoulder of another skutatos and the pair broke off to lift a hay bale with a length of rope wrapped under it. The hay bale was dripping with pitch, as Procopius had ordered, and when one of the villagers touched his torch to it, the bale ignited. With a grunt, the pair heaved the flaming mass over the spear wall and into the Seljuk crush. The bale disintegrated on contact, showering burning pitch over the Seljuk warriors. Men screamed, pulling back from the fray, skin bubbling. But as quickly as the bale had been ignited, the flames died and the Seljuks rallied.

Then a spear snapped and a handful of Seljuk infantry tumbled through the gap. The next spear began to bend and the Seljuk cavalry were pushing through as well. Apion's eyes narrowed and he roared to the two villagers by the pig pen. 'Let them out!'

The two stepped away from the pen gate and at once the pigs burst free, some thirty animals, racing as a pack, snorting, squealing, trotters sliding over one another.

'The gate!' Apion roared. 'Herd them to the gate!'

The villagers had already taken care of it, a woman and a small girl brought crackling torches to them. The two men then each took to jostling a side of the herd, thrashing a torch at any animal that tried to make a break and head back towards the centre of the village. The animals' terror seemed to swell at this and they raced, splitting through the skutatoi, through the spear wall and in between the legs of the Seljuk horses. The mounts whinnied, rose on their hind legs, bucked and leapt at this and the riders were hurled from their saddles, falling on their heads, snapping bones or being pierced on the spear wall.

The skutatoi roared at this, then pushed to close the gap on the sprawling mass of Seljuks. As Apion joined the swell, he could see the ghazi commander beat his sword into his shield, crying out to his riders as the pigs fled off across the plateau. The Seljuks were wavering, their number halved, but their leader was rallying them. Apion was overcome by a now familiar certainty: he had to live through this while Bracchus still walked the earth. He hoisted himself onto a riderless ghazi stallion, then heeled the beast to turn. He held out his scimitar and galloped for the ghazi commander. A guttural roar burst from his lungs and he saw everything ahead with a tinge of crimson, the dark door open, flames licking out. He mustered all his strength as he swiped his sword down onto the commander's shield. For a moment, their eyes locked, wide, whites bulging. It was him, Bey Soundaq, from the pass.

Soundaq butted his shield out. Apion pulled back and then swiped with his blade, shattering the man's shield, then again, and this time his and Soundaq's scimitars clashed with a rasp of iron. He drove the man back from the gates with each hack. He barely noticed the rumble of hooves as the other ghazis fled, leaving only Soundaq. With another strike, the Seljuk's scimitar snapped and he backed up, hands aloft as Apion's blade hovered at his throat.

'Gut 'im,' one toxotes called. Apion blinked, looking round at the blood-spattered remnant of the Byzantines. All eyes were upon him. His heart warmed to see Sha, Nepos, Blastares and Procopius standing. Then he heard the familiar wail of the buccina from below the edge of the mountaintop plateau, the reason for the sudden Seljuk retreat.

'Riders, ours! Not a moment too soon!' one of the skutatoi yelled.

He turned to Soundaq. 'If your men had not fled just now, I would already have this blade in your throat. Yet the last time we met, you said you had seen enough blood?'

'That was then. Since that day I returned to my village, on the edge of the Colonea Thema. I found my village in ruin, burned by Byzantine torches, my family slain.'

Apion felt the fury inside him temper.

'So you've got your victory, Byzantine,' Soundaq grimaced, 'now end it with my blood.' He tilted his neck to the point of the blade.

Apion lowered his sword. 'Ride,' he pointed to the opposite mountain path where the rest of the Seljuk party had fled, 'and ride fast.'

Soundaq's eyes widened a little; he nodded and made to ride off, but turned back. 'I say again what I said to you that day: Byzantium's time is over.' With that, he heeled his mount and galloped off.

Apion spun round at the sound of a stretching bowstring, his eyes falling on an opportunistic toxotes. 'Loose that arrow and you'll be sorry!' The toxotes glared at him momentarily, hesitating, then dropped his gaze to the ground and relaxed his bow.

Nepos wandered over, tucking his sword away. 'A fine act, Apion. He was the ghazi from the pass, no?'

Apion looked down at the Slav and relaxed the tense scowl on his face. 'He was dead. I was ready to tear his heart from his chest until I realised it was him.'

Nepos frowned, then took a deep breath. 'It's over, Apion.'

Yet Apion knew it was only the beginning, and he shivered at what the coming war might summon from within him. He made to touch the prayer rope, seeking calm, then frowned again at the etching of the *Haga* on his skin. Did God truly hold sway over the fates of men or was it a much darker force? Then the words of the old lady from the river echoed in his mind.

You may not see it now, but you will choose a path. A path that leads to conflict and pain. Much pain.

The commotion was widespread as they marched back into Argyroupolis. Townsfolk wore panicked expressions and clamoured around the barracks. They had all heard the bell peal from the mountaintop village and knew exactly what it meant. When Apion and the beleaguered column had staggered through the gates, bloodied, weary and depleted, murmurs of concern grew into a panicked babble.

'We've got worse to come,' Sha spoke in a hushed voice as they entered the barracks, the iron gates clanging shut behind them.

Apion looked up; Bracchus stood in the centre of the courtyard, flanked by Vadim and his cluster of towering bodyguards. The rest of the garrison were formed up into a depleted bandon, holding their fluttering crimson Chi-Rho banner in silence. They looked tense.

'They're readying for an attack on the town?' Apion assumed.

'I don't think so,' Sha growled. 'Look!'

Apion followed the African's gaze; a circle had been demarcated in the dust in the centre of the muster yard. Bracchus' glare turned on Apion.

'A death bout? Now? Is the man insane?' Blastares growled, pushing forward.

'Blastares, no!' Sha pushed a hand over the big man's chest to halt him. 'Challenging him results in only one thing. Remember what happened to Basil?'

'I remember,' Procopius cut in, 'but who is it this time?' The old soldier bundled forward, peering across the ranks.

Apion felt an odd chill: usually two men would be stood by the edge of the circle at this point, ready to fight. This time there was nobody, just two piles containing a helmet, sword and a shield each.

'Dekarchos, report!' Vadim barked.

Sha stopped before the big Rus and the tourmarches. He fired that distant but intense stare off over Bracchus' shoulder. 'Ghazi riders, sir, they made an attempt to take Bizye. Not just raiding either, sir, they had a division of spearmen with them too.'

Bracchus' expression was both gleeful and enraged at once, a manic grin under his blade of a nose, lips twitching in unrest. 'Raiders. Dealt with now?'

'Yes, sir, but...'

'As I would expect.' Bracchus flexed his fingers inside the studded gloves and punched one fist into his palm. 'What I would not expect,' he boomed, all those formed up behind him silent, 'is for my garrison, *my* garrison, to be roaming the mountains, engaged in idle gambling? Neglect of your duty while the enemy hovers nearby... it does not sound good at all, does it?' He dragged a finger across the line of battered and bruised survivors of the skirmish.

'We were off-duty, sir. No rules were broken.'

'Oh, I'll be the judge of that,' Bracchus hissed. 'You are *my* subjects, you are *my* army!'

Apion tasted fury on his lips. His fists balled and he realised he was shaking.

'Easy, lad,' Nepos whispered. 'He's looking for an excuse.'

'So let's gamble on the outcome of the next contest...'

Procopius' eyes bulged in realisation. 'Oh, shit!'

'...where the neglectful dekarchos will show his skill with the sword against another.' Bracchus dragged his glare across the party, then lifted a finger and stabbed it at Apion. 'Come forth.'

'Never.' Blastares grappled for his sword.

Apion clasped a hand over the hilt before he could draw it from its sheath. 'No, Blastares.' With that, he stepped forward, drew his scimitar and staked it in the circle, then stooped at one of the piles of armour to hoist the kite shield and place the helmet on. Sha followed suit, then turned to him, spathion in hand. Apion saw a mix of fear and resignation in the African's eyes. He nodded to him, holding his gaze. 'Don't hold back, sir,' he said, sincerely.

Bracchus, grinning, waved the gathered garrison around the circle. When formed, he raised a hand and then dropped it. 'To the death!'

The pair sidestepped around the circle in a silence only broken by the scuffing of their feet in the dust. Apion felt nauseous at the reality of this and tried to see Mansur before him, imagining this as a friendly duel. His mind steadied, he tried to measure his next move: to fight Sha or to lunge for the tourmarches. Every time he circled past Bracchus, he noticed the veins in his jugular, so close.

Vadim and Bracchus' men began to grumble and heckle at their hesitancy. 'Perhaps one of my men will be less coy about ending one of your lives?' Bracchus mused. One of the giant bodyguards stepped forward, drawing his spathion, the rest forming a wall around Bracchus.

The chance was gone and Apion knew straight away that the big guard would be ruthless. He had only one choice. He read Sha's next footstep and lunged, bringing his sword smashing down on the dekarchos' skutum. Sha roared and pushed back with the boss of his shield, then smashed his sword down at Apion, who dodged just beyond the blade. A pained frustration was etched across Sha's face, enraged and apologetic all at once. At the edge of the circle, Blastares, Procopius and Nepos winced as they looked on. Apion saw the three of them eyeing Bracchus' bodyguards. He parried a blow from Sha then spun to shake his head briskly at them.

Apion pushed forward again, shield on shield with Sha. Then the pair swung their swords at each other's flanks, then both leapt back with a roar. Apion's tunic was split over his ribs and the underlying wound gushed red. Sha's garment had lost a handful of armoured plates from the back, the skin underneath pumping blood.

'At last, some action!' Bracchus roared. 'This, men, is what I want from all of you. Undying commitment and devotion to your tourmarches.'

Face etched with desperation, Sha rushed for him again, and Apion had but an instant to react; if he had still been wearing his brace he would have been dead already. He swiped his shield up and threw himself to his right at the same time, leaving one leg trailing. The shield caught Sha's sword and dulled the African's blow, the dekarchos then tripped over Apion's leg, thudding to the dust.

In a flash, Apion was up and had his scimitar at Sha's throat. The African gulped, eyes wide in realisation, then dropped his weapon.

'Unexpected,' Bracchus spoke in a curious tone.

'Finish him!' the guards jeered.

The rest of the garrison stood still and silent. Apion looked up to them, catching the eyes of each one on the front row. 'This man fought like a lion today, saved the lives of hundreds in Bizye, some maybe even your kin?'

'My mother lives in the village,' one soldier said, bunching his way forward.

'So you want me to push my sword through this man's throat?' Apion asked.

'Of course not,' the soldier replied.

'So the cripple boy has become a man?' Bracchus spat. 'The boy who carries a Seljuk sword. Lives with a Seljuk family.' Some in the crowd broke into a murmur at this. 'That's right, the *Haga* speaks the Seljuk tongue because he is one, in all but blood.'

'My actions have spoken for me, sir, every time I have donned the armour and arms of the thema.' Apion turned to Bracchus, sheathing his sword. 'If any man thinks less of me for such a trivial aside as living with a peaceful Seljuk family then let them come forward and face me,' his eyes narrowed on Bracchus, 'then you will have your measure of blood; but I will not kill Dekarchos Sha.'

Bracchus' eyes grew cold and he clicked his fingers. 'Vadim. Finish them. Finish them both!'

But before Vadim could step forward, the clatter of hundreds of swords being grappled and partially drawn filled the air. The garrison moved forward, flanking Apion as he helped Sha to his feet. Vadim hesitated and then looked to Bracchus.

At that moment, Apion saw a glimmer of fear in the tourmarches' eyes. It lasted for just an instant, then it transformed into something darker than he had ever seen, even within himself. If Bracchus was to die here at the hands of many, then the entire garrison would be to blame. And he knew all too well the punishment the Agentes could inflict on those who crossed or harmed one of their own. No, Bracchus would die as planned tonight, on the end of his dagger alone.

He held his hands up to the men of the garrison and then turned to Bracchus again. 'The tourmarches is our senior officer. We must respect his word.' Apion kept his expression firm despite the scowls from some of the men at this. 'What happened here was an unfortunate misunderstanding.' He cocked an eyebrow to Bracchus. At last the blackness in the man's eyes faded and he nodded.

'As you say, soldier. Men, at ease. This is an issue for myself, the dekarchos and this soldier to deal with.'

The garrison remained braced until Apion turned to them, nodding. With a muted sigh, all half-drawn swords were replaced. He clasped an arm to Sha's shoulder and then looked to Bracchus. 'We will accept the harshest punishment associated with our crime of what? Disorder while off-duty?'

'Oh yes, you will,' Bracchus seethed.

Apion offered him a humble nod, as the rasping voice echoed in his mind.

You will take no more lives. And tonight, you whoreson, I will drink your blood.

The summer night was balmy and the cricket song was loud indoors as well as out. From a few bunks away, Procopius groaned some sleepy nonsense-talk about the war against the sheep. Apion shook his head clear of the distraction. His muscles ached from the skirmish and then the aborted death bout during the day, but his mind and his heart were alert and honed on one thing.

He heard the muttering of the change of guard. It was time.

He untied the prayer rope and mouthed an oath and then an apology to his parents. For tonight he was to become a cold-blooded murderer. He lifted his dagger, tucked it inside his belt and crept from the sleeping quarters to lurk in the shadow of the main doorway.

Outside was dark apart from the torch ablaze on the watchtower by the gate. An ordinary evening, like any other. Only tonight, when Bracchus made his way to the officers' quarters with Vadim, both would have their throats opened. He felt shame as he realised he was grinning at the prospect, welcoming the image of the dark door, flexing his own fingers as he saw the knotted arm reach out for it.

He watched the guards on the tower until they turned to look out over the fortified town. Then he scuttled across the muster yard to crouch in the shadows of the hay bales by the stables, back pressed against the wall of the storeroom adjoining to the officers' quarters. When Bracchus walked past, he would spring. All this time, all that pain, all the angst, it would be let tonight like a poisonous cyst. He peered around the corner. Still nothing. He frowned, scanning the muster yard. There were no other guards in the compound. Something didn't feel right.

Suddenly, an arm wrapped around his throat and a sharp point pressed into his neck.

'So the hero tries to flee the barracks under cover of night?'

His vision cleared to reveal Bracchus, stood before him. Vadim held him from behind, grunting in amusement, a ham-like hand clutching at Apion's throat, the other hand holding a dagger, the tip resting on his jugular.

'Well, not in my realm, you Seljuk-loving whoreson; here you pay for your crimes and you pay heavily.' His words grew into a snarl as he gripped Apion's hair and wrenched his head back. 'You tried to humiliate me on my own territory. Shrewd and bold, I'll give you that. But, as countless souls would tell you if their throats had not been ripped out, I do not hesitate to stamp out those who displease me. That is not good news for you.' Bracchus nodded and Vadim wrapped his arm around Apion's chin.

Staring at the star-studded night sky, Apion knew it was too late to shout, too late to plead. The knife blade pressed deeper into his jugular and he winced at the hot blood that escaped and trickled down his neck.

'That's not all; I've got *two* reasons to cut your throat, end your pitiful life.' Bracchus' words stung in Apion's ear. 'A business friend of mine, a very profitable business friend, old Kyros – used to make me a fortune taking money from the fools riding the highways near Trebizond – went missing some years ago. My men used to collect a cut of his takings every winter, then one time he didn't show. I sent word round to look out for him, and then I heard he and his mob had been found, slain in the grass by the Piksidis. When I heard this I was distraught; I'd have to do without the old bastard's money. I put a price on the head of those responsible, but nobody had seen a thing. Last they'd heard he had set out to shake the coins from some fool.' Bracchus' glare sharpened. 'Now, years later, when it is all forgotten, I get word that a farmer has been telling of what he saw that day. Two young boys, one a cripple and the other a Seljuk, fleeing from the valley just before Kyros and his band were found.'

Apion's thoughts swirled, then he hardened his expression. 'I set out to buy information from him, the man tried to kill me. He got what he deserved for that.'

'In turn, I could easily end your life in return for the lost revenue from Kyros.' Bracchus nodded to Vadim, who pushed the knife blade in further, stinging Apion's flesh.

Apion fixed a glare on the tourmarches. How many had been slaughtered and buried by him and his network, all with the emperor's blessing? If he was to be the next victim, then he had failed. Rage boiled in his veins.

His muscles contorted and he thrashed backwards, kicking up from the ground. A dull crunch reverberated through the back of his skull and Vadim released his grip with a moan, staggering back. The big Rus clutched at the squashed mass of his nose, cupping the blood that gushed from his nostrils and the fine line where the cartilage had snapped. Then he slumped to his knees.

Apion's heart hammered as he stood locked in a glare with Bracchus. Both of them darted glances to the dagger, discarded in the dust. Apion heard a rasping voice scream inside him. *Take it.* He spotted the glint in Bracchus' eye and dropped to one knee, snatching the blade, just as Bracchus made to do likewise.

Turning the blade over in his hand, a gleeful lust raced through Apion. This was the moment. The tourmarches would be found tomorrow, throat cut back to his spine, eyes gouged from his face. Apion shivered with desire for blood.

'Think very carefully about what you do next,' Bracchus spat, eyes trained on the glinting tip of the dagger. 'A soldier breaking night curfew? What was he doing? What happened when his superior officers questioned him? He attacked them, tried to kill them?' Then the tourmarches' face curled into a grin under his razor of a nose. 'You're already covered in evidence, boy.'

Apion touched a hand to his scalp, warm and wet with Vadim's blood.

'You'll die a disgrace, your Seljuk-loving head on a spike, no doubt...' Bracchus said.

'You don't even know why I'm out here tonight, do you?' Apion hissed. He heard his next words in his mind before he spoke them. *Let me tell you of my murdered parents, while I watch your lifeblood spill at my feet.*

But Bracchus cut in before he could say it. '...and I can assure you that they will die for this.'

Apion's frown fell, the mist in his thoughts parted. 'What did you say?'

'Your dirty Seljuk farmer and his whore of a daughter.' Bracchus pushed up against the blade, the point resting by his heart. Apion's mind raged with the fires from behind the dark door and his fingers curled tight around the blade's handle. Vengeance was within a dagger's length. 'Spill a drop of my blood and they will die on my order, an order that is already with my men across the thema.'

Apion flinched as Vadim also stood tall again, wiping his ruined nose with the back of a shovel-like hand, drawing his spathion.

'You heard him,' Vadim growled, 'drop the blade or your family will be a pile of blood and bone... after we've all had a shot of the girl, of course.'

A thousand voices screamed inside Apion's mind. His chest heaved, spit jumped from his gritted teeth and his muscles seemed to be harder than iron, the blood raging through them.

'My colleagues in and around Trebizond, they know who you are now, and I have an understanding with them,' Bracchus said. 'All they are waiting on is for my word. I just wanted us to have this little discussion before deciding whether to give that word or not. So if you somehow use that toothpick to kill both of us,' Vadim grumbled in laughter at this, 'then your family will be food for the vultures within a handful of days.'

'You *whoreson*!' Apion spat.

'Well, my reputation rides on these qualities.'

Bracchus was back in his element and Apion fell to his knees, the dagger sliding from his wrist. Mansur, Maria, what had he brought upon them? Like a pestilence, these murderous dogs had followed him from the corpses of Mother and Father to his new family. *No, you have followed them*, the rasping voice countered.

'So,' Bracchus stooped, prodding the dagger away with a jab of the foot, 'I have every reason to end your life. You have every reason to keep me healthy and in a fine mood. So you will become the dog that you are. You will follow my orders above anyone else's. I see potential in you; you could be very useful...'

252

Apion's mind spun as he looked up into the tourmarches' rapacious gaze. His lips moved but no words were forthcoming. The chance to end it all had evaporated like a mist.

Bracchus' face remained unchanged. 'When the strategos finally comes here, he will give the orders, but he knows his place with me as much as the next man. Let's just say that I carry the weight of the imperial seal with me, and I have work for you, Seljuk lover, *bloody* work. So make no mistake, I am to be your master!'

Apion's blood ran cold, but what choice was there? To retaliate would be a death sentence to those he loved. He pushed up to stand level with the man. There would be another time, and next time there would be no mistake. All the dark fury would be let on this murderous whoreson.

He nodded briskly. 'You have spoken your piece. So let me return to my bunk.'

Bracchus' grin turned up horribly to dominate his features, then he patted Apion's cheek. 'Good dog.' Apion shivered at his touch.

Then the tourmarches turned to Vadim. 'See the mutt has a good sleep, will you? He and his dekarchos have one hundred lashes to be ready for in the morning.'

Vadim grinned, and then slammed his ham of a fist into Apion's nose.

A dull crack of breaking cartilage filled his head and then all was black.

–

'Twenty-three!' Vadim roared. The iron-tipped tendrils of the whip dug into Apion's back again, gouging deep into his flesh before being wrenched out, pink strands of tissue flailing from their ends. Every strike brought a groan from the garrison, formed up and forced to watch the spectacle.

Apion stared straight ahead, through the iron barrack gates, through the town walls and through the mountains. A cold sweat bathed his skin and he saw the farm, he saw Mansur and Maria and knew what he had to do: he would have no choice but to be the lap dog that Bracchus was to make him. And this was just the start of it.

'Twenty-four!'

Bracchus walked around to stand between Apion and the gates, his eyes searing.

Apion closed his eyes and sought the images of the farm again. Perhaps he would lose consciousness, he hoped. Then he thought of poor Sha who was to be next up.

'Twenty-five!' Apion felt the blackness close in on him and his head drooped. Then a bucket of cold water crashed over him, jolting him back to the present.

'Twenty-six!'

'This is the fate of any man who does not obey me entirely!' Bracchus boomed to the garrison as Vadim pulled the whip back for the next strike. 'Remember this and remember it well.'

'Twenty-sev—'

'He is coming!' an excited voice roared; a citizen stood, gripping the gate bars, eyes wide. 'The strategos is coming, the thema is mustered!'

The garrison looked up in unison to see the thick dust cloud approaching from the west as the gate top buccina wailed out to herald the sighting of friendly forces.

Apion held his head up despite the thick nausea in his gut and the stinging agony of his back. Bracchus had not shifted his glare from him, the tourmarches was testing him. Apion kept his expression blank.

—

By afternoon, the hubbub surrounding the strategos' arrival had settled down. Cydones had arrived with five hundred kataphractoi cavalry, over three thousand skutatoi infantry, nearly one thousand toxotai bowmen and two thousand light infantrymen – nearly every fighting man in Chaldia. The thema was mobilised for Tugrul's invasion, the soldiers swarming around the sea of pavilion tents that filled the pass outside Argyroupolis. The first thing the strategos had done was to demand an instant report on the recent events from Bracchus, and his eyes had narrowed at the talk of the raid on Bizye. So Apion and Sha had been called into the officers' quarters to join Cydones, Ferro and Bracchus in discussing the matter. The strategos had not offered any greeting to Apion when he entered, instead simply offering a knowing nod. Then the group had got down to the discussion.

'There was a scout rider patrol nearby. The town was saved,' Bracchus said, his tone flat and his expression cold. 'Does that bring to an end your questioning, Strategos?'

'You'll do well to respect your commanding officer,' Ferro replied, leaning over the table.

'Easy, Ferro,' Cydones spoke evenly, then looked to Bracchus. 'I am not looking to apportion blame, Bracchus. We nearly lost an important hilltop site. It may not be key, but what concerns me is that had the garrison soldiers and the scout riders not been nearby, the raiders could have wiped the place from the mountain. Then they would have done the same to all the settlements dotted around Argyroupolis, snaring us here like rabbits and we wouldn't have known until it was too late.'

Apion sat back from the table, touching a hand to his battered nose, still swollen with congealed blood from Vadim's knockout punch. Without thinking, he leant back to rest his weight on the back of the seat, then winced as the raw flesh stung at the pressure. His back had been cleaned and bandaged by the medic, but the pain was still sharp and he needed rest. However, this meeting could not be refused.

Apion had heard the men of the garrison talk of how they had heard the faint pealing of the warning bell from Bizye. But they complained that the noise seemed to echo from every direction through the mountain pass and nobody knew for sure from which town the noise was coming. He envisioned the mountainous area around Argyroupolis and tried to graft a shatranj board on top of it. He couldn't though; the mountains were a new dimension.

He imagined the king trying to signal his cavalry, to tell them he was in danger and to come to his aid. Then it clicked.

'We need beacons,' he offered.

'Soldier?' Cydones cocked an eyebrow and turned to Apion.

Apion searched for the hubris he had felt during combat but could only feel the weighty positions of the men in the room push down on him. Then he noticed a keen glint in Cydones' eye, and this spurred him on. 'We need to be made aware of any attack on the outlying towns as early as possible…'

Cydones nodded. 'Go on.'

'…so we need beacons.' His mind flashed back to the flaming torches the villagers had used to herd the pigs. He imagined a man stood at the lip of the mountain, just before the gates of Bizye, waving a larger torch. 'We should build watchtowers on all the highest peaks near each settlement. Have a man tend to a pile of brushwood atop the tower, ready to set it alight should an enemy approach. Then we, here, will know of them as soon as the outlying villages do, and there will be no confusion over which village is in danger.'

'A fine idea.' Cydones nodded, then turned to Bracchus. 'What do you think, Tourmarches, can this be implemented easily?'

Apion noticed that Bracchus' expression was darkening, and cut in: 'My tourmarches showed me the reasoning behind the idea earlier; he has had it in mind for some time.'

Cydones looked to Apion and then to Bracchus again, his eyes narrowed. 'Well, Bracchus, you should have said. A wise idea is always best shared.'

Bracchus kept his tone even, darting a furtive glance at Apion. 'Yes, fortunately the skutatos remembered.'

Cydones shook his head. 'His days as a skutatos are over.'

Apion frowned. 'Sir?'

'From what I have heard of his endeavours yesterday, young Apion has proved that he needs more responsibility.' Cydones spoke firmly to Bracchus, then turned to Apion. 'What is it the men call you?'

Apion felt his face flush. '*Haga*, sir. It means...'

'Two-headed eagle, yes, I know.' Cydones' expression was firm, his gaze unwavering. 'Apion, you are to lead a bandon. You are now a komes.'

Apion's mind reeled with pride and terror at once as Cydones handed him the white sash that denoted the rank. He glanced at Bracchus.

'I will serve under the tourmarches with pride, sir.' He stood to salute Cydones and then sharply to Bracchus as well.

Bracchus glared at him.

CHAPTER 18

Lost

The wagon trundled along the highway, a handful of soldiers lining the benches either side of the open cart, most of them catching up on sleep or lost in their thoughts. At the rear, Apion dangled one leg from the back of the vehicle and his gaze hung on the eggshell-blue sky. The strategos had insisted that the garrison soldiers take a brief spell of leave before the campaign that was to come and the soldiers were elated at this. Apion, however, realised that Cydones was giving the men what could be a last chance to see their families.

He cupped his now healthier purse: four nomismata remaining from his pay as a skutatos, plus an advance of thirty nomismata for his new role. A komes! Yet instead of pride, he felt only a relentless and sharp anxiety needling at his stomach. Bracchus had been undermined by the strategos and Apion feared the consequences. Only his open show of fealty to Bracchus had quelled the immediate rage in the tourmarches' eyes. After Cydones retired to his quarters it was all Apion could do to convince Bracchus that he would be loyal despite his promotion; he had struggled to keep the food in his stomach and his scimitar in its sheath as he knelt before the man, insisting that he would obey the tourmarches without question. It was his reasoning that, as a komes, he could offer more to Bracchus than he ever could as simple skutatos of the ranks. Bracchus had grinned like a shark at this, imagining the possibilities. Apion had kept his own expression blank, seeing only Mansur and Maria in his mind, praying that he had done enough to keep them from the tourmarches' thoughts.

The wagon jolted over a bump in the road, the lip of the cart grating against his lash wounds, healing, but still tender. He refused to wince at the pain, noting the frequent looks from the other soldiers. The garrison held him in high regard, still calling him that name, *Haga*. Yet still he wondered how he would fare when he returned from leave to take up his duty as leader of a bandon of mainly newly mustered men. One thing he would not have to fear was lack of support from the four of his current kontoubernion. Sha had grinned knowingly when the news was broken. Then, when Apion got back to the barracks to pick up his belongings, Blastares, Nepos and old Procopius were waiting with equally broad smiles; the four had recommended him for promotion. A selfless gesture he would never forget from them. He hoped that his insistence on having them in his bandon would go some way to showing his gratitude, and the first thing he had done was to have them all promoted to the rank of dekarchos, with Sha declared as the senior of the four. He had still to work out the detail but he knew each of their strengths and they would have important roles to play in the unit: Sha was the diplomat of the four; Nepos the thinker; Procopius the artilleryman and Blastares the infantry lion. He felt for a moment as if he was almost missing them, then shook his head with a chuckle, and took to looking over his new armour. To cap his new role he now had a fresh and polished iron klibanion to replace his stinking, torn and barely effective cotton vest. Then there was a crimson cloak, a helmet that actually fitted him with a well-oiled scale aventail and new, supple leather boots. Now some three hundred men would be his to lead, to lead and inspire. Not for the first time since his promotion, he gulped back the flurry of self-doubt that clawed at his chest.

The wagon juddered and shook his thoughts clear. He looked across the tapering mountains, the sun warming his skin. The flatlands around the Piksidis were coming into view again, bursts of greenery and shimmering farmland marking the height of summer. The uncertainty over Bracchus and the leading of a bandon would have to wait, because for the first time in a long time, Apion realised he was coming home. He inhaled the nutty scent of barley and let the chatter of cicadas dance on his ears. Then there was the tink-tinking of tools as a farmer and his workers set out posts for a fence. He heard laughter and saw them jibe and play-wrestle as they worked. One of them was dark-skinned and bearded – a Seljuk by the looks of it – the others clearly Byzantine. Something about the rare scene warmed his heart. It all felt so right.

When they reached the crossroads near the valley of Mansur's farm, Apion hitched his satchel over one shoulder and leapt to the ground as the wagon slowed.

'Be seeing you next week, sir?' the driver grinned.

Apion frowned for a moment. *Sir?* Then he relaxed in real-isation. How different was this to the irritable exchange with the driver who took him to the barracks over a year ago? Then he thought again, suddenly aware he was standing tall and balanced on his legs, both knotted with muscles; how different had he become? He fished out a pair of folles and tossed them to the driver with a grin. 'Until then.' He waved to the wagon and the garrison soldiers inside cheered him as the vehicle moved off.

He descended into the valley and crossed the stone bridge. Without the breeze from the moving wagon, the heat was intense, so he removed his helmet and wiped the sweat from his brow, then roughly combed his sun-bleached beard with his fingers. The hills here seemed so much smaller after a year in the mountains. He wondered what else might have changed. Then, there it was: the farm. His heart tingled at the sight of the place, as run down as ever but beautiful in every other sense. The white-grey dots of the goats grew as he approached and their bleating sounded like a chorus of welcome. Smoke puffed from the chimney. *Salep and stew?* He wondered with a grin, his stomach gurgling.

Mansur was sitting in the doorway, lazily carving at a piece of wood with a dagger. Apion put his helmet back on and adopted his best soldierly march. 'Imperial soldier requesting billet!' he chirped.

Mansur squinted up, half-blinded by the sun, then put his wood and dagger down and stood. His face was blank, then he nodded, removing his felt cap to wipe the sweat from his brow, examining the figure before him. 'Apion,' he said softly.

Apion took his helmet off, grinning.

'You have been through a lot in the last year, I can see.' Mansur eyed him with a tired smile. The old man was getting older. 'I knew you could overcome the injury, Apion.' He nodded to what used to be the withered leg, and then tapped a finger to his temple. 'Remember what I said? The injury was up here more than it was down there.'

Apion nodded, pride swelling in his chest.

'You've seen a few fists and swords, I can tell.' His gaze danced over the broken nose and the fine battle scars etched on his hands. Then his eyes fell on the stigma of the *Haga* and he cocked an eyebrow, tilting his head to one side. 'This is what they call you? Then you have earned a fine reputation!'

'But the beard!' another voice trilled behind him from the shade of the doorway. A sweet voice, like honey to his ears. 'Are you trying to look as ugly as possible?'

He opened his arms and beckoned her. Her mock scowl fell away and she ran into his arms and together they laughed, Mansur embracing the pair. Apion's soul glowed. This was it. He was home.

After eating a Mansur-sized portion of stew and snatching conversation in between mouthfuls, he pushed his pay into Mansur's hand and waved away the old man's attempts to refuse it. After that, they played a game of shatranj that ended in stalemate. Then he felt a heavy tiredness settle upon him and retired to his old bed. He slept like a bear in hibernation for the rest of that day and only woke near noon the following day, feeling refreshed as never before. As he lay in the warm comfort of the bed, he prodded the bedding, only then realising the stark contrast between it and the musty and concrete-like bunks at the barracks. When the sleep had cleared from his mind, he stretched and slid from the bed, eyes hungrily taking in the sun-baked lands outside the shutters. He wanted to drink in the surroundings, have every part of it bottled in his mind to escape to when he was away again. Then he swatted the thought of the dwindling time he had here from his mind. *Live for the day!*

He sauntered out through the hearth-room, picking up a fig from the table and filling a cup with chilled water before walking out into the sun. Mansur was set to attack a pile of logs with his axe.

'Allow me,' Apion said, licking his fingers of fig juice. 'It'd be a fine alternative to daily training.'

Mansur stepped back, then grinned. 'Well, aye, if you insist.'

Apion swung the axe at the first chunk of wood while Mansur sat back to watch. The blade sunk about halfway in and he dug it back out using his foot for leverage.

'So, life in the ranks; is it what you hoped it would be?' the old man asked tentatively. 'Did you find what you sought?'

'That has not yet come about,' Apion said, flicking a glance up to Mansur. The old man nodded. Apion felt a surge of guilt: his quest to exact revenge on Bracchus had cast a dark cloud over his relationship with the old man and his daughter for so long now. He would tell Mansur everything, he affirmed, tomorrow, first thing, before Maria had risen. Apion turned back to the logs, his mind suddenly chattering with the bitter dilemma. He tried to clear his mind but could see only images of all the blood he had let in the last year. His next axe swing clove the chunk of wood in a single strike, the blade embedding in the chopping stand, quivering. Apion stared through the axe, sweat dripping across his eyes.

Mansur hesitated before replying. 'That is a pity. You seemed buoyed yesterday. It warmed my heart to see you like that. I was worried for you when you left and I wondered if you would ever return.'

'Every day I thought of this place, of you and Maria.' Apion wondered at the old man's thoughts. Then he remembered Giyath that night before he left. 'How are Kutalmish and his boys?'

Mansur's silence sent an icy shiver up his spine.

'Mansur?'

'Giyath fell in battle last autumn.'

Apion's thoughts darkened. How many faces had he seen of those Seljuks he had killed? 'Where was he?'

'In the deserts to the south-east. Your emperor saw fit to commission an offensive campaign, so the Hikanatoi Tagma were despatched on a fleet that sailed to Trebizond. Then they marched through this way; four thousand kataphractoi, trampling the grass from the land. They joined the infantry of the Lycandus Thema in the south and then fell upon Edessa, where poor Giyath was stationed. The assault failed, but the Seljuk Garrison took heavy losses. Giyath's body was never recovered. Kutalmish is shattered with grief, even though he had known for some time that his first born was doomed to die on the end of a sword.' Mansur held his gaze on Apion.

Apion remembered Giyath's haunted features on that last night. Something had already died in him by that point. 'What of Nasir?' he asked, brow furrowed in concern.

Mansur lifted a weary half-smile. 'Nasir is well. He has become a fine rider, soon to be a bey, leading many other riders, I hear. He is due to return in the next few days. Also, he…' Mansur stopped. 'No, I will let him tell you the news.'

Apion cocked an eyebrow, confused but relieved that his old friend had not fallen. He turned back to the wood and chopped.

The next morning he was up at dawn when the air still held the cool of night. Dressed in a grey woollen tunic, he ate a quick breakfast of yoghurt, honey and bread, washed down with fruit juice, then headed for the stable shed.

He ruffled the old grey mare's mane, muttering words of comfort to her, saddened a little by the sight of her bowed legs and cracked hooves.

'You gave me legs when I had none.' He kissed her nose. The mare spluttered and turned back to her hay. 'And I bet you're delighted you don't have to take my weight anymore?' he laughed. 'You've earned your rest. Enjoy it!' He turned from the stable and took a few short strides and then broke into a jog and then a sprint.

The air whistled in his ears as he gathered speed and he welcomed the distant tingle on his scar. He ran without let-up, round the valley floor, skirting the highway and the low-lying Piksidis, before rounding on the hill to the north of the farm. He pushed through the beech thicket and reached the boulder cairn at the centre. His lungs rasped and his eyes stung from the fresh sweat, but a grin touched his lips as he set eyes on the etching of the *Haga*.

It had taken him just a short while to run the land and crest this hill, when it used to take him twice that time just to hobble to the top of the hill with his brace, and many times longer in the days when he needed the crutch. He rested back against the cairn and wondered at that one brief but delightful encounter with Maria. Right here, where they had been together. Her scent and her soft, smooth skin. He realised he was grinning again.

Suddenly, a rabbit bolted from the ground by his thigh.

Apion started and then chuckled as its tail bobbed frantically in flight. 'Lucky for you I have a full belly and have left my bow at home.' He stood, then noticed the hole where the rabbit had darted from, under the boulder cairn. He pulled at a boulder near the base and saw it was not a rabbit warren but a bigger hole, and something white inside caught his eye. Curiosity piqued; he lifted away the surrounding boulders and gawped at the small cave it revealed underneath. He slithered through the opening. He could only stand with his neck bent but it was a cosy little space. Then he noticed the pure-white animal bones on the remains of a makeshift hearth. Long disused, probably some traveller's temporary shelter from the distant past. *The fun I could have had with a den like this, and I must have ridden past it every day*, he mused.

He shook his head and climbed from the opening, then sat again to take a swig of his water skin. He saw the shadow of an eagle trace the grass ánd glanced up, but the sky was a brilliant, unbroken blue. Yet as he looked, three black eagle feathers floated from the glare of the sun, and he reached up to catch them. His skin rippled as he examined the feathers; they would make a fine plumage for his helmet, he smiled. Fighting for the empire had evoked a new sense of being in him. Perhaps when he had his vengeance, he might remain in the armies of the empire. He let his gaze wander through the trees, off to the eastern horizon.

Then he realised he was not alone. The silver-haired lady with the milky eyes was sitting beside him. She too gazed east. Apion felt at ease despite her sudden appearance, and their last conversation seemed like only days ago when it had in fact been some six years earlier.

'I know now that you speak only the truth,' he said to her. 'I had a choice, just as you said I would. But what is a choice to a man when he knows he will only be able to live with himself if he takes one particular path. That path for me has meant pain and hardship in every minute of my life with the army.'

She nodded at this. 'That you have understood heartens me. So what will you do now you know where your life is headed?'

Apion frowned. 'But I don't know where the rest of my life is headed, not yet. After I have had my revenge, I am still unsure of what I will do next.'

Her face fell at this. 'Oh, Apion, I wish it were only a few years of pain you were to endure. Don't you remember what I told you? When the falcon has flown, the mountain lion will charge from the east, and all Byzantium will quake. Only one man can save the empire...'

'...the *Haga*,' Apion finished her sentence, gazing at his stigma with a frown. 'But how? What does it truly mean?'

265

She shook her head. 'It means what it means, and I have learned that nothing can change the truth of it. You know this too.'

He clutched at the three eagle feathers again and examined their structure, then glanced east, a tear gathering in his eye. 'I will never come home from the ranks, will I? Tell me, old lady,' he spoke, closing his eyes, touching his prayer rope, 'what part does God play in all of this?'

She did not respond.

'Who are you talking to?' a voice called out.

Apion jolted, turning to see Maria. The old lady was gone.

'Lots of old memories, eh?' Maria shrugged nervously.

Apion looked down at the grass. A long silence ensued.

Finally, Maria spoke. 'What happened before you left for the thema, Apion, with Nasir; I just wanted to say that I'm sorry for that. I didn't want to hurt you.' She eyed his new frame. 'You know that what happened had nothing to do with your old limp, don't you?'

Apion snorted. 'Eh? I left to find glory, Maria. I'm an officer now.' He hated himself for those words. 'I'd forgotten about this place and us,' he lied. 'There are so many women that loiter around the barracks and the inns that it all merges together.' The words were tumbling out despite his heart screaming at him to stop.

She nodded, eyes fixed on the grass underfoot, then she sat next to him without replying. Together, they picked the grass in the still heat and time passed, morning becoming midday. Then the sky slowly greyed with clouds that darkened and then the air grew muggy. The first rumble of thunder split the air, then thick blobs of rain showered down around them.

'Come on!' He grabbed Maria's hand, pulling her towards the cave under the cairn as the rain turned sheet-like. They scrambled into the cave and shivered, shaking the water from their bodies.

'What is this place?' Maria asked as Apion kindled a fire from the brushwood that had collected in the space.

'Shelter!' he chuckled as the fire sparked to life. He saw sadness in her eyes and fixed his gaze on her. 'I know you didn't want to hurt me Maria, but you did. You are like family to me and I felt betrayed. Yet that was not why I left for the thema.'

'I'll always be here for you, Apion.' She rested a hand on his and her gaze locked on his eyes.

'And I will always protect you, Maria. I love you.' The words seemed to numb his lips.

She did not reply. He leaned across and kissed her, her lips tasted salty. He ran his hands over her hips and pulled her close. She put her arms around him loosely. His fires ignited, Apion laid her on the bracken-coated cave floor.

'Apion,' she started.

He hesitated, his tunic halfway off. 'Yes?'

Her eyes seemed to glass over a little, then she looked away and loosened her robe. 'Nothing.'

They made love. It was slow and gentle and Apion's mind flitted with all of the fantasies he had had of this moment. His love for her was being fulfilled at last. But something didn't feel quite right. That hunger she had shown the last time just wasn't there. He climaxed and for that moment his mind was free of troubles. Blissful and fleeting. Then he lay down next to her and took her hand in his.

Some time later, the storm still raged. Apion sat up and opened his satchel, breaking a loaf of bread and a round of cheese and offering half of each to Maria. They munched quietly and washed the meal down with water.

He turned to her. 'I don't want to be without you again, Maria.'

'But you're in the thema, Apion!' She shook her head. 'You will be gone from here in days!'

He thought of the few words of the silver-haired lady and of his own realisation. *I will never come home from the ranks, will I?* At this he frowned and shook his head firmly. 'No, I'll be in barracks and on campaign for some time to come, but a day will come, soon, when I will return here, to live and to farm. I don't want to be lost to you again.'

'Apion...' Her brow furrowed.

'I want to look after you. I want you to be my...'

'I'm betrothed to Nasir.' Her words were spoken shrilly and they hung in the air.

Apion's heart iced over and a chill ripple of realisation crept over his chest.

'I'm sorry, Apion, I tried to tell you,' she started.

'Tell me this is a joke, Maria, please!' His words were faint.

'I love you, Apion, but I also love Nasir. Can you understand how hard that is?'

No! His mind screamed, he could not understand. He loved Maria and only Maria and how could she feel any differently about him? She looked at him, eyes moist but resigned.

His arms fell limp by his side. 'Then I should not have come back here.'

'Apion, don't be so foolish. Remember, we're here for each other?'

Her pleading eyes stabbed at his heart. He looked away and stooped to lift her from the cave. 'The storm is abating. Come, we should go back to the farm.'

Outside, the land still shimmered from the storm and light-grey clouds scudded across the sky. They walked side by side but Apion felt utterly cold and alone. He could see her wiping tears from her cheeks in his peripheral vision and wanted so much to dry her eyes for her. He searched for some words, something that could make this better, when a whinny broke the silence.

'Komes?'

Apion spun around. A drenched imperial messenger held his mount's reins tightly, the beast frothing and sweating. 'Yes?'

'The strategos has sent for you personally. He wants all of his officers in Argyroupolis by dusk.'

'What's happening, rider?'

'Tugrul is advancing, he has destroyed the army of the Colonea Thema utterly and completely, and now he moves for Chaldia as we speak.'

Apion felt the iron veneer crawl over his skin. His sorrow brewed into a black anger.

Leave was over.

War and vengeance beckoned.

The wagon rumbled far more hastily through the valleys on the return journey and the land was gloomy and grey like his thoughts. Mansur had not returned before the wagon had called to pick him up; he had planned to tell the old man of Bracchus' threat so that some form of protection could be arranged. Then there was something else. Not just the news of Nasir and Maria. He couldn't put his finger on it, but he felt sure there was something else the old man had wanted to talk about. Then again, he mused, it had seemed that way since they had first met back in the filthy drinking hole in Trebizond all those years ago.

He looked up: the soldiers sat across from him in the wagon bore equally disgruntled and anxious looks, each torn from their loved ones after only a few days of their promised week of leave.

'Take heart,' he encouraged them, 'we travel to fight with the strategos. With his leadership, victory is ours for the taking and soon enough we will be back with our families.'

The wagon rumbled on for some time, then slowed in the muddy slop by the roadside. 'Stopping for a piss-break!' the driver bawled.

The soldiers dropped out to empty their bladders but Apion simply stretched his legs, gazing along the south-eastern track. As he did so, he noticed a lone rider trotting towards them, coming north-west. The rider grew clearer as he approached. Wearing mail armour and with a pointed Seljuk rider's helmet hanging from his saddle; he had dark skin, broad shoulders and a swinging pony tail. Apion knew it was Nasir before he saw the rider's grey eyes.

The rest of the garrison soldiers bristled, some touching their hands to their swords.

'Easy,' Apion called. 'He is a good man and rides in peace.' Then he turned back to Nasir.

Nasir gawped for a moment, then burst into a wide grin, sliding from his horse, arms extended. 'Apion!' He wrapped his arms around Apion in a bear hug, then grasped his shoulders to behold him. 'You... you are so different?' he stammered, noticing Apion's height, build and balance. 'And what do you call this,' he laughed, pulling at his beard.

Apion shook his chin free of the grasp with a snarl, then felt ashamed as his friend flinched, suddenly wary. 'I'm sorry,' he sighed, 'it's just this damned wagon-ride, and that my leave is over.'

Nasir smiled warily. 'The clouds have pissed on me all the way from Edessa, but I can't stop smiling because I'm headed in the right direction!'

Then Apion remembered Mansur's news and felt further shame. 'I heard about Giyath. I'm so sorry.'

Nasir's face fell stony. 'He died a hero. That's all he ever wanted.'

'I hope that softens the grief for you and Kutalmish.' Apion saw the pain in Nasir's eyes and left it at that. Then he braced himself. 'But I believe there is good news too,' he started, feigning a smile, 'congratulations are in order?'

Nasir's face lit up again. 'We are to wed at the end of the summer!'

Apion clasped his friend's forearm, then embraced him to disguise the reddening of his eyes.

'Will you come to the ceremony, if you can? You have to be there. Without Giyath, you are the closest thing I have to a brother.'

Apion's heart softened at the tender words. 'Of course I will be there. Just make sure you get word to me before the day?'

Nasir nodded.

Apion thought of the war that was to come and wondered what might happen before then. 'You know what is coming, don't you?'

Nasir's expression darkened. 'War? Yes, I know what awaits me when I return to my posting. My riders and I are to join with the *Falcon* in seven days.'

'Tugrul already advances on Chaldia, Nasir.'

'We cannot divert fate, friend. Let us not fret over what we cannot control.'

'Right, everyone back on the wagon!' the driver yelled.

Apion looked to the wagon, then back to Nasir. The rain came on again ferociously. 'Nasir,' he grasped his friend's wrist, 'there is something you must know.'

Nasir frowned.

'Bracchus, he may come back to the farm.'

'That vile bastard? You haven't dealt with him yet after what he did to you and your parents?'

Apion leaned in closer to whisper to his friend. 'I planned to have his heart on the end of my dagger on the first day I joined the thema, but the man is a wily opponent and I have not been able to get at him. More importantly, he and I have a… situation.' Apion fixed his gaze on Nasir. 'He's threatened to have Maria and Mansur killed if I disobey him.'

Nasir's face paled and his eyes darted around the ground in puzzlement. Then he looked up to glare at Apion. 'Then you must break the hold he has on you, you must remove the threat.'

'Sir, we must be going,' the wagon driver yelled through the downpour.

'Bracchus is a shrewd operator but I will do everything in my power to do that. You know I will. I promise you, they will not be harmed.'

He held Nasir's gaze as he walked backwards and hoisted himself onto the wagon.

Nasir remained, wide-eyed, fixed on Apion, who stared back likewise as the wagon trundled off to the east.

CHAPTER 19

The Assassin

The first day back at Argyroupolis saw the summer heat return with a vengeance, the ranks of the mustered thema seeking respite from the baking sun inside the sea of pavilion tents. Meanwhile, inside the town barrack compound, a newly formed bandon readied to stand before its komes and the strategos for the first time.

Apion stood in the centre of the muster yard, boiling inside his plumed helmet, cloak, klibanion, tunic, leggings and boots, tongue welded to the roof of his mouth as his new charges filed from the bunk block. Flanking him was a *buccinator* bearing his bronze horn, a drummer and a standard-bearer. Behind him stood Cydones, Ferro, Bracchus and Vadim. This was his first address to his men and he had been dreading it all morning.

The first file lined up, shields freshly painted with the Chi-Rho and a crimson backdrop. At this point he felt well, but then the next file lined up, then the next and the next, his heart clenching at every one. In all his men numbered just over two hundred with the last six files depleted of their full complement. The majority of these men had been mustered from their farms by the strategos over the last year. This, like every other bandon, was carefully seeded with members of the garrison, tasked with disseminating drill, tactics and procedure.

Finally, his unit was fully formed, front ranks glistening in the scarce klibania and helmets, the rest in felt caps and padded vests and jackets. He resolved to address the poverty of equipment

– so stark in comparison to the well-equipped Seljuks he had encountered – when the time was right.

To a man they stood before him in silence, eyes forward as protocol demanded, but he caught many of them snatching glances at him and the white sash around his torso. While the garrison soldiers loved him, the newly mustered men would surely have their doubts, waiting on the words of this young lad promoted from the ranks, eager to dismiss him or keen to see his words stutter and fail. Sha had warned him about that. He removed his helmet and held it underarm, his hand resting on his sword hilt. His words seemed to be stuck somewhere deep down and the silence crept on his skin. Then he ran his eyes over the front rank of dekarchoi from left to right; Sha, Nepos, Blastares and Procopius stood front-centre, newly promoted and bristling with pride. They wore their best soldierly expressions but their eyes were on him. Then Sha gave him a disguised nod of encouragement. The four were with him.

At that moment he knew the bandon would follow him.

He called to the skutatos holding the bandon standard and took hold of it. The wooden staff bearing the Christian Chi-Rho emblem on crimson cloth had three coloured tails: crimson for the thema, gold for the tourma and crimson again for the bandon. His bandon. He hoisted the standard into the air and glanced up, seeing the shimmering sunlight dance through the frayed edges of the prayer rope on his wrist and illuminate the stigma of the *Haga* on his forearm. He filled his lungs.

'*Nobiscum Deus!*'

The men of the bandon were silent only long enough to suck breath into their lungs, then they barked back with gusto.

'*Nobiscum Deus!*'

The first address over, the bandon broke up, heading back to the sleeping quarters to polish and hone their armour and weapons. Apion kept his stance true and proud as he marched back into the bunk area. As a minor officer, he would still live with the rest of the men and he was glad of that.

'You held yourself well out there, sir.' A voice spoke as he stepped into the shade indoors.

Apion turned to Sha, still not used to the African referring to him as an officer. He glanced around: only Procopius and Nepos were nearby. He let his lungs empty and his shoulders sag a little but he resisted the urge to show too much complacency. 'Aye. It was good to see you in those lines though.' At this, Nepos gave a wry hint of a smirk and Procopius issued a baritone chuckle.

'It's hotter than the bloody sun out there!' Blastares croaked as he sauntered into the bunk room, his scowl shimmering with sweat. He lifted an arm to sniff his armpit and then winced, choking at his own stench. 'Cotton tunics, that's the way ahead!'

'If we had them in the storeroom then you'd all have one by now,' Apion nodded, 'but the last supply train was all essentials: grain for the rations and ore for the smiths.'

'Yes, war dictates,' Nepos added.

'Whatever. I just pity the poor bugger who has to march behind me,' Blastares chuckled, uncorking his water skin and sucking thirstily on the contents. Then he stopped, belched and grinned wryly at Apion. 'Oh yes... sir,' Blastares was still getting used to Apion's new rank, 'I've got bad news; that whoreson wants a word with you.'

Apion followed Blastares' nod outside; Bracchus stood with Vadim in the centre of the muster yard, deep in conversation.

'Something about going out with a detachment from the bandon. Today, unfortunately.'

Apion nodded in silence.

'He's got it in for you, sir,' Procopius said. 'Be on your guard.'

Apion looked to his trusted four. They had surely noticed the artificial obedience he had shown Bracchus. They knew something was wrong. But this was his battle and his alone.

'Then I have my first sortie.' He flicked his eyebrows up, trying to sound casual as he made for the doorway.

The cicadas trilled like an unseen army as he emerged again into the white heat of the afternoon, his skin stinging at the dryness of the air. As he approached, Bracchus looked up, breaking off his words with Vadim. The man's features sharpened under the shade of his helmet. He saw Vadim off with a hand on the shoulder and then beckoned Apion with a grin.

'You wanted to see me, sir?' Apion stopped a few paces from the tourmarches and adopted the over-the-shoulder stare into the distance that Sha had taught him. It avoided confrontation, apparently.

'You're going on scout patrol today, Komes, with a detachment from your new charges.'

Apion remained firm and focused on a two-storey tenement at the other side of the town but a blur in his peripheral vision marked the gathering of sixteen men. He nodded. 'Yes, sir. I await my briefing, sir.'

Bracchus' grin widened. 'Good, I see our understanding is mutual. I command, you obey.'

'Yes, sir!' Apion barked.

Then Bracchus leant in. 'You have your first job to do for me. There is a young lad you will be marching alongside, by the name of Sidonius. You see him, the shaven-headed one? Seems his father would rather not pay his debts. Shame he doesn't realise his boy has been posted to my tourma.'

Apion broke his stare and shot a glance at Bracchus, then around at the forming men. Mostly veterans, going by their scars and otherwise lined faces. Then there was the odd one out: slight, shaven-headed and sporting a set of caterpillar-like eyebrows. Sidonius was busying himself tying on his padded corselet, trying to keep up with his colleagues. The lad looked nervous. Apion felt a horrible apprehension that those nerves were all too appropriate.

'You go out from the town today as a sixteen. You return as a fifteen.'

Apion's blood chilled. *Never*, a voice rasped in his mind. What kind of nightmare was this?

'Don't engage your mind.' Bracchus' words were icy. 'That will only lead to one thing. All it needs is my word. Just one word and they're dead.'

Apion's mind swam. His stomach heaved and every muscle wanted to engage: to prise Bracchus' chest open with his dagger and rip out his heart; to scream warning to Sidonius; to shout and shout until Cydones, Ferro, Sha, Nepos, Blastares and Procopius came running with their swords; to roar so loud that Nasir would hear him and come too, so loud that Mansur and Maria would hear and run for safety. He turned back to Bracchus and not a sound escaped his lips as he held the tourmarches' glare. He swallowed the sickness inside. He thought of Mansur and Maria.

'Yes, sir.'

—

'Keep pace; focus on your breathing, not the heat!' he roared, his words echoing through the mountain pass. He remembered the early days of his running routine and sympathised with his men; they would be feeling the burning in their muscles, the fire in their lungs, the afternoon heat like shackles, but he could not show anything but steely resolve to them. The veterans behind him were good soldiers it seemed, silent and steady, yet to fall out of line even once. Then, at the rear there was Sidonius. The soldier was red in the face, panting and spitting phlegm every hundred paces or so.

'Keep it up at the back!' he growled. The men seemed to respond to gruff and booming tones more readily.

They continued at the unrelenting pace until the sun was starting to drop from its zenith and the path came out of the eastern side of the mountain and into a wide, dusty plain. He saw the sizeable palm thicket, the usual stopping point for patrols to the east, the babbling of the spring in its midst audible over the panting men. Apion raised a hand and croaked: 'Fall out to slake your thirst and fill your skins.'

They approached the palm thicket, shading a series of man-sized limestone boulders and the spring. The soldiers dropped their ration packs with a groan, some too tired even to drink from their skins, others kneeling to cup handful after handful of water. Apion strolled in behind them, welcoming the cool shade offered by the broad fronds. He ached to sit but his mind would not rest.

He eyed Sidonius. The refreshed skutatoi started to poke around in the thicket, bantering about the possibility of finding fruit. Then the young, red-faced soldier went off in his own direction, climbing over the first boulder then dropping down behind it into the thicket and out of sight. Apion's heart ached, for the lad was as shy and ill-prepared for life in the thema as he had been just over a year ago. Yet only a short time remained before they were due back at Argyroupolis. There would be no other stop, no other opportunity. *Opportunity?* He almost retched at the word. He closed his eyes and searched for an answer. Mother and Father were not there in the darkness. Mansur was not here to offer his sound advice, nor was Cydones. Apion was alone. *Do it for them*, he reasoned, desperate to feel some sense of justification.

'Fill your water skins and then we move out again,' he barked to the men.

While the rest of the sixteen groaned, Apion's face fell stern and he stalked over to climb the boulder heap. The current of the spring grew into a gurgling, then a gushing, as he dropped onto the bed of pebbles on the other side. Only a patchwork of sunlight made it through the canopy of leaves overhead and a musty tang of rotting vegetation entered his nostrils, an oddly welcome change from the arid air of the march. He saw the lad, crouching by the source of the spring, washing the dust from his face, but staring into the water, his eyes heavy and sad. Then Sidonius picked up a pebble and plunged it into the water, his face forming a scowl. Apion wondered if he could find some reason to believe there was sufficient badness in the lad to vindicate what he had to do next. His fingers trembled as he touched his sword hilt, his breath shallow.

'Sir, you startled me!' Sidonius leapt to standing, eyes wide but with a grin stretching across his face.

Apion stopped, only paces from the lad. He noticed Sidonius' eyes fall on his hand, fingers resting on the scimitar hilt. Shame crept over his skin.

'God walks with us, eh, sir?' Sidonius pointed to the prayer rope on Apion's wrist, then lifted the length of rope he wore around his own neck clear of his clothing. 'I have prayed that war will not come, as I fear for my family if it does.'

Apion's heart slowed, his head cleared. There would be another way. There had to be. Surely he could get back to the barracks and engage Cydones immediately, explain everything. But, within a heartbeat, doubts muddied his chain of thought: *the Agentes are answerable only to the emperor; by the time you have spoken to Cydones, Bracchus will know you have failed and the order will be given*. He shook his head clear of the squabbling and fixed his eyes on Sidonius.

'War is here, soldier. Praying will not change it. You are here now and you can fight to protect your family. But you need to build some muscle though; believe me, I know.' He rummaged in his ration pack, but there were no betel leaves in there and there hadn't been for some weeks now. Instead, he pulled out his last almond, oil and honey cake, breaking it in two and offering one part to Sidonius. 'Are you hungry? This will keep your energy up, and it tends to stave off thirst too.'

'Aye, my stomach is bottomless it seems.' He nodded to the crumbs scattered atop his own pack by the spring. 'We could stop for the rest of the day and I don't think I'd be able to take in enough water or food.'

'Ha – maybe you could hide in here! There's enough fruit and water for a man to live on?' he joked, and then wondered at the possibility. *You go out from the town today as a sixteen. You return as a fifteen.*

Sidonius did not reply, his face riddled with guilt.

'You didn't come in here to eat, did you? You came to slip away.'

The lad's shoulders slumped and he held out his hands. 'I'm not cut out for army life.'

'When you've signed up, you have no option.' Apion kept his face stern.

'I've tried, but I feel like a child amongst all these veterans. My father is a rich farmer in Trebizond, but I am not cut out for that life. So I came here to prove I was more than a rich man's son, but I don't fit in here either.'

'I see,' Apion sighed. 'Then you've answered the question already. Run for home and you will not find happiness. Stay here and at least you can protect your family by protecting the borders. Neither option is pleasant, but the latter is the correct one.'

Sidonius' head dropped and he kicked out at a pebble. 'You're right. I'm sorry, sir, for being weak, I mean. I am sorry I spoke of this. I will not show such weakness again.' He stepped forward to pick up his pack and leave the spring.

Apion stepped forward and grabbed his wrist. 'Sidonius, wait. There's something you need to be aware of. If we go back to the barracks you are in danger.' His eyes darted and then he pinned the lad with his gaze. 'Perhaps you should remain here after all.'

Sidonius' eyes widened and then he tried to laugh it off but stopped as Apion's expression remained firm under his jutting brow. Then panic set on the lad's face. 'What are you talking about?'

'I'm in as much danger as you. It's the tourmarches.'

'Officer Bracchus?'

'You have not been here for a week yet, Sidonius, but you have probably heard the rumours already; he has no honour and his heart is black.' His expression intensified and his grip on Sidonius shoulder grew vice-like until the lad's face wrinkled in fear. Then a thud shook the pair, followed by a gurgling. Sidonius' eyes grew wide and a hot crimson spray jetted from his mouth and nostrils, covering Apion's face. Apion stepped back, mind spinning. Had the fire behind the dark door made him do it without realising? He leapt back and touched a hand to his sword hilt and dagger – both were still sheathed, but doubt laced his veins as he noticed his sword arm: knotted, scarred, sun burnished and adorned with the red stigma of the *Haga*.

Then his eyes locked on the arrow quivering in the lad's neck, arterial spray fountaining from the wound. Sidonius grasped at the arrow shaft, mouthing silent cries for help, before slumping to his knees, his eyes distant. By the time the lad's body crumpled onto the pebbles, Apion was crouched and scanning the undergrowth, a rhiptarion held horizontally, eyes narrowed. Then he saw a figure in the foliage: a Seljuk archer, fumbling for another shaft, darting glances at his weapon and then up at Apion. The Seljuk raised his bow just as Apion launched his throwing spear. With a thwack of cracking ribs and a shower of blood, the Seljuk was thrown back into the foliage. Apion dropped his shield and spear and leapt into the green. He whipped the dagger from his belt to land on the man, who was already shivering in his death throes, pink foam bubbling from the javelin wound, the cotton vest the man wore useless from a strike at such close range. Apion held his dagger to the Seljuk's throat but the light in the man's eyes was already dimming. Then a cry rang out.

'*Allahu Akbar!*'

Then the same cry rang out in a hundred foreign tones all around the thicket, followed by a chorus of swords rasping from their scabbards. The ground rumbled and Apion's eyes narrowed on the foliage all around him, his skin anticipating the first lick of a sword blade or arrowhead. Then it happened. A scimitar split the air above his forehead and he ducked just as a Seljuk swordsman chopped the weapon down into the bark of a palm. Apion then leapt up to crunch an uppercut into the man's jaw, sending teeth spraying across the spring. The Seljuk pulled his scimitar free of the bark and jabbed at Apion, who leapt back just too late, but his klibanion saved him, the blade chinking from one of the iron plates. Apion grasped for his own scimitar, then pulled his hand back from the hilt with a roar as the Seljuk's blade tore across his knuckles. The Seljuk came again and again, ripping the blade past Apion, scoring the flesh on his forearms as each strike came closer. At either side, more and more Seljuk fighters poured into the thicket, ignoring the duelling pair and heading for the other fourteen skutatoi. Between parrying blows he shot glances around for his shield. Then he stepped on a wet pebble, his boot slid out from under him and he was prone. A Seljuk warrior leapt for him. Apion swiped his scimitar round with a guttural roar, drowning out the snapping of sinew and bone as the Seljuk's leg was sheared in that one blow. The Seljuk fell, screaming until Apion silenced him with a strike through the heart.

All around: desperate roaring and clashing of iron sounded from back over the boulder pile. Apion stooped to pick up his kontarion and shield, then splashed through the crimson shallows of the spring.

He slid over the boulder pile and saw it: five skutatoi remained standing, backs pressed together in a last stand as some twenty Seljuk spearmen harried and jabbed at them. The other nine of his charges lay like broken flotsam in the spring, punctured with arrows and their flesh ripped open by scimitar blades. In the shimmering heat outside of the thicket, a dust cloud billowed up from a moving mass. Blinking, he made out the seemingly infinite train of heavily armoured spearmen, archers and cavalry, a sea of banners bearing the horizontal bow emblem of the Seljuks. The akhi in the thicket were merely a light vanguard. He remembered briefly Bey Soundaq's words at the mountain pass.

A storm approaches from the east, and the Falcon soars on its wrath. Byzantium's time is over.

He turned back to the last stand, only two skutatoi stood now. This would be the end, surely. He gripped his scimitar hilt firmly, rushing for the nearest Seljuk with a roar. His blade sunk into the warrior's neck and before the Seljuk next to him could turn to meet the attack, Apion had his sword free and scythed it round and into the man's chest, bursting the unarmed ribcage, showering the ground in a shrapnel of bone and gore. The next man he fought mouthed screams but Apion heard only the blood pound in his ears, feeling the heat of gore on his face and the dull shudder of every blow he hacked into the man's lamellar.

281

Then the next man came at him, shield raised, scimitar hooked over the top. Apion butted forward with his own shield and the man staggered but remained composed. Then Apion lunged forward for a killer strike. The Seljuk took a step back and let the blow fall through the air, sending Apion sprawling into the midst of the Seljuk mass pressing on the last two skutatoi. He scrambled to stand but slipped on the carpet of gore. Clawing at the crimson mush, he tried to pull his way clear of the melee until a pair of hands grappled on his ankles and pulled him back. A sea of snarling faces roared, jabbing their scimitars down at him. He grasped a shield from a dead skutatoi and, like a desperate animal, he tucked his torso behind it and kicked out as the Seljuks rained blows on the battered skutum. One scimitar ripped into his ankle and he could barely hear his own pained scream. He tucked his leg in and saw another skutatos drop to the ground beside him, eyes staring, jaw missing and blood haemorrhaging from the wound. He roared at the impotence, the certainty of death. Then he pushed to standing with a roar, lifting his scimitar and swiping round at the cluster of Seljuks. If he was to die then he would die fighting. Then a hand wrenched at his neck, yanking his entire body up and off the ground.

He retched as his midriff landed on the back lip of a saddle, legs and arms dangling either side. Suddenly the acrid stench of blood was pierced by horse sweat. He righted himself to see what chaos his world had fallen into. He saw a stern grimace and forked beard of the rider. *Cydones!* He caught sight of some thirty other kataphractoi riding with the strategos. The akhi party lay shattered where they had stood just moments before. Then the wind grew into a whistle and the horse juddered as it thundered back through the mountain pass. The patter of arrows smacking into the dust around them thinned and then stopped and the jeering of the massive Seljuk column fell away behind them.

'Ferro!' Cydones cried over the wind. 'Break off detachments of three, get word to each of the tourmae. The campaign army will not be enough – not nearly enough – we need all of our reserves, even the garrison from Trebizond. Send word to the emperor: tell him we need the support of the tagmata or the eastern frontier *will* fall!'

'Aye, sir!' Ferro slowed and yelled orders to the rest of the kataphractoi. Sub-groups of riders splintered off and shot ahead at full gallop, lowered in their saddles.

'Sir,' Apion said, righting himself to sit in the saddle, 'the Seljuk army, they're not coming through the pass for Argyroupolis. They look to be headed south, around the mountains?'

'Tugrul means to draw us out into the field,' Cydones replied. 'They are forcing us to break one of the tenets of the art of war; they are forcing us to fight them on their terms.'

'Do we have the strength to meet them on the field?'

'They outnumber us vastly, four of them to one of us. The *Falcon* means to crush us,' Cydones said. 'But we will face them. We must!'

Grey clouds scudded across the sky, driven by a warm summer wind. The wall guard at Argyroupolis stood stiff-jawed and attentive, looking over the sea of tents massed on the flat ground outside the town walls. Meanwhile, inside the town, the barracks had been transformed: a contraflow of wagons and mule trains entered and left the enclosure, the warehouse their destination, laden with bare essentials such as tents, mallets, sickles, spades, axes, cookware and hand-operated grain mills along with caltrops, disassembled artillery, spare bows, swords and armour.

Every patch of free space in the muster yard and the space outside the barracks was packed with the fully mustered thema army and the shattered remnant of the Colonea Thema that had staggered in the previous evening. Thick clusters of infantry and riders stood, chattering nervously and drinking from their skins. Some nibbled carefully on their rations, cracked wheat and yoghurt cakes being a cheap favourite given their ease of being cooked down into a nourishing stew as needed or eaten solid while on the move. The occasional whinny came from the loose rabble of five hundred cavalrymen. These dark-skinned riders were Pechenegs – Turkic mercenaries that Cydones had managed to hire when it became clear that the emperor would not be sending the tagmata to support them. These riders were swift and deadly with their bows, if lightly armoured and liable to digress from orders. The populace crammed around the perimeter, eager to hear the latest word on the war. Fathers, mothers, wives, sons and daughters with faces wrinkled in concern for their kin who readied to engage the Seljuk advance. Tucked into the corner of the enclosure by the officers' quarters, Apion stood shoulder-to-shoulder with Sha, Nepos, Blastares and Procopius. The rest of the depleted bandon stood behind him.

'Come on, come on.' Procopius shuffled in discomfort, hands clasped over his groin. 'I've got two jugs of the amber stuff sloshing around in here!'

'Keep a lid on it, you're just making it worse,' Blastares hissed, breath reeking of the ale the pair had been quaffing all morning to calm their nerves. Then he jabbed a finger up to the battlements. 'The big man's about to speak.'

Three blasts on a buccina drowned out the rabble of soldiers and whinnying of horses and at once the crowd fell silent, the ranks inside the barracks rippled into neat bandon squares, Chi-Rho banners lifted high. Then the wall guard about-faced to glare into the city.

'Warriors and citizens of the thema!' Cydones strode along the battlements, fully armoured and gleaming, plumage whipping in the wind. He stopped at a crumbling section that straddled the barrack compound and the market square. He held his arms outstretched, his face shaded under the brow of his helmet. 'Tugrul means to claim glory for his god and his people, but the fire is with us. *God* is with us! By the end of the month, the Seljuk threat will have been extinguished, these pretenders driven from our lands and back to the east. As you can see, our armies number greatly and our men hunger to wield their swords.'

'The Seljuks number greater though!' a lone voice heckled.

The skutatoi punctuating the throng of the populace surged for the man who had spoken out. Apion knew the man had a point though. The emperor had not sent any reinforcements, not even a token detachment of kataphractoi to raise morale.

'That they may,' Cydones countered, halting the soldiers with his words, 'yet we have won fine victories against greater number before, and we will win many more.'

'But while you're out there, who'll be left to defend the cities?'

Cydones paused before replying and the citizen seemed to shrink back into the crowd in the ensuing silence. A smart technique, Apion noted. 'A garrison will remain in each of the population centres. Should Tugrul fall upon one of our cities or towns, then this army you see before you will fall upon him, dashing his army against the walls. He and his horde will not be allowed to roam freely in our lands!'

The crowd murmured, unconvinced. They all knew that a skeleton garrison, fewer than half of the normal number at barely two hundred men – half a bandon of infantry and a handful of archers – would be remaining while the thema army moved out. 'The emperor must send more forces! We need the tagmata!'

'The emperor knows well of our situation, the tagmata are being readied.'

'Bullshit,' Nepos muttered under his breath. 'All of it. The tagmata aren't even mobilised from what I've heard. The emperor sits in Constantinople scratching his arse and letting us take a battering from the Sultanate. The Armenians, fifty thousand men, would have been marching with us but for the purple-blooded fool's ridiculous decree.'

Apion tilted his head back a little to direct his words to Nepos. 'Cydones' hands are tied though, are they not? He has to feed these people with hope or the battle is lost before it has begun.'

'Aye, this is true. I wish it were not,' Nepos concluded. 'Yet I fear even the strategos cannot stir victory from the number he has mustered.'

'Have faith. He won't engage unless he knows he can win,' Apion replied.

'May God above march at the head of our ranks!' Cydones roared, beating his spathion against his shield, freshly painted with the Chi-Rho. Two priests walked to flank the strategos and together they raised an enlarged, crimson standard, decorated with the image of the Virgin Mary, rippling as the cloth caught the wind. At last the populace cried out in fervent support.

Procopius sighed from behind as the fervour died, then there was a rhythmic patter of urine hitting the dust. 'Bloody ale!' the old soldier grumbled. 'Knew I should have stuck to wine.'

Blastares groaned and Nepos grimaced. Apion tried to ignore the warm spray showering his boots, noting the kataphractoi readying for the signal to move out. 'Bandon!' he roared, nodding to the standard-bearing skutatos. 'Prepare to move out!'

Apion sucked in a breath, pulled on his helmet then hoisted his pack, kontarion, rhiptaria and skutum. The men of the bandon rustled into readiness and he stood to one side as they marched forward past him. Then a hand landed on his shoulder.

'Not so fast. You've got more business to take care of,' Vadim sneered, then leaned in to his ear. '*Bloody* business.'

–

The thema had set out in good spirits, marching to the war drums, priests flanking the strategos, chanting and raising the Chi-Rho and Virgin Mary standards to cheers from the bristling column in their wake. Over seven thousand fighting men followed the strategos and the symbols of God: three and a half thousand skutatoi, one thousand toxotai, two thousand light infantry, five hundred kataphractoi, five hundred Pecheneg horse archers and then the massive train of mules, siege engineers and the detritus of traders and merchants who clung to the mobilised army like pilot fish.

As feared, Tugrul's forces had skirted the towns and cities of Chaldia and turned back, drawing the thema army from its homeland and into the south-eastern reaches of the defenceless Colonea Thema. Then they marched east for three days, into southern Armenia, the familiar mountain ranges tapering into an arid brushland. Rumours swept round that Cydones had expected to meet a contingent of one hundred mercenary Frankish heavy cavalrymen – the kataphractoi of the west – but they were never sighted. Nerves were frayed as soldiers worried about their own lives and those left behind. Somewhere here Tugrul's army was camped, but it was another kind of army they came across; the decaying remains of the Colonea Thema.

Carrion birds formed a dark cloud above the never-ending heap of bones, flesh and putrefying guts. So Cydones ordered the dead be buried, an enormous and morale-sapping task, but one that not a single soldier griped at. After a day, the deed was done and the priests had blessed the graves. When they set off again, the arid ground and burning sun sapped the bluster of the thema and even rallying calls and shows of the Virgin Mary standard from Cydones and his officers had seemed to lose their gravitas.

At the end of the most brutally hot day yet, they stopped to set up camp on a yawning plain, dangerously exposed but utterly necessary given condition and morale. While the kataphractoi and the Pechenegs patrolled the area, the banda set to work on the standard marching camp. The exterior ditch and rampart was dug, then the palisade wall and four gates were erected, then caltrops, roped together, were sown into the dust outside the walls.

Before the sun dropped the weary infantry were finally relieved. Then the thema had gathered as usual to sing the hymn to the Trinity. After that, they settled in their respective tents with their wooden cups and bowls to eat an evening meal of millet porridge and hard tack bread, washed down with a sparing amount of their water ration, then nuts and honey to replenish the energy lost in the day's march.

Now, the sun was dropping, illuminating the dusty plain and painting the camp in a lazy orange. Apion and his trusted four were sitting in silence inside his pavilion tent, and he and Nepos were locked in a game of shatranj. The tent was one in a sea of hundreds, with the standard ten sets of quilted bedding laid out, feet around the centre pole, spears dug into the ground by the head of each set of bedding, shield and armour balanced alongside it. As officers, the four no longer shared a bunk section or a kontoubernion tent and would soon have to disperse to their own tents, shared with the men they each led. Yet every night so far they had congregated like this.

'Ah!' Nepos broke the silence.

Apion looked up; the Slav was lifting the war chariot piece to hold it over a square for a moment, then he looked up with a wry grin. 'Hmmm... nice try,' he said, replacing the piece.

Apion leant back with a sigh, wiping the sweat from his brow; this shatranj game had become an epic. Six nights of this had seen them play alternately cagily and aggressively, but still no outcome. Now as the sun slipped into the horizon it was the same again. Staying engaged with Nepos like this was both a tonic and a pox on his mind. Since Vadim had given him his latest order, Apion had a third, darker concern.

For by the sunrise, the Slav was to die.

Bracchus had found out Nepos' dark secret: back in his home thema, the Slav had led a mob in the beating of what Bracchus called 'one of his chosen men', which Apion took as a euphemism for an Agente. So the Slav had fled east, seeking refuge in the border garrisons, unaware that the master Agente himself ran the very barracks he had fled to. Bracchus' diatribe rang in his thoughts. *Once again, the truth comes to me late, but it always comes to me. It seems that your Slav friend dared to stand against one of my... chosen men. As the years passed, Nepos may have thought he was to go unpunished for his crime. Not so. I will spare him the fate I have laid out for you, though, and instead grant him a swift death. So he will die tonight. Open Nepos' throat before sunrise or your whore and her father are as good as dead. Riders in the camp will take word back west and it will be done.*

He tried to focus on the shatranj board but his stomach turned over again at the order. Surely there had to be some way to get past Bracchus, get word to Cydones, to end this cycle. Yet in his heart he knew Bracchus' men were all over the land, ingrained like a tumour. Nepos would have to die, Apion concluded with a swimming nausea. He glanced around the tent for something, anything to distract him from what lay ahead.

Sat at the other side of the tent was Blastares. Roaring drunk only a short while ago, he seemed to have blunted his inebriation with tomorrow's ration of bread. The big soldier had watched the shatranj game, but with glassy eyes and a distant smile; no doubt his mind was replaying some rutting session. Procopius was snoring violently and Sha buffed his armour by the tent flap, eyes narrowed as he gazed into the setting sun.

'What do you see on the horizon tonight, Sha?' Apion asked with a smile, but his words sounded terse.

'A very red sunset.' The dekarchos replied. 'I see us sleeping tonight, waking tomorrow, filling our bellies... and then I sense bloodshed.'

Apion's skin crawled and he darted his gaze to the floor when Sha looked to him.

'But with a pair of master tacticians like you two in our ranks,' he grinned, nodding to the shatranj board, 'the blood will surely be shed on our swords.'

Nepos chuckled throatily, studying the shatranj board with a wrinkled brow. 'Don't listen to a word I say; this bugger is the cunning one. Like a fox, he is. Looks like this game will have to continue over into tomorrow night.'

Apion forced a smile. 'Agreed. I say we get our heads down early, keep our minds sharp. Tonight might be the last opportunity for a good sleep for some time.'

Blastares lent weight to the order, his head already lolling forward, a crust of bread hanging from his lips and a grating snore filling the gaps of silence in between Procopius' chorus.

Nepos yawned then tapped the board. 'Wake that pair and we can all get back to our own tents. Tomorrow we will finish this once and for all, eh?'

Apion nodded with another weak smile. 'Until tomorrow.'

The air was fresh under the clear sky and despite the waning moon, the myriad stars helped Apion pick his way through the shadows and web-like ropes between the tightly packed pavilion tents. He settled by the edge of one of the blocks and fixed his eyes on Nepos' tent. Coughing and snoring came from the tent sentries and sleeping soldiers, and all around the palisades and temporary timber platforms serving as watchtowers, crackling fires outlined the double-strength camp perimeter sentries. There was no evidence that there would be a night attack, but nobody seemed to know where the Seljuk horde lay and anyone doing anything other than visiting the latrine would be challenged for being out of their tents.

He waited for what seemed like an eternity, crouching, watching as man after man sauntered from their tents, bleary-eyed, across the wide crossroads that divided the camp, over to the latrine pits by the eastern side. But still Nepos' tent remained closed. The nominated sentry for the kontoubernion was standing by the tent entrance, shivering, eyes fixed on his boots. Then the tent flap opened. Apion crouched into the shadows and clutched at the dagger handle in his boot for reassurance. The Slav emerged, pulling his locks back from his face, shivering, his breath clouding in the air as he grunted to the sentry. The Slav wore only a tunic as he shuffled for the latrines. Apion shut out his thoughts and scuttled after him.

He moved quickly, closing in on Nepos across the wide walkway. He flicked a glance one way and then the other. The starlight seemed to shine on him accusingly, following his every step. The Slav wandered behind the mound of earth that had been piled conveniently to shield the latrine pits and Apion stopped for a moment by the last of the tents. He was by the middle of the camp's western edge and the customary walkway dissecting the camp west to east lay between him and the latrines like a chasm. He glanced up the walkway to the centre, where the larger tents were pitched. The officers. The strategos. Bracchus.

He hesitated for a moment. To go after Nepos, to make for Cydones and tell all or to drive his dagger into Bracchus' black heart while he slept. The image of the last option lingered in his thoughts. But Bracchus' men all across Chaldia would know of the order that hung like an axe over Mansur and Maria and would carry it out on hearing of his death. He had no choice. He had to go after Nepos. He would have to be stealthy, to sneak up on the Slav before he could make a noise. It would be easier that way. He pulled the dagger from his boot, stood up and stalked into the latrines. He summoned the image of the dark door.

In the starlight, he could make out Nepos hiking his tunic back down. Only a few moments to spare. He blocked out the foul stench of the pits and rushed for his friend. Only at the last instant did the Slav turn, eyes bulging, hands clasping for his missing sword belt. Apion wrapped an arm around Nepos' throat and the Slav struggled in vain.

'Apion,' he croaked, his tone hurt and desperate.

'Shut up!' Apion glanced all around. Good, they were enclosed within the earth ridge as he had hoped. 'Someone could come at any moment. So shut up and listen, for your sake and mine. Do you understand?'

Nepos slackened a little in his struggle and nodded briskly. Carefully, Apion let go. Nepos staggered back, his face white in panic at the sight of Apion's dagger. 'Apion?'

Apion shook his head firmly, thumping a fist onto his heart, tucking the blade away. 'Never, Nepos, my friend. I just had to make it look real. Here, have this.' He pulled his satchel from his shoulder and lifted a package of salted meat, a portion of hard tack bread and a water skin from it.

'Rations? What is this?' Nepos shook his head.

'You told me that first day I came to Argyroupolis that you had come here to get away from a situation at home. Well I know what happened; that man you beat, he was an Agente!'

Nepos' eyes widened. 'How do you know of my past? Only I knew that man was an Agente!'

Apion grabbed the Slav's shoulder. 'Because Bracchus is an Agente, he is the master Agente, he controls them all! He knows all about you. You've got to trust me. You need to get out of the camp. Tonight!'

Nepos started. 'Bracchus? All this time I have been living under the gaze of one of the men I have been running from?' Then the Slav's eyes narrowed. 'Then what does he have on you, Apion? Ever since that day we defended Bizye, you have seemed cowed under his influence.'

Apion gripped the Slav's shoulders. 'There is no time, Nepos. You have to trust me, and despite all of this I know you do.' He held his gaze firmly on Nepos' eyes.

At last, Nepos' gaze softened and his shoulders slumped. 'You are correct.' He touched a finger to his lips, his eyes darting in thought, then he nodded. 'So I have to disappear tonight? Then it starts here. Only you leave this pit. The rest – slipping from the camp – I will make good.'

'You will need my help in slipping out of the camp…'

'No, I can manage that, but there is one thing you can do,' Nepos urged. 'Go to Blastares' tent, give him a nudge, press his bladder or tell him to go take a shit. Tell him it's cold and to take an extra cloak – a dark one. Then return to your tent. I will do the rest.'

Apion nodded. 'I get it, but where do you hide until then?'

'Well I'm not hiding in the pit, that's for sure.' Nepos rolled up his half-sleeves and rubbed his hands together, then nodded to the earth bank. 'I tell you though, Blastares is going to get one hell of a fright when he does come by this way.'

Apion looked to the loosely piled earth; easily shifted by hand to allow the Slav to hide under a thin coating of the stuff until Blastares arrived. He turned back to Nepos. 'When you escape, head back west and north, past Argyroupolis. Then stay true to the valleys until you reach the source of the Piksidis.' Apion described the route back to Mansur's valley, the hill with the beech thicket, the cairn marked with the *Haga* and the cave. He took the carved

292

wooden chariot rider shatranj piece from his satchel and pressed it into Nepos' palm. 'Mansur will know you are genuine if you give him this. He will provide you with food and anything else you need. But you must be discreet, stay in the cave and visit Mansur only at night, for Bracchus has contacts everywhere. I will come for you when the army stands down, when Tugrul's army is defeated...' He grinned, then his words trailed off and shame overcame him at the troubled look in Nepos' eyes. 'You, Sha, Blastares and Procopius trusted me, supported me, lifted me on your shoulders for me to become your komes. Then one of my first acts is to force you to desert, like a criminal or a coward – as far from the truth as possible – all because of that black-hearted whoreson.'

Nepos gripped him by the wrist. 'I trust you, lad, like a younger brother. Go and be safe in that knowledge.' Nepos held out a hand.

He clasped his hand into Nepos'. 'I will sort this out, Nepos, I promise you that.'

'We will meet again, Apion.' Nepos stepped back towards the earth rampart.

With a last look, the pair parted and Apion hurried from the latrine and made straight for the tents.

Stood by the marching camp's western gate, Peleus felt his eyelids grow heavy and he pushed the tip of his dagger into his palm. At once he was awake again. He glanced across to Stypiotes by the opposite gatepost, whose eyes were red-rimmed with tiredness but at least he was awake. Peleus suppressed a chuckle; his friend had been in a foul mood ever since the two had been chosen to go on guard duty. God help any Seljuks who might attack this entrance to the camp, he mused.

'Tomorrow night, Stypiotes, we eat then we sleep,' he croaked, 'deep, dark sleep!'

Stypiotes scowled at him. 'Stop talkin' about it!'

'But I need to do something; every time I stare out at the darkness I start to nod off.' Peleus stopped, noticing Stypiotes' eyes widening. 'Stypiotes?'

'Somethin' moved, behind you!'

Peleus spun on his heel, nothing was there, but a small, round pebble spun on the spot, slowing then stopping. Stypiotes stalked over to Peleus' side of the gate and the pair braced, holding their spears out, eyes prying into the blackness.

They did not notice the black-cloaked, and stealthy figure that climbed to perch on the edge of the gate. Nor did they hear the figure drop silently out of the camp and then sprint, bare-footed, into the night, slipping into the wilderness.

'Ah, it's nothing,' Peleus said, pointing back into the camp. 'Look, it must have been one of the lads acting up.'

Stypiotes screwed his eyes up to peer at the shadowy figure that stood just to the side of the central walkway, glaring at the pair and the fleeing figure's wake. 'Who's that?' he barked, unable to make out the features of the man.

But the shadow melted into the darkness without reply.

–

Night passed in a heartbeat and Apion did not sleep, instead lying, eyes wide open, bathed in a slick of sweat. Packs of wild dogs howled in the brush and every one struck panic into his heart. Then the buccina cry had split the air at the first orange of dawn. But instead of the usual morning roll-call, it was the emergency call for muster. At once the camp sprung to life in a babble of shouting and clattering of iron.

'To your feet!' Apion shouted to the nine men of his kontoubernion.

Footsteps, panting and a gruff horking up of phlegm sounded outside and then came a familiar voice. 'Where's the pointy-faced bastard?' Procopius croaked, poking his head into the tent, wiping the sleep from his eyes. 'He's not in his tent. A bit keen to get promoted is he?'

Apion pushed out from the tent, heart thumping. 'What do you mean?' He shot a furtive glance to each side of the camp. Good, he thought, no commotion and no sign of Bracchus.

Sha was there, pulling on his klibanion, looking round, face wrinkling. 'Nepos? No, I haven't seen him either.'

Blastares stumbled from his tent, frowning, lifting a finger to point at Apion.

Panicked, Apion cut in. 'Blastares?'

'My head is pounding!' the big man groaned, rubbing a hand over a purple lump on his temple. 'If that's not bad enough it looks like some bugger stole my cloak as well. Last thing I remember is staggering to the latrines. And before that I had this disturbing dream about you, pressing my bladder!'

Apion disguised his relief.

'Bloody ale!' Blastares continued. 'Though if I see some whoreson nicking around in my cloak I'll fuc—'

A second buccina cry pierced the air, drowning out his words.

'It'll have to wait,' Apion said. 'Come on, something big is happening!'

—

By the time dawn was fully upon them, the Chaldian Thema stood in formation, the only noises were of horses scuffing and snorting and the iron rattle of armour. The ranks were tense; nobody knew for sure why the emergency muster call had been used, but many craned their necks to scan the horizon outside the camp. Empty.

Then Cydones and Ferro strode to the front of the army. 'This morning, we seize our destiny!' The strategos gave one of his customary pauses before continuing. 'The dawn scouting party has returned. The Seljuk army has been located. Some eight miles to the south. We are in fine shape, men. Fine shape to seize victory. We march to victory, and God marches with us!'

Apion's eyes narrowed. The strategos' rhetoric seemed to rouse the ranks, but he knew that if the numbers of the Seljuk horde were to be believed then the wives and mothers of Chaldia would lose a lot of husbands and sons today. The defeated Colonea Thema had numbered not much less than the army mustered here today, he shivered, remembering the swarm of carrion birds that had feasted on their corpses. Then something caught his eye. He glanced over the ranks. There, about twelve men to his left, stood Bracchus at the head of the tourma. The tourmarches stared dead ahead, face pointed and cold, no hint of emotion.

He closed his eyes and prayed that Nepos was far to the west by now. He had his story ready: he had slit Nepos' throat in the darkness and dropped his body into the latrine pits. Now he just had to avoid Bracchus until the latrine pits were filled in, so his story could not be refuted.

Then realisation sparked in his mind; it could all end today – the clash with Tugrul's hordes presented the opportunity he had been waiting for. He flexed his fingers on his scimitar hilt and prayed that the battle would see him and Bracchus in close proximity.

CHAPTER 20

The Falcon's Hordes

The war drums rumbled in the intense morning heat and Tugrul's Seljuk horde shimmered like an ethereal mirage across the plain. *By God let the heat be exaggerating their number,* Apion thought as he studied their ranks. At least twenty-five thousand, they didn't just blanket the horizon, they seemed to be swallowing it, arcing around the land to cover three sides of the Byzantine square formation. The Seljuk flags with the golden bow emblem licked at the sky like an inferno.

'We need more men,' Blastares said in a low tone, swatting at the incessant cloud of black flies attacking his face.

It was what they were all thinking, Apion was sure. His bandon were placed at the south-eastern corner of the square, facing towards the right arm of the Seljuk arc. His trusted three stood alongside him at the head of their files, the other files making up the bandon on either side. Every man on the front rank had been afforded an iron klibanion to go with the red sash that marked them out as dekarchoi. Those in the ranks behind had to make do with padded jackets or vests and the knowledge that they were marginally less likely to die than their officers. This and all the other banda of the thema formed the outer wall of the square. Inside the iron-human bulwark, the toxotai and light infantry waited, knowing they would have to slip outside the square to shower their missiles on the approaching enemy before slipping back inside when the two forces clashed. In the centre of the square, beside the cluster of medical tents, artillerymen and supply wagons, the kataphractoi and the mercenary Pecheneg horsemen waited patiently; they were to be the hammer that would sally forth from the formation and then strike the enemy upon the anvil of the infantry square.

Upon sighting Tugrul's horde on the horizon, Cydones had not hesitated in making the call to fall into this classic defensive formation, but as expected, morale dipped at the order. Yet Apion could see straight away that the strategos had no choice due to weight of numbers; the army they now faced had only a week previously utterly destroyed the army of the Colonea Thema. They were Tugrul's finest, not the light ghazi riders but the elite and shimmering ghulam, equal in every way to the kataphractoi. They were armed with fine composite bows, scimitars and well-honed spears and their number was far greater than the clutch of one thousand riders Cydones had at his disposal. Yet the meat of the Seljuk army was in the swell of iron-scale-clad akhi infantry, thousands upon thousands of them, at least four men to every one of the thema skutatoi. The enemy ahead troubled Apion – perhaps no Byzantine soul on this plain would live beyond today – what troubled him more though, was the enemy behind. He had caught sight of the distinctive golden plumage of Bracchus only fleetingly since they had adopted this formation, floating somewhere by the back ranks of the bandon to the right of Apion's. The tourmarches was responsible for the four banda on this side of the square. *Close enough*, Apion decided. But perhaps this was all meaningless thought, he mused. The massive Seljuk horde had the manpower to crush the Byzantine square swiftly if they were orchestrated in just the right way.

He wondered what the *Falcon* would be thinking right now as he eyed this Byzantine square from across the plain. His eyes narrowed, again considering the blurring of the Seljuk banners in the heat haze. An idea formed in his mind. They could not increase their number, but they could induce over-confidence from the Seljuks. He called to a scout rider and gave a message to be passed back to the strategos.

As the scout rider set off, Apion twisted round to see the mounted, green-cloaked and green-plumed Cydones, mail veil across his face, flicking his attention across his lines from every angle, as if searching for something he had lost. This was the strategos' real-life shatranj board.

'Kataphractoi,' Cydones roared, waving a hand to the left wing of the formation. He made a pushing motion and the rider by his side waved his banner towards the southern and northern sides of the square that would effectively be the Byzantine flanks. Like iron-scaled creatures, each of the two cavalry wings moved out, away from the centre of the square, to position themselves by the gaps among the banda on those sides.

Apion wondered at the strategos' plans. The key would be to lure the Seljuks into making the first move, to make them present a weak spot in what looked like a wall of iron. They would only do so if the Byzantines themselves offered a weakness. Shatranj indeed.

Then he noticed the scout rider talking to the strategos. Cydones seemed to consider the message for a moment, then nodded and raised his sword. 'Banda!' he roared. 'Lower every second standard then close the gaps between.' A buccina keened a series of notes to reinforce the order.

Apion bristled with pride. The strategos had taken his advice. In the heat haze the Seljuks would doubtless be struggling to ascertain the exact number of Byzantine banda they faced. Thus lowering every second standard meant the Seljuks would be likely to count only half the true number of that stood in opposition to them. It was a glimmer of hope. The lure was set.

'Engineers, mark our range!' the strategos yelled back over his shoulder. The ground shuddered and a cracking of stone and grinding of dust rang out. The banda on the front of the square parted and ten clusters of siege engineers strained behind their ballistae, small wooden wagons with yawning timber bows mounted horizontally across them.

'Come within three stadia and you'll get a bolt through your chest.' Procopius nudged Apion with an elbow. 'Finely constructed aren't they? Could do with a couple of trebuchets too, even just to scare the shit out of them, eh?'

Apion nodded at the old soldier's words; the giant stone throwers, the city-takers as they were called, were capable of hurling man-sized rocks over eight hundred feet. Almost four times the height of a man and with a throwing arm the same height again, they could shatter men and walls alike. But they were rarely brought out for a field battle given their monstrous weight, questionable accuracy and lack of manoeuvrability, even when deconstructed.

Then the ballistae fired, bolts whistling through the air and troughing into the ground between the Byzantine front lines and the Seljuks, sending puffs of dust from the earth where they landed.

'Let's see how brave they are now, eh?' Blastares said.

'Aye but let's hope first they don't have any long-range devices of their own,' Procopius countered.

'I suppose,' Blastares grudgingly backed down, fleetingly eyeing the skyline for any sign of approaching missiles.

Apion offered a sly grin at Procopius; not many could shut Blastares up with one line. Then he noticed a group of some fifteen unarmoured men shuffling forward, each stooped under the weight of the iron cylinders they carried, flexible piping coiling from the tip of the cylinders to a handle on the side, some kind of pump for whatever was inside. Apion assumed they were some kind of devices to aid the ballistae. When the men carrying them forked out to stand not on the front of the square with the artillery, but on the flanks, one just to the side of his own bandon, he cocked an eyebrow.

'You've never seen the Greek fire before?' Procopius asked. 'Because when you have seen it, you'll never forget.'

The old soldier's words were drowned out by the gallop of the Byzantine scout riders, who hared out into no-man's land, unarmoured, bearing only a clutch of spears with strips of purple cloth tied to their base. One by one, the test missiles were located and marked by a spear.

'How much do you reckon he's holding back?' Procopius squinted over at the strategos.

'Holding back?' Apion asked.

Procopius smirked wryly. 'I reckon there's another hundred, hundred and fifty feet in those devices if we get the right tension.'

'I pray you're right,' Sha muttered, his attention taken by the sudden rippling on the Seljuk horizon. 'They're coming!'

'And we're waiting,' Apion spoke evenly. Then the Seljuk war horns moaned like an army of lost spirits. Apion's skin rippled and the ground started to shake as if a thousand titans were coming for them. The ethereal blur on the horizon sharpened and the closer the mass came, the more ferocious it appeared. He glanced along his ranks: the skutatoi were braced, faces etched with doubt. A murmur of fear rippled through the air. This would be his first full-scale battle and as an officer too. Doubt surfaced in his mind and his tongue shrivelled in his mouth. At the same time he tried to resist squirming as his bladder seemed to have swollen suddenly, pressing, demanding to be relieved.

'Ha, not so funny now, is it?' Blastares whispered, leaning in to him. 'Don't worry, you'll get used to it. By the time you've got blades swinging in your face, it'll be the least of your worries. Besides, one of their lot might be kind enough to open your bladder for you.'

He turned to Blastares and saw the grin of nervous excitement and determination on the big soldier's face. Hearing words of encouragement being shouted by komes up and down the front line, he realised that the rest of his bandon needed to feel ready like Blastares. He turned to them and to a man, their eyes were fixed on him, expectant. He gulped back the terror that tried to catch his tongue, took a breath deep in his lungs and drew his eyes across their number, then bellowed. 'Stay strong in your hearts, men. The *Falcon* of the proud Seljuks comes to show us his power, but we have our mighty strategos,' he stabbed his scimitar towards Cydones, 'the legend of Chaldia!'

Blastares gripped his shoulder and punched a fist into the air. 'And we have the *Haga*! The ferocious two-headed eagle flies with us!'

Apion's bandon erupted in a cheer, rousing and far louder than the surrounding units. Then the banda flanking his also erupted in a cheer. '*Stra-te-gos, Stra-te-gos!*' was mixed with chants of '*Ha-ga!*'

'Just remember,' Blastares added with a wink to Apion on one side and Sha on the other, 'I've got your flanks covered. You cover mine, eh?'

Apion flashed a grin in return but the burly soldier's words were drowned out by the Seljuk advance, as the war horns died the trilling battle cry of the Seljuk infantry filled in with an even greater noise. The Seljuks were still within a fair distance of the outer artillery range markers when another buccina wail came from Cydones' cavalry wing. At once the artillery units buzzed around their devices and, like an angry snake, the line of ballistae recoiled across the square front. To a man, the Byzantine square held their breath. Then the Seljuk infantry centre was riven with a series of troughs, the dust thrown up tinged with crimson and the air filled with screaming.

'And again!' Procopius yelled, bashing his sword hilt on his shield. The rest of the ranks around them joined in the chorus of celebration. But when Apion glanced to Procopius, the old soldier's face had returned to its usual puckered expression.

'Procopius?'

The old soldier leaned into his ear. 'We'll take encouragement where we can get it, but Tugrul isn't that stupid. They're testing our true range at the expense of a few hundred cheap infantrymen.'

Apion squinted until he could see the battered Seljuk front ranks: barely armed men, similar to the Byzantine light infantry. Some clutched daggers, some were empty handed. Behind them, the glimmering ranks of iron-clad soldiers were untouched and safely out of range.

'How can they fight for their leader when he treats them like that?' Apion barked through the dust cloud that whipped back over the thema ranks.

'They've got no choice. Beggars, brigands and the like,' Sha said. 'They run forward, they may live. They run back, they will die. Tugrul demands, they obey.' Volley after volley of ballista bolts pummelled the wretches and the sun was dulled momentarily by the dust thrown up. The thick ranks of Seljuk light infantry were already in chaos. Those who chose to continue forward slowed as their fleeing colleagues hared past them in the opposite direction. At the same time, the Seljuk archers loosed volley after volley of arrows into the deserters. Chaos reigned.

'Bastards!' Blastares spat. 'A few less mouths to feed, that's all they were brought here for.'

Apion wondered at the men of the light infantry in the Byzantine ranks, currently tucked inside the skutatoi outer wall. On another day would they not have been committed to death in the same fashion? Mansur's words echoed in his mind. *These are the choices of the strategos.*

There was then a lull until the dust cloud swept past them. The cream of the Seljuk ranks stood, still cupped in a crescent like a viper's jaws around the rough crater of the longest lying ballista strikes. The Byzantine cheers fell flat and the plain was still and silent. Then, suddenly, the silence was shattered with the terrible wail of the war horns and raucous jeering of the Seljuk ranks. The Byzantine buccinators filled their lungs and blasted a howling response from their instruments. The Chi-Rho banner bearing the image of the Virgin Mary was hoisted high in the air and, to a man, the thema cried out in defiance.

'Clever buggers,' Procopius roared over the cacophony.

Apion assumed Procopius was talking of the Seljuk's wise decision to keep their best men out of ballista range, but then he followed the old soldier's gaze; his eyes were still narrowed on the artillery squads, who had remained at their machinery, knuckles white. Added to this, Cydones was poised, one hand gripping the reins of his mount, the other ready to be raised to give an order, eyes darting along the enemy lines as the Seljuk cavalry filed into a high flanking position, ready for the kill.

The Seljuk flags for the advance were being hoisted, war horns being brought to mouths.

Then the strategos' cry pierced the air. 'Again! Loose!'

The air was filled with the coordinated twang and pained creaking of the ballistae as all of the devices shot their missiles, this time they exploited the absolute maximum range and the extra fraction of tension that Cydones had secretly asked them to withhold in the last barrage. The effect was devastating. On the front foot, the Seljuk ranks were caught cold by the hail and despite their fine armour, the first ten ranks of densely packed heavy infantry were shattered like toys, men were sprayed into the air and officers skewered. There was no let-up; as the Seljuk infantry curled around to flee, they stumbled over the dead, fell to the dust and blocked those behind. Then the artillery barked once more and another wave of desolation ruptured the Seljuk lines.

'Double bluff,' Apion whispered as he eyed the strategos, sat motionless in the saddle, plume flitting in the breeze.

'Led them right into it,' Procopius was grinning like a shark.

To a man, the thema roared. '*Stra-te-gos! Stra-te-gos! Stra-te-gos!*'

Cydones wheeled round on his mount and pumped a fist in the air. The words tumbled from Apion's chest too. '*Stra-te-gos! Stra-te-gos!*'

The ballistae hail slowed, leaving a carpet of gore across the plain. Apion wondered how many they had taken from the Seljuk number. At least a quarter of the infantry, he hoped. But the ballistae had fallen silent, and were now being rolled back inside the square.

At this, the shimmering band of Seljuks rippled, units reorganising and repositioning, no doubt lifting their dead back from their lines. Then they were still again, a dense wall. Many of their number had fallen but many more still stood. Too many.

'This is it,' Apion said.

'By your side, sir!' Sha replied, steadying himself, pressing his shoulder against Apion's, just as they had practised. Procopius and Blastares bunched up likewise and the whole bandon followed suit, as did the rest of the outer square.

Then the war horns cried again. The trilling Seljuk war cry filled the air once more and immediately the akhi infantry poured towards the front of the square and the ghulam wings rushed for the flanks.

As the ground shook, Apion heard the strategos' cry over the din of thundering hooves. 'Kataphractoi, break!' Cydones bellowed. The order was reaffirmed by a buccina blast and at once the two wings of cavalry burst from the flanks of the square, the Pechenegs following Ferro's wing. They sped out beyond the pincers of the closing Seljuk arc.

'Where d'they think they're going?' a soldier yelped from behind Apion.

The rest of skutatoi around Apion murmured in concern and this grew into a panicked squabble as the jaws of the Seljuk arc raced ever closer. He blocked out his own creeping doubt and pictured himself as an eagle soaring, seeing the field from high above. Clarity soothed his doubts. 'They're positioning to counter the Seljuk charge. It's just as we've trained for since the mustering, but this is for real.' He barked back to the dissenting voices. This seemed to ease their concern a little. 'We pin the enemy on our spears, then the strategos and his riders will hit them in the flanks and from the rear, cut them to pieces!' His tone sounded firm and assured, but inside he knew it was all too simple to speak of how things should work. Added to that, the bulk of the men who stood in the ranks had been farming in the five years since the last campaign and had only had a handful of sessions of training since being rounded up by Cydones. The men of the garrison – those in the front ranks – would be critical, he realised.

Perched at the corner of the square, Apion's eyes were fixed on the riders thundering for them, but he was all too aware of the dark mass of infantry growing in his peripheral vision. The *Falcon*'s claws were closing around them. The banda at the front of the square opened to allow the light infantry to rush out, ready to meet the Seljuk infantry advance with their axes, slings, bows and javelins. Meanwhile, the toxotai spread themselves thinly around the inside of the square, giving scant but welcome archer cover to all sides. Apion then glanced to the closing gap at the pincers of the Seljuk arc, spotting Cydones' standard shrinking as the cavalry wings burst clear of the noose just in time.

'He's drawing them out,' Blastares growled. 'Less for us to bloody our swords on!'

Apion craned to Blastares' height to see. The back ranks of the Seljuk ghulam cavalry had indeed peeled off to meet the threat, but the dense front ranks of the riders were only a handful of paces away. Thousands of them, spears lowered, hurtling forward to smash the square. A sea of taut bows rippled up from the rear of the ghulam charge and then at once the twang of a thousand bows filled the air.

'Shields!' Apion cried, glancing up just in time to see the dark storm cloud of arrows that hurtled for them. He wrenched his shield up and three iron tips hammered into its surface an instant later. His heart thundered, hearing the choking cries of the stricken; if the ghulam wished they could wheel back and forth from the Byzantine square, firing upon the banda until their quivers were empty, thinning the skutatoi at their leisure. The hail slowed and he looked up, eyes widening at the snarling wall of riders, spears lowered for the charge. No, the ghulam were not for waiting, he realised with a swirl of terror and hubris, they were coming for the kill. The dark door rushed for him, the knotted arm punched forward to knock it from its hinges, the fire engulfed him.

'Rhiptaria ready, loose! Front ranks, brace!' he roared. The front two ranks rippled, kontarion spears jutting forward like a porcupine. At the same time, the ranks behind coiled and then hurled their throwing spears like a dark cloud and these were joined by the arrow hail from the toxotai.

The rhiptaria hammered home, punching Seljuk riders from their mounts, smashing through bone and sending jets of crimson into the air, stopping many a man and beast in their tracks, terrible whinnying and screaming ringing out. Then the hail slowed until it was only the thin spray of archer fire: the Seljuk riders were thinned, but only a little.

The ghulam wall hurtled forward. Apion grappled his kontarion and braced for the impact. Dead ahead, a conical-helmed and scale–clad giant of a rider on a frothing stallion, demonic behind an iron-plate mask, hooves rapping like hammers on the earth, burst a few strides ahead of the charge. The rider then made to leap the spear wall and plunge into the bandon. With a roar, Apion and the men of the front line punched their spears forward. The impact was colossal, Apion felt his entire body jar and he was thrown back as the mount was punctured through the chest by the spear thrusts, some of the shafts snapping. The rider was thrown into the bandon where he was butchered in an instant.

Apion staggered to his feet and his heart froze; the front line of the bandon was broken and the rest of the ghulam charge was only strides away. He lunged forward to rip an unbroken kontarion from the convulsing stallion, then pressed up against the next nearest skutatos, others bunching up on his other side.

'Come on then, you whoresons!' he roared with all the breath in his lungs.

With that, the Seljuk charge smashed home and the land turned red.

Byzantines disappeared under hooves, heads spun free of bodies, riders were thrown from their horses to skate across shields or to be catapulted into the Byzantine ranks.

The bandon could not hold its shape due to the weight of the charge and dissolved into a swirl of combat. Apion smelt the hot and sour breath of the Seljuk steed pressed against him. The skutatos engaged with the rider fought manfully, but was then struck with a death blow, cleaved from shoulder to stomach, sending gristle and gut slapping across Apion's face. Apion pounced on the rider's momentary distraction to smash his shield boss into the mount's mouth, and then leapt to pull the rider from his horse. But the rider smashed his scimitar hilt into Apion's temple, felling him to the dust. Blinded by the blow and seeing only the dark shape of the mount rounding on him, he jabbed out with his spear. Hooves smashed down by his head and he rolled clear, then a spear ripped down past his shield, through a plate in his klibanion and across his ribcage to crack into the ground. The blood soaked him and his own pained snarl barely registered in the cacophony all around him. Still grounded, he glanced around to find his lines; skutatoi boots stamped and skidded several paces away, then bodies fell in a mire of skin, white bone, grey matter and pink tissue as the Byzantine line compressed under the charge. The spear shot for him again and in a clatter of wood and iron, his shield shattered. When the spear came again, it was aimed right at his heart, the snarling features of the rider behind the thrust. This time he butted the shaft with his palms, diverting the thrust into the ground, and then he heaved on the shaft with all his weight to pull himself to standing, dragging the spear from the rider's grasp. The rider fumbled for his sword but Apion leapt up, ripping his scimitar from its scabbard and plunging the blade into the rider's chest. A blood cloud burst over the riders behind as the body slid and thudded into the carpet of gore, convulsing.

His limbs shaking, his mind roaring, Apion looked up for his next opponent. At that moment the furore of the battle fell away.

He saw Bracchus.

The tourmarches was barely ten paces away, panting, teeth bared, blood coating his face. Apion locked eyes with Bracchus. This was the moment he had prayed for. He stalked forward, gripping his scimitar so hard that his arm trembled. Then a blur of movement caught his eye: a wedge of ghulam galloped for Bracchus and Apion saw that the tourmarches was the one man plugging a gap between two banda. His mind raced. If the ghulam got inside the square, the battle was lost, every Byzantine was as good as dead. But revenge was right here for the taking. *Kill him*, the now familiar voice rasped in his head. He hefted his kontarion like a throwing spear, eyes still fixed on the master Agente, then hoisted it forward with all his might.

Bracchus' eyes bulged and his mouth opened to scream, when the spear travelled over his head and into the stomach of the lead rider of the ghulam wedge. The rider fell with a cry, pulling his mount's reins with him, the beast tumbling with a pained whinny under the hooves of the mounts behind it. At once the wedge dissolved into a mass of felled riders and thrashing beasts. A group of skutatoi rushed forward to despatch them. The square was saved.

Bracchus was left standing, gawping at him, the blood of the felled ghulam dripping from his brow. Apion realised he had saved the tourmarches' life. Then the rasping voice cried in his thoughts. *And now it is time to take it!*

Apion lurched forward, eyes fixed on the tourmarches. He realised that the Seljuk riders closing on either side of him, scimitars raised, would cut himself and Bracchus off from the square, and doubtless hack the pair to pieces, but Apion was sure he could strike the master Agente down by his own hand first. If he was to die here too then so be it; as long as none of Bracchus' contacts knew of the true manner of the master Agente's death on the battlefield. Bracchus' glare curled into a frown as Apion approached. He held his expression blank until he was within striking distance, then filled his lungs to scream. But at the moment he made to raise his sword, something barged him to one side.

Apion gasped, startled; one of the soldiers bearing the curious cylinders had shoulder-charged him from the sword-swipe of a ghulam. Now the man pushed up to be back-to back with him, lifting the nozzle, waving it at the circling riders, a lit torch in his other hand.

'Stay with me, sir!' the man cried.

Apion shot glances all around but in the blur of swirling cavalry, Bracchus had disappeared back into the square.

The cylinder-bearing soldier then pressed a lever attached to the nozzle. 'Brace yourself, sir!' What happened next matched the fury in Apion's mind: like a demon serpent, fire spewed from the device, engulfing more than ten ghulam riders, each one igniting like a torch. The air rippled in the intense heat as the riders' screams peaked and then stopped suddenly, blackened bodies crunching onto the ground with a stench of burning flesh, horses fleeing, whinnying in terror, still ablaze.

The ghulam riders behind hesitated. Then, like an ebb tide, the Seljuk horsemen wheeled to turn away, their leader crying out an order.

'They're retreating!' one voice roared in hope.

But Apion heard and understood the ghulam cry. *Their square is faltering. Reform and then crush them with another charge!*

Looking to either side, Sha, Blastares and Procopius still stood, but he could see huge gaps where previously there had been a white-sashed komes at the head of each bandon. The officers of the other banda had fallen in heavy number with the charge and the ranks seemed to be hesitant as the riders withdrew. *Now*, Apion realised, *Now is the crucial moment.* To allow the cavalry to disengage and then charge once more to equally devastating effect would be the end, for certain.

'Don't let them pull back! Charge!' he roared.

He was already running forward, breaking from the ranks, scimitar drawn, blood hammering in his ears. He leapt for the back of the nearest ghulam and wrapped an arm around the rider's waist, pulling him to the dust and punching the scimitar into his throat. Like a wall of fury, the Byzantine line swept along behind him, leaping for the Seljuk riders before they could break away. Men screamed in bloodlust and battle horses whinnied in agony as iron upon iron rang out, sword on sword, spears breaking through bone. The Byzantine line bit hungrily and the Seljuk riders fell in their hundreds, hamstrung by the strike.

The fire raged in Apion's veins and his limbs numbed, feeling only the dull judder of his scimitar as it struck through armour and flesh again and again, while the screaming of the Seljuks rang out unbroken. Then the earth rumbled once more. Apion's blood ran cold and he looked up. But what he saw filled his heart with hope: barely a hundred feet away, Cydones led his kataphractoi from the tip of a wedge as they galloped at full pelt for the disarray of the Seljuk cavalry retreat. The strategos' eyes were narrowed and he lay low in his saddle, spear dipped, cloak billowing in his wake. The riders to the rear of the wedge were upright, arrows nocked to bows and then loosed as one dark cloud. The disorder that was the Seljuk cavalry line fell into utter chaos under the resultant hail, then they crumpled as Cydones' wedge hammered into them, momentum overcoming numbers. Men flew from their horses, shields splintered; bodies of riders and horse alike were swept under the stampede of Byzantine hooves. Apion hacked and stabbed and the Seljuk ranks seemed to vanish before him. At last he pulled upon the reins of a Seljuk mount, hauled himself onto its back and heeled the beast into a charge for the last clutch of ghulam. One swiped for him and he parried, then ripped his blade across the rider's throat, the blood spraying across his eyes. As the body toppled and the ghulam broke into a retreat, Apion raised his sword to strike his next opponent, but was faced with Cydones, braced and dripping in crimson like some gory reflection.

All around the battered Byzantine square, the Seljuk ranks broke into a panicked retreat, harried by Ferro's riders and the Pechenegs. Cries of victory rang out all around Apion and the strategos. '*Nobiscum Deus!*'

Both men's eyes stayed fixed on each other as they panted, teeth gritted.

After what seemed like an eternity, the cheering died and the army broke out in a hoarse and baritone chant of the ritual thanksgiving to God. The prayer made the land tremble and Apion shuddered as the dark door swung shut. He held up his sword hand, the muscles knotted with tension and laced with a myriad of new cuts, the blood mixing with the red ink of the *Haga* stigma.

Then his eyes dropped to the prayer rope; it seemed to be biting into his wrist. The stench of burning flesh was rife and all around, and a carpet of dead eyes stared up at him.

—

The spacious pavilion tent provided cool respite from the afternoon sun. Apion swirled his cup, the wine was spicy. Even the few sips he had taken had him feeling giddy. He welcomed the intoxication, washing the bloody events of the day from his eyes and softening the cries of the wounded around the camp.

'A young lad might want to water his wine,' Cydones said, tearing at a chunk of bread.

'Don't discourage him, sir,' Ferro winked, tilting the wineskin into Apion's cup once more.

'I think I've learned my lesson when it comes to ale and wine, sir.' He cocked an eyebrow, remembering the foul illness that seemed to cling to his whole body for a full day after the evening drinking in Trebizond.

'You've learned many lessons, it seems.'

Apion studied his cup, still uncomfortable with praise.

'The men are talking about you again. That call for the counter-charge was pivotal, Apion. Without it, we may not be sat here right now. It's a special officer who can apply such thinking to his actions *and* inspire men to follow him. The *Haga* indeed!' Cydones chuckled and swigged at his wine.

Apion remembered the battle like a vicious nightmare. For all the blood that was spilled, Bracchus still lived. The glory was meaningless. 'Anyone could have made that call, sir.'

Cydones smirked. 'They could have but they didn't. You did. That was an impressive act of courage and I admire you for it, I really do. You could have died on the end of a hundred Seljuk lances for that moment of inspiration. And most often those overcome by bloodlust do tend to find the blood they seek – their own!'

Ferro chuckled and crunched into a fresh loaf of bread. 'Aye, but what a swordsman… from what I've heard anyway.'

Apion knew from his aching limbs that he had fought well. He made to sit a little taller but winced as the movement caused his bandaged ribs to rub together. His old, serrated scar would have many cousins now.

'I saw it, Ferro. The lad was like a demon in the ranks! But as I say, that's not the reason Apion is here. We've got plenty of good fighters.' The strategos leaned forward. 'It's good men and good thinkers that we need. That charge, it wasn't just bravado, was it?'

Apion looked up; the strategos' eyes sparkled. He thought of the shatranj board. 'It was a simple decision really, if they had come again, our square would have collapsed.'

'It is simple,' Cydones nodded, '*if* you can see the field in your mind. Impossible if you cannot. You would not have been able to orchestrate a rabble of bloodied and emotional men if you shared their state of mind. That is what makes you special, Apion. And the call to drop every second bandon? I salute you for that.'

'Aye, you'll be in for a long game tonight, sir.' Ferro nodded to the wooden shatranj box on the table beside Cydones. 'I've heard he has quite a talent for it.'

'No surprise,' Cydones nodded sternly. 'He had a fine teacher.'

As the strategos opened the box to reveal a polished marble chequered surface, he started to place beautifully carved marble pieces on opposing sides of the board. 'Tugrul is formidable, a shrewd man with a long trail of victories behind him, but today he was a fool. He let his guard down and assumed he would win an easy victory because of his numerical superiority. One slip, after years of seeming invincibility. That's all it takes to turn a legend into a fool. He may have survived the battle going by the scout reports, but his reputation died today.'

'Then he will be wounded, sir. A wounded enemy is to be feared. The need for vengeance is like a disease.'

Cydones nodded, face falling stony. 'I fear as you do that we have only injured the *Falcon*. Yet the thema cannot remain fully mobilised, the lands need to be tended to keep the populace fed. So the ranks are to return to their lands, but on high alert. Garrisons will be tripled and the forts will be rebuilt and manned where the budget will allow it. We will be ready for the next wave of invasion. Today was but the first wind of the storm.'

'Many died today, sir.' Apion had washed in a stream but could still smell the metallic stench of the day's gore. 'I slew more than I could count, but I can still see each of their faces.'

'I have the faces of thousands in my head, Apion.' Cydones nodded solemnly. 'They talk with me in my sleep. I can offer them no answers.' The strategos placed each of the pawns on the board carefully, then looked up. 'That's something you can change, Apion. One man can save thousands of lives.'

'Or end them,' Apion added abruptly, remembering Mansur's words.

Cydones nodded. He held the cavalry shatranj piece before placing it down. 'To do the former, you need the right tools.' He placed the cavalry piece on the board. 'You are to be a rider, Apion.'

Ferro clapped a hand on his shoulder and left the tent with a chuckle. Apion's skin tingled.

'I have a fine chestnut Thessallian gelding, ideal for your new role.'

Apion searched the strategos' eyes.

'You led men well today. A bandon followed you, yes, but those around your bandon followed you also.' He leaned forward. 'They fought for you, Apion. A man who can lead many banda makes a fine tourmarches. Like Ferro, you will lead an army for me as part of the thema. You will report to me, directly.'

Apion's body was numbing with the wine but his mind reeled. Then he thought of the reality of it.

'But I have been a komes for such a short time, sir. The men, they respect me and I know they will follow me, but would this not stretch their loyalty too far?'

'Your words echo my doubts, Apion, when I was promoted from a skutatos to a strategos in the space of a few years. But you can lead them. You know this, you have already said it: you command respect,' Cydones' face fell firm, 'and you have the mind to lead them wisely. And one day you will lead the thema, Apion, you will be a strategos. I know this now.'

Apion nodded, Cydones belief in him was like a tonic. He wondered how the strategos could be so sure.

'So you accept the role, soldier?' Cydones said.

Apion's first thoughts were of the men who had supported him. Good men. 'If I am to be a tourmarches then I want my men with me,' he spoke firmly. 'They've got something, each and every one of them. I want them alongside me.'

Cydones held out his hands. 'Ferro has been my right-hand man since I was in the ranks, Apion. I understand completely.'

'Then I gladly accept the role, sir.' He leaned forward, then thought of the missing man of his trusted four. Had Nepos made it to the farm safely? Then he looked up at the strategos; was this the juncture to speak candidly with Cydones about Bracchus? He opened his mouth to speak, leaning forward, when a pair of bloodied and bandaged tourmarchai strode into the tent, jabbering and hauling documents and bags of coins. He shook his head, now was not the time. But seeking out Nepos could not wait. 'But I must ask for one more thing: will you grant me a leave of absence, before I take up my new position, a week at most? There is something I must tend to, back home.'

'Granted,' Cydones nodded, 'and be sure to come back focused and ready for the struggle that lies ahead.'

Apion sucked in a deep breath. 'I will, sir.'

–

Apion left the tent and headed for the latrines, walking through the sea of bandaged and bloody men being attended to by the medics.

'God bless you, sir.' One man held out his hand. 'You saved us!'

Apion clasped the man's hand, his brow furrowed at the praise after such bloody work. As he walked on more and more men called out to him, then a chant started. '*Ha-ga! Ha-ga!*'

He was glad to be clear of the men as he reached the latrines, then a familiar voice barked at him.

'Congratulations on your promotion… sir.'

Apion turned to face Bracchus. His eyes searched the tourmarches' face. For once, his nemesis' expression was blank, the inky pools of his eyes empty. The he saw it, something buried deep inside, just the merest glint of some long-buried sadness.

Apion swallowed his hatred for an instant. 'Thank you, sir.'

'And you saved my life as well. I should thank you for that.'

Apion wondered at how to reply to this. 'I am a soldier, I carried out my duty. Now, I have been granted leave,' Apion said, his chest tightening as he saw Bracchus' features harden back to that familiar, icy expression. 'I imagine we will speak again when I return?'

Bracchus fixed his eyes on Apion. 'Perhaps…'

Apion frowned as the tourmarches walked away.

CHAPTER 21

The Journey Home

The army had reached the crossroads after three days' march to the west. Here, the bulk of the thema made their own way back to their farmsteads, while three banda were sent to garrison Argyroupolis and further divisions were sent to bolster the other forts, towns and cities of the thema against any sudden Seljuk counterattack. After this, Apion and Blastares had ridden together on their new mounts for a further four days. The big soldier had asked for and been granted leave to sort out some issue with the plot of farmland he had leased, but had left untended since he had joined the permanent garrison of Argyroupolis. So they were to ride together, through the mountain pass and into the farmlands of the thema, as far as the crossroads for Trebizond. And Apion was grateful for the big man's company.

With the spectre of war temporarily removed, the air had a freshness and lightness, like the land drying after a storm. They had dressed in comfortable linen tunics and felt caps for the first few days – just enough to keep them cool and shade them from the blistering sun – but today, Apion was in his full military garb: tunic, iron klibanion and crimson woollen cloak, boots and leggings, helmet with a scale aventail and a black eagle-feather plume. He wanted to look his best for his return to the farm. He thought back to his recent chat with Cydones over what made a fine soldier: give a man armour and fine weapons and he will be braver and more loyal for it. He wondered at the often rag-tag garb of the banda ranks, far removed from the elite kataphractoi, and he thought back to the damp and mouldy cotton vest and boots Vadim had shoved in his arms on first joining the thema. Then he thought of the shimmering rock he had found up in the mountain cave when sheltering with Kartal the Seljuk. Armour and weapons required funding. Generating funds required initiative. His eyes narrowed. As soon as he returned to the army he would discuss with Cydones the commissioning of new silver and iron mines high up in the mountains, untapped of their riches. Yes, every man in his ranks would march with a fine klibanion, helmet, spathion, good boots and a freshly painted shield.

He sat high and straight in his saddle, remembering Father riding home from campaign like this. Then he shuffled in discomfort as the sweat trickled down his back and the klibanion bit into his neck.

Blastares eyed Apion and chuckled. 'Whoever she is, I hope she's worth it?'

Apion cocked an eyebrow, thinking of Maria. She was worth it. If only she was not to marry his best friend, he mused wryly, then he saw Blastares' wicked grin. 'And I suppose you won't be using your new kit to impress the ladies?'

Blastares shrugged. 'Fair point. As soon as I sort out the patch of dust they gave me instead of a proper farm, and the arsehole kataphractos who leased it to me and now thinks he's my master, then I'll be heading into the city – the wage of a *droungarios* weighs heavy on the purse!'

Apion grinned. Despite the gruffness of the big soldier and his initial doubt at Apion's worthiness, they were like brothers now. Blastares had masked his joy at being promoted to a droungarios, commander of two of Apion's twelve banda, behind a flurry of increasingly sordid insults. But it was the glint in Blastares' eye that told him all he needed to know: he could entrust the big man with his life, just as he could with Sha and Procopius, also newly promoted to the same rank. Then he thought of Nepos, the man who should have shared in the glory with them. Blastares had not brought up the topic of the missing Slav, and Apion guessed this was because the gruff soldier was missing the 'pointy-faced bastard' but did not know how to properly express the sentiment.

His musings were interrupted when Blastares lifted a leg and let rip with a forced release of foul gas. 'I'm not eating hard tack bread again for at least a month...'

Apion cocked an eyebrow, eyeing the empty wine sack jiggling below Blastares' saddle; the bread was doubtless only part responsible for his flatulence.

'...no, I'll be spending my days eating pheasant, then my evenings drinking good wine... and the rest...' He winked, flashing a stumpy-toothed grin and motioning with his hands as if testing two pieces of fruit for ripeness. 'So what's your plan for this spell of leave?'

Apion wished more than anything that the week ahead was for nothing other than spending time with Mansur and Maria. 'Many neglected duties, Blastares, but I'll just be happy to get back to the farm. It's been a while since I rode regularly and my arse is yet to become re-callused from the saddle!'

'Aye,' Blastares snorted, shuffling in his saddle, 'who'd have thought it, eh? Riding like emperors on horses and it feels like you're getting buggered by an elephant. Give me a march any day.'

'Well you're going to have to get used to it, Blastares, we all are. There's going to be a long spell of campaigning when we return at the start of the new moon.'

'Tchoh! Bloody spoil it before it's even started why don't you?' Blastares moaned and then pulled the last of his wineskins from his pack. 'Right, I'm starting early.' With that, he pulled the cork from the skin with a *plunk* and proceeded to gulp at the contents.

The day grew hotter and the dust lined their throats. Then, at last, they reached a crossroads and a desiccated timber signpost with etchings on each of its pointers. Blastares ambled towards the road for Trebizond, then he stopped and turned in his saddle. He cleared his throat and then issued a brisk salute. 'Until the new moon, sir!'

Apion nodded sternly then broke into a grin. He reached out a hand. Blastares looked puzzled at first, then he broke out into a matching grin. The big soldier extended a ham-like hand and clasped Apion's forearm. 'Until the new moon, Blastares. I look forward to serving with you again.'

'I might have sobered up by then.' With that and a throaty cackle, Blastares heeled his mount into a trot onto the highway. Then the big man spurred the beast into a gallop and was soon no more than a dust trail.

Apion watched him go. At last he could think freely without the responsibility of the other men. He heard the faint babble of the Piksidis and a warmth spread in his chest, he sucked in a breath and looked west.

The farm was a short ride away.

But first, he had to seek out Nepos.

—

The ghazi rider slid from his mount and knelt in the centre of the courtyard in front of Muhammud and his broad-shouldered bodyguard, Kilic.

'Speak,' Muhammud said. He kept his voice stern and peered down his nose at the rider, just as his uncle had always taught him. But under his cool facade, his heart thundered; something was very wrong.

The rider craned his neck up. His eye was misted and still seeping from a small cut. His clothes were filthy and his skin caked in dirt and his mount trembled from exhaustion. 'Mighty Alp Arslan, I bring news of Great Sultan Tugrul. The Byzantines were strong, too strong. Our mighty leader has been defeated,' the rider panted.

Muhammud's eyes bulged. Tugrul, the man who had taught him the very essence of honour, had been defeated? Then his blood chilled; had the *Falcon* fallen? *No, it is too soon*, his mind screamed. At the same time, the possibilities raced through his thoughts. *You are their leader, now is your time, Mountain Lion.*

'Does the *Falcon* live?' Muhammud heard his own words, flat and hoarse.

'He lives,' the rider nodded fervently.

He felt a wave of relief, but then a burning shame crept over his skin as he realised he was also disappointed. 'What of his armies now?' he demanded. 'They are regrouped, I presume, but where?'

The rider shook his head. 'The armies were routed, only the Sultan and his retinue remain intact and they have taken refuge in eastern Armenia. The survivors from the ranks, they have scattered and will not be returning. The Sultan, he is…' the rider glanced to Muhammud and then back to the ground, '…he is broken. He spends his nights in silence, gazing to the west. The Byzantine strategos has another who fights by his side. The *Haga*, the ferocious two-headed eagle. The Sultan's men say he fought like a *djinn*, bringing men with him like a wall of fire.'

'Enough!' Muhammud snapped, cutting the rider short and sweeping a platter of goblets and dishes from the table by his side to shatter on the courtyard.

Some twenty-five thousand men. Lost. Whittled down to barely a thousand by the swords of an outlying army of this ancient empire of Byzantium, not even close to their emperor or the seat of power in Constantinople. So his uncle had got it wrong, assuming one army could break Byzantium. *You should have taken me with you, Falcon.*

He glanced up to see Nizam, who had paced silently out behind the rider. The vizier's eyes were heavy and he gave the faintest shake of his head. Muhammud looked from the vizier to the rider and assessed his next move. Word could not spread of the Sultan's defeat. Muhammud sensed a shadow pass over his soul. He had to be a ruthless leader now, like his uncle.

'You rode alone?' he asked the rider, who nodded.

'Take him back to the ranks. Have him bathed, clothed and fed,' he sighed to Kilic. As the giant of a man moved to usher the rider to his feet, Muhammud gave him a firm and familiar nod, eyes cold as ice. Kilic nodded back.

Muhammud turned away and looked to the strategy map laid out on the ground before him. He gazed over the map, then closed his eyes at the gurgling protests of the rider as Kilic tore a blade across the man's throat. When the rider fell silent, he opened his eyes again, looking over the fifty shatranj pieces currently set around the large red dot representing Isfahan. His eyes narrowed; did the Byzantines really believe they had broken the Seljuk spirit, routed the core of their armies? Fire raced through his veins as he thought of the emperor and his armies rejoicing at his uncle's humiliation. But their joy would be short lived; Byzantium had seen but the tip of the blade that was to strike through its heart. He glanced up at the battlements of the city walls and could see the dust haze from the swell of activity outside. Then he barked at Nizam. 'Come with me.'

Muhammud strode from the palace and across the square, ignoring the salutations and cries of praise from the crowds. Then he flitted up the steps to the battlements, Kilic and Nizam hurrying to keep pace with him. At last they stopped as Muhammud rested his palms on the crenelated stonework. 'Yes,' he purred, his eyes sparkling as he drank in the scene before him.

The fertile plain was invisible under a blanket of military: a sea of tents, warhorses, men in shimmering armour and an endless line of siege towers and stone-throwers. He had spent the last months whipping them into a frenzy, telling of the glory to be had in toppling the ancient empire of the west. As the weeks had rolled by and word had spread around the Seljuk lands, new divisions were formed to accommodate the influx of warriors who wanted to be part of this glory, to march with the *Mountain Lion*. He thought again of the strategy map: fifty pieces, each representing two thousand men and all of them hungry. Hungry to crush Byzantium.

'Sultan Tugrul was to call on me when the time was right, to solidify his holdings in Byzantine lands,' he spoke evenly to Nizam. 'Well that call will not now come, but the fruit has never been riper. We will crush those who seek to unhinge our glorious destiny and the *Falcon*'s honour will be restored under my banner. Our siege engines will shatter the crumbling walls of Byzantium's cities and their armies will die under the hail of our arrows.

Should this army of Chaldia, or any other, choose to meet me in the field. Well, then they will face the wrath of the *Mountain Lion!*'

He grappled the Seljuk banner from the nearest guard on the wall and hoisted it up over his head, the golden bow emblem fluttering in the gentle breeze. First the soldiers camped directly below the walls saw it and leapt to their feet, raised a chorus of cheers and rapped their scimitar hilts on their shields. Then, the cacophony rippled outwards across the plain like thunder.

Muhammud glared into the setting sun. This strategos of Chaldia would pay. And the *Haga*, this so-called invincible warrior? Muhammud vowed that he would seek him out and crush his army. Then take his head.

'Glory awaits us in the west!' he cried out to the horde.

The horde cried out until the city walls shook.

Muhammud drank in the scene, eyes wide. Then Kilic leaned in towards him.

'Another rider has come in, master. A straggler from the armies of the *Falcon*.' The bodyguard nodded to the bearded rider who climbed the last of the steps onto the battlements. 'He is alone. Just give the word.' The bodyguard showed Muhammud the dagger tucked into his wristband.

Muhammud nodded to Kilic then frowned, eyeing the rider. He did not seem to be nervous.

The rider knelt on one knee. 'Alp Arslan, I trust you already know of the... situation... in the west?'

Muhammud's eyes narrowed at this. He looked to Kilic, hesitated, then almost imperceptibly shook his head. Kilic's shoulders slumped and the bodyguard moved away. 'I do. So, why do you come before me?' He motioned with his hands for the rider to stand.

The rider stood. 'I am Bey Soundaq, and I have fought in the west for many years now. I come before you to tell you of the man who you must destroy if our glory is to be realised.'

'One man?'

323

'One man, Alp Arslan. I have spoken with him, he is no ordinary soul; he is one man who fights and leads an army like no other I have seen.'

Muhammud's eyes narrowed.

'The *Haga* stands between us and glory.'

Peleus lifted his skin and poured another handful of the brackish water over his face but the desert air dried him like crackling in seconds.

'Bloody murder, this,' Stypiotes croaked, slumping back onto the sand. 'Did I cark it in the battle and get fired down to hell? That's what it bloody feels like. If the strategos reckons this is such a good idea then he should have stayed out here to build the bleedin' towers himself!'

'Well, the strategos likes the new beacon system around the town and this is just an extension to it. Apparently the idea came from Apion,' Peleus said.

'Aye, the *Haga*. Well he's certainly got something about him, I'll give him that. Remember the hobblin' runt that turned up at the town gates last spring? Now he's a tourmarches? That takes some doin'. They're even sayin' he'll be the next strategos. Still though, he could have hauled his arse out here and helped.'

Peleus nodded, eyeing the wooden stumps marking out the four corners of this tower, rope joining them to form a square. He saw the point in the initiative of building the chain of desert watchtowers, but Stypiotes would take none too kindly to being lectured at the moment, he figured.

A bandon of infantry, four master carpenters, two blacksmiths, an architect and an engineer were accompanied by a detachment of fifty kataphractoi and some thirty Armenian camel scout riders. Numbering nearly four hundred, this group had been sent out east by Cydones while the rest of the thema returned to Chaldia. Everyone was less than delighted but the strategos had won over the majority with a promise of triple pay for a month. The idea was to stamp home the advantage gained during the usual lull after such a decisive victory. So while the Seljuks licked their wounds, Byzantium would stake its borders physically with these wooden watchtowers, the lantern chain would act as an early warning system against the next attack, whenever it came. After a few days marching they had now delineated the first leg of the chain, coming in from the borders of Armenia and out into the sands and hills of the eastern reaches of Anatolia.

With a grimace, Stypiotes scratched roughly at his crotch. 'There's no bloody point in wearin' this armour. It makes my arse really itchy in this heat. We could walk about with targets on our backs; there's nobody around for miles. The Seljuks are broken, for now.'

Peleus chuckled and pulled the parcel of smoked fish and dried fruit from his ration pack. Cydones had been keen to give the detachment privileges and these prime rations were one such measure. 'Take a seat, Stypiotes, you're making me nervous pacing around like that and you'll only make yourself hotter.'

'Cah!' the big soldier grunted, flopping down onto the sand next to Peleus. 'Here, let's have some of that.' He pulled a strip of smoked fish for himself. 'I tell you, when you've been dreaming of sitting in the inn at Argyroupolis, sinking wine, cup after cup, before picking your woman, then you get this.' He widened his arms to the endless dunes that rolled out ahead and shook his head.

Peleus wondered just what orders Cydones would relay next. If these watchtowers were to be of any use, someone would have to man them permanently. He felt a moan coming on.

'Peleus, Stypiotes!' a voice called. It was young Atticus the skutatos, on the back of a camel ridden by a swarthy Armenian. 'We're setting up camp at the next watchtower site. The komes wants you to gather your tools and fall in to help prepare the camp.'

'Grand! More graft!' Stypiotes grumbled.

'Come on,' Peleus nudged him with a grin, rolling up his ration pack and standing up to offer a hand to his friend, 'they might have stashed a secret barrel of ale on the mule train?'

Stypiotes clasped his forearm and hoisted himself to standing. 'Aye, one barrel would do *me* but what about y...' The big soldier's words trailed off as he squinted into the coming dusk.

'Stypiotes?' Peleus frowned, and then spun round.

The dark-blue horizon of the coming twilight seemed to writhe. Peleus' skin rippled. 'Get down!' he hissed, pushing Stypiotes and himself to the sand.

The zip of an arrow ended with a thud and then a gurgling. Young Atticus clutched at his throat and the dark-red froth that bubbled from the shaft. Another arrow hammered into the chest of the Armenian rider and with that, the camel took flight, the two bodies sloping from its back and onto the sand.

'Ghazis!' Stypiotes gasped, clutching at his sword hilt.

'A raider party?' Peleus replied, then poked his head just over the lip of the dune. His brow furrowed at the dusk-masked plume of a marching column, far to the east. 'No, a vanguard!' He and Stypiotes' stayed locked in a wide-eyed stare.

'They wouldn't come west again so soon?' Stypiotes started.

Peleus's eyes grew wide in terror. 'We've got to get word back to the strategos!'

—

Apion fixed his eyes on the horizon, willing the valley to roll into view, but resisted heeling his mount, weary as the gelding already was. He wondered how Nepos had fared since fleeing the camp. His instructions had been garbled and panicked at best, though that was understandable given the life or death cusp they had both stood on at the time.

Stay true to the valleys until you reach the source of the Piksidis. Be wary, for Bracchus has men everywhere and they are cold killers. Believe me, I've faced them. You will come to a small farm just off the highway to Trebizond, you'll recognise it as the only one for miles that looks like it's about to cave in on itself. The valley side behind this farm rises to a modest peak a quarter of a mile to the north. Climb this peak. Up there, there is a beech thicket. Push through the thicket and you will come to a small clearing. You will come to a cairn with an ancient emblem of the Haga on it. Pull the rocks from the base. You will see what looks like a rabbit warren, but loosen the earth around it. There is a cave where you can shelter...

It was now well into the afternoon and a heat haze rippled the land in front of him. The hill and the cluster of beech trees shimmered up ahead. Every ounce of his will was pulling him just south, the farm obscured by the rise of the valley.

'Only a little longer,' he whispered, inhaling the familiar summer scents of the place. He slid from his mount and rubbed a hand along the gelding's nose. 'Easy, boy. You'll be fed and watered soon, and then you can meet with my old mare. Then you can rest or run for the next few days.' With that, he stalked up the hillside, armour chinking.

The air was still and his breath quickened as he walked, blinking sweat from his eyes, removing his plumed helmet and untying his plaited hair. Nepos would be too smart to come running out, he was sure. The man was a shrewd creature; thanks to God he was good-hearted. Between them they could surely plan a way to rid themselves of Bracchus. One thought had nagged him the whole way home: perhaps he should have been candid with the strategos about Bracchus when he had the chance; surely there was a way that the man could be outed as the poisonous cyst he was, despite his imperial connections? Then Bracchus' fate could be decided by others, perhaps? He shook his head clear of the rabble of thoughts. That was all to come.

The hilltop came into view and he pushed through the beech grove. With a grin, he considered calling for his friend or sneaking up on him. He pushed into the clearing then stopped, blinking.

A still, shadowy and inhuman form filled the space in front of the cairn, and the carving of the *Haga* was spattered with crimson. His heartbeat died to nothing, the blood thudding in his ears changed to a piercing ringing.

Apion stared.

Nepos' lifeless body hung limp, impaled upon a kontarion dug into the earth. The Slav's eyes stared hopelessly skywards.

Apion retched, unable to tear his gaze from the horror.

Then a weak bleating rang out. Apion looked up. A lone goat, barely more than a kid, stumbled along the hillside. On its fleece it bore Mansur's woad marking. That and a foreign, crimson streak.

The sweat on his skin felt like ice-water as he turned to the dip in the valley. Then he sprung into a sprint. He leapt up and onto the Thessallian's saddle and heeled it into a gallop, guttural roars accompanying every kick. Their speed sent a howling wind past his ears as he ducked low in the saddle, his hair and the crimson cloak whipping behind him. The valley opened out in front of them. Then the bowed roof of the farm appeared. Terror grappled his heart.

Please do not let it be true.

A ringing in his ears grew into a shrill whistle as he saw it all: the ground outside the door was a carpet of crimson. The goat herd was scattered, many lying motionless or thrashing in their death throes. The grey mare lay still, a broken spear shaft embedded in her guts, entrails spread across the ground where she lay. Apion felt his chest bellow and then sting and he heard his own roar, distant and other-worldly. The front door was ajar, hanging on one hinge. He slid from his mount and stumbled inside, seeing his scimitar held out before him, his arms numb, the world around him shaking, buzzing.

Inside, the darkness blinded him, but he clawed forward, feeling for first the old oak table and then the hearth. Panting, he glanced around at the dimness that was slowly sharpening before him. Then he saw it.

Proud Mansur lay sprawled across the hearth, an awful wound in his belly gaped from where the dagger had gone in to where it rested now, just below his throat. His face bulged; swollen and discoloured in a frenzy of cuts and his eyes had been gouged from their sockets. Four bodies of irregularly armoured men lay around him, torn with scimitar wounds. So the old man had fought one last time. Then he saw the tiny wooden shatranj piece clutched in the old man's palm; the war chariot given to Nepos. Apion trembled where he stood. Fear was no part of it.

Then he saw the dark red robe. Maria's robe. It lay, discarded, torn and soiled with gore. Beside it a tuft of her dark hair lay in a pool of blood. Before he could piece together what would have happened to her, his mind washed clear of thought, his vision narrowed. He felt the thud of his knees hit the flagstones, the sting of his hands slapping over his eyes, the stabbing pain of the flesh in his throat tearing from his own screaming.

As the afternoon dimmed towards dusk, Apion remained on the floor. His chest heaved and his heart emptied what was left in it. After that, he remained there still, gazing up at the old oak table, his mind replaying the times long past when they had sat together. He saw Mansur and Maria, smiling, laughing. Beside them he saw Mother and Father. Father held Mother's hand as they all ate together.

When Apion reached out a shaking hand towards the image, it all disappeared, leaving only empty twilight.

—

The air changed as night descended on the valley and a warm drizzle broke the drought at last. A hooded figure on horseback trotted down the hill behind the farm. Then the figure dismounted and entered the farmhouse.

Inside, Apion heard the scraping of a footstep on the flagstones, then sensed a shadow stand over him. He did not realise that the figure was really there until it spoke.

'I come here to honour their bodies,' the voice seemed to be shaking, enraged, 'but you… you have the nerve to come back here now?' The figure lowered the hood to reveal Nasir's contorted features, shaded in the half light. He held blankets, brushes and a spade.

'Nasir?' Apion stammered, pushing himself up to stand. Then a rasp of iron sent sparks across the gloom. Nasir held his scimitar out, pointed at Apion's throat.

'Another step and I'll tear your throat out. By Allah, I should have slain you where you lay.'

Apion stepped back, shaking his head. 'Nasir, I came home to this, I...'

'You did not do this, but you brought this upon them!' Nasir roared.

'Never! They were everything to me!' But even as he spoke, Apion felt the truth of Nasir's words burn on his neck. He retched, then doubled over to spew out the trickle of bile left in his belly.

Nasir arced his scimitar round and down onto the oak table, the blade embedding in the wood and the frame cracking. 'You should have been here to protect them.'

The words cut like a blunt dagger through Apion's soul. He had failed Mansur and Maria just as he had failed Mother and Father. The *Haga* they called him, the ferocious two-headed eagle, the demon swordfighter, the leader of men. All names unbefitting of a man who could not protect those he loved most.

He stood tall under Nasir's gaze and cleared his throat. 'You are right. I should have been here. You know how much they meant to me, Nasir. You more than anyone else.'

Nasir's shook his head. 'No. There can be no excuses for what has happened here.' He wrenched his sword clear of the table and sheathed it. 'We may once have been as close as blood kin. I remember our oath.'

'...until we're both dust...' Apion mouthed.

'I said I remember!' Nasir roared. 'But this changes things, it changes everything. Nothing will be the same anymore.'

What's left? A hoarse voice whispered inside Apion's head.

'Your presence offends their memory,' Nasir spat.

There is something left, isn't there? The voice sounded rapacious.

'Leave this place. Leave and never come back.' Nasir's shoulders broadened and he took a step forward. 'Because I'm making a new oath, this time to myself. If our paths cross again after tonight,' his brow wrinkled, 'I *will* kill you.'

Apion heard his old friend's words and deep down inside, a distant voice cried out, pleaded for Nasir to reconsider. But in his head the rasping voice was in full flow. *Yes, there is something... something sweet, something long, long overdue... revenge! Nothing stands in your way now.* His eyes were fixed on a distant point, far beyond the shattered table. 'Those responsible for this will die, Nasir. What happened to Mansur will happen to them. I swear it. This is my oath.'

Nasir sneered at this.

'Everyone who played a part will be cold and still, by my sword. The man who orchestrated this, all of this, he is a walking shade.'

'You talk of death as if you were the reaper?' Nasir spat, his eyes narrowing.

Apion felt a coldness wash through his veins and he looked his old friend in the eye. 'Everything you have lost, I have lost also, Nasir: Mansur, like a father to me, and Mar...' Apion moved forward, Nasir shook his head.

'Don't you dare say her name!'

'Maria. Maria was my closest companion as a child. Then she was my lover, the woman I dreamt of every night I was away. Her face, her scent, they soothed my mind.'

'She was to be my *wife*!' Nasir roared, then lurched at him, one fist crashing into Apion's nose.

A metallic wash coated his throat as he stumbled back against the hearth. 'I won't strike you back, Nasir. You've done nothing wrong. You've got every right to hate me,' he said as Nasir towered over him, chest heaving, fists balled, 'but I warn you, stand back and let me leave.'

Nasir tilted his head back, grimacing. 'So you ride out of the valley, leaving destruction in your wake.'

Apion stopped as he passed Nasir. 'My words won't help today, but I want you to know and remember that I am sorry, so, so sorry.'

'Until we meet again, Apion.' Nasir's face was stony. 'If it is on the battlefield then that would be apt.'

Apion nodded, pulled his crimson cloak around his body, then stepped out of the farm and into the warm drizzle. He stopped to glance back at the shattered door, for an instant his mind cruelly played back the memory of little Maria, her fawn hand pulling the door open on that first day.

Then the memory was washed away with the image of the dark door. This time it did not rush towards him. No, this time he beckoned it forward. He reached out for it, his scarred and knotted arm with the *Haga* emblem fitting perfectly over the arm in the image. Apart from one thing.

He drew his hand closer, he saw the prayer rope on his wrist flicker to the white band of skin in the image. That God could let this happen all over again sickened him to his soul.

Something inside him snapped.

In silence, he pulled the prayer rope until it ripped free of his wrist, then threw it to the ground.

With that, he leapt on his Thessallian and heeled the gelding into a fierce gallop. He would not rest until he had hunted them down.

All of them.

—

'He was my good friend. Let me help dig,' Kutalmish pleaded.

Nasir's palms were blistered and his eyes stung with sweat. Yet he waved his father away without reply and continued scooping earth from the spot where old Mansur was to be buried.

'You are a strong-headed boy, Nasir; you are turning out like your brother was before he died. Why did you react to young Apion as though he was the perpetrator of this vile act?'

Nasir stopped digging and turned to his father, bathed in the pale orange of the coming dawn. 'How can you defend him? Bracchus and his men came here to collect a debt of blood from him. He knew they would come here and he had a choice to stop this.'

'Everything is black and white with you, isn't it?'

'I know that I am honouring Mansur by forever ridding this valley of Apion.'

'What does she think of this?'

Nasir bristled; Maria lay in his bed, being nursed back from near-death by the old woman with the milky eyes and healing hands. 'Maria should not be concerned with him anymore.'

'So you did not tell him she lives? You let him ride off with a weight of guilt he does not deserve?'

'It's a blessing that I didn't cut his throat from ear to ear.'

'My, Giyath shines through in you, indeed, son.'

Nasir glared at his father, the old man looking frailer than ever, eyes red from weeping. 'He'll use his rage, he'll thunder off and find the bastards who carried out this act *and* slaughtered his parents. I've gifted him that rage.'

Kutalmish frowned then whispered. 'Forcing a man to face Bracchus is no gift.'

Nasir scowled and made to reply, then stopped as he noticed his father close his eyes and shake his head. 'Father?'

'A dark truth has been hidden, son.'

Nasir climbed from the grave. 'Speak!' he barked.

Kutalmish looked to the shrouded form of Mansur's body. 'Forgive me, old friend,' he whispered, 'but our oath was until death.'

'Father, what do you know?' Nasir realised he had his father by the scruff of his robe.

'Apion will destroy Bracchus, son. Bracchus is a vile and dark creature who has brought misery upon our lives. Yet Apion will hate Mansur even more than Bracchus if he finds out the truth. A truth he was never meant to discover.'

'How could he hate Mansur, how could he hate him as much as Bracchus? Bracchus killed his parents!'

Kutalmish's features fell stony. 'Bracchus was not alone that night.'

Nasir stood back, wide-eyed, then he frowned, glancing to the form of Mansur's body. 'Mansur? Never!'

Kutalmish closed his eyes, tears escaping and dancing down his lined cheeks. 'He was a troubled man for a long time, Nasir.'

'How could he be involved in killing Apion's family? Bracchus is a black-hearted dog. Mansur was anything but!'

'And maybe one day, long past, Bracchus was also a good-hearted soul. Just as, that one night, Mansur was as black-hearted as Bracchus. Life changes people, Nasir, brutally.'

'What happened?' Nasir demanded.

Kutalmish mouthed a prayer and then looked his son in the eye. 'Apion's father was the cavalry commander that led the charge on our caravan, Nasir. He was responsible for the death of Mansur's wife... and your mother too...' His words trailed off with a sob.

Nasir's mind raced. His hatred of Apion swirled with this revelation.

'His father made a mistake, a big one. He saw Mansur and I, riding armed, took our caravan for a Seljuk supply train... and attacked. He realised his mistake and tried to call off his men, but by then it was too late. Since that day blackness welled in Mansur's heart, it was all I could do to quell it in mine.'

'I cannot imagine Mansur as a murderer.' Nasir shook his head, then looked up to his father. 'Apion told me of that night. He spoke of one masked figure that stood back from the slaughter of his parents. Could that have been Mansur?'

'Mansur came to me that night, his mind in pieces. He never spoke of his part in the events of the night. Yet, when he fell into a troubled, exhausted sleep, I lifted his scimitar from its sheath...'

Nasir's eyes widened.

'...the blade was clean, Nasir.'

'Then he took no part?'

'He was there, Nasir. Whether or not he took part in the butchering of Apion's family is secondary.'

'But Mansur tried to do the right thing, to make amends – that's why he brought Apion back to the farm, isn't it? Yet it all came back on the old man like a blade,' Nasir snarled, 'the Byzantine people are poison!'

'Nasir, it was not the Byzantines who started this. It is simply the way of man. Just as the healer lady said when she brought Maria to us. *Man will destroy man.*'

'No, our people are different.'

Kutalmish's head fell to his chest. 'That is what Mansur said, all those years ago, on the night he lost his wife.'

Nasir's eyes burned. 'The difference is that I will not yield! I will fight these people until their empire is no more!'

CHAPTER 22

The Wrath of the Haga

Inside the officers' quarters in Argyroupolis, Bracchus and the bearded, cloaked man glared at one another in the guttering candlelight. The imperial Agente had ridden from the west, escorted by fifty tagma-quality kataphractoi. He and his party had breezed into the town then beckoned Bracchus and dismissed the guards and the strategos with a flash of the imperial seal on his papers. Once they were alone, the man's message had riled Bracchus to the core. *You are to go east, far to the east*, the Agente had purred.

'You effectively want me to walk into the Sultan's heartland, into the lion's jaws?' Bracchus reiterated, stifling a gasp of derision.

'The emperor wills it, Agente Bracchus. He granted you your power and so you must obey him.'

Bracchus struggled to suppress his rage. Here he stood, on the cusp of ultimate power, already the master Agente of the eastern borders, and one step from becoming a strategos. Yet this man sought to take it from him. His chest tightened as he remembered the last time anyone had taken from him, his mother's words echoing in his mind. Before he realised it, he had already clasped a hand to the hilt of the dagger strapped to his thigh. 'I am only too well aware of my duty to the emperor,' he hissed, eyeing the man's jugular, within easy swiping distance.

'Then be aware that he can take your power from you, as fast as… the swipe of a dagger.'

Bracchus' hand froze as he noticed the Agente's eyes on the movement of his arm. The man spoke a bitter truth: the emperor

336

could turn every Agente against Bracchus on a whim. He gulped back the impotent fury he felt. Only when the emperor was at his mercy would he be truly untouchable. Perhaps, he mused, he should play this game. 'Very well,' he spoke evenly. 'If this mission is so crucial then perhaps the emperor will take requests for certain things that will aid my future service when I return.'

'Naturally,' the Agente replied.

'Good. I choose my men for this mission; I take as much coin as I feel necessary.'

The Agente nodded.

'And see to it that I return to a post of strategos.' The Agente frowned at this, but Bracchus cut in before he could continue. 'One other thing, very important.' He leaned forward, his grin spreading in the candlelight. 'I want impunity. Total impunity. Right to the top.'

The Agente nodded uneasily. 'It can be arranged. You will be gone from the empire for some time, Bracchus. Years in all likelihood. When you come back,' he broke into a cold grin, '*if* you come back, you will be furnished with these things.'

Bracchus grinned and nodded. 'Then we leave before the sun has fully risen, as planned. I will evaporate into the eastern sands.'

Cydones stood beside the skutatos on the gate tower, watching the column of fifty heading away from Argyroupolis, headed east. His heart lifted at the sight and he knew the feeling was mutual among the ranks. The tourmarches Bracchus was a pox on the garrison no longer. He thought over the conversation he had overheard, concealed in the storeroom adjacent, then smiled: the imperial Agente could bend the thema to his will no more. He looked skyward and wondered at the piety in praying for Bracchus to be exposed and executed in the Seljuk court. Then he started as the skutatos beside him grappled the edge of the watchtower.

'Lone rider approaching from the west,' the man shouted, peering at the figure, pale orange in the dawn light. 'Ah, all is well, he is one of ours.'

Then Cydones broke into a wide grin. 'He certainly is. Look, the black plumage... it's the *Haga*!'

The gates swung open before Apion. The men cheered him as he entered. Then their voices fell silent at the sight of the bloodstains coating his face and armour as the Thessallian galloped past. The six giant riders Bracchus had despatched to ambush him at the edge of the mountains had been fierce fighters, but their strength could not overcome his fury as he hacked them down, face stony, eyes staring.

He heeled his mount on through the town at a gallop. The place was just coming to life but everything around him was a blur of noise and colour. His eyes were focused on the barrack compound. He slowed at the iron gates, he and his mount panting, and roared up to the east-gazing skutatos in the watchtower. 'Open the gates!'

The skutatos spun round and called down to the men in the compound. The gates opened with a weary iron moan and Apion slid from his mount, striding across the muster square towards the officers' quarters.

'Can't keep away, can you?' a familiar voice called.

Apion spun to see Sha, whose face fell at the sight of his friend's bloodied features and burning glare.

'Apion... what happened?'

'Where is he?' Apion growled. When Sha hesitated Apion grappled the collar of his tunic and snarled, blood dripping from his beard. 'Bracchus, where is he?'

Sha's brow wrinkled. 'You haven't heard? He's gone, Apion, you don't need to worry about him anymore.'

Apion pushed back from Sha and snarled. 'Gone?'

338

'It is true, he is headed east and will be gone for years,' Cydones cut in, descending the staircase from the town walls.

Apion spun to face the strategos. 'How long ago did he leave?'

'Not long, just after daybreak.' Cydones halted as he saw the gruesome apparition that was his new tourmarches. 'Apion, what is wrong?'

Apion looked to him. 'He had them killed. Mansur, Maria. They're dead. Nepos too.'

Cydones' eyes fell to the ground, searching, then he glanced back up. 'Old Mansur? Who killed them? And Nepos, he deserted did he not?'

Apion shook his head. 'No, no! It's Bracchus, sir. He is an Agente. He has engineered all of this.'

Cydones shoulders sagged and he sighed, a tinge of redness touching the rims of his eyes. 'I knew of his imperial connections, but this? This makes him a darker soul than I ever realised.'

'Sir,' Apion croaked, the whites of his eyes stark against the congealing blood caking his features, 'where is he headed?'

'East,' the strategos replied.

He affixed the strategos with a firm look, then hauled himself onto the saddle. 'Then I must ride, sir.'

Cydones nodded. 'Yes. Ride fast, Apion.'

Bracchus gripped the reins of his mount, squinted into the rising sun and wondered at the indignity of it all. He, the puppet master for so long, had been mastered by the emperor. Or more likely the Agentes based in Constantinople who had the bend of the emperor's ear, he mused wryly. Still, all options were open. He could follow his mission objectives to the letter and then he would return to the empire to a position where nobody would have power over him. Or he could infiltrate the Seljuk palace as ordered, and then negotiate with the Sultan. The power was still in his hands, he smirked.

'Sir, messenger approaching,' Vadim said, twisting in his saddle, squinting over his shoulder.

Bracchus raised a hand and the column of thirty – Vadim, six of his finest skutatoi bodyguards, plus squires and slaves – stopped. Bracchus twisted in his saddle. 'This messenger wears armour?' he muttered. Then he noticed the rider wore a crimson cloak and black-plumed helmet. Then he saw amber locks billowing from under the aventail and the rider's features and garb were spattered in crimson. His eyes narrowed and he clicked his fingers and nodded to the two nearest bodyguards. The column turned to face the approaching rider and the two bodyguards moved to stand in front of Bracchus.

When the rider did not slow, Bracchus' eyes widened. When the rider ripped his scimitar from its sheath and roared, Bracchus felt a long-buried sensation. Terror.

Apion gathered all his might and smashed the blade down on the first bodyguard, the giant of a man spinning on the spot, his helmet falling to the ground in two pieces, skull cleaved. The second bodyguard stumbled back in fright as his colleague's body crumpled to the dust. Apion thundered away then circled back around and came charging for the column again.

'Protect your superior!' Bracchus roared, kicking a boot into the bodyguard's back. At this, the rest of the bodyguards drew their spathions and rippled into a line across the mounted figures of Bracchus and Vadim.

Apion hared directly for the centre of the line. Then at the last moment he swerved, swooping past the end of the line and beheading the man at the edge. He galloped on and up the mountain edge before racing back. The four remaining skutatoi moved round to form a line in front of Bracchus, but this time their eyes betrayed panic. Then Apion sheathed his scimitar and pulled a bow from his back. Riding at full pelt for the centre of the line, he nocked an arrow to the bowstring, stretched and loosed it. The missile punched through the face of the bodyguard directly in front of Bracchus, who flinched at the spray of blood. Then he loosed another arrow that caught the next bodyguard in the throat.

'Take him down!' Bracchus roared to his two remaining men and Vadim.

'With pleasure, sir,' Vadim growled and heeled his mount into a gallop after Apion, the two bodyguards stalking out to the flanks.

Apion saw the three only as dull shapes. Only one being existed in the world right now and that was Bracchus. Vadim's sword came smashing down at him as the big Rus tried to intercept, but Apion swiped his scimitar blade to parry, then smashed the hilt of the sword into Vadim's face. As the big Rus toppled from his mount, moaning, Apion lay flat in his saddle and heeled his mount into a charge for the unprotected Bracchus, who was grappling for his sword, eyes wide in panic. He raised his scimitar, then closed his eyes, seeking out the faces of Mother, Father, Mansur and Maria. Then he tensed his shoulder to stab through Bracchus' chest when suddenly a white-hot pain streaked through his leg. In a heartbeat, his world was turned upside down in a thrashing of hooves and pained whinnying.

He scrambled back from the Thessallian; the beast was writhing on the ground, chest punctured by a rhiptarion thrown by one of the bodyguards. The spear had also ripped into Apion's thigh, tearing across the old scar. He heard Bracchus roar with delight, then he felt the ground shake from thunderous footsteps. He looked up just in time to see Vadim's double-headed axe arcing down on him. He scrambled away just as the hefty blade split a rock where he had lay. Then he pulled round to face the big Rus, feeling his weight push down on the thigh-wound, urging him to crumple to one knee. The other two bodyguards completed a circle around him.

'Now finish him, just like his Seljuk whore and her father!' Bracchus' face was pinched in malice.

Apion sought out hidden reserves of energy to spin at the flurry of sword thrusts and axe swipes, enough time only to defend, no time to strike out. Vadim's axe blade ripped across his neck and for an instant he feared it was all over, hot blood washing down his chest. But it was not arterial and his strength stayed with him at first, though his limbs began to tire and each parry became weaker, slower as his blood drained into the ground.

Panting, he saw what looked like a dust cloud approaching from Argyroupolis. Then he braced as Vadim's face curled into a grin and the big Rus lurched for a death blow, hoisting his axe two-handed. Apion ducked back and let his foe's momentum carry him past, the blow falling to the dust, then he saw the glimmer of opportunity; before Vadim could turn to face him again, Apion wrapped his scimitar blade around the Rus's neck and ripped it back. Vadim spun to face him, snarling, but the lifeblood was already flooding from the gaping wound, soaking the dust. His face greyed and his expression changed to one of confusion, and then he crumpled to his knees. The axe toppled to the ground first, then Vadim fell forward and was still.

The two remaining bodyguards looked less certain now as Apion faced them, emerald eyes searing under his frown. He lurched for the first and hacked down on his shoulder, the man falling in a fit of convulsions. Then he spun to chop into the second's neck but he hesitated as this man dropped his sword, hands raised. The scimitar blade hovered at his neck. Apion saw terror in the man's eyes, and a twinge of pity formed in his heart. Then he remembered the catalogue of atrocities he had been involved in as Bracchus' bodyguard. In one swipe he beheaded the man.

Panting, he turned to Bracchus. He saw the image of Mansur's body, Maria's bloodied dress, Father and Mother's butchered corpses. He lifted his scimitar and pointed it at the mounted figure.

He did not notice the hundreds who emerged from the approaching dust cloud: members of the garrison, who quickly formed a circle around the confrontation, Sha marshalling them. Then there was one figure on horseback. Cydones.

Bracchus looked to them all and then to the strategos. 'This man has murdered my bodyguards and now he turns his blade on me. Arrest him!'

The watching garrison shuffled but nobody spoke.

'I said arrest him!' Bracchus' words were hoarse.

Cydones held Bracchus' stare, then quietly heeled his mount round into a gentle trot back towards Argyroupolis. Bracchus' eyes bulged. The squires and slaves of Bracchus' column melted through the circle and followed the strategos.

'A death bout seems fitting?' Apion said, his chest shuddering.

'You have no idea, do you, boy?' Bracchus heeled his steed into a gentle trot, circling Apion. 'I answer to nobody and nobody defies me. My blood is sacred. You could not comprehend what suffering I could bring upon you if you were to spill a drop of it.'

Apion's glare was unblinking. 'You can bring no more suffering on me, Bracchus. Everything I have is gone and now I live only to see your heart torn from your chest.'

Bracchus grimaced, darting glances to the watching garrison. To a man they stared back stonily. He shook his head and laughed. 'All for the lives of the Seljuk whore and her father? How many Seljuks did you slay in the field, *Haga*? How many have lost fathers, sons, husbands because of you.' Bracchus leaned forward and spat: 'You are everything you hate about me.'

Apion gritted his teeth, his whole body shaking as he turned, his eyes fixed on the master Agente as he circled. 'Never!'

'You brought it upon them,' Bracchus continued. 'I gave you an order, a simple one, and you chose not to obey it. You made that choice. Your Slav friend died along with them... all your doing.'

The words stung Apion. He remembered Nasir's diatribe to the same effect. Then he shook the thought from his head and fixed Bracchus with a fiery glare. 'And my parents? Did I choose for them to die on your blade?' The words felt like a fire in his throat.

Bracchus frowned. 'Your parents?'

'You've never worked it out, have you?' Apion snarled. 'You remember the boy who cut the finger from your hand?'

Bracchus stopped circling, his face falling. 'You… you!' His eyes searched the dust for a moment. 'Of course…' he muttered. Then he looked up again, a terrible grin creeping across his features. 'Then it is you who has never worked it out, boy.'

Apion snorted. 'Speak, before you die.'

'Did you never wonder why your beloved Mansur took you under his wing? Fed, clothed and cared for you?'

'He did it because he was a good man. That is why you will die for his murder.'

Bracchus shook his head. 'He did it because he could not live with his guilt! A weak man to his core! He did it because he was there that night, he was there when your parents paid the price for borrowing from me more than they could repay.'

Apion's blood seemed to freeze in his veins. The other men with the Agente that night. They were Seljuk. They were masked. *No*, he pleaded in his mind. 'Never!' he roared. 'Mansur would never do that. He would never be part of your dealings in any case.'

'Unless,' Bracchus grinned, 'he had another reason to see your parents die.'

Apion shook his head. 'These will be your last words, Agente.'

Bracchus hefted his spathion in his hand, gripping his legs around the flanks of his mount. 'He asked me if he could come that night, for he had sought vengeance for the death of his wife for years. He lusted after the blood of the man who led the cavalry charge that saw his wife slain. He longed to see your father dead.'

Apion's body numbed from blood loss and realisation. His lips tingled in expectation of a retort but there was none. The truth had its claws in his soul. His grip on the scimitar fell slack and the blade dangled from his hand, his vision spotting over.

'It started nineteen years ago, with your father's misguided but welcome attack on Mansur's caravan,' Bracchus spoke evenly, eyeing his opponent's lethargy, heeling his mount into a brisk trot to circle Apion. Then he hefted his spathion back, eyes bulging. 'And on my sword point, it ends now!' he roared and swept the blade down.

Apion saw the blade coming, but his mind was in another place, stood in the dark doorway. He leapt for the flames with a roar. He barely saw Bracchus' sword spin up and away from his lightning-fast parry. Time seemed to slow as he leapt to grapple the tourmarches by the throat, pulling him down from the saddle and throwing him prone. As Bracchus struggled to pull a dagger from his belt, Apion stamped on his gloved hand, the bones crunching under his boot, Bracchus' screams distant. He lifted his scimitar to Bracchus' chest, fixed his eyes on the master Agente and then, with a guttural cry, he thrust down, pushing with all his might until the blade dug deep into the ground below.

With that, he collapsed onto all fours, panting. He uncoiled his fist and stared at the chariot shatranj piece, still stained with Mansur's blood.

Then a hand clutched at his sleeve. Bracchus glared at him, eyes dimming, blood foaming from his lips. 'Now you truly know darkness…' he hissed as the life left his body.

Every day I soar over the mountain town I see him, the lone figure standing on the battlements at the break of dawn, gazing east, looking for answers he will never find. Where once he saw beauty in daybreak, he now sees only pain. Having cast aside his god and purged the earth of the twisted soul Bracchus, he has shed what had kept him human. Now he lives in a netherworld where he is ever seeking outlet for his fury.

The Haga has risen, just as fate decreed.

Then, as I look to the rising sun, I can feel the rage of the Mountain Lion, marching west.

This land is on the cusp of a collision that will echo through the ages.

Author's Note

First of all, I would like to thank you warmly for reading my book and I hope it was enjoyable for you.

If I could ask just one small favour of you, it'd be this: please spread the word! A short review or recommendation on Amazon or Goodreads, or a simple tweet or mention to your friends would be great — all these things are a massive help to me.

Now — to the history. The following is intended to shed a little light on some of the thinking and choices I made over how to present certain elements of the period in which the story is set.

In researching this book I soon came to the conclusion that Byzantium simply refuses to be defined. I quickly realised that this probably sums up why I find the empire so intriguing, in that you can look at any aspect of its history time and again, and each time come away with new meanings or ideas. This isn't the easiest basis for writing historical fiction, but I found it fascinating nonetheless, trying to envisage how the devout Christians of the empire would have seen the world they lived in, pursuing the ideals of old Rome without the means or circumstance to uphold them.

In my anachronistic use of the terms 'Byzantine' and the 'Byzantine Empire' (first coined by modern historians), my aim was to steer the reader away from any preconception or imagery that may have been conjured by the terms that the Greek-speaking inhabitants of the empire would have used to refer to themselves, namely Romans or Romaioi. Although Byzantium was absolutely and seamlessly the heir to the Roman Empire, it also became very, very different and far removed from the position of might and power of the high principate and the classical Caesars.

The Byzantine military underwent numerous reforms in its long history, starting as something akin to the classical Roman legions and ending up as a desperate handful of medieval militias fighting on the walls of Constantinople at the dusk of the empire. Thus, when I write of the armies of the themata, I am aware that there are many definitions of exactly how these armies were composed, based on time period and information source. In putting shape to this shifting world I would like to offer my sincere thanks to Dr Timothy Dawson, whose knowledge of the period is quite simply astounding. In this aspect I have used the bandon as the standard battlefield infantry unit of the time, despite some evidence that suggests that by the 11th century AD, the thousand-strong chiliarchy may have been preferred to – or used in conjunction with – the bandon following the reforms of Nikephoros Phokas and Nikephoros Ouranos in the 10th century AD. I preferred the bandon for the simple reason that the structure seemed more mature and aligned to the historical reference materials detailing the period in which the story is set.

For my use of the shadowy wing of imperial agents known as the Agentes, I admit a hearty dose of speculation, though not without foundation: in the classical Roman Empire, the *frumentarii* served as a secret service for the Caesars, spying, informing, sowing dissent and assassinating on the emperor's command. They grew to be hated by the populace of the empire and its armies until they were disbanded by Diocletian in the 3rd century AD. How substantial this disbandment was is questionable though, as Diocletian almost immediately went on to form the *Agentes in Rebus*, a group thought by some to have been personal messengers for the emperor, and by others to have been a rebranded and far more effectively organised version of the *frumentarii*. Both theories have their merits, but that their title means 'those who are active in matters' tells me all I need to know. The *Agentes in Rebus* remained in existence as Rome fell, and served the Byzantine emperors until they were officially abolished in the 9th century

348

AD. However, given that subterfuge had been inherent in Rome and Byzantium for over a millennium, and the word 'duplicitous' had become synonymous with the word 'Byzantine', I find it hard to believe that an organisation like the Agentes of this book were not still in existence in some form.

At this point I would once again like to thank you for reading. Apion will return, and I hope that you will join me for the next instalment of his story. Until then, please feel free to visit my website where you can find out more about me and my writing.

Yours faithfully,
Gordon Doherty
www.gordondoherty.co.uk

Glossary

Abbasid Caliphate: An Islamic caliphate that controlled the lands of ancient Persia before the 10th century AD. In the following years, much of this control was ceded to the *Daylamids*.

Agente: A Byzantine imperial agent, tasked by the emperor with spying, sowing dissent and dealing ruthlessly with troublemakers.

Akhi: Seljuk infantry armed with long anti-cavalry spears, scimitars, shields and sometimes armoured in lamellar.

Ballista: Primarily anti-personnel missile artillery capable of throwing bolts vast distances. Utilised from fortified positions and on the battlefield.

Bandon (pl. banda): The basic battlefield unit of infantry in the Byzantine army. Literally meaning 'banner', a bandon typically consisted of between two hundred and four hundred men, usually *skutatoi*, who would line up in a square formation, presenting spears to their enemy from their front ranks and hurling *rhiptaria* from the ranks behind. Banda would form together on the battlefield to present something akin to the ancient phalanx.

Bey: Seljuk military commander, subordinate to an *emir*.

Buccina: The ancestor of the trumpet and the trombone, this instrument was used for the announcement of night watches and various other purposes in the Byzantine forts and marching camps as well as to communicate battlefield manoeuvres.

Buccinator: A soldier who uses the *buccina* to perform acoustical signalling on the battlefield and in forts, camps and settlements.

Buskins: Calf length boots. The Byzantine Emperors famously wore purple buskins decorated with golden thread.

Chi-Rho: The Chi-Rho is one of the earliest forms of Christogram, and was used in the early Christian Roman Empire through to the Byzantine high period as a symbol of piety and empire. It is formed by superimposing the first two letters in the Greek spelling of the word Christ, chi = ch and rho = r, in such a way to produce the following monogram:

Daylamid Dynasty: An Islamic Persian dynasty that originated in Daylaman in modern-day Iran and grew to take control of the Abbasid Caliphate. Also known as the Buyid Dynasty.

Dekarchos: A minor officer in charge of a *kontoubernion* of ten *skutatoi* who would be expected to fight in the front rank of his *bandon*. He would wear a red★ sash to denote his rank.

Djinn: Islamic demon.

Droungarios: A Byzantine officer in charge of two *banda*, who would wear a silver★ sash to denote his rank.

Emir: Seljuk military leader, equivalent to the Byzantine *strategos*.

Fatimid Caliphate: Arab Islamic caliphate that dominated modern-day Tunisia and Egypt in the Middle Ages.

Follis: A large bronze coin of small value.

Foulkon: The Byzantine heir to the famous Roman *testudo* or 'tortoise' formation.

Ghazi: The Seljuk light cavalry, whose primary purpose was to raid enemy lands and disrupt defensive systems and supply chains.

Ghaznavid Empire: A Persian Muslim dynasty of Turkic origin who ruled much of Persia, Transoxania and Northern India prior to the rise of the Seljuks.

Ghulam: The Seljuk heavy cavalry, equivalent to the Byzantine *kataphractos*. Armoured well in scale vest or lamellar, with a distinctive pointed helmet with nose-guard, carrying a bow, scimitar and spear.

Haga: A ferocious two-headed eagle from ancient Hittite mythology. Also the basis for what would become the emblem of both the Byzantine Empire and the Seljuk Empire.

Kampidoktores: The drill master in charge of training Byzantine soldiers.

Kataphractos (pl. kataphractoi): Byzantine heavy cavalry and the main offensive force in the *thema* and *tagma* armies. The riders and horses would wear iron lamellar and mail armour, leaving little vulnerability to attack. The riders would use their *kontarion* for lancing, *spathion* for skirmishing or their bow for harrying.

Kentarches: A Byzantine officer in charge of one hundred Byzantine soldiers. A descendant of the Roman centurion.

Kentarchia: A notional unit of one hundred Byzantine soldiers, commanded by a *kentarches*.

Klibanion (pl. klibania): The characteristic Byzantine lamellar cuirass made of leather, horn or iron squares, usually sleeveless, though sometimes with leather strips hanging from the waist and shoulders.

Komes: An officer in charge of a *bandon* who would wear a white* sash to denote his rank.

Kontarion: A spear between two and three metres long, the kontarion was designed for Byzantine infantry to hold off enemy cavalry.

Kontoubernion: A grouping of ten Byzantine infantry who would eat together, patrol together, share sleeping quarters or a pavilion tent while on campaign and would be rewarded or punished as a single unit.

Mangonel: Catapult-style siege engine that shot heavy projectiles from a bowl-shaped bucket at the end of the arm. Used for both anti-personnel and anti-fortification purposes.

Nomisma (pl. nomismata): A gold coin that could be debased by various degrees to set its value.

Protocancellarius: Chief clerk in charge of Byzantine military *thema* administration.

Protomandator: The chief of heralds in a *thema*, responsible for despatching messengers and relaying communication.

Rhiptarion: A short throwing spear. *Skutatoi* carried two or three of these each.

Salep: A hot drink made with orchid root, cinnamon and milk.

Shatranj: A precursor to modern-day chess.

Skutatos (pl. skutatoi): The Byzantine infantryman, based on the ancient hoplite. He was armed with an iron helmet, a *spathion*, a *skutum*, a *kontarion*, two or more *rhiptaria* and possibly a dagger and an axe. He would wear a lamellar *klibanion* if positioned to the front of his *bandon*, or a padded jacket or felt vest if he was closer to the rear. *Tagma* skutatoi may well all have been afforded iron lamellar armour.

Skutum: The Byzantine infantry shield that gives the *skutatoi* their name. Usually teardrop-shaped and painted identically within a *bandon*.

Spathion: The Byzantine infantry sword, derived from the Roman *spatha*. Up to a metre long, this straight blade was primarily for stabbing, but allowed slashing and hacking as well.

Strategos (pl. strategoi): Literally 'army leader'. The *themata* armies of Byzantium were organised and led by such a man. The strategos was also responsible for governance of his *thema*.

Tagma (pl. tagmata): The tagmata were the professional standing armies of the Byzantine Empire. They were traditionally clustered around Constantinople, but in the 11th century they were moved closer to the empire's borders to counter emerging threats. These armies were formed to provide a central reserve, to meet enemy encroachment that could not be dealt with by the *themata*, and also to cow the potentially revolutionary power of those *themata*. They were well armoured, armed, paid and fed. Each tagma held around five thousand men and was composed of exclusively cavalry or infantry.

Thema (pl. themata): In the 7th century AD, as a result of the crisis caused by the Muslim conquests, the Byzantine military and administrative system was reformed: the old late Roman division between military and civil administration was abandoned, and the remains of the Eastern Roman Empire's field armies were settled in great districts, the themata, that were named after those armies. The men of the themata would work their state-leased military lands in times of peace and then don their armour and weapons when summoned by the *strategos* to defend their thema or to set out on campaign alone or with the *tagmata*. When mustered, each thema could field around ten thousand men, primarily infantry.

Tourma (pl. tourmae): A subdivision of a Byzantine *thema*, commanded by a *tourmarches* and comprised of some two thousand soldiers of the *thema* army and encompassing a geographical subset of the *thema* lands.

Tourmarches (pl. tourmarchai): A Byzantine officer in charge of the military forces and administration of a *tourma*.

Toxotes (pl. toxotai): The Byzantine archer, lightly armoured with a felt jacket and armed with a composite bow and a dagger.

★The use of a sash to denote rank is backed up by historical texts, but the sash colours stated are speculative.